DEAD
LOCK

ALSO BY DAMIEN BOYD

As the Crow Flies

Head in the Sand

Kickback

Swansong

Dead Level

Death Sentence

Heads or Tails

DAMIEN BOYD

This is a work of fiction. Names, characters, organizations, places, events, and incidents are either products of the author's imagination or are used fictitiously. Any resemblance to actual persons, living or dead, or actual events is purely coincidental.

Published by Thomas & Mercer, Seattle

www.apub.com

ISBN-13: 9781542047029
ISBN-10: 1542047021

Cover design by @blacksheep-uk.com

Printed in the United States of America

For Peter

Prologue

Coal smoke. It was a familiar smell – comforting somehow – swirling in the fog of his dreams every morning when the crows dragged him back to his senses, even before he opened his eyes. Was it the same bloody lot following him along the cut these past several weeks? Sitting on the cabin roof every morning, squawking for all they were worth.

Mutton headed coveys.

He glanced across at Jack, fast asleep in his bunk. He was never up before dawn. It must be the grog. He reached over, picked up the jar and took a swig. Just the dregs. He grimaced.

Disgusting.

Tam's bunk was empty, as usual when they reached Combe Hay. Selling coal to the lock keeper's wife, no doubt. And more besides.

He slid his feet out from under Sikes, the smelly brindle Lurcher who kept them in rabbits in return for the scraps, and yawned.

Time to sort out Bess. Poor Bess. She comes first.

He slipped his feet into his boots and crept out of the cabin, finding the horse where he had left her last night, tethered to a tree along the towpath eating the wet grass, as far from the water's edge as he could get her. She'd been in the canal again last week, but then it was Tam's proven remedy for a buckled shoulder.

'Works every time,' he always said. 'Get her in the water and let her swim it off. It'll soon pop back in.'

It was happening more and more often these days. Poor old Bess. The old nag was starting to struggle to get the barge moving when it was full of coal.

All twenty ton of it.

He filled her nosebag with the last of the oats from the barrel and slipped it over her head. They should get to Paulton today and he'd make sure he filled it up good and proper for the return trip.

He left Bess eating her breakfast in the half light of the dawn and wandered back along the towpath towards the barge. He slid back the tarpaulin and dropped down into the empty hold as quietly as he could. It was either that or wake up Jack and get another basting for his trouble.

He picked up the last few bits of coal. The dregs.

Again.

One day he'd have his own boat – it was the life of a bargee for him – then there'd be no more dregs. For him, or Bess.

He tiptoed along the gunwale to the back cabin, trying not to rock the boat. Smoke billowed out of the stove when he opened the door, which explained why everything – and everyone – was covered in a thin layer of black dust. Coal safely in, he gave it a prod with the poker, closed the door and then placed the kettle gingerly on the top. Jack didn't mind the whistle of the kettle if it was followed by a nice cup of 'Rosie', as he called it. And the stronger the better to mask the taste of the coal.

'Nat, are you in there?'

He poked his head out of the back cabin to find Tam running along the towpath, doing up his belt as he ran.

'Get Bess harnessed up, then get up to the next lock. It's against us.' Tam was banging on the side of the cabin with his fist. 'Get up, Jack. We need to get moving. I'll meet you at the top of the flight.'

Then he watched Tam disappear through a gap in the hedge and sprint off across the field.

Lock keeper on your tail again, is it?

Here we go again, Bess.

Nosebag off, harness on. Then he ran along the towpath to the next lock. They had stopped for the night in the middle of the flight so it was only a short dash. He closed the top gate and then ran back to the bottom gate to open the paddles, emptying the water from the lock.

First the nearside, then across the top of the gate to the offside. With both paddles open the lock would empty twice as fast.

He looked back to the barge. Jack was already getting Bess moving. Easier for the old girl today, with no cargo on board.

He glanced down at the top of the gate as he cranked the windlass lifting the nearside paddle, the water swirling as it roared out through the opening. The gate was crumbling and split where it had been rammed by barges coming into the lock too fast over the years, the splintered wood just visible through the piles of wet leaves lying along the top.

He could step over them.

It'd be no bother.

Chapter One

Skylarks; seagulls in the distance; a blackbird somewhere behind him – he was sure he could hear a blackbird; and a flock of crows on the roof, *giving it large*. Much more of that and he'd switch the siren on, that'd sort the buggers out. A murder, that was it, a murder of crows; it had come up at the pub quiz the week before. Louise had got it – she'd been good at collective nouns – but couldn't explain why it was a 'murder'. Now he knew, though, and he'd cheerfully shoot the bloody lot if he had a shotgun.

He reached up and banged on the underside of the roof. Then settled back to listen to the patter of the rain on the windscreen.

And the crackle of the radio.

'QPR three-ten from Control. Over.'

It was not the dawn chorus he had been hoping for.

'QPR three-ten, this is Control. Over.'

He rubbed his eyes – sleeping with his contact lenses in again – he must get some more eye drops. And he winced when he tried to lift his head – an inflatable neck pillow would be good too. No matter how far you wind the seat back, sleeping in a car is still bloody uncomfortable.

'QPR three-ten from Control. For God's sake, Nigel, wake up! Over.'

He sat up and fumbled for the radio with his left hand, still rubbing his eyes with his right.

'Bugger,' he muttered, as he dropped the handset into the passenger footwell. He opened his eyes, blinking furiously, and peered out into the fog – or were the windows steamed up? 'Control, this is QPR three-ten. Go ahead. Over.'

'We've received a report of a missing child. Alesha Daniels. One-zero years of age. Repeat, one-zero years of age. Father's name is Ryan Daniels. Address three-three Tyler Way, Highbridge. Over.'

'Control, received. Three-three Tyler Way. Will report back when we arrive. Over.'

'He has a record of violence. Over.'

It just gets better and better.

'Received, record of violence. Over.'

Police Constable Nigel Cole dropped the handset into the lap of PC Sandra MacIntyre, who had managed to sleep through the entire radio exchange as well as the squawking of the crows.

'What is it?' she asked, stifling a yawn.

'Missing girl.' Cole started the engine and switched the fans to full blast.

'How old?'

'Ten.'

'How much longer have we got left?' MacIntyre was sitting up now, cranking her seat forward with her left hand.

'Two hours.'

'It's six o'clock?'

'Nearly.'

Cole began wiping the inside of the windscreen with a handful of tissues. 'Here, do your side,' he said, passing the packet to MacIntyre.

He jabbed the buttons on the driver's door, opening both his window and MacIntyre's.

'Shut that, Nige, for God's sake.' She was leaning forward in her seat, trying to reach the bottom of the windscreen with the tissues. 'It's bloody freezing.'

Cole shut the windows, relieved to see that the rubber seal had cleared the condensation from both anyway. Another minute or so and the rear demist would have done its job too. He adjusted the fans to blow on the windscreen.

'Who is it?' asked MacIntyre, throwing the sodden tissues into the footwell.

'Alesha Daniels.'

'Not Ryan's kid?'

Cole was putting on his seatbelt. 'Ryan Daniels. Thirty-three Tyler Way. D'you know him?'

'He's moved house if it's him. Bit free with his fists. Worse when he's been on the lager. His partner – shit, what was her name?' MacIntyre shook her head. 'She must've had us over there three times.'

'Where?'

'Worston Lane. It was a flat down the Burnham end. Can't remember the number. She never pursued it though.' MacIntyre shrugged her shoulders. 'Usual story.'

'Control said he had a record?'

'GBH. He headbutted an old bloke who cut him up at a roundabout. Broke his nose.'

'Grievous bodily on an elderly man? Sounds like a nasty piece of work.'

'First thing I did when I got there was breathalyse him. Nicked the tosser for drink driving too.' MacIntyre grinned. 'He was sent down for two years and got a five year ban. I'm sure his daughter's name was Alesha. Social Services were all over them.'

Cole waited for her to put her seatbelt on, then turned out of the gravel car park behind the River Huntspill on to the narrow country lane, craning his neck to watch the drainage ditches on either side of the cattle grid.

'Clear this side,' said MacIntyre. 'Nice spot, that one. Off the beaten track.'

'You have to watch it when the fishing season opens. The pumping station is only a mile or so that way.' Cole was pointing out of the back of the patrol car with his thumb. 'You're likely to wake up to find some bloody fisherman's tweeted a photo of you.'

'It doesn't help that you sleep with your mouth open.' MacIntyre smiled. 'You'd go viral in a jiffy.'

Cole looked up at the red brick terrace – three storey with dormer windows, steps up to the front door, thin brown streaks running down the flaking white paint from the rusting screws that held the numbers on, loosely by the looks of things. There were four sets of two – 33, 34, 35, 36 – and none were on straight.

Three of the letterbox covers on the wall were missing, but the Entryphone system looked new.

'I remember this when it was a derelict factory and scrubland.'

'When was that?'

'Ten years ago. More probably.' The door flew open and a figure appeared, leaning over the wobbly railings at the top of the steps.

'Is that him?' Cole wrenched on the handbrake.

MacIntyre looked up and sighed. ''Fraid so. Looks like he's had a few too.'

'Will he remember you?'

'Oh yes.'

'Better let me do the talking then,' said Cole, switching off the engine.

MacIntyre picked up the radio. 'Control, this is QPR three-ten on scene. The father appears drunk. Over.'

'QPR three-ten, he rang again and was very agitated. Proceed with caution. Over.'

'What time was she first reported missing? Over.'

'Zero-five-four-two. Over.'

MacIntyre replaced the handset. 'That's not bad,' she said, turning to Cole. 'It's only just gone six now.'

'Tell him that.'

Ryan Daniels was hanging over the railings, waving his arms and shouting. Several days of stubble, food down his T-shirt, jogging bottoms and bare feet; he was jabbing his TV remote control at the patrol car.

'And why'd he wait until the morning to report her missing?' continued Cole.

'Pisshead probably fell asleep,' muttered MacIntyre. She frowned. 'He's had a few more tattoos by the looks of it.'

'Let's get this over with.'

'I love your optimism.'

Cole climbed out of the driver's seat. 'Mr Daniels, is it?'

'Yes, it bloody well is. What time d'you call this? How long does it take, for fuck's sake? My daughter's out there somewhere, you useless—!'

MacIntyre slammed the passenger door. 'Let's take this inside, Ryan,' she said, stepping forward.

'It's Mr Daniels to you. He can come in, but you can fuck off.'

'Calm down, Ryan.'

'I'll deal with it, Sandra.' Cole's eyes widened. 'You wait here. All right?'

Cole squeezed past a bicycle chained to a radiator in the narrow hallway and followed Daniels, flicking a light switch on the wall at the bottom of the stairs.

'Bulb's gone,' said Daniels. 'You'd better watch out for the bottles.'

Two plastic crates filled with empties and unopened post, then another on the bottom step; Cole stepped over them and followed Daniels up the stairs, relying on light that was streaming in through a door at the top.

'I hadn't realised these were flats,' he said, admiring the stack of washing up in the kitchen sink.

'Rented,' replied Daniels. 'I've been here two years, since me and Tanya split up.' He cracked open a can of cheap lager with a label Cole didn't recognise and leaned back against the sink, sending the pile of plates crashing across the draining board.

'May I?' asked Cole, gesturing to a small table.

Daniels nodded, can to mouth.

'When was the last time you saw Alesha?'

'She stayed last weekend, as usual, and left on Sunday. She comes here every Saturday night, goes home Sunday. And I had to fight for that.'

'What d'you mean?'

'In court.' Daniels was lighting a cigarette. 'I had to get a Child Arrangements Order or whatever the fuck they call it.' He blew the smoke out through his nose. 'To see my own bloody kid.'

'When was that?'

'A year or so ago.'

'And she's ten?'

'Yes.'

'Lives with her mother then. Is that Tanya?'

'Yes. She's got a flat in Worston Lane.'

'Tanya who?'

'Stevens.'

'Does she live alone?'

'There's a boyfriend who stays. Kevin Sailes.' Daniels sneered. 'Wanker. You'll find them both on your database.'

Cole raised his eyebrows.

'Yes, and me.' Daniels took another swig of beer.

'How does Alesha get here?' Cole cleared a space on the table in front of him, piling up several empty foil trays, and opened his notebook.

'She cycles from Tanya's.'

'It was raining last night.'

'That doesn't bother her. She loves her bike, she does. She's always out on it.'

'Whose is this?' Cole picked up a wine glass and turned the red lipstick on it towards Daniels.

'Monica's. What's that got to do with Alesha?'

'Where's Monica now?'

'She went home about midnight.' Cole flicked his ash into the sink. 'She drove me over to Tanya's about eleven thirty, dropped me back here and then went home.'

'How much had she had to drink?' Cole looked up.

'My daughter's missing and you're asking me how much my girlfriend had to drink? You must be fucking kidding me?' Daniels slammed the can down on the worktop, sending two plates and associated cutlery crashing on to the floor. The can followed, the dregs dribbling on to the lino.

'What time was Alesha due here?' asked Cole, changing the subject.

'Six.' Daniels sighed. 'She comes at six every Saturday evening.'

'So, why wait nearly twelve hours to report her missing?'

'Look, it may have been a bit later when Monica went home.'

'What difference does that make?'

'You work it out.'

Cole glanced into the foil tray on top of the stack on the table in front of him. Several cigarette butts, soaked in sauce, were in amongst the noodles, two of them hand rolled with a small roll of cardboard in the end.

Daniels lunged forward, snatched the trays off the table and dropped them in the bin. 'We thought . . . I thought . . . she'd gone to a friend or something. She's done it before and forgotten to tell anyone.'

'Does she have a mobile phone?'

'I had an upgrade so she's got my old Samsung. It's switched off.'

'You've tried it?'

'Of course I bloody have!'

'And you haven't seen her since last Sunday?'

'She came to my work on Thursday afternoon. Scrounging money for sweets.'

'Where's that?'

'Jester Prints in Love Lane. We do screen printing. T-shirts and stuff. She was only there a few minutes. I gave her a couple of quid and off she went on her bike.'

Cole glanced at the can of lager in Daniels's hand.

'I only drink at weekends. All right?'

Cole nodded. 'And when did you last hear from her?'

'She sent me a text yesterday morning to say she'd be over later as usual. Here,' replied Daniels, handing Cole his phone, 'see for yourself.'

Cole peered at the message and then copied it into his notebook.

C u later dad xx

'What time was that?' he asked, handing the phone back to Daniels. 'It just says "yesterday".'

Daniels clicked on the message, holding his cigarette between his teeth. 'Saturday twenty-fifth April, ten forty-two,' he said, wincing as the smoke drifted up into his eyes.

'And she just never turned up?'

'No. I kept ringing and ringing, but no one answered.'

'What was she wearing?'

'How the fuck would I know that? I haven't seen her since Thursday!'

Cole took a deep breath. 'Does she have a favourite coat?'

'A green padded jacket. It's dark green, shiny, with a fake fur band around the hood.' Daniels dropped his cigarette into an empty can of lager on the side, picked it up and shook it, listening for the hiss as the dregs soaked the burning tobacco. 'Jeans too. She always wears light blue jeans, torn at the knees, y'know.'

'What about her bike?'

'It's too small for her, really. Bright pink with a white plastic basket on the front. There's stuff like tinsel hanging from the handlebars too.'

'Any other distinguishing marks, stuff like that?'

'Braces on her teeth. Fixed, like the train tracks. I've got a photo of her on my wall. D'you want it?'

'Yes, please.'

Cole was still scribbling in his notebook when Daniels returned with a small framed photograph. 'That's her on the left.' Alesha was smiling at the camera, cheek to cheek with a friend. 'It's a selfie. That's Evie, I think.'

'Can I keep this?'

'I'd like it back though.'

'When was it taken?'

'Six months ago. The half term before Christmas. They're on the beach.'

'And is her hair still the same?'

Daniels nodded.

'Has Alesha ever gone missing like this before? Even for a short time?'

'She's had a sleepover at a friend's once or twice and forgotten to tell me, but she's always answered her phone straight off when I've rung.'

'Have you tried ringing Tanya?'

'Yes. I told you I went over there too. Monica took me. And I walked over there again this morning. Nothing. There are no lights on even. That's why I rang you lot.'

'Have you been out to look for Alesha?'

'I walked the route she'd take, yes.'

'Which way is that?'

'Through the Catholic church, along Marine Drive then through Apex. If she was in town with her friends then it's just Marine Drive and Apex. The path through the park is at the end of the road here.'

'Can you try her again now?'

Cole watched while Daniels dialled Alesha's number and held the phone to his ear.

'It goes straight through to voicemail,' said Daniels, shaking his head.

'Have you left a message?'

'Loads. D'you want me to leave another one?'

'No.' Cole handed his notebook and pen to Daniels. 'Write down Tanya's full name, address and phone numbers.'

'The landline's been cut off.'

'Give it to me anyway. And Alesha's mobile.'

'Here,' mumbled Daniels, handing the notebook back to Cole. Then he cracked open another can of cheap lager.

'Does she have her own room here?'

'Yes.'

'Can I see it?'

'It's the only tidy room in the flat,' said Daniels, holding open the door. Cole peered in. It was small, just wide enough for a single bed and a bedside table, with a few teddy bears on the pillows and posters on the walls. The cries of the seagulls outside carried through the open fanlight.

'Her stuff's in here,' said Daniels, sliding open a small built-in wardrobe behind the door. A few piles of clothes, a pair of trainers on the floor – the ones with wheels in the heels – odd bits of make-up, an iPod and a pair of headphones.

'Make-up?' asked Cole, frowning.

'She'll have pinched it from her mum, I expect. Monica gave her the lipstick though. It was an old one she was going to chuck out, I think.'

'What about her friends?'

'Evie and Mia are her best friends, but I don't know their surnames. They're in the same class at school.'

'St Andrew's?'

'Yes. Tanya will know who they are.'

'Does Alesha have a computer?'

'An iPad. I gave it to her for Christmas the year before last.'

'Is she on Facebook?'

'Used to be, but it's all Snapchat these days,' replied Daniels. 'Never really got the hang of that.'

'Me neither.' Cole smiled. 'Where is this iPad?'

'She keeps it at home now. She kept it here for a while when Tanya was threatening to sell it.'

'Sell it? What for?'

'You'll find out.'

Chapter Two

'I had a look up and down,' said MacIntyre, 'but none of the neighbours are up yet.' She was walking back along the pavement as Cole ran down the steps outside Daniels's flat.

'You drive.' He threw the car keys to MacIntyre and jumped in to the passenger seat. Then he picked up the radio. 'Control, from QPR three-ten, database check. Over.'

'Go ahead. Over.'

'Tanya – *Tango-Alpha-November-Yankee-Alpha* – Stevens – *Sierra-Tango-Echo-Victor*; and Kevin Sailes – *Sierra-Alpha-India-Lima-Echo-Sierra*. Acknowledge. Over.'

'Control, reading back. Tanya Stevens and Kevin Sailes. Over.'

'That is correct,' said Cole. 'Children and Vulnerable Adult check, Alesha Daniels – *Alpha-Lima-Echo-Sierra-Hotel-Alpha*. Over.' He turned to MacIntyre. 'Drive.'

'Where?'

'Burnham. Worston Lane.'

'Control, received. What is your position? Over.'

'Checking the mother's address in Worston Lane. Stand by. Over.'

MacIntyre flipped the siren on as she accelerated along Burnham Road.

'We don't need that at this time in the morning,' said Cole.

'Spoil sport,' muttered MacIntyre. A few minutes later, she turned right in to Worston Lane and slowed. 'It's the upstairs flat on the end there. I remember now.' She pulled on to the grass verge. 'What number is it?'

'Thirteen B'.

'That's it.'

A new front door and windows on the ground floor contrasted with the original metal-framed windows upstairs, the glass cracked in one corner and the black paint peeling off. Cole climbed out of the patrol car and looked down the side of the property.

'The front door's at the top of those steps,' said MacIntyre. She opened the front gate and Cole followed her along the garden path, glancing down at the immaculate front lawn as he walked past. The back garden, visible beyond the bottom of the steps, was a jungle: grass and weeds almost up to the seat of a child's swing; a shed in the far corner, the roof collapsed.

'The back belongs to upstairs,' said MacIntyre, shaking her head.

'Better check it out.'

Cole walked up the steps and banged on the front door, watching MacIntyre wading through the grass while he waited. Then he squatted down and opened the letterbox.

'Tanya, it's the police. Are you in there?'

Silence.

He heard MacIntyre on the steps behind him and stood up as she reached the top. 'Garden's clear,' she said, brushing her trousers.

Cole banged on the door again.

'Two doors up there's a van with a ladder on the roof. See if we can borrow it, will you?'

MacIntyre sighed and trudged down the steps, leaving Cole peering through the letterbox. He took out his notebook and phone, then dialled Tanya's number.

'That's fine,' said MacIntyre, when Cole appeared around the corner of the block. 'He's just throwing some clothes on.'

'Her *mobile*'s in there. I can hear it ringing.' He looked up at the front window. 'We'll try round the back first.'

'I've never understood why people pin blankets up at windows,' said MacIntyre. 'I mean, get some bloody curtains at a charity shop. It's probably cheaper anyway.'

Cole watched the neighbour standing on the rear wheel of his van to unlock the ladder on the roof. Then he helped him lift it off and carry it around the back of number thirteen.

'Sorry to wake you on a Sunday, Sir.'

'No worries, mate,' came the reply.

'D'you know them?'

'Not really. They say "hello" if you bump into them, but that's it.'

'What about the daughter?'

'Nice kid. Seen her out on her bike. Gotta feel sorry for her, though, living in that shithole. It's no place for a child to be.'

'Why not?'

'You should know.'

Cole nodded.

They propped the ladder up between the windows at the back and Cole started climbing, with MacIntyre holding the bottom.

'This must be Alesha's room.' Cole was holding on to the ladder with his right hand and the window ledge with his left. He noticed a damp patch on the wall, opposite the end of her bed, peeling wallpaper, and a poster for some girl band he had never heard of lying on the floor, the Sellotape having given up the fight to hang on. Apart from that, the room was tidy, except for the goldfish floating upside down in his or her bowl. He turned and looked down at MacIntyre. 'It's empty and the door's closed.'

Then he leaned over to his right. 'Kitchen.' He shook his head. 'At least, I think there's a kitchen in there somewhere. Can't see anything.'

'D'you want me to carry the ladder round the front?' asked the neighbour.

'There's a blanket up at the window,' said MacIntyre.

'The fanlight's open,' said Cole. 'I can reach in and pull it down.'

'Are you sure we should be doing that?'

'There's a ten year old girl missing, Sandra.'

'Yeah.'

Seconds later Cole was at the top of the ladder at the front of the property, standing on the top rung, which was resting on the brickwork beneath the window. He was holding on to the open fanlight with his left hand, pulling at the old tartan blanket with his right. Judging by the hairs on it and the smell, some poor dog was missing its bed.

'It's just drawing pins by the looks of it,' he said. 'One more.' Then the blanket fell down inside the flat. 'Oh, shit.'

'What is it?'

Cole looked down at the woman slumped on a brown leather sofa held together with duct tape. Her head was tipped to one side and she was drooling on to a pile of vomit on the cushion behind her. A belt was looped around her left arm, a syringe still clamped in the fingers of her right hand. An empty bottle of vodka lay on its side on the floor in front of her.

'Battering ram,' shouted Cole, as he reached down for the top of the ladder.

MacIntyre left the neighbour holding the bottom and raced over to the patrol car, opening the boot with the remote control as she ran. She returned with the battering ram and handed it to Cole, just as he was stepping off the bottom rung of the ladder.

'And an ambulance,' he said. 'Suspected overdose. She's unconscious. Vomited at least once.'

MacIntyre nodded and ran back over to the car.

'I can put this back. You carry on,' said the neighbour.

'Thank you, Sir.'

Cole ran around to the side of the flat and up the steps to the wooden front door, hitting it just above the lock in one movement. It splintered and swung open. Cole retched, turned away and took a deep breath.

That's all you need at this time in the morning.

MacIntyre was behind him now. 'Shit, what's that smell?' She put her hand over her nose and mouth.

'Right first time,' mumbled Cole.

'Is she dead?'

'I don't think so. You check the other rooms.'

'Will do.'

Once in the sitting room, Cole kicked the empty bottle of vodka away and checked the woman for a pulse. 'She's alive,' he said, when MacIntyre walked in.

'No one else here.'

'Is there a loft hatch?'

'Don't know.'

'You'd better check. Then stay with her and keep her airway clear.'

Cole ran down to the patrol car and picked up the radio. 'Control from QPR three-ten. We are at the mother's address, Tanya Stevens. She's unconscious, suspected drug use, ambulance requested. No sign of male occupant, Kevin Sailes, or Alesha. Repeat. No sign of Alesha. Acknowledge. Over.'

'QPR three-ten, received. Alesha is the subject of Child Protection Plan. Positive ViSOR match Kevin Sailes. Acknowledge. Over.'

'Received.' Cole took a deep breath and puffed out his cheeks. 'Is he on the register for violence or sex offences? Over.'

'Not known at this time. You're the officer on scene, Nige. What is your report? Over.'

Cole glanced up at the flat and watched MacIntyre opening the front window.

Why me? Why bloody me?

The sound of a siren in the distance brought him back to the present. That and the radio.

'C'mon, Nigel. What's it to be? Over.'

Cole nodded. He'd got it wrong before, and been a laughing stock for a few weeks, but that was a small price to pay.

Fuck it.

'Control, Alesha Daniels confirmed missing. High risk. Repeat. Missing. High risk. Suspected child abduction. Acknowledge. Over.'

Chapter Three

'Who's the reporting officer?'

'I am, Sir,' replied Cole, spinning round to see Chief Inspector Bateman striding towards him along the garden path.

'Let's hope you've got it right this time, Cole.'

'Yes, Sir.'

'Are you on your own?'

'Sandra MacIntyre went in the ambulance with the mother.'

'Good.'

'She's still out of it.'

'And there's no sign of the boyfriend?'

'No, Sir. He's on the Sex Offender Register at this address, but gave his mother's address in Weston when he was on bail. There's someone on the way over there now.'

'What about his mobile phone?'

'The registered number's dead, but he must have another one.'

'Well, you did the right thing, Cole.' Bateman sighed. 'Let's get the dogs out and the helicopter up too. Tell them to use their thermal imaging camera and start over at Apex Park.'

'I tried the helicopter, Sir. It's tasked elsewhere.'

'Doing what?'

'Following a stolen car on the M5.'

'Tell them the Bronze Commander is authorising an immediate divert.'

'Yes, Sir.'

'What about CCTV?'

'Someone's checking the town cameras now.'

'Does Sailes have a car?'

'Not according to DVLA, Sir.'

Bateman nodded. 'We'll need Family Liaison over at the father's flat, preferably before I get there. And let's page the Coastguard and BARB Search and Rescue as well. Get them searching along the Brue and the beach.'

'Yes, Sir.'

A police van screeched to a halt in the middle of the road and four uniformed officers jumped out of the back.

'You lot, on foot,' said Bateman. 'Which way did she go?' he asked, turning to Cole.

'We don't know where she started from, Sir, but from here it would have been through the Catholic church car park, along Marine Drive and through Apex Park.'

'Right. You two go that way. You two follow the same route starting from the town.' Bateman leaned in the passenger window of the van. 'The rest of you can start at the other end and fan out across Apex. All right?'

'Yes, Sir.'

'Check the reeds along the water's edge and the undergrowth—'

'We haven't got a description yet,' interrupted Cole, 'but she was probably wearing jeans and a dark green shiny jacket with a fur edging on the hood.'

'Remember that's not been confirmed yet,' said Bateman.

'We do know her bike was pink with a white plastic basket on the front and tassels on the handlebars,' continued Cole.

He watched the van speed off along Worston Lane towards Highbridge.

'What about her friends?' Bateman asked, turning back to Cole.

'I can't find anything in the flat, I'm afraid, Sir. I've got the mother's phone, but it's locked and she's unconscious.'

'What about the school?'

'St Andrew's. I rang the emergency number and they were going to get Alesha's teacher to ring me.'

'How long ago was that?'

'Ten minutes.'

'Ring them again. And stay on it. We need to know what Alesha was wearing.'

'Yes, Sir.'

'Have you spoken to the father about a Child Rescue Alert?'

'Not yet, no.'

'All right.'

Cole watched Inspector Bateman walking up the steps and into the flat while he waited for his call to be answered.

'Erica Bawden.'

'Miss Bawden, it's PC Cole again. You were going to get Miss Tapper to ring me?'

'I can't get hold of her, I'm afraid. She's not answering her phone. I don't think she was going away.'

'What's her address?'

'She got one of the new houses in Gielgud Close. Number forty-nine, I think.'

'Thank you. And her phone number?'

Cole scribbled the number in his notebook as Miss Bawden read it out from her emergency list.

'Thank you.'

'D'you want me to keep trying her?' she asked.

'No, leave it to me.' Cole rang off and ran up the steps into the flat to find Bateman standing in Alesha's bedroom, looking at the posters on the wall.

'She's seems like a normal kid,' he said, shaking his head, 'which is quite something when you look at the parents.'

'Yes, Sir.'

'And this must be a health hazard,' he said, pointing at the black mould on the wall, much of it hidden behind a wardrobe. He wrenched open the door. 'Her clothes smell damp. Would you want your child sleeping in here?'

Cole shook his head.

'Me neither,' muttered Bateman. 'What about the teacher?'

'I've got an address for her. Shall I go?'

'Send someone else. You're reporting officer, so you'll be staying with me. Have you notified Somerset Direct?'

'Not yet, Sir.'

'Better do it. Social Services will need to know. And the Safeguarding Coordination Unit. Then you can knock on the door of number ten opposite. The curtain's been twitching pretty much non-stop the whole time we've been here.'

Cole was sitting in his patrol car twenty minutes later with his phone clamped to his ear when Chief Inspector Bateman dropped into the passenger seat; the sound of a helicopter in the distance cut off when Bateman closed the car door again.

'Well?'

'I've notified Somerset Direct and the SCU, Sir. And we've got addresses for her friends, Evie and Mia. Officers are on the way now.

The hovercraft's out along the waterline and the Coastguard are working their way along the River Brue.'

'What about the nosy neighbour?'

'Mrs French. Lots of background information about Alesha, but she's not seen her since yesterday morning.' Cole opened his notebook. 'She keeps an eye out for her, feeds her when Tanya is otherwise engaged. Social Services have been involved and she gave me the name of the social worker, Diane Bradshaw.'

'When did she last see Sailes?'

'Not for a couple of days, but she rarely sees him anyway.'

'Nothing from the lot on foot?'

'Not yet.'

'What about Family Liaison?'

'Karen Marsden is with the father now, pouring black coffee down his throat by all accounts.'

'Well, we'd better go and see him,' said Bateman, fastening his seatbelt.

Bateman raised his eyebrows when Karen Marsden opened the front door wearing jeans and a red fleece top. 'No uniform, Sergeant?'

'I live in Burnham, Sir, so I came straight here when I got the shout. My uniform's in my locker at Express Park.'

'How is he?'

'Still conscious, which is an achievement in itself when you see how much he's had to drink.'

'Don't tell me he's still drinking.'

'He hasn't had one since I got here and I just made him another coffee.'

'Well, that's something, I suppose.' Bateman sighed. 'Lead on.'

Cole and Bateman followed Karen up the stairs and into the lounge. Daniels was slouched on a black leather sofa in front of a coffee table that was covered in empty cans, leaving just enough room for an ashtray and the TV remote control.

'Ryan, this is Chief Inspector Bateman,' said Karen. 'And you've met Nigel Cole?'

'Where's the other one?'

'She went to the hospital with Tanya,' replied Cole.

'Is she all right?'

'She'd been using, Ryan.' Karen sat down next to Daniels and put her hand on his arm. 'She was unconscious, but we think she's going to be OK.'

'What about Alesha?'

'We've got search teams out looking for her, Mr Daniels,' said Bateman. 'We're tracing her mobile phone and the helicopter's up with its thermal imaging camera. The hovercraft and Coastguard are out looking too.'

'We're checking the town CCTV,' said Cole. 'And we've tracked down her friends, Evie and Mia. Officers are over there now.'

'We're doing everything we can,' said Karen.

'We need to talk about a Child Rescue Alert,' said Bateman.

'What's that?'

'Local news, radio and television. We use her photo, a press conference with you. It's the fastest way of getting the public to keep an eye out for her.'

'I'm not sure I—'

'It really is the best way,' said Karen.

Tears began trickling down Daniels's cheeks. 'All right, all right. Anything,' he said.

'I'll set that up now,' said Bateman.

Daniels sat up. 'Where's Kevin?'

'We don't know.'

'So, he could be with Alesha?'

'We're checking his mother's address in Weston.'

'D'you know his mobile number?' asked Cole. 'We've got Tanya's phone but it's locked and she's still unconscious.'

'The code's twenty-two twelve. Always used to be anyway. It's her date of birth.'

'We can't access her phone without her consent,' said Bateman.

'Why not arrest her for possession of a Class A drug?' asked Karen. 'Then we could.'

'She'd need to be conscious for that.'

Cole stepped backwards out of the lounge door unseen and tiptoed down the stairs. Once out on to the street, he opened the boot of the patrol car and picked up Tanya's iPhone. He tapped in 2212, unlocked it, then went to 'Contacts' and scribbled down Sailes's mobile number in his notebook.

He arrived back at the top of the stairs just as Bateman was coming out of the lounge.

'Where have you been?'

'I just remembered, Sir. This was last number redial on the landline in Tanya's flat.' He handed his notebook to Bateman, open at Sailes's mobile number.

'The landline's been disconnected,' said Daniels, still on the sofa just inside the door.

'It may have been on a piece of paper by the phone.'

'Where's that piece of paper now?' asked Bateman, frowning.

'I may have mislaid it, Sir.' Cole shrugged his shoulders.

Bateman smiled. 'Just find that phone.'

'Yes, Sir.'

Cole was leaning back against the patrol car with his eyes closed when he heard footsteps coming down the stairs, and lurched forward just as Bateman wrenched open the front door.

'Well?'

'Alesha's wearing blue jeans, a white T-shirt with *The Walking Dead* on it and her green—'

'*The Walking Dead*? What the bloody hell's she doing watching that at her age?'

'Dunno, Sir.'

'Some people,' muttered Bateman. 'Go on.'

'And her green shiny coat with the fake fur on the hood,' continued Cole, reading from his notebook. 'Evie left them outside the pavilion and cycled home. She got home about five fifteen. Then Mia was picked up by her Mum outside Fortes in Pier Street just after five thirty. That was the last time anyone saw Alesha.'

'Well, at least it gives us a starting point for the CCTV.' Bateman was pacing up and down on the pavement in Tyler Way. 'Let everybody know and let's start some house to house. Marine Drive and the houses facing on to Apex Park. Worston Lane too.'

'Isn't it a bit early, Sir?'

'What time is it?'

'Eight thirty,' replied Cole. 'And it's Sunday, don't forget.'

'Tough.'

Cole nodded and opened the driver's door of the patrol car.

'And we'd better put the dive team on standby,' continued Bateman.

'What about the helicopter, Sir? It's found nothing at Apex.'

'Get them searching back gardens between here and Worston Lane, if they've got enough fuel left.'

Cole picked up the radio, watching Bateman in his rear view mirror briefing the press officer, Vicky Thomas. 'All units, all units, this is QPR three-ten, stand by for observation message. Over.'

Bateman opened the passenger door of the patrol car and leaned in. 'Where's the photo of her?'

'I sent it down to Express Park to be copied, Sir. It's on its way back now with the house to house team.'

Bateman nodded and slammed the door of the patrol car before disappearing inside thirty-three Tyler Way with Vicky Thomas.

'All units, this is QPR three-ten, description confirmed. Blue jeans, dark green shiny bomber-style jacket with fur lining to hood. White T-shirt with zombie logo. Shoulder length brown hair, not tied back. Jeans ripped at the knees. Over.'

Cole looked at his watch. On another day he'd have fifteen minutes left, then it would be home to bed. He sighed. Not today.

'QPR three-ten from QPN two-nine-two. Over.'

'QPN two-nine-two, this is QPR three-ten. Go ahead. Over.'

'We're in an area of dense undergrowth opposite Parsons Road, repeat Parsons Road, behind the narrow channel into the boating lake. Acknowledge. Over.'

'QPR three-ten, received. What is your status? Over.'

'We've found something. Over.'

Chapter Four

'Sorry to interrupt.' Cole peered around the lounge door.

Karen Marsden was sitting next to Daniels on the sofa, with Vicky Thomas sitting on the one armchair in the room. Bateman was standing with his back to the window.

'What is it, Cole?' he asked.

'I wanted to ask Mr Daniels about the tassels on Alesha's handlebars.'

'Is it urgent?'

Cole hesitated.

'They're pink streamer things,' said Daniels, looking up at Cole over his shoulder. 'I got 'em on eBay. They've got a plastic thing on the end that pushes into the end of the grip.'

'And they're pink?'

'Pink and silver. Shiny, like tinsel.'

'Thank you.' Cole ducked back out of the room.

'Give me a minute,' said Bateman, following him. He closed the door and lowered his voice. 'Have we found something?'

Cole nodded.

'Where?'

'Apex Park. In the trees opposite Parsons Road. It sounds like one of the tassels.'

'We'd better get over there now.'

Cole had turned the car round by the time Bateman appeared at the top of the steps. He ran down and jumped in the passenger seat.

'I didn't tell him,' he said, fastening his seatbelt. 'What've they found? Exactly.'

'Just a tassel, Sir, hanging in a tree. One of the dogs—'

'How far from the lake?'

'Twenty yards or so.'

Bateman picked up the radio handset as Cole raced out of Highbridge on the A38, coming up behind a queue of traffic at the junction with Burnham Road. 'Put the siren on.'

'Yes, Sir.'

'Control, from—' Bateman frowned. 'What's this car's call sign?'

'QPR three-ten.'

'Control, from QPR three-ten, this is Bronze Commander requesting underwater search unit. Immediate assistance required. Parsons Road, Highbridge. Acknowledge. Over.'

'Received. Stand by.'

Less than sixty seconds later Cole screeched to a halt behind a police van parked in Parsons Road. Several officers were talking to residents on the doorsteps of houses off to his right, and a dog van was parked on the grass to his left.

A small copse overlooking the lake had been cordoned off with blue tape, the grass around it recently mown, giving the appearance of dense undergrowth in the trees. One hundred yards or so from the houses opposite, and perhaps eighty from the two bungalows on the corner, it would have been deserted on a rainy Saturday night in April.

'What about fishermen?' asked Bateman.

'It's closed season, Sir,' replied Cole.

'Bloody well would be, wouldn't it.' Bateman unfastened his seatbelt and opened the passenger door. 'Let me know what the dive team say.'

'Yes, Sir.'

He was watching Bateman striding across the grass when the radio crackled.

'QPR three-ten, dive team en route. ETA fifty minutes. Repeat. ETA fifty minutes. Over.'

Cole ran across the grass, a rumble of thunder in the distance just carrying over the helicopter that was moving slowly north, high above Marine Drive. Cole glanced up as he ran, looking for the flash of lightning, then he caught up with Bateman just as he was ducking under the police cordon.

'Dive team will be here in fifty minutes, Sir.'

'That'll have to do.'

They followed a uniformed officer along a muddy path through the undergrowth to a small clearing in the middle of the copse. Several footprints and a single bicycle tyre track had been taped off on another path coming in from the other side of the trees.

'She came in that way, Sir.'

'What about the footprints?'

'They're not a child's that's for sure. We've marked off what we can see, but it's been raining all night.'

'Let's get Scientific Services out here straightaway.'

'Yes, Sir,' said Cole.

'The streamer thing's round the other side, Sir,' said the officer, pointing at a small conifer where the paths crossed.

The tassel was hanging from a branch near the top of the conifer, but no more than three feet off the ground; several of the streamers tangled around the branch above.

'And nobody's touched it?'

'No, Sir.'

Cole looked along the path that led down towards the lake where several more footprints had been cordoned off. He was able to follow the bicycle tyre track for a few yards, then it stopped.

'Looks like he picked up the bike and carried it,' said Bateman.

'Must've thrown it in the lake, Sir,' said the uniformed officer.

'Well, we'll soon see.'

◆ ◆ ◆

'What time is it?'

'Nearly midday, Sir,' replied Cole.

'What time does your shift end?'

'Four hours ago.'

Bateman smiled.

'Alesha's mother has woken up,' continued Cole. 'But she's had to be sedated.'

'Didn't they get anything out of her?'

'Only that she didn't know where Alesha was. She had a row with Sailes last night and he'd gone off in a huff.'

'What time?'

'We don't know.'

'We can't rule him out then.'

Cole turned back to the water and watched the air bubbles breaking the surface twenty yards from the bank. He had spent the last half an hour watching the line of bubbles and following the diver's progress as he crawled along the bottom of the lake feeling with his fingertips, searching for a child's bicycle or a phone. Or a child's body.

The diver was following a rope with a weight on the end. Follow it out from the bank, move the weight two feet to the right, follow the rope back to the bank, each time fanning out across the lake from a gap in the reeds usually occupied by an angler.

A second member of the dive team was feeding a line out to the diver and retrieving it as he swam back towards the bank. 'Compressed air and comms', apparently. A third was crawling through the reed bed along the margins.

Maybe the life of a police diver wasn't so glamorous after all?

A small crowd of dog walkers was watching from the far bank, some of them pointing cameras.

'I'd better go,' said Bateman. 'The press conference is set for twelve thirty to catch the lunchtime news. Let me know straight away if they find anything.'

'Yes, Sir. D'you want the car keys?'

'I can walk back from here.'

'Yes, Sir.'

'And send someone round to move that lot on.' Bateman gestured to the onlookers on the other side of the lake. 'Ghouls,' he muttered.

Seems a bit harsh, thought Cole, turning to watch the camera flashes in the trees behind him. One minute he's doing a press conference to ask the public for their help, and the next he's calling them 'ghouls'. Still, searching for a missing child was hardly a spectator sport. He walked down to the edge of the water and waved at the group to move on, which they did. Hastily.

'He's got something!'

The shout came from the dive team officer on the bank.

Cole spun round to see a pink streamer emerging from the water, followed by a set of handlebars and behind them a diver, the torches on either side of his full face helmet still on. He carried the bicycle to the bank and passed it up to another dive team member, who placed it on a plastic sheet.

Cole watched a Scenes of Crime officer taking photographs of it, while he waited for Inspector Bateman to answer his phone.

'They've found the bike, Sir.'

'Are you sure?'

'Yes. It's got the other tassel.'

'What about the phone?'

'That's going to take a lot longer, Sir. He could've thrown that forty or fifty yards out.'

'I'm going to have to tell Daniels. I don't want to spring it on him in the press conference, and he can identify it afterwards. Where is it now?'

'On the bank here. SOCO are looking at it.'

'Good. Look, I've arranged for someone to take over from you. Brief them when they get here, then you can go home.'

'I'd rather stay, Sir.'

By mid-afternoon more than fifty local people – friends, neighbours and dog walkers – were out searching Apex Park and along the River Brue, long lines of them covering different areas under the watchful eye of a uniformed constable.

Cole had added the role of search coordinator to reporting officer and didn't feel so bad now about sleeping through much of his night shift. He was watching Scientific Services complete their search of the copse and listening for a shout from the divers still combing the bottom of the lake for Alesha's phone, the line of bubbles in the murky green water now over fifty yards from the bank.

The occasional rumble of thunder in the distance broke the silence, but it had stayed dry, which explained the crowds arriving to help with the search.

He noticed Sandra MacIntyre walking towards him along the footpath from the end of Tyler Way.

'What're you doing here?' he asked.

'The mother's still out of it. One of the Weston lot turned up so I got a lift back. I thought you'd be in bed by now?'

'No such luck.'

'Have they found anything else?'

'Not yet.'

'Well, we've got Kevin Sailes,' said MacIntyre. 'Picked him up at a friend's house in Bridgwater.'

'When?'

'About an hour ago.'

'Nobody tells me anything.' Cole shook his head. 'And I'm supposed to be the reporting officer.' He handed his clipboard to MacIntyre. 'Take over the search, will you?'

'If I must.'

'You can see where I've sent people. Just send any others who arrive somewhere else and mark the map. You know the drill.'

'I'll be fine. Where are you going?'

'I want to find out what Sailes is saying.'

'He's at Express Park,' shouted MacIntyre, as Cole ran over to his patrol car. 'Says he's not seen her since yesterday morning.'

Cole slowed to a walk. That made it a stranger abduction, if Sailes was telling the truth. He leaned back against the side of his car and closed his eyes.

'Let's go home, Nige,' said MacIntyre. 'We're not going to find anything now. She's either miles from here or—'

'Don't say it.'

'We did our best.'

Cole nodded. 'Did you check the loft in the flat? There was that case where a girl went missing and they found her in the loft days later.'

'I checked it.'

'And the shed?'

'Yes. And the helicopter's been over it with the camera.'

'I know, I know.'

A large white lorry turned into Parsons Road behind them and they watched it bounce up the kerb and pull on to the grass adjacent to the footpath.

'Looks like we can go now anyway,' said MacIntyre.

Chief Inspector Bateman climbed out of a patrol car that had been following the lorry.

'You've heard about Sailes?'

'Yes, Sir.'

'We're setting up the mobile command unit. You two have had a day and a night of it, so brief Sergeant Dean and bugger off home, the pair of you.'

Dean was behind them, pulling out an expanding section from the side of the trailer. Then he unfolded a set of steps on to the path and clipped them into place. 'Ready when you are, Sir,' he said.

'One last thing,' said Bateman. 'We'll need whoever's dealing with Alesha in our Safeguarding Unit. Who is it, d'you know?'

'Jane Winter, Sir,' replied Cole. 'She's on holiday. She went with—'

'I know that. Where've they gone?'

'The Lake District, I think.'

'Better get her back then. It's not as if she's gone to Australia, is it.'

Chapter Five

Change at Oxenholme – it was going to be a long day – then Birmingham New Street and Bristol Temple Meads. Bridgwater by lunchtime, Dixon had said. Trust him to book a cottage in the middle of nowhere that had a landline and satellite broadband. There really had been no escape.

Six hours sitting on the train. It had taken less than five on the way up in his new Land Rover, once she had got over the embarrassment of being seen in it.

Not just mushy pea green, but metallic mushy pea green!

'It's Heritage Green. And it's a damned good spec for the price, so you'll just have to get used to it,' had been his excuse. Still, the bonnet was new and needed a re-spray, so she had time to persuade him to get the rest of the car done at the same time.

Detective Sergeant Jane Winter settled back into her seat and watched the streaks of rain on the window slowly change from vertical to horizontal as the train picked up speed. To be fair to him, Dixon had said that she could take the Land Rover. There were plenty of walks he could do straight from the cottage in Hartsop, then at the end of the week he'd hitchhike down to Windermere and take the train home.

Jane would like to have seen that. She smiled. Hitchhiking with a rucksack on his back and a large white Staffordshire terrier on a lead. It would have been quicker walking home. Monty would have hated it too. And besides, she'd had far too much gin last night to drive at this time in the morning, making the 06.45 from Windermere the safer bet.

Yesterday had been a good day, the only day of her holiday, come to think of it. She slipped off her shoes and stretched her toes out on the cold floor of the train carriage in a feeble attempt to numb the pain now the medicinal gin was wearing off.

'We'll start with something easy, don't worry.' She should have known she was in trouble from the cheesy grin that went with it and a few hours later she had found herself halfway along Striding Edge on the way to the summit of Helvellyn. She had looked down only once during her trip along the knife edge ridge, coincidentally right after Dixon had shouted, 'Don't look down!' Mercifully, he had been too slow with the camera to capture the look on her face.

The summit itself had been cold, the icy wind whistling across the top and sending them scuttling for the crowded summit shelter. Roger Poland, the Home Office pathologist and a close friend, had rung Dixon when he had a mouthful of ginger cake, but he couldn't make himself heard over the roar of the wind anyway, although the intermittent signal hadn't helped. Jane had snatched Dixon's phone just in time to hear Roger shout, 'Have you asked her yet?' then the signal had been lost.

'Asked me what?'

'No idea.'

Yeah, right.

Today was to have been a rest day, taking a motor boat out on Lake Windermere, then tomorrow a trip up Scafell Pike. Much to her surprise, Jane had found herself insisting. 'You can't come to the Lakes and not go up the highest one.'

'If you say so.'

But instead she was on her way back to work, to help in the search for Alesha. Poor Alesha.

What the bloody hell have you been up to this time?

'They'll have found her by the time you get there,' Dixon had said, 'so you can turn round and come straight back.'

Jane frowned. The worst part about it was that they still hadn't cleared the air. A few short weeks ago he had been talking about marriage, in a roundabout sort of way, a subject he had not mentioned since. But it wasn't her fault. She had thought he was dead and had told him straight. She could hear herself even now. *'You're doing my head in, you really are. You go out sometimes and I never know whether you're coming back.'* She winced. Then had come the line that hit home. She knew that. And it had changed everything. *'I'm not sure I can do this any more.'*

Both of them had deftly avoided the subject ever since. Or at least Dixon had. She had tried to get around to it, but somehow never got there; the conversation stopped by an offer of tea or gin. Or a bloody film. Monty was getting even longer walks on the beach than usual. And more of them too.

She hadn't pushed it, though. Dixon had booked the week away and that would be the time to sort it out, or at least it was supposed to have been. And now that chance was gone. The chance to tell him that, yes, he was doing her head in, and, yes, his film collection was crap, but that she loved him despite that, or because of it. She just loved him.

It had been a bumpy ride, the last few weeks, one way or the other.

Then there was Lucy, the sister she'd met for the first time at their mother's funeral. She had only met her birth mother twice, the second time when Sonia turned up at the cottage scrounging money for drugs. Then a few days later her probation officer had phoned with the news that she was dead.

Jane sighed. Thinking about it, it was only a few days afterwards that Louise was telling her Dixon was dead too. Surely he could understand her reaction?

It had been Dixon who had spotted Lucy sitting with her foster parents at the back of the crematorium at Sonia's funeral. Jane smiled. But then who else would it have been? He had been by her side through it all. And that must count for something. Mustn't it?

Jane noticed the rain running down the window instead of across it as the train slowed on the approach to Oxenholme station. She slipped her feet back into her shoes and stood up, dragging her bag off the luggage rack above her head.

Only five and a half hours to go.

◆ ◆ ◆

'Sorry, Jane.'

'You've not found her then?' She opened the back door of Detective Constable Louise Willmott's car and threw her bag on the seat.

'Not yet,' replied Louise, looking over her shoulder. 'Deborah Potter's putting together a Major Investigation Team.'

'Detective Chief Superintendent Potter . . .' Jane hesitated by the car door, her voice tailing off.

'It's not looking good. We found Alesha's phone this morning.'

'Where?' asked Jane, slamming the back door shut.

Louise waited until she wrenched open the passenger door. 'In the lake.'

'No sign of her?'

'No.'

'Where's the mother's boyfriend?'

'Express Park. We've got no real reason to hold him, though, apparently. Potter wants you to sit in on an interview this afternoon, but if nothing comes of that she'll have to let him go.'

'What's he said so far?'

'He and Tanya had a row and he went to a friend's house. It all checks out.'

Jane was putting on her seatbelt.

'Says he hasn't seen Alesha since Saturday morning,' continued Louise. 'Did Tanya know he was a convicted paedophile?'

'She did.'

Louise turned the key, her loud sigh lost in the roar of the engine. 'How was your holiday?' A forced smile was the best she could muster.

'One day of it.'

'Did you sort things out?'

Jane shook her head. 'We hadn't got round to it yet.'

'What did you do yesterday?' Louise turned out of the railway station car park.

'We'd start with something small, he said. Then he took me along Striding Edge. A knife edge ridge with huge drops on either side. I nearly shit myself.'

'What about Monty?' Louise frowned.

'He was fine in his nice padded harness. Nick even carried him some of the way.'

'And you?'

'I had to look after myself, but it wasn't that bad, really. There's a path along the side.'

Louise smiled.

'It was a lovely cottage,' continued Jane. 'In a little place called Hartsop, right in the mountains. The living room's upstairs with huge windows looking straight out.'

'But it's got a landline.'

Jane scowled. 'And satellite broadband.'

'Sorry.'

'It's not your fault. And besides, if we can find her quickly I can go back.'

'I wouldn't hold your breath.'

'What d'you mean?'

'I've just got a bad feeling about this one.' Louise grimaced. 'We all have.'

'Who's "we"?'

'Me, Mark and Dave. We've all been seconded to the MIT until further notice.'

'Really?'

'It's a huge team. DCI Lewis told us to drop everything and go.'

'Maybe they know something we don't?'

'While there's a chance she's still alive . . .' Louise's voice tailed off.

'The first seventy-two hours and all that,' muttered Jane.

'Have you met Alesha?'

'A couple of times. I went to the flat with the social worker, Diane. It became high risk as soon as Tanya got involved with Sailes.'

'I wouldn't get involved with someone I knew had done that.'

'Tanya came up with all sorts of crap to try to justify it.'

'I can imagine.' Louise was leaning forward, peering up at a set of traffic lights. 'How was Nick anyway?'

'Fine.'

'And you've left him up there?'

'Didn't have a lot of choice.'

'He'll get himself killed in those mountains on his own.'

'He promised he wouldn't. And he's going to text me every morning with his route for the day.'

'What's today's?'

Jane fished her phone out of her handbag and read the message aloud. 'Blencathra via Sharp Edge and down Hall's Fell.'

'Have you googled it?'

'No.'

'Don't.'

◆ ◆ ◆

'That's Deborah Potter talking to the cameras,' said Louise, as she turned into the Bridgwater Police Centre on Express Park.

'She tried to get Nick to go to Portishead. Offered him a job at HQ after the Manchester thing.' Jane was looking over her shoulder at the gaggle of journalists while Louise waited for the huge steel gates of the staff car park to open.

'What'd he say?'

'Nothing yet, I don't think.'

'Don't you know?'

Jane shrugged her shoulders. 'Car park's full,' she said, changing the subject. Louise was driving round looking for a space, then turned up the ramp on to the top floor.

'It's the Portishead lot who've come down, and some from Bristol. There's a briefing at one o'clock.'

'Odd time for a briefing,' said Jane.

'They were waiting for you.' Louise parked in the only vacant space and switched off the engine. 'Leave your bag in the car and I'll give you a lift home later.'

'Thanks.'

'The Incident Room's on the second floor.'

'I'll just grab a sandwich from the canteen on the way up. I haven't eaten all day.'

'OK.' Louise swiped her ID card, opened the back door and followed Jane along the landing. 'I'll see you up there.'

Jane listened to her footsteps on the stairs. Then DCS Potter's voice.

'Where's DS Winter?'

'She's on her way, Ma'am.'

Mercifully, only Detective Chief Inspector Lewis was in front of Jane in the canteen queue.

'Sorry about your holiday,' he said.

'It's fine, Sir, really. I'd have come back anyway. Alesha's one of mine and I need to be here.'

Lewis nodded. 'How's Nick?'

'In his element up on the fells somewhere, I expect.'

'Lucky sod.'

Jane smiled, paid for her sandwich and a can of Diet Coke, then headed for the stairs, listening to Deborah's Potter's voice.

'We need to expand the timeline. The last sighting of Alesha is on the Reeds Arms' CCTV at five thirty-four yesterday afternoon. Where did she go after that? What did she do? There's been enough publicity now to run the house to house again, so let's see if we can't jog someone's memory.'

The open plan office on the second floor was a sea of faces, all of them turned towards Jane as she appeared at the top of the stairs chewing on a mouthful of egg and cress sandwich. Officers were sitting at workstations, on workstations and it was standing room only at the back. Jane recognised DCs Dave Harding and Mark Pearce, sitting at the front with Louise, but no one else.

'Ah, there you are,' said Potter. She was standing at the front of the room. 'Everybody, this is Detective Sergeant Winter from our Safeguarding Unit, and when she's finished her lunch I'm sure she'll—'

'It's fine, Ma'am,' interrupted Jane, dropping the rest of her sandwich in the bin.

'Right, well, for those of us who don't know, you can start by telling us what Safeguarding is and how it operates.'

'We're an intelligence unit,' said Jane. 'We gather information on vulnerable people and children. Then we identify those who might be at risk, do a risk assessment and put in place a safeguarding plan. We also liaise with Social Services and the NHS to make sure nothing is missed and act as a central point of contact for referrals. Our office is downstairs and the team includes social workers and clerical staff from the NHS. It basically means that if a child turns up at hospital with bruises, we get to hear about it. Or if there's an incident of domestic violence reported to us and children are there, Social Services get to hear about it. It ensures the exchange of information between the various agencies.'

'And what do you do?'

'I'm in charge of the children's team within the Multi-Agency Safeguarding Hub.'

'So, you can tell us everything we need to know about Alesha?'

Jane hesitated. 'Yes.'

'The floor is yours,' said Potter, stepping back.

'I can prepare a summary for circulation later on today, but she's been on the at risk register pretty much since she was a baby. Her father took her to Weston hospital with bruises that he couldn't explain and the doctor called in Social Services. The SCU didn't exist back then.'

'What happened?' asked Potter.

'The suspicion was that she'd been shaken, but the medical report was inconclusive. Social Services investigated and she was returned to the family. The social worker monitored the situation for a time and, although there were various reports of domestic violence, none involved Alesha and Tanya refused to make a formal complaint so there was no further intervention.'

'Anything else?'

'When she was six, teachers reported some odd remarks she made at school and a further investigation concluded that Tanya was now a drug addict, but no formal steps were taken to remove Alesha from the home at that stage.'

'Why not?'

'She wasn't deemed to be at risk.'

'No shit.' Jane recognised Dave Harding's voice.

'A neighbour in Worston Lane has been in regular contact with Social Services since then.'

'That'll be Mrs French at number ten.' Potter nodded. 'What about the maternal grandmother?' she asked.

'There's no mention of a grandmother, Ma'am.'

'Go on.'

'Then when the SCU was formed we began to get a proper picture of what was going on. Her father served nine months of a two year sentence for GBH. It was a road rage incident with two aggravating factors – a headbutt and the victim was elderly. While he was inside Tanya was nicked for possession of Class A, so Social Services stepped back in and Alesha was taken into care.'

'But she went back?'

'Her father left the family home when he got out of prison and Tanya agreed to go to rehab, so the court said she should go home. Then there was a fight over child arrangements between Ryan and Tanya, which was resolved by the court, and all seemed reasonably calm. The social worker had even considered downgrading her risk classification. That is until Kevin Sailes moved in.'

'Nonce.' This time Jane didn't recognise the voice.

'We know about him,' said Potter.

'That was earlier this year. January, maybe. It coincided with me joining the SCU.'

'And you've met Alesha?' asked Potter.

'Several times, yes. She's just a normal kid. Fascinated with make-up and celebrities. She's had a few brushes with the law, but nothing to be concerned about.'

'What?'

'There were some wing mirrors damaged along Marine Drive and the community support officer thought she may have been involved. That was over Easter. Then there was a shoplifting incident last year. The suspicion was that Tanya had sent her in there.'

'Not sweets then?'

'Razor blades. The expensive ones that sell well on eBay.'

Potter nodded.

'We couldn't prove Tanya was behind it,' continued Jane, 'and the shop agreed to drop it, given Alesha's age. There were allegations of bullying last year too, but those were dealt with by the school.'

'She was being bullied?'

'She was doing the bullying,' replied Jane. 'Allegedly.'

'Let's speak to the teachers then, and the parents of the children involved.' Potter turned to an officer perched on the corner of a workstation at the front of the room. 'Bob, you and your team can pick this up.'

'Yes, Ma'am.'

'And she's never gone missing like this before?' asked Potter, turning back to Jane.

'She's stayed out a couple of times, but she's always texted Tanya or rung Mrs French. And she's never thrown her bike and phone in the lake first either.'

Potter scowled at Jane, then turned back to the gathered officers. 'Right, well you all know what you've got to do, so let's get on with it. We're coming up on forty-eight hours since she went missing, so we need to find her today. All right?' She waited until the officers began talking amongst themselves, some of them heading for the exits, before she turned back to Jane. 'You're with me. Kevin Sailes is in custody downstairs so we'll see him first. Then we'll go and see Tanya.'

'Yes, Ma'am.'

'And just so you know, I don't appreciate sarcasm.'

'Yes, Ma'am.'

Chapter Six

'Will someone please explain to me why my client and I are still here?'

'For the tape, my name is Detective Chief Superintendent Deborah Potter. Sitting to my left is . . .'

'Detective Sergeant Jane Winter.'

'And to my right is – will you please confirm your full name for the tape?'

'Kevin John Sailes.'

Jane still hadn't got used to the new interview room layout, with the interviewing officer sitting next to the suspect and opposite the tape recorder. 'Nice and cosy,' Dixon had called it. 'And designed by an idiot.' Jane leaned forward and looked across at Sailes, sitting on the other side of Potter. He was sitting on his hands, gently rocking backwards and forwards in his chair, his eyes fixed on something on the floor in front of him. Or nothing, more like, thought Jane.

A light grey tracksuit replaced his own clothes – taken for forensics – his blond hair was matted and his beard patchy at best. Mercifully, Potter's perfume was masking the smell. Almost.

'And to his right is . . .' continued Potter.

'His solicitor, Michael Curry.' He sighed. 'Now, why are we still here?'

'Your client has been arrested on suspicion of an offence contrary to section 91 of the Sexual Offences Act 2003, Mr Curry.'

'He has already explained that. It was inadvertent. He simply forgot to notify the police when he changed his mobile phone.'

'He also appears to have overlooked that his registration as a convicted sex offender prohibits access to the internet.'

'That was a mistake on the part of the phone company,' said Curry.

Potter glanced at Jane and shook her head. 'Made three months ago.'

'There's nothing sinister on it,' mumbled Sailes. 'Check it if you don't believe me.'

'We are,' said Potter. She leaned forward and looked across at Curry. 'Your client is also helping us with our enquiries into the disappearance of his girlfriend's daughter and would be well advised to continue to do so.'

'We've been through this,' muttered Sailes.

'And we'll go through it again,' snapped Potter. 'Tell me about Kelly.'

Curry leaned across and whispered in Sailes's ear. 'No comment.' Jane's lip reading must be improving.

'There's no need for that.' Sailes turned to Curry. 'I thought she was sixteen, she told me she was sixteen.'

'And the photographs?' asked Potter.

'She let me take them. It was just a bit of fun. I never did anything with them.'

'That's all right then.' Jane was impressed with the sarcasm Potter was able to pour into such a short sentence.

Thought you didn't like sarcasm?

'Look, we kept in touch and when I got out of prison we started seeing each other again. That's got to count for something?'

'Then what happened?'

'We split up.'

'And why was that?'

'She met someone else.'

'Someone her own age?'

Sailes nodded.

'If you would confirm your agreement, for the tape.'

'Yes.'

'Let's talk about age then. She was fifteen, and how old were you?'

'I was thirty-three when we met.'

'How did you meet?'

'On the internet.'

'There's a word for that,' said Potter.

'I didn't groom her. She groomed me, if anything. But it was wrong. I know that now.'

'When did you meet Tanya?'

'About a year ago, I think.'

'How?'

'We have a shared interest.'

'In drugs?'

'It started when I was in prison. I was fine until I went in there.'

'And when did you meet Alesha?'

'Look, I never laid a finger on Alesha. I never touched her.' Tears were beginning to trickle down Sailes's cheeks. 'She was nine, for fuck's sake.'

'But you didn't tell Tanya you were a registered sex offender?'

'It's not exactly a great opening line, is it?'

'How about when you moved into the flat? That was January, wasn't it?'

'I didn't really. I used to doss there a few nights a week, but I wouldn't say I ever moved in, as such. I'd be at Darryl's a few nights a week too, depending on what was going on.'

'Depending on what you'd been able to score?'

Sailes sighed. 'Yes.'

'And what do you use?'

'Anything I can get my hands on.'

'And Tanya?'

'The same.'

Potter turned to Jane and raised her eyebrows.

'How would you describe your relationship with Alesha?' asked Jane.

'What's that supposed to mean?'

'It's not supposed to mean anything, Kevin. You have a relationship with Alesha. What is it?'

'We get on all right, I suppose. I don't see her that much. She's usually in bed when I arrive at the flat and then gone to school when I wake up.'

'Where do you sleep?'

'Sometimes on the sofa, sometimes in Tanya's room. It depends.'

'On what?'

Sailes took a deep breath. 'How far gone we are.'

'What happens in the morning, if you and Tanya are too far gone?'

'Alesha gets herself ready and goes off to school. It's not far.'

'Were you aware she was in trouble at school?'

'What for?'

'Bullying.'

'No.'

'What about the razor blades? Was that you or Tanya?'

'What razor blades?' asked Curry.

'Alesha was caught shoplifting before Christmas, Mr Curry,' said Jane.

He leaned over and whispered in his client's ear.

'No comment,' mumbled Sailes.

'Did you ever meet any of Alesha's friends?'

'No,' replied Sailes. 'They never came to the flat.'

'Has Alesha ever stayed away before?' asked Potter. 'Run away, perhaps?'

'No. And if she did, she'd just go to her dad's.'

'What about your associates, do any of them ever come to the flat?'

'No.'

'A neighbour has reported two men, both seen at the property on more than one occasion.'

Sailes was staring at his trainers, laces removed, which had almost slipped off the end of his feet. Trainers and no socks – it added to the smell. 'Suppliers. And before you ask, no, I won't tell you who they are. They've got nothing to do with Alesha. I'm not sure they've ever even met her.'

'Let's start with your whereabouts on Friday, then, Kevin,' said Potter.

Sailes leaned back in his chair and puffed out his cheeks. 'Alesha was at school when I woke up. I went to Bridgwater on the bus, scored some . . . stuff. Then I hung around with Darryl for a while. She was already in bed by the time I got back.'

'Did you see her?'

'No.'

'So, how d'you know she was in bed?'

'I don't, I suppose. Maybe Tanya said something, I don't know. Or maybe I just assumed she was. Anyway, I didn't see her.'

'And Saturday?'

'She was gone before we woke up.'

'What time was that?'

'Lunchtime.'

'And you've not seen her since?'

'If I had, I'd bloody well say so.'

'Saturday then. Where did you go when you woke up?'

'Darryl's.'

'Until what time?'

'Five or so, I suppose. Then I went back to the flat, but me and Tanya had a row, so I walked back to Darryl's.'

'Walked?'

'It's only twelve miles. She'd had all my money so I had nothing for the bus.'

'What was the row about?'

'Money and drugs. She'd taken all my cash and my stash. The whole bloody lot. So, I went back to Darryl's to see what I could scrounge off him.'

'Where was Alesha during all this?'

'I didn't see her. She usually goes to her dad's on Saturday anyway.'

'When did you tell Tanya you were on the Sex Offender Register?'

'I didn't.' Sailes leaned forward and jabbed the index finger of his left hand at Jane. 'She did.'

'Did Tanya ask you about it?'

'I told her the same as I told you. The truth.'

'And she accepted that explanation?'

Sailes nodded.

'For the tape?'

'Yes.'

◆ ◆ ◆

Potter waited until the interview room door closed behind her.

'Let's get him released on police bail. That'll give us twenty-eight days, then we can charge him with the Section 91 offences, if nothing else.'

'Yes, Ma'am.'

'Tell them he can be released once we've seen Tanya. And we'll have a condition on it that he stays away from the flat. Is she at home yet?'

'Yes, Ma'am.'

'Get the drug squad to put a tail on him too. He'll probably lead them straight to his dealer.'

Jane nodded.

'It's starting to look random,' said Potter, shaking her head. 'Did you believe him?'

'Some people lie for a pastime. All that crap about walking from Burnham to Bridgwater, for a start.'

'We've got him on CCTV at a petrol station on the edge of Bridgwater, but how did he get there?' Potter was checking her phone for messages. 'Right, well, let's go and see what Tanya's got to say for herself.'

◆ ◆ ◆

PC Cole lifted the blue tape at the end of Worston Lane and Jane ducked under it, following DCS Potter.

'Sorry,' mouthed Cole.

'It's fine, really,' said Jane.

'She's got her mother with her,' said Cole. 'And Karen Marsden's in there with the social worker.'

'About bloody time she put in an appearance,' muttered Potter. 'Has Tanya said anything?'

'She's not seen Alesha since Friday night. She was off her trolley on Saturday morning and Alesha was gone when she woke up.'

'Makes you wonder why some people have children at all.' Potter frowned.

The image of an empty crematorium flashed across Jane's mind. There had been seven mourners at Sonia's funeral, including herself and Nick. She'd met her three times, if she included being born; the file said she had been given up for adoption at birth. She knew why, though, and it was a sobering thought to know you were a mistake.

Jane hesitated at the top of the steps and looked down at the back garden, the grass flattened by a fingertip search, then strimmed and searched again. 'It was nearly up to the swing when I was here last,' she said. 'Quite an achievement in winter.'

'At least she's had it cut for free.' Potter turned and knocked on the front door. 'Family Liaison?' she asked, when an officer in uniform opened the door.

'This is Karen Marsden, Ma'am,' said Jane.

'How is she?' asked Potter.

'It's difficult to tell, really, Ma'am. She's not had a fix today and is a bit shaky. She left hospital with a methadone prescription, but she hasn't taken it.'

'Has she said anything?'

'Nothing of note. Her mother's here and she's a right pain in the arse. Seems to think Alesha can look after herself.'

'She's bloody well had to,' said Jane.

'Who is it?' The voice was shrill and came from inside the flat.

'That's the mother,' said Karen. 'Sonia. It's no bloody wonder Tanya's turned out the way she has.'

Another Sonia?

Jane stifled a wry smile. When she got home, she'd ring her mother – her adopted mother – just to find out how she was.

'What about the social worker?' asked Potter.

'She got here just after lunch, Ma'am. Between you and me, I think she feels a bit responsible. We were in the kitchen and she said they should've got Alesha out of here when Sailes came on the scene.'

'Hindsight is a wonderful thing,' said Potter, glancing at Jane.

'We told them to intervene, begged them, but it was their decision.'

'Well, we are where we are.' Potter shook her head. 'Let's get on with it.'

They followed Karen along the corridor and into the gloomy living room, one small lamp offering the only light. Two women were sitting on the sofa, the older with her arm around the younger woman, who was shaking, her face partially hidden behind large sunglasses.

'Can we get that down?' asked Potter, gesturing to the rug pinned up at the window.

'It's her eyes,' said the older woman, presumably Sonia.

'You'll be Tanya?' asked Potter, turning to the younger woman.

She nodded.

'Rest assured we are doing everything we can to find Alesha. All right?'

'Where's Kevin?'

'He's still in custody, but he'll be released later this afternoon on condition that he stays away from here. Is that clear, Tanya?'

'He's got nothing to do with Alesha.'

Jane couldn't tell whether her eyes were open or closed behind the sunglasses. And she'd overdone the peroxide since she last saw her, that much was clear; her straggly bleached hair visible even in the near darkness.

'He'll be charged with two offences relating to breaching the terms of his registration. I understand you knew he was a registered sex offender?'

'It was all a mix up,' snapped Sonia. 'He's not a paedophile, if that's what you mean.' No need to wonder where Tanya got the peroxide habit from.

'We know what he is and what he's done,' said Potter. 'And the fact remains he was convicted of two counts of sexual activity with a child, served three years of a five year sentence, and is now on the Sex Offender Register for life.'

'He thought she was sixteen.'

Missing front teeth too. Jane's eyes must be adjusting to the gloom.

'So he says, but the jury didn't believe that, did they?'

'He told me he pleaded guilty,' mumbled Tanya.

Potter turned to Jane. 'You know Jane Winter, I believe?'

Tanya nodded.

'We'll find—'

'Oh, she'll turn up somewhere,' said Sonia, cutting Jane off mid-sentence. 'She'll be fine.'

'What can you tell me about Saturday morning, Tanya?' asked Potter.

'Nothing, really. I didn't wake up until lunchtime.'

'We're going to get you some help, Tarn.' Sonia pulled her daughter towards her. 'She can't go on like this.'

'No, she can't.'

Jane spun round to see the social worker, Diane Bradshaw, standing in the doorway.

Potter squatted down and put her hand on Tanya's knee.

'Where was Alesha when you woke up?'

'Out.'

'Where?'

'I dunno. On her bike somewhere.'

'She's always out on her bike,' said Sonia. 'Sometimes she meets her friends, or she goes over to see *him* in Highbridge.'

'Who's "him"?'

'Her bloody useless father.'

'Had she complained of anyone following her?' asked Potter, looking up at Tanya.

'No.'

'Said anything unusual about anything unusual?'

'No.'

Tanya began swaying backwards and forwards, her head lolling from side to side.

'She's going again.' Sonia allowed Tanya to slump back into the leather sofa.

'Should we call a doctor?' asked Potter.

'She'll be fine in a minute or two.'

'What about the press conference later?'

'I'll make sure she's all right for that.'

Potter stood up and walked over to the door. 'Are you the social worker?'

'Yes,' replied Bradshaw.

'Follow me.'

Jane closed the door behind them and stepped back. She knew what was coming and it had been a long time coming. Far too long. She had done her best, but she had to work with social services. Potter didn't.

'Mrs Bradshaw, is it?'

'Yes.'

'Can you please explain to me what Alesha is doing living in this dump with that for a mother?'

You go for it, girl.

'Er, well, I—'

'If ever a child was at risk . . .'

'She was monitored closely.'

'By a neighbour, from what I can see.' Potter checked her phone and threw it into the bottom of her handbag. 'I mean, if this doesn't qualify as "at risk", I don't know what the bloody hell does.'

'You can't talk to me like that.'

'Yes, I bloody well can, because I'm the one clearing up your mess. And you'd better hope we don't find ourselves pulling Alesha's body from a lake.'

Chapter Seven

'She's dead, poor kid,' muttered Potter, switching off the engine. 'But don't tell anyone I said so.'

'What makes you say that?' asked Jane.

'Two days and not a sign.' Potter grimaced. 'I've just got a horrible feeling . . .' Her voice tailed off as she wrenched on the handbrake. 'Let's get in there and see if anyone's come up with anything.'

Jane followed her across the top floor of the car park, then stepped forward to open the staff entrance with her pass. 'We've still got the reconstruction and then there's the press conference,' she said, holding open the door.

'Not much use if we're looking for a body,' muttered Potter. 'You got children?'

'Not yet,' replied Jane.

Not yet? Where did that come from?

She shook her head. It had always been a straight 'no' to that question before. 'How about you?' she asked, hurriedly.

'Two. And one grandchild.'

'You don't look old enough.'

'If I didn't know better, I'd think you were chatting me up.' Potter forced a smile. 'Puts a different complexion on it, though.'

'I bet.' Jane watched Potter trudge along the landing. She paused at the bottom of the stairs, wiped under her eyes with the knuckles of her index fingers and then turned to Jane.

'Game face on. All right?'

'Yes, Ma'am.'

'Not a word.'

'No, Ma'am.'

Once at the top of the stairs Potter dropped her handbag on to the nearest workstation. This silenced those officers sitting at the front of the room, but not the rest.

'Right.' Potter clapped her hands and then looked at her watch. 'We've got the reconstruction along Marine Drive at five and the press conference at five thirty. Is everything ready?'

'Yes, Ma'am,' replied Dave Harding. He was standing behind Mark Pearce holding a plastic cup in each hand.

'And the child?'

'It's Alesha's friend, Evie. They look very similar. We've got the same bike, tassels and everything, and the same coat too.'

'Good.'

Louise appeared at the top of the stairs behind Jane. 'Everything's ready for the press conference downstairs. The TV crews are just setting up. The father's here and I've left him in a private room with the press officer.'

'What about the school, Bob?' asked Potter. 'Did you find anything out about the bullying?'

Bob, slumped on a swivel chair at the back of the room, sat up sharply. 'It wasn't anything serious and the school dealt with it. We've got statements from the parents involved and there's nothing there.'

'Anything else?'

'A few sightings, Ma'am.' DCI Chard was sitting at a workstation in the corner. A bloody good job Dixon is two hundred and fifty miles away, thought Jane. She could do without the aggravation.

'Some more promising than others,' continued Chard. 'All of them followed up and none of them Alesha, sadly.'

'Thank you, Simon.'

'It's not looking good, is it, Ma'am,' said Chard. 'The longer it goes on.'

'I'll have none of that talk in my team, Simon.'

'No, Ma'am.'

'She's alive until we find her body. Is that clear?'

Chard nodded.

'Are we any further forward with the timeline?' continued Potter.

'No, Ma'am,' said Chard.

'Well, you know what you've got to do, so let's get on with it.'

'D'you want me at the reconstruction, Ma'am?' asked Jane.

'Yes,' replied Potter. 'How long will that note on Alesha's background take you?'

'Half an hour.'

'You've got twenty minutes,' said Potter, looking at her watch.

◆ ◆ ◆

The Safeguarding Coordination Unit on the first floor was the only office in the building with soundproof walls and a door. Jane closed it behind her, leaned back against it and closed her eyes.

'Not found her yet, then?'

She opened her eyes to find the one other person in the room staring at her.

'No.'

'You will.'

'I hope so, Sandy.'

Jane sat down at a workstation, switched on the computer then tapped out a text message on her phone while she waited to log on to the network.

Where are u? Jx

She placed the phone on the desk next to her keyboard, staring at it while she typed in her username and password. Then she started on Alesha's report, still glancing at her phone from time to time. She'd told Potter it would take half an hour, but the reality was ten minutes at most. She just needed to cut and paste a few paragraphs from Alesha's Child Protection Plan summary into a new document. All those hours keeping her reports up to date had not been a waste of time after all.

Dixon's reply came just as she was emailing the document to Potter.

At the cottage. Monty knackered. Watching telly. Found her yet? Nx

Jane tapped out a reply with one hand while she scrolled through her emails with the other.

No. Don't take him too far. What you watching? Jx

Jane sighed. Whatever it was it would be in black and white. And poor Monty. She tapped out a second message and sent it.

He's not a mountain goat!

She'd switched off her computer and was counting down the last of the twenty minutes when Dixon's reply arrived.

The Ladykillers. Carried him most of way lazy bugger. Gray Crag, Thornthwaite Crag, Caudale Moor and Hartsop Dodd tomorrow

There was just enough time to wind him up a bit.

The remake? Jx

Jane smiled as she dropped her phone into her handbag. 'See you, Sandy,' she said, closing the door behind her.

'Good luck.'

Jane stayed back behind the TV camera crews as they followed Evie along Marine Drive towards Apex Park. Teams of officers were knocking on doors on either side of the road, with still more talking to dog walkers in the park. She watched Potter pacing up and down, glancing expectantly at the officers supervising the house to house enquiries.

'You'd expect to get something from this. Anything,' she muttered.

'It may come later when it's been on the news, Ma'am,' said Jane.

'It'd better.'

Mark Pearce and Louise were part of the team doing the odd numbers on the far side of the road. Jane watched Louise scribbling on her clipboard while Mark was speaking to a middle aged man at number fifty-one.

'Looks promising,' said Jane, nodding in that direction.

She followed Potter across the road to meet Louise, who was running down the garden path.

'What is it?'

'Mr Randall,' replied Louise. 'He's visiting his elderly father. Hasn't been over since Saturday afternoon. When we knocked here before we just got carers who said Mr Randall senior has dementia and wouldn't have seen anything.'

'But the son was visiting?'

'He was. And he remembers a white van.'

'It bloody well would be a white van, wouldn't it,' said Potter.

'It's quite a distinctive one. Old, and possibly continental. He thinks maybe a Citroën or a Renault. It had a square front.' Louise looked down at her clipboard. 'With a faded grey plastic trim. Transit size, but squarer.'

'Did he see the driver?'

'No.'

'What time was this?'

'He saw it a couple of times, driving up and down. The last time was just before he left at about five o'clock.'

'It fits.' Potter snatched the clipboard from Louise. 'I'll take it from here. You join the rest of the house to house team.'

'Yes, Ma'am.'

'What about me, Ma'am?' asked Jane.

'You'd better stay for the press conference. And you can make sure they ask the people in Parsons Road about the white van, all right?'

'Yes, Ma'am.'

They watched in silence as Potter strode down the garden path and invited herself into number fifty-one. Pearce followed.

Louise spoke first when the front door closed behind them.

'D'you get the feeling she's clutching at straws?'

'Can you blame her?' replied Jane.

'I suppose not.'

'It's the first possible lead we've had in forty-eight hours.'

Louise nodded.

'You'd better get over to Parsons Road,' continued Jane. 'I'll hang on here for Potter.'

'I've still got your bag in my car.'

'Leave it there for now and I'll catch up with you later.'

Jane watched Louise run back to her car and then reached into her handbag when she felt her phone buzz.

What remake? Nx

Microwave from frozen: Cat E – Full power – 6 Minutes. Cook for 3 minutes, stir, replace film lid and cook for a further 3 minutes.

The only edible thing Jane had been able to find in the cottage was one of Dixon's Slimming World chicken tikka masalas. It'd have to do. She took out her phone and sent him a text message.

What category is this microwave? Jx

Then she leaned back against the worktop and closed her eyes. The press conference had started at 5.30 p.m. and had lasted no more than twenty minutes, allowing ten minutes for editing before the early evening news. Tearful parents pleading for the safe return of their daughter, followed by footage of the Alesha lookalike cycling along Marine Drive.

Tanya had at least remained conscious throughout, although Jane suspected this was down to some illegal substance. Her tears were genuine though. There had been no doubt about that.

There had even been time to narrow down the description of the white van and find a photograph of one similar, so maybe that would jog someone's memory.

'You might as well go home, Jane,' Potter had said.

'To what?'

A long evening by the phones had followed, hoping for the one call that might lead them to Alesha.

Alive would be a bonus now.

It was only after she sent the text that Jane noticed the time. Gone midnight. She was not going to be popular. Still, at least she wouldn't be putting on weight.

No idea. You just got in? Nx

Yes. Phones all night. Reconstruction on evening news. One good lead. Uniform staking out caravan park at Glastonbury. There's no milk. Jx

Jane stirred the masala sauce while she waited for a reply.

There's a beer in the fridge :-)

She slid the plastic tray back into the microwave and set it going for another three minutes.

Slimming world? xx

It's the sugar content. I'm diabetic!

I know, I know. You get some sleep. Speak tomorrow xx

Will do. Don't forget to get bread out Nx

Jane felt the roof of her mouth with her tongue and winced. She'd waited until the bloody sauce had stopped bubbling. Maybe she should

have left it to stand a bit longer than the one minute it said on the packet?

Sleep would come. It always did. Eventually. But she never understood why it took so much longer when she was exhausted. 'Too tired to sleep' was a phrase Dixon had used before and now she understood.

The streetlights had gone off, plunging the bedroom into pitch darkness. A bit like that cave, although it was warmer, mercifully, even without him next to her and Monty on the end of the bed.

She rolled over on her side and closed her eyes. At least she hadn't had to set the alarm.

'You've had a long day,' Potter had said. 'Just get here when you can tomorrow.'

Nice of her.

She tried to picture Alesha somewhere. Anywhere. The last time Jane had seen her she had been standing in the doorway of the flat. Eavesdropping probably, although she said she hadn't been listening.

Poor kid.

Tanya's mother Sonia had been a bit close to home too. Pictures of Jane's birth mother began flashing across her mind, of Sonia slumped across the bonnet of a car – that'd been the last time she'd seen her – then standing in the crematorium at Sonia's funeral, Dixon holding her up. And then there was her half-sister, Lucy, with her nose stud and hair dyed jet black. Or full sister maybe, the only one who knew – possibly – dead from a drug overdose.

Shit. They were supposed to be calling in on Lucy on their way back from the Lakes.

And she'd forgotten to ring her mother, her adoptive mother. Her real mother. The one who had been there. Always. She hadn't said anything – she wouldn't – but Jane knew she had been nervous about her meeting Sonia.

Random thoughts and pictures popping into her head. It was either that or sheep jumping over a gate.

Chapter Eight

Black coffee and toast. The bread had been frozen, but she'd managed to break off a couple of slices. And she would need a few more coffees if she was going to get through the day. It must've been gone one when she finally got to sleep and she was awake by seven.

Jane yawned as she waited for the steel gates of the staff car park to open. Then she parked in the open on the top level and took her phone out of her handbag. A full signal. Shame. It was a call she had been dreading.

'Lucy, it's me.'

'Who?'

'Jane. Your sister. Remember?'

'I was winding you up.'

'Sorry, it's been a long night.' Jane was watching Potter standing on the far side of the car park, stubbing her cigarette out on the top of the wall.

'What's up?' asked Lucy. 'You'll be here at the weekend, won't you?'

'I've had to come back to work. We've had a child go missing.'

'I saw it on Facebook.'

'She's one of the ones I look after so I was called back, but it means we won't be stopping in to see you this time, I'm afraid.' Jane paused. Silence. 'There'll be other times, though. Lots of them. All right?'

'I get it. She comes first.' A loud sigh.

'Don't be like that, Lucy. It's my job. Listen, if we find her quickly then I'll be coming back up and we can . . .' Jane's voice tailed off when she heard the familiar beep, beep, beep. She looked at the screen – 'Call Ended' – and was about to redial when she noticed Potter staring at her.

'Good morning, Ma'am,' said Jane, dropping her car keys into her handbag. 'Didn't they give you a pass?'

'It's in my handbag.' Potter was standing by the staff entrance, waiting for Jane to open it. 'You're early.'

'Too tired to sleep,' she said, swiping her ID card and opening the door.

'Got that T-shirt,' muttered Potter.

'Anything come from the caravan park?'

'It was empty.' Potter sighed. 'We've got a few samples off to the lab to see if Alesha had been there, but she sure as hell wasn't there when they kicked the door in.'

'There are a few other sightings to follow up.'

'Plenty.'

'I'll be up in a minute.' Jane continued along the landing to the canteen, while Potter went upstairs to the Incident Room on the second floor.

'Coffee, please.'

'Takeaway or—?'

The rest of the question was lost in shouting coming from upstairs.

'Better make it a takeaway,' said Jane, raising her eyebrows.

'Pay me later.'

'Thanks.'

Jane snatched the coffee and ran. 'Have we found her?' she gasped, at the top of the stairs.

'Sailes has gone missing and his friend Darryl just reported his car stolen.' Potter snatched her handbag off the desk. 'Want to come?'

'Why not?'

Potter stopped at the top of the stairs. 'Louise?'

'Yes, Ma'am.'

'Check with Family Liaison and find out if he's been to Tanya's flat.'

'It's a breach of his bail conditions if he has,' said Jane.

'That'll be the least of his worries when I catch up with him.' Potter took her car keys out of her handbag. 'Number thirty-two Drakes Close. D'you know it?'

'It's down behind the docks.'

Ten minutes later they were sitting in Potter's car looking up at a line of blue garage doors with flats above; four garages in all, with a glazed front door at either end set in an extension just wide enough to accommodate a staircase.

'I wonder what an estate agent would call these?' asked Potter.

'Coach houses, I expect,' replied Jane.

'You missed your vocation.'

'Thanks.'

A patrol car was parked further along Drakes Close, and beyond that a dog van.

'I thought we might threaten him with a sniffer dog,' said Potter.

Jane smiled.

'We'll have that bin bag too,' continued Potter, pointing at a bulging bin liner sitting on top of a grey bin behind a low wall. 'We'll leave this here,' she said, switching off the engine.

'Anyone would think they'd never seen a police car before,' muttered Jane, gesturing towards a small crowd that had gathered on the corner.

'Get uniform to speak to them.'

'Yes, Ma'am.'

'And the neighbours.'

Potter waited until Jane had briefed the uniformed officers, then knocked on the door.

'It's open.'

Jane raised her eyebrows.

Darryl was waiting for them at the top of the stairs. Bare feet, torn jeans, and an AC/DC T-shirt; long fingernails, tattoos on the knuckles and nicotine stains.

Haven't you heard of shampoo?

'Spring cleaning is it, Darryl?' asked Potter, noticing the vacuum cleaner on the landing.

'I always run the hoover round when I've got important guests coming.' He grinned.

'I bet you do.' Potter smirked. 'We've got a sniffer dog outside.'

'Look, I've just reported my car stolen. I don't want any trouble.'

'May we . . . ?'

'Yes, come up.'

The living space at the top of the stairs was open plan, with a bathroom visible through an open door on the far side. The kitchen was set against the back wall, the kettle boiling.

'Coffee?'

'No, thank you.'

'Have a seat.'

'When did you first notice your car was missing?' asked Potter.

'This morning. Just before I rang.'

'Do you know who's taken it?'

'Not for sure, no.'

Potter waited.

'Kevin came here yesterday after you lot released him. We smoked a bit of this and that, had a few beers and he left about nine or so. I heard a car start, but didn't make the connection. It was only this morning I noticed my keys were gone.'

'And he's a friend?'

'I'm worried about him. He can hit it pretty hard and . . .' Darryl hesitated.

'What?'

'I can't claim on the insurance without a crime number. That's what they said when I rang them.'

Potter looked at Jane and took a deep breath.

'What had he been smoking?'

'A bit of weed. Nothing much. But he said he needed something a bit stronger. I don't do that.'

'We know, Darryl.' Potter nodded. 'Remind me, what's your conviction for?'

'Possession. It was a tiny amount. One joint. A fine, that's all I got. A fine.'

'Did he say anything about Alesha?'

'Look, he was pissed before he got here, going on about how you lot were going to fit him up for it. With his past and everything.'

'Fit him up for what?'

Darryl frowned. 'He didn't say, just that he didn't stand a chance, with his record.'

'How much did he have to drink?'

'Three or four cans.'

'What of?'

'Special Brew.'

'Did he say where he was going?'

'No.'

'Where was your car parked?'

'In the road, where yours is now.'

'And what is it?'

'An old Renault Clio V6 Sport. Black.'

'Has he taken it before?'

'No. I'd never let him take it anyway. Not in the state he's in.'

◆ ◆ ◆

'Well, he's got his crime number,' said Potter when the front door closed behind her.

'With friends like that . . .' Jane shook her head.

'You can't blame him. Kevin pinched his car and I'm guessing he has no intention of bringing it back either.'

'What d'you mean?'

'He's done a runner. Probably miles away already if he took the car at nine last night.'

'With Alesha?'

'If she's still alive. That's my guess, anyway. My phone's buzzing.' Potter began rummaging in her handbag. She looked at the screen. 'Louise. I'd better ring her back.'

Jane waited. She was getting good at piecing together a conversation from listening to one side of it.

'You rang?' . . . 'What time?' . . . 'For fuck's sake.' . . . 'What time did he leave?' . . . 'Did he say where he was going?' . . . 'She's lying. Tell them to stay there. I'm on my way. Then I'll be over to see Tanya.'

Potter dropped her phone back into her handbag.

'He turned up at Tanya's?' asked Jane.

'Family Liaison went home at eight, would you believe it? Tanya's bloody mother told them to, apparently.' Potter pointed the key fob at her car and opened the doors. 'He got there about nine thirty and left just after midnight. Said he was going to his mother's, only she says she hasn't seen him.'

'At least it gives us a starting point for the traffic cameras.'

'They're already on it.'

The drive to Weston, two junctions north on the M5, took no more than twenty minutes and Jane spent most of the time watching the familiar landmarks flashing by: Brent Knoll, the lighthouse, Brean Down. She knew what Dixon would say: 'You're not going to find him looking where you know he isn't.' It was a good point, but maybe Sailes's mother would know where he might have gone. It was worth asking, even if there was a touch of the headless chicken to the investigation. That was another of Dixon's gems.

'What are you thinking?' asked Potter, as she turned off the motorway.

'Nothing, Ma'am.'

◆ ◆ ◆

'Is this Moorland Road?'

'Yes.'

'What number is it?'

'It'll be that one up there, with the patrol car parked across the drive,' replied Jane, looking along the line of almost identical grey stone houses, the only difference between them the colour of the cornicing on the bay windows.

Potter parked behind it, blocking the drive of the next door property, both cars astride the faded double yellow lines.

The front door opened just as Jane reached up for the bell.

'You can't leave that there.'

'I think you'll find I can, Mrs Birch,' snapped Potter.

'The neighbours'll give me hell.'

Potter turned to the uniformed officer standing in the hall. 'Have you spoken to the neighbours?'

'Not yet, Ma'am.'

'Now would be a good time.'

'Yes, Ma'am.'

Mrs Birch sat down on the bottom of the stairs, flicked off her slippers and began rubbing her bunions. Too many years in high heels, thought Jane. Black leggings and a black T-shirt that was far too tight; yesterday's make-up. Jane glanced along the corridor at the collection of empty wine bottles on the kitchen table.

Potter frowned. 'Birch?'

'I married again. Twice, actually.'

'And when was the last time you saw Kevin?'

'I've been through this.' Mrs Birch sighed loudly. 'Last week.'

'His sex offender registration gives this as his place of residence.'

'Well, it isn't.'

'Have you spoken to him on the phone?'

'No.'

'Whose is that Fiesta parked out front?'

'Mine.'

'Does he ever use it?'

'What? Let him use my car? The state he's in most of the time? No bloody fear.'

'What state is that?'

'You know.'

Potter nodded. 'We do.'

'How often does he visit?' asked Jane.

'Once or twice a week, I suppose.'

'Does he ever stay the night?'

'On the sofa. There was a bed in the spare room, but I got rid of it, hoping he'd take the hint.'

'Which one is Kevin?' Jane was pointing at a photograph on the wall of two children astride donkeys on Weston beach, the pier visible in the background.

'Neither. They're my children by my second husband.'

'Any photos of Kevin?'

'No.'

'How does he get here?' asked Potter.

'Bus.'

'Has he ever owned a car?'

'He used to have a Mini, one of the old ones, but it packed up.' Mrs Birch leaned back on the stairs, her elbows propping her up.

'Which way would he come, if he was driving?'

'The main road. Why?'

'He was driving a stolen car last night and left Tanya's saying he was on his way here.'

'He must've changed his mind then.'

Potter waited until the front door slammed behind her.

'Fancy having a mother like that.'

'Fancy,' muttered Jane.

'I told you you were wasting your bloody time.' Sonia slammed the front door behind them, leaving them standing on the concrete steps outside Tanya's flat contemplating the dash to the car.

Tanya was still unconscious, making the visit a complete waste of time, according to Potter. Add to that Sonia's insistence that she had been asleep in Alesha's bedroom the whole time Kevin had been at the flat, and the best that could be said about it was that it was on the way back to Express Park. Jane preferred to look on the bright side.

Karen Marsden was there and stood her ground as best she could. Of course it wasn't ideal to leave them on their own, but she'd done an eighteen hour shift yesterday and there was no one else available in Family Liaison to take over. DCS Potter could always take it up with the Police Commissioner.

Risky, Karen, but Jane had enjoyed that last line all the same.

'You got a brolly?' asked Potter.

Jane shook her head.

'Me neither.'

'Let's go for it.'

Potter unlocked her car as they ran along the garden path and Jane jumped in the passenger seat. 'We must've learned something from that,' she said, when Potter jumped in and closed the driver's door behind her.

'Like what?'

'Tanya told Karen he turned up at nine, drank a bottle of vodka, pinched some of her methadone, had a row with her mum and left just after midnight.'

'Without saying where he'd been or where he was going.'

'Karen also said the neighbours heard a row, but couldn't make out what was being said.' Jane was putting on her seatbelt.

'That's my phone.' Potter reached over and took her handbag off the back seat, dropping it into Jane's lap. 'Answer it, will you. It's in the side pocket.' Then she switched on the engine.

'Jane Winter.'

'Is the chief super there?'

'She's driving, Lou. What's up?'

'Another child's gone missing.'

Chapter Nine

Potter screeched to a halt at the end of Worston Lane. 'Where to?' she asked, revving the engine.

'Catcott.'

'Where the fuck's that?'

'Just head out to the M5 and go south,' replied Jane.

'Have we got a name?'

'Hatty Renner. Ten years old. Walks to school and never got there.'

'Is she known to Safeguarding?'

'No, but I'll need to check.'

'Another ten year old . . .' Potter was edging out on to the roundabout, watching the traffic coming from her right.

'Chief Inspector Bateman is Bronze Commander.'

'Good.'

Once off the M5, Jane glanced across at the King's Sedgemoor Drain as Potter raced down Puriton Hill heading east on the A39. More blue lights were screaming out of Bridgwater, just as they had done that night before Christmas when Dixon had got to her just in time. Not that she could remember much about it or see anything from the boot of the car. Still, she'd returned the favour since then.

'D'you think it's Sailes?' she asked.

'He's a convicted paedophile and he's done a runner.'

'He's not doing himself any favours, is he?'

'No, he bloody well isn't.'

The junction at Catcott was blocked by a patrol car that quickly moved when Potter waved her warrant card at it.

'Where do we go now?' she shouted across to a uniformed officer on foot.

'Left at the crossroads, then next right into Old School Lane. It's Old School House, up on the right.'

Another officer stepped out into the road and flagged them down as they raced along the lane. 'Park over there, please, Ma'am. Chief Inspector Bateman is expecting you.'

'Thank you.'

Jane wondered how many parents had pulled into the same lay-by to collect their children before it had been converted into a private house. And a big one at that. Grey stone again, with sandstone cornicing to the windows and doors. Jane imagined the windows plastered with art projects. The vegetable garden at the side must have been the playground.

Bateman came striding across the lane as Potter locked the car.

'We've got house to house going already between here and the school.'

'Tell them to ask about a white box van or a black Renault Clio.'

Bateman nodded.

'Where's the new school?' asked Potter.

'About half a mile that way,' replied Bateman pointing along the lane. 'The helicopter's on its way and when we've got more boots on the ground we'll start a search of the surrounding fields.'

'Where are the parents?'

'The mother's inside. Not too good, as you might imagine.'

'And the father?'

'At work.' Bateman shrugged his shoulders. 'She hasn't told him yet.'

'He'll hear it on the bloody news soon if she's not careful.'

'Family Liaison aren't here yet, either. They're a bit short staffed, apparently.'

Potter turned to Jane.

'What about that young DC, Louise somebody?'

'Willmott. I'll call her.'

'What's the mother's name?' asked Potter, as Jane turned away with her phone clamped to her ear.

'Adele.'

'Has she got anyone with her?'

'Her mother's here. She lives in Stawell just over the A39 there. Got here before we did. And there's a neighbour in there too. Ros somebody. She lives a couple of doors down, with her husband, Bob.'

'Louise is on her way, Ma'am,' said Jane, dropping her phone back into her handbag.

'Let's get in there then.'

Jane followed Potter through the open front door and into a large living room with a spiral staircase in the far corner leading up to a galleried landing. Beneath that a passageway led through to the kitchen.

At the other end of the room, to Jane's left, leather furniture surrounded a wall mounted television with two tall stained glass windows either side of a wood burning stove. Sitting with their backs to Jane were two women, mother and daughter, the older with her arm clamped around the younger as she rocked backwards and forwards. An all too familiar sight.

'Mrs Renner?' Potter stepped forward.

'Yes.' She turned her head slowly, her eyes staring into space from behind the tears.

'Detective Chief Superintendent Potter. I'm leading the investigation into the disappearance of—'

'We've seen you on the telly,' said the older woman.

'And this is Detective Sergeant Winter,' continued Potter. 'Does Hatty have a mobile phone?'

'Yes. I gave the other officer the number.'

'Good. We'll get a trace on it.' Potter sat down on the edge of the sofa next to Adele. 'You really need to tell your husband before he hears it from someone else.'

'I know.'

'D'you want me to ring him?'

That was brave, thought Jane.

'No, I'll do it.' Adele stood up, took a deep breath and walked over to a table in the window. 'I'll take this in the kitchen, if you don't . . .' Her voice tailed off.

'We can send a car for him if that would help,' said Jane, watching her staring out across the garden, her eyes fixed on nothing in particular. Blue jeans and a cream cable sweater, hand knitted probably, her mousy brown hair held back in a band. No make-up to run in the tears that were drying on her cheeks.

'Thank you.' Adele picked up the telephone and trudged across the flagstone floor.

'You need to tell your father too,' said the older woman over her shoulder.

'Later, Mum.'

'He may be able to—'

'Later.'

Adele stepped to one side in the doorway, allowing another older woman out of the kitchen. She was holding a mug in each hand.

'The police are here, Ros,' said Adele.

'I was just making tea. Can I get you a cup?'

'No, thank you.' Potter turned to the older woman who was still sitting on the sofa. 'You'll be Hatty's grandmother?'

'Geraldine. I live over at Stawell.' Wooden beads hanging round her neck jangled like wind chimes when she stood up.

'Has Hatty ever gone missing before? Gone somewhere she shouldn't have and not told anyone, perhaps?'

'No.'

'How about over to Stawell?'

'Maybe when she's older. She's too young to be crossing the main road on her own.'

Jane watched Ros sit down at the dining table with her back to the window. 'Can I make a note of your name, please?' she asked.

'Ros Hicks. I live at Gable Cottage, three doors down. I'm just here to see if there's anything I can do, really.' She shrugged her shoulders. 'Not sure there is, though, apart from making the tea.'

Jane wondered whether she had ladled on her make-up before or after she'd got the call. She settled on before, giving Ros the benefit of the doubt. Those highlights would have taken several hours in the hairdressers too.

'Was she christened Hatty?' asked Potter, turning back to Geraldine.

A scream of 'I know, I bloody know' echoed along the short passageway from the kitchen followed by the sound of plastic smashing on a tiled floor.

'Harriet,' said Geraldine, grimacing. 'They've got another phone upstairs.'

'Is there anything we should know?' Potter gestured towards the kitchen.

'They'd only just started letting Hatty walk to school on her own.'

Potter nodded. 'Any brothers or sisters then?'

'She's an only child.'

'Can you think of any connection between Hatty and Alesha?'

'No.' Geraldine shook her head.

'A sports team perhaps?' asked Potter.

'No, she's—'

The sound of wood being dragged across a stone floor stopped her mid-sentence. 'He's on his way.' Adele was pulling a chair out from under the large oval dining table. She sat down opposite Ros, her head in her hands. Ros reached across the table and rubbed the side of her arm.

'We're doing everything we can,' said Potter.

'We know,' said Geraldine.

'We're going to have some more questions. Difficult ones, I'm afraid, but we'll wait till your husband gets here, if you prefer.'

Adele looked up, tears trickling down her cheeks. 'He was in the Plymouth office, so he's going to be an hour and a half.'

'At least,' said Geraldine.

'Well, let's hope we've found her before then,' said Potter. She looked at Jane and nodded towards the door. 'We'll come back later. I've asked Detective Constable Willmott to come and sit with you. She'll be here in a minute and will be able to answer any questions. All right?'

'Fine.' Geraldine was standing behind her daughter with her hand on her shoulder.

The rain had stopped by the time they were back out into the lane, Louise parking in the lay-by behind Potter's car.

'You're going to have to fill in for Family Liaison, Louise. All right?'

'Yes, Ma'am.'

'The husband's on his way from Plymouth. In the meantime, find out what you can, but be subtle about it.'

Louise nodded.

'C'mon, Jane, we'll follow Hatty's route down to the school.'

A leafy lane, trees overhanging, no pavement and four houses set back in their own grounds, but far too close to home perhaps; then out on to Manor Road, the main road through the village – wide, pavements on either side, houses, other children going to school, parents going to work. It would have been a bold move snatching her here, thought Jane. She frowned.

'Are you thinking what I'm thinking?' asked Potter.

'Probably.'

'It must've been in the lane.'

'Was it raining this morning?'

'We'll find out. The road's dry, though.'

'It's too open here.'

'Unless she knew him?' Potter looked up and down Manor Road, watching uniformed officers going from house to house, others stopping traffic. 'Someone must have seen something.'

Jane nodded.

'Get everyone together for a briefing at two,' continued Potter. 'Full team. The press officer had better be there as well.'

'Yes, Ma'am.'

'Right then.' Potter clapped her hands. 'Everybody!'

DCI Chard slammed his mug down on his workstation. 'Shut up!'

'Thank you, Simon.'

Jane sat down on an empty swivel chair at the front of the room and glanced at her phone. One text message – from Lucy.

Sorry about earlier x

Jane smiled. She had her back to the glass balustrade and turned to look down into the atrium below. The CID area on the first floor was all but deserted – everyone seconded to the MIT, probably. Several uniformed officers were milling about on the ground floor, but the workstations were empty. Still, that meant more boots on the ground in Catcott, as Bateman had put it.

'When you're ready,' shouted Potter. She was standing at the front of the room, which was now only marginally fuller than it had been at the last briefing. Jane had been sitting in Potter's car when she took the call from the Assistant Chief Constable. 'Five more officers? Is that it? How the hell am I supposed—?' The call ended abruptly, the closed windows saving Potter's phone from the ditch at the side of the road.

'You'll see some new faces. Not many, but we'll have to make do. Bob, I want you and your team to stay on Alesha.'

'Yes, Ma'am.'

'Superintendent Guthrie, where are you?'

'Here, Ma'am.' Never heard of her, thought Jane. Guthrie stood up at the back of the room; tall, short dark hair and a two piece trouser suit – pinstripe. Jane smiled. Dixon had been right about pinstripe suits and promotion.

'Sally has brought her team down from Bristol. I want you to focus on Sailes. Find him.'

'Yes, Ma'am.'

'That leaves my team on Harriet Renner, otherwise known as Hatty. She lives in Catcott – it's a small village just off the Glastonbury road, the A39 – and walks to school. It's not far and her route takes her right through the middle of the village at a busy time in the morning. Lots of people around, you'd have thought, but today she never arrived. There's a photo somewhere.'

'Here,' said Jane, holding it up.

'Dave, can you get that copied for everyone?'

Jane leaned forward and handed the picture, still in its frame, to Harding.

'She's similar in appearance to Alesha, and was last seen wearing the school uniform you see in the photo. But that's where the similarities end. Her parents are well-heeled. The father works for Svenskabanken AB as their area sales director. The mother doesn't work.'

'Is she an only child, Ma'am?' asked Bob. He was sitting at the front this time, but still slumped in his chair.

'Yes. And on the face of it her situation couldn't be more different to Alesha, but there must be a connection between them somewhere. Find it.'

Bob nodded.

'We've got a Child Rescue Alert press conference lined up for later today and we can follow that up with a reconstruction in forty-eight hours. Let's hope we don't need to.'

'Any news on Sailes?' asked Jane.

'Nothing on the traffic cameras,' replied Harding, shrugging his shoulders. 'He leaves Tanya's and disappears off the face of the earth.'

'Let's get the helicopter to have a look. And a thorough search along the main road. That's the route he'd have taken. Sally?'

'I can organise that with uniform, Ma'am.'

'Get 'em to do it on foot.'

Sally Guthrie nodded.

'We had surveillance on his friend, Darryl. Josh, where are you?'

'Here, Ma'am.'

'Anything?'

'Nothing. He stayed in the whole time. Billy-no-mates too, by the looks of things.'

'What about his phone?'

'We're waiting for the call log now, Ma'am.'

'Keep on him.'

Josh nodded and sat down.

'Anything on the white van?' asked Potter.

'We've got one on the traffic camera at junction twenty-two,' replied Bob. 'Saturday afternoon at three twenty-four p.m.'

'What about the number plate?'

'False.'

'Would be, wouldn't it?' Potter sucked her teeth. 'Get the photo over to the house to house team at Catcott.'

'It's done, Ma'am.'

'What is it, do we know?'

'It looks like an old Volkswagen LT31. Most of them left these days have been converted into camper vans. This one hasn't, so it should be quite distinctive.' Bob sat up. 'Well, as much as any white van is.'

Jane was distracted by a door slamming below her on the first floor. She looked down through the glass balustrade, her attention drawn by raised voices coming from meeting room 2, where DCI Lewis was sitting with his back to the glass partition. One of the receptionists appeared at the top of the stairs from the ground floor, ran along the landing and opened the door. Lewis raised his arm, then she backed out of the room.

Jane watched the officer sitting opposite Lewis close a file on the table in front of him, get up and leave the room, revealing a figure pacing up and down, his lower half all that was visible from Jane's vantage point.

'Jane?'

'Yes, Ma'am. Sorry,' she said, turning back to Potter's briefing. 'You were saying?'

'I was telling them that Hatty is not known to Safeguarding. That's right isn't it?'

'It is. I checked. She has no record with us or Social Services.'

'Good.'

Jane turned back to meeting room 2 just in time to see the door open and Lewis stride along the landing towards the stairs. Once at the top, he walked across the Incident Room and whispered in Potter's ear.

'You'll have to excuse me,' she said. 'I'm needed downstairs. We've finished anyway, I think, so let's get on with it.' She followed Lewis back to the top of the stairs.

'What about me, Ma'am?' asked Jane, standing up.

'You'd better come too,' replied Lewis, glancing over his shoulder at Potter.

Lewis waited until Jane closed the meeting room door behind her.

'Detective Chief Superintendent Potter, this is the senior Home Office pathologist for this area, Dr Roger Poland.'

Poland was leaning forward, his elbows on his knees and his head in his hands. He looked up, his jaw clenched, breathing heavily through his nose.

'Are you all right, Roger?' asked Jane.

He opened his mouth to speak, but the words caught in the back of his throat. He coughed, releasing the tears that had collected in the corners of his bloodshot eyes.

'Take your time,' said Jane.

'That's the one thing we haven't got,' muttered Lewis, shaking his head.

'What is it?' asked Potter.

Poland took a deep breath. 'Hatty . . .' He swallowed hard. 'Hatty . . . is my granddaughter.'

'Oh, shit, Roger.' Jane squatted down next to his chair and put her arm around him.

'We're doing everything we can, Dr Poland,' said Potter.

'Not everything,' replied Poland.

'What d'you mean?'

He turned to Jane and mumbled, his voice almost a whisper, 'Where is he?'

Chapter Ten

Detective Inspector Nick Dixon sat down on a boulder just below the summit of Hartsop Dodd and slid his rucksack off his shoulder. He looked around at the various summits poking out of the clouds all around him while he rummaged in the bottom for a banana. There should be a bottle of water in there somewhere too.

Two tiny dots, coats probably – one red, one blue – were visible in the distance on the summit of Caudale Moor, where he had stood less than an hour ago. And the summit of Helvellyn a few miles away to the west, where he had stood on Sunday, with Jane.

Monty was on the end of his long lead, drinking from a small stream that trickled across the path just below them. A waterfall then took it to the bottom of a deep gully next to the path where it joined the beck that was cascading down the mountainside.

He smiled. It had been a good day. Not as good as Sunday, though. That had been fun. Striding Edge with a large white Staffordshire terrier tucked under his arm was something he would remember on his deathbed. And Jane's face! Shame he had been too slow with the camera.

'Don't you dare!' He could still hear her voice. 'It didn't help that you were reading out the mountain rescue reports in the pub last night.'

Monty collapsed on to the grass next to him, closed his eyes and was asleep before Dixon could offer him a biscuit. He envied him that ability sometimes, but this was not one of them. It was a view to savour, not sleep through.

Sunday had been a cold day. He thought about them arriving at the summit shelter wearing woolly hats, gloves and coats, a freezing cold easterly wind racing across the top of Helvellyn. Another walker had done the honours with the camera for the obligatory summit photographs and then it was down Swirral Edge – or, as Jane had put it, 'the quickest way to the pub'.

Too much gin in the Travellers' Rest had been her undoing. She'd been asleep by the time they arrived back at the cottage in Hartsop, so Dixon carried her in and laid her on the bed in the downstairs bedroom, hoping she wouldn't be unconscious the next time he carried her over the threshold. If there was to be a next time.

That was a conversation he had been avoiding. After all, it was only a few weeks ago she had let rip when she thought he was dead, and the memory was still fresh. Maybe his legal training hadn't been a complete waste of time? He smiled. Solicitors were supposed to be good at delaying things – 'masterly inactivity', the senior partner had called it – and putting it off reduced the risk of getting the wrong answer.

He unzipped the top pocket of his rucksack and took out a small black velvet jewellery box. He opened it and looked at the diamond glinting in the afternoon sunlight.

The time would come, but not yet perhaps?

Then he snapped the box shut. Monty jumped up and started growling.

'Sheep, matey, that's all.'

'He's on holiday.' Potter folded her arms.

'He'll come back,' said Jane.

'Look, we've got fifty officers working on it already. What difference can one more make?'

Jane frowned at her. 'Do we really need to answer that question?'

Potter turned away.

'Manchester?' continued Jane.

'He's my friend and he'll find Hatty,' said Poland. 'Do I have to ring David?'

'Who's David?' asked Potter, turning to Lewis.

'Charlesworth.' Lewis raised his eyebrows.

Jane watched her mulling it over. Another run-in with the Assistant Chief Constable, and for what? She'd already been complaining the team was short staffed for such a major investigation.

'I told Dixon he'd got something that makes the rest of us nervous,' said Potter, shaking her head.

'What?' asked Poland.

'God knows,' she replied. 'But we could do with it now, whatever it is.'

'He makes things happen,' said Lewis.

'Get him on the phone, Jane,' snapped Potter.

'He'll have his mobile switched off. There's no signal unless you're up on the tops. Down in the valleys there's nothing.'

'How did we get hold of you?'

'The cottage has got satellite broadband and a landline, but he'll be out and about.'

'Try them anyway.'

'Yes, Ma'am.'

'And get the local lot to send a patrol car if you have to.'

Poland stood up, looked at Potter and nodded. 'Thank you,' he said.

Either Dixon was descending faster than usual or the cloud was racing up the ridge towards him. It didn't happen often in the Lakes, getting up above the cloud, but it was a sight to behold when it did. He sat down by the path and admired the last of the view until the cloud was swirling all around him.

He smiled. Jane would shit herself, he thought, lost on the mountains in the clouds. Thank God it hadn't happened when they'd been halfway along Striding Edge.

'All we've got to do is stay on the path and we'll be fine, old son,' said Dixon, convinced that even Monty was frowning at him.

A few minutes later they were below the cloud again, Dixon looking down through the drizzle at the lake off to his left, Brotherswater, and Hartsop, a tiny hamlet nestling in the valley.

Weaver's Cottage was clearly identifiable 1,000 feet below him, not least because of the flashing blue light in the car park.

He unzipped his coat pocket, took out his phone and switched it on. Then he rang Jane.

'Oh, thank fuck for that. Where are you?'

'On the side of Hartsop Dodd looking down at the cottage. There's a patrol car next to my Land Rover.'

'They're looking for you.'

'What's going on?'

'Another girl's gone missing.'

He sighed. 'When?'

'This morning. Listen, Nick . . . it's Roger's granddaughter, Hatty.'

Dixon closed his eyes.

'He's here,' said Jane, 'and he won't go until you—'

'Tell him I'm on my way.'

Chapter Eleven

'Where are you?'

'Stafford Services,' replied Dixon, through a mouthful of tuna sandwich. 'I had to stop for something to eat.'

It had taken him twenty minutes to get down off Hartsop Dodd, and then another twenty minutes to clear out the cottage; open the back door of the Land Rover, bung everything in, sort it out later.

'What about Monty?'

'He's had his.'

'Roger's still here, wearing a hole in the carpet in meeting room two,' said Jane.

'Tell him to go home and I'll come and see him later.'

'I tried that.'

'I'm going to be another three hours or so, and that's depending on the traffic at Birmingham. Why not take him to the pub for a bite to eat?'

'I tried that too.'

'Where's Potter?'

'They've had the press conference downstairs. Roger's daughter and son-in-law are here. It's finished now, I think.'

'Is there any connection between the two girls?'

'Not that we can find.' Jane sighed. 'Yet, anyway.'

'Do they look alike?'

'Not really.'

'I'll drop Monty off at home and ring you when I'm on the way. I should be at Express Park by nine thirty.'

'I forgot to tell you, DCI Chard's staffing again.'

'Oh, joy.'

'Ring me when you get home.'

'I will.' Dixon rang off, dropped his phone on to the passenger seat and picked up a chocolate bar. He tore open the wrapper with his teeth as he accelerated down the slip road on to the southbound M6, hoping that he would have missed the Birmingham rush hour.

Two girls, no obvious similarities and no connection between them, snatched within twenty-four – forty-eight – 9 a.m. today . . . The maths eluded him. Another bite of chocolate was called for. Sixty-four hours of each other; that was it. Tiredness was creeping in and he needed the extra sugar.

It reminded him of his days in the Met and the Friday night drive to the Lakes or North Wales, climbing all day Saturday and Sunday, followed by the race home on Sunday evening, just in time for the night shift sometimes. Still, he'd been younger and fitter then.

Poor Roger. He must be climbing the walls.

Dixon glanced into the back of the Land Rover. Monty was fast asleep, his head resting on the corner of the Scrabble box. Lucky sod.

And DCI Chard again? Dixon shook his head. Still, third time lucky. He'd made Chard look like an idiot twice now – first at the school, then Manchester – but that was likely to be the least of his worries.

Twat.

The sudden urge to vomit held Dixon in a vice-like grip for a few seconds. He leaned forward over the steering wheel and grimaced, then it was gone. Taking with it the vision of him standing in front of Roger, telling him that he'd found Hatty's body.

It was the movement that caught his eye as he turned into the visitors' car park at Express Park just after 9 p.m. Dixon glanced up at the floor to ceiling windows on the first floor just in time to see Roger jump up from his swivel chair and head for the stairs, Jane close behind him.

'You're supposed to use the staff entrance,' said the receptionist when Dixon pressed the buzzer.

'Just open it.'

He heard the loud sigh over the intercom, followed by the telltale click of the door unlocking.

'Thanks, Reg,' said Dixon, wrenching open the door.

'We keep them locked at this time of night for a reason, y'know.'

Dixon let it slam behind him as he headed for the security door at the side of the reception desk.

'You haven't noticed the lights.' Reg was grinning and pointing up at the ceiling. 'They've been fixed.'

'Maybe later.'

'Fair enough.'

Roger was halfway down the stairs behind the security door when Dixon opened it. He slumped down on to the step behind him, put his head in his hands and began to sob.

'We'll find her, Roger,' said Dixon.

'Dead or alive?'

'He's been holding it together all night.' Jane was standing above Roger, watching his shoulders heaving. 'He wouldn't go home.'

'Where's his daughter?'

'She went home with her husband. Her mother's there as well. And Louise is filling in for Family Liaison.'

'What about Potter?'

'She's still here.' Jane raised her eyebrows. 'Waiting for you, I think.'

Dixon squatted down in front of Roger. 'Look, it's going to take me a couple of hours to get up to speed, then we'll have a chat. All right?'

Roger nodded.

'We'll get someone to take you home. Or would you rather go to your daughter's?'

'Home.'

'Leave him with me,' said Jane.

Dixon stepped over Roger on to the step above him. It was a tight squeeze with Jane standing on the same step. He put his arm around her waist and pulled her close to him as he went past. 'I missed you,' he whispered.

'Me too,' said Jane, moving her lips but making no sound. 'I'll catch you up when I've got Roger into a car.'

'I'll be on the top floor.'

'I know.'

Dixon was walking past meeting room 2 when the door opened behind him.

'In here.'

'Yes, Sir.' Dixon recognised Lewis's voice.

'Long drive?' asked Lewis, closing the door behind him.

'Long enough.'

Dixon pulled a chair out from under the table.

'Don't sit down; you won't be staying,' said Lewis. 'Just watch your back and remember Deborah Potter's running the show.'

'Yes, Sir.'

'Roger went out on a limb to get you assigned to the MIT.'

'On a limb?'

'Let's just say he threatened to pull a few strings.' Lewis sat down. 'Seems to think no one else can find her, which won't go down well with the rest of the team.'

'I don't give a flying f—'

'I know you don't,' snapped Lewis. 'Just watch your back, that's all I'm saying.'

'Yes, Sir.'

'And keep out of Chard's way. I've got enough on my plate without having to bail you out of another disciplinary.'

'Yes, Sir.'

'And for all our sakes, just find her.'

'I was hoping to find them both, Sir.'

◆ ◆ ◆

The sound of telephones ringing, being snatched off desks and slammed back down again carried from the Incident Room on the second floor, the conversations merging into a low murmur, getting louder all the time as Dixon took the stairs two at a time. All of the workstations were occupied, some officers speaking on their phones, others leaning back in their chairs, eyes closed, if only fleetingly until the phone rang on the desk in front of them and they lurched forward to answer it.

Dixon spotted DCI Chard out of the corner of his eye, watching his every move. And Deborah Potter sitting at a workstation – scrolling through the call logs, probably – the grey streaks in her dark hair gone, replaced by highlights. Bags under tired eyes too.

Two large whiteboards had been mounted on the wall to his left, a photo of a ten year old girl at the top of each. Beneath, different coloured arrows led in different directions to other photographs, more on the left, Alesha's board – which Dixon had expected; the investigation had been going on longer, after all.

'Where's Jane?'

Dixon spun round to find Potter standing behind him. 'Putting Roger in a car. I said I'd see him later.'

'We're getting a good response on the phones, by the looks of things.'

Dixon nodded.

'Jane can bring you up to speed,' continued Potter. 'Then we'll speak tomorrow.'

'Yes, Ma'am.'

'It's Deborah when no one's listening. I've told you that before.'

'Thank you.'

'Just remember you report to me and no one else.' Potter smiled. 'And I'll try to keep Simon Chard out of your hair while I'm about it.'

'That would be appreciated.'

'I bet it would. All the statements are on the system. A password should've been emailed to you by now.'

'I'll check.'

'I'll be going home in a minute, but you've got my mobile number?'

'I have.'

'Have you thought any more about Portishead?'

'Not yet.'

'Well, the offer's there if you want it.'

'Thank you . . .' Dixon hesitated and looked over his shoulder. 'Deborah.'

He was still standing in front of the whiteboards when Jane appeared next to him, holding a coffee in each hand.

'Here,' she said, passing him a mug. 'What d'you want to do first?'

'What d'you think of Kevin Sailes?' asked Dixon, stepping forward and peering at his photograph.

'He's a registered sex offender living in a flat with a ten year old girl. They'll tell you he doesn't live there, but he does. And why's he done a runner? Where the bloody hell is he?'

'Get me everything we've got on him, will you?'

'Paper copies?'

Dixon nodded. 'You've met him before?'

'Once, at Tanya's flat a couple of months ago. Then I sat in when Potter interviewed him yesterday.'

'Can I see the tape?'

'It's on the system. Give me a minute.' Jane glanced over her shoulder. 'We'll need to find a vacant workstation downstairs.'

'Is this the best shot of the van?' Dixon was pointing at a black and white photograph, taken on a traffic camera at junction 22 of the southbound M5. It was grainy, at best, and impossible to identify the driver.

'There's another one at the motorway roundabout, which shows the number plate, but that's it.'

'And it's false?'

'Registered to a Datsun 120Y that was written off in 1991.'

'Surprised it lasted that long,' said Dixon, frowning at the photograph. The registration number had been scribbled on the whiteboard underneath. 'A244 AEG,' he muttered.

'What?'

'Who's looking at the van?'

'Bob somebody. Dave's in his team.'

'I'll be down in a minute.' Dixon was scanning the workstations, looking for Harding.

'He's at the back,' said Jane, heading for the stairs. 'Sitting next to Mark.'

'Thanks.'

Mark Pearce saw him first, reached over and tapped Dave Harding on the elbow. He swivelled round on his chair, with his phone still clamped to his ear, and smiled at Dixon standing behind him.

'And you saw this when?' asked Dave, turning back to his notepad. Dixon watched him making notes as he fired questions at the caller.

'What was she wearing?' . . . 'And what did the man do?' . . . 'What sort of vehicle was it?' . . . 'An estate car?' . . . 'Colour?' . . . 'Did you get the registration num—?' . . . 'Let me make note of your phone number, Mrs Calvert, and someone will be in touch with you tomorrow to take a statement.' He wrote it down on the bottom of the note. 'In the meantime, please try to remember anything else you can, no matter how insignificant it may seem.' . . . 'Thank you.' . . . 'And thank you for your call.'

Harding replaced the handset. 'Another well meaning time waster.' The telephone rang again almost immediately. 'Nice to see you, Sir,' he said, turning back around to face Dixon. 'How was your holiday?'

'Short. Tell me about the van.'

'It was spotted by a witness in Marine Drive and we picked it up on the traffic cameras from that. Why?'

'Who checked the registration?'

'I did.'

'Did you check any others?'

'No. It's false, a dead end.'

Dixon sighed. 'If I gave you a roll of black insulating tape and a pair of scissors, how long would it take you to change an "L" or an "F" into an "E"?'

'Oh shit.'

'Just for argument's sake, you know.'

'Two minutes, at most,' said Pearce, grinning.

'C'mon, Dave, it's the oldest trick in the book.'

'But it'd be obvious—'

'To everyone except a traffic camera,' interrupted Dixon. 'And that's all he cares about.'

'That "G" could be a "C", couldn't it? For fuck's sake.' Harding threw his pen on to the desk. 'Shall I run it past Bob Rutledge?' he asked.

'No, just do it.' Dixon turned towards the stairs. 'And if you find anything, tell him you used your initiative.'

Chapter Twelve

'Hello, Sir.'

'They said you were filling in for Family Liaison over at Catcott.'

'Someone turned up in the end,' said Louise. She was perched on the corner of Jane's workstation. 'What time did you get here?'

'Nineish.' Dixon pulled up a chair next to Jane. 'How were Hatty's family?'

'Not good. The mother's had to be sedated.'

'She's Roger's daughter,' said Jane.

'I know.'

'And the father?' asked Dixon.

'Much the same, but he refused a sedative.'

'Did Roger turn up?'

'No, his ex-wife rang him and he said he'd come straight here. I'm assuming he did, which is why you're here?'

'Something like that.'

'Well, I'd better get upstairs.'

'Stay,' said Dixon. 'You might as well watch this too.'

'What is it?'

'Sailes's interview.'

Dixon watched the tape in silence, only once leaning forward and scrolling the film back. That was the bit when Sailes was running through his whereabouts when Alesha disappeared. He'd had to lean forward too when Sailes's voice dropped to a whisper as he was explaining why he hadn't told Tanya he was on the Sex Offender Register. The noise of the printers on the shelf behind them hadn't helped.

'Well?' asked Jane.

'Who's looking for him?'

'Superintendent Guthrie.'

'How big's her team?'

'Eight.'

'Well, that's eight officers wasting their time.' Dixon shook his head.

'How d'you know?'

'I don't *know*,' replied Dixon. 'Are those the statements?' he asked, gesturing to the printers.

'That's them.' Jane jumped up and took the piles of papers off both, together making a bundle an inch thick. She dropped it on the workstation in front of Dixon.

'Does it include the ones you took this morning?'

'Only the handwritten versions.'

'They'll do.'

Dixon began flicking through the bundle.

'We'll leave you to it,' said Jane. 'We'll be upstairs.'

'Thanks.'

He was still reading when Jane and Louise reappeared, each holding a strong black coffee. The phones had long since gone quiet. There had been a debriefing from Potter, after which officers who had been on duty all day began to drift off home.

'Anything?'

'Six good leads,' replied Jane. 'Potter's got uniform following up two now and the rest tomorrow.'

A loud click came from Dixon's neck as he looked up at the ceiling and yawned.

Jane winced. 'Long day?' she asked, raising her eyebrows.

'Very.'

'What now?'

'You go home and get some sleep. I need to see Roger.'

'But, it's nearly one in the morning.'

'D'you think he'll be asleep?'

Jane shook her head.

'Then we find Sailes.'

Jane was standing by the passenger door of Dixon's Land Rover, pulling on the handle. He leaned across from the driver's side and flicked the lock.

'Stop that, you'll break it.'

'I thought these things were supposed to be indestructible,' Jane said, jumping in.

'And I thought you were going home to bed.'

'I'm coming with you to see Roger.'

They were out on the M5 before Jane spoke again. 'Makes it more than just a job when something like this happens, doesn't it?'

'It's never just a job, but I know what you mean.'

Dixon watched the headlights of traffic passing on the opposite carriageway flickering in Jane's eyes as those on full beam lit up the passenger compartment, before it was plunged into semi-darkness again, lit only by the lights from the dashboard and the moon reflecting off the white bonnet.

'You did ring Lucy and tell her we wouldn't be calling in?' he said, without turning his head.

'She put the phone down on me.'

Maybe now was the time to chance his arm? Just a little.

'You thought any more about what you said?'

'What did I say?'

Dixon smiled, watching her out of the corner of his eye.

As if you don't know.

'You said quite a lot, but "I can't do this any more" sticks out.'

'I was angry. Devastated, if you must know. I thought you were dead, for fuck's sake.'

'So, can you do this any more?'

'Can you?'

'I never said I couldn't.'

Dixon waited, allowing the conversation to hang while he listened to his new diesel engine; much quieter than the old one, and without the annoying rattle.

'Of course I can.' Jane was looking out of the passenger window. 'There, I've said it.'

Dixon smiled.

'And I'm sorry,' continued Jane.

'What for?'

'Everything.'

'Don't be daft.'

Dixon decided that he had pushed it enough.

'So, what happens now?' asked Jane, as he drove down the off slip at Taunton.

'We find Sailes.' That was not the answer she had been expecting; he could see her frown in the orange glow from the streetlights on the motorway roundabout. The time would come to take the conversation further, but this was not it. Not now, not while Hatty was missing and his best man was in pieces.

'How?'

'You'll see.'

Dixon parked in the gravel drive, behind Roger's Volvo, and looked up at the house. All the lights on the ground floor were on. 'See, I told you he wouldn't be asleep.'

By the time they had climbed out of the Land Rover, Roger was standing on the doorstep, a glass of whisky in his hand.

'You came,' he said, appearing to sway from side to side.

Dixon stepped forward and put his arms around him. 'Let's get you inside.'

'I'm fine, really.'

Jane's phone buzzed in her handbag just as Dixon was lowering Roger on to his sofa.

'What is it?' he asked.

Jane was peering at the screen. 'Briefing at six. Full team.' She frowned. 'I wonder what that's about?'

'We'll soon find out.'

Roger reached forward for the whisky bottle on the coffee table, but Dixon snatched it away and put it on the mantelpiece.

'Have you got a post mortem tomorrow?'

'Cancelled it.'

'Have you eaten?'

'Nope.'

'I'll see what's in the freezer,' said Jane.

'What about Adele? Have you seen her today?' asked Dixon.

Roger shook his head. 'Geraldine's there. I never get a look in when her precious mother's there. Turned Adele against me when we got divorced. All tie-dye and joss sticks she is. She'll do you a tarot reading too, if you want. I tried ringing earlier but *she* answered the phone and wouldn't let me speak to her.' He sat up. 'Wouldn't let me speak to my own daughter, would you believe it?'

'Louise was there earlier, Roger, and she said Adele had been sedated.'

Poland sighed. 'Poor kid.'

'How often do you see Hatty?'

'Every now and then, but I never get party invitations. Geraldine will be there and she comes first. We can't be in the same room together.'

'Can't?'

'It's not a pretty sight.' Roger slumped back into the cushions. 'You be careful when you get married.'

'I bunged a chicken korma in the microwave, Roger. I hope that's OK,' said Jane, appearing in the doorway.

'Thank you.'

'I'm going over to Catcott tomorrow,' said Dixon, sitting down next to Poland on the sofa. 'Then I'll go and see Alesha's parents. All right?'

'Who's this Kevin Sailes everyone's looking for?' asked Roger, sitting up.

'Tanya's boyfriend.'

'Is he a paedophile?'

'I don't think he's got anything to do with either Hatty's or Alesha's disappearance.'

'But they're looking for him?'

'In the wrong place, but we'll soon see.'

Roger's eyes glazed over. 'Is she alive?'

'Don't ask me that question, Roger. You can't ask me that question.'

Poland nodded.

'As soon as I know for sure she isn't I'll tell you. Until then, she's alive.'

'I understand.'

'Can you think of any connection between the two girls?'

'No.'

'What about sport?'

'Hatty played rugby for the under twelves at Bridgwater rugby club. And she was in the panto group.'

Dixon glanced up at Jane, who shook her head.

'Anything else?' he asked, turning back to Roger.

'No.'

'I'll be back in a sec,' said Jane, when the microwave pinged.

'What if there's no connection?'

'Then we've got to consider the possibility it's random.'

'The worst case scenario . . .' Roger's voice tailed off.

'Look, we've got some good leads being followed up as we speak and more tomorrow. There's a briefing in . . .' Dixon looked at his watch. 'Five hours. So maybe something else has come up in the meantime too.'

'You'll find her. I know you will.'

Jane handed Roger a tray with his microwaved curry steaming. 'I'd give it a minute,' she said. 'Is there any mango chutney?'

'No.'

'What can you tell me about Jeremy?' asked Dixon.

'They've been married fifteen years or so. He's a nice lad. Works for a Swedish bank, on the sales side.'

'How long have they lived at Catcott?'

'Hatty was two. They moved down from Bath. He'd been working in London doing the daily commute into Paddington.'

'And what's your relationship with Adele like, when Geraldine's not there?'

'Better than it was. Cordial after the divorce, I suppose, but it's getting better.'

'You never mentioned any of this before,' said Dixon.

'It's not really the sort of stuff you broadcast, is it.' Roger was pushing the rice around his plate. 'Every family has its dirty laundry.'

'How old was she when you divorced?'

'Fourteen.'

'Who divorced who?'

'I divorced her.'

'Why?'

'You'll find out when you meet her.' Poland grinned through a mouthful of curry.

'I'm going to go now, Roger, but I'll be back tomorrow. All right?'

He nodded.

'Try to stay off the Scotch.'

'I'd better stay with him,' said Jane.

'D'you mind?' asked Dixon.

'No, it's fine. You go to the briefing at six and then pick me up.'

'Will do.'

Jane was standing in the porch, several moths slowly battering themselves to death on the light bulb above her head, when Dixon turned back and kissed her on the lips.

'You will find her, won't you?' she asked.

'He has to believe I will, for now at least.'

Chapter Thirteen

'Good morning, everyone.'

Dixon was sitting at the back of the crowded Incident Room flicking through the last of the witness statements that Jane had printed off the day before. Four hours' sleep on the sofa would have to do, although he was still wearing the same clothes and hadn't had time to shave either. He had fed Monty, though, and let him have a run in the field behind the cottage.

'As you all now know,' continued Potter, 'Hatty Renner is the granddaughter of the Home Office pathologist Dr Roger Poland, and at his request we're joined by Detective Inspector Dixon.'

He stood up.

'He looks like he's just got down off the side of a mountain, because he has. Cooperate with him at all times, please.'

Dixon glanced across at Chard as he sat down and watched him shifting in his seat, the scowl exaggerated for the benefit of anyone who might be watching.

'Now then, Devon and Cornwall raided the caravan park at Pentewan Sands.' Potter shook her head. 'Nothing, sadly. And we got the same result at Ilminster. Good intent on the part of the informant, but a waste of time all the same. We've got four more sightings that we're following up this morning.' Potter paused. 'But . . .' she shouted.

Dixon looked up, as did everyone else.

'Thanks to Dave Harding and a bit of old fashioned police work we have a solid lead. The van. Take a bit of black electrical insulating tape and change the "L" to an "E" and you get A244 AEG. So, Dave, bright spark that he is, checked A244 ALG and, lo and behold, it's a white VW LT31 commercial van registered to one Edward Buckler. Does that name ring a bell with anyone?'

'Didn't he used to be on TV, Ma'am?' The voice came from the front of the room.

'That's right. Ted Buckler. He did the local weather on ITV,' said Potter. 'And three years for a string of historic sex offences. He runs a flower wholesale business now from a yard at Watchfield. He's ViSOR registered at Tanner's Farm, Westhill Lane. Anyone know it?'

Silence.

'Looking at it on Google Earth, there's a couple of sheds and some polytunnels. Or at least there were when the photos were taken.'

'When do we pick him up, Ma'am?' asked Harding.

Potter looked at her watch. 'Ten minutes ago. And Scientific Services will be tearing his place apart right about now.'

Several officers leaned forward and patted Harding on the back. Dixon even spotted a high five.

'News blackout for the time being, for obvious reasons,' continued Potter. 'Sally, where are you?'

Detective Superintendent Guthrie stood up.

'We need to know if there's anything connecting Buckler and Sailes.'

Guthrie nodded.

'Preferably before we interview him.'

'Yes, Ma'am.'

'Where have you got to with Sailes?'

'He's vanished. Nothing on number plate cameras, his bank account's got a few quid in it but it's not been touched and none of his friends will admit to having seen him.'

'Calls on his mobile?'

'None. No trace on it either.' Guthrie shrugged her shoulders.

'Well, keep trying.' Potter turned to Chief Inspector Bateman sitting at the front. 'Where have we got to with the search, Mike?'

'We're into day four in Highbridge,' he replied, standing up. 'The search area is expanding and we've got the Coastguard and hovercraft out again today. We're searching campsites, the holiday park, farmland; and now we're split between two sites, of course. We've had lots of help from the public, though, and the helicopter. That'll be over Catcott today.'

'If we get anything from Buckler we'll let you know straightaway.'

'Thank you.'

'Who's going to interview him?' asked Harding.

'I am,' replied Potter. 'With Inspector Dixon. We'll need everything we've got on him, though, Dave, if you could rustle that up for me?'

'Yes, Ma'am.'

'Right, that's it, I think. Get to it.'

Dixon headed for the stairs at the back of the room, he hoped unnoticed.

'Where are you off to?' asked Potter, leaning over the balustrade.

'I left Jane at Roger's last night. We didn't think he should be on his own.'

'You'd better get her then. I'll be heading over to Watchfield at nine.'

'Can I meet you there?'

'Yes, fine. All being well I want to interview him this morning.'

Dixon nodded. He'd be at Roger's before seven. Plenty of time.

'How is he?'

'Asleep,' replied Jane, jumping in the passenger seat of Dixon's Land Rover. He was parked across Roger's drive, engine running.

Monty stood up with his paws on the back of the front seats and began licking her ears. 'He said he'd come down to Express Park later,' continued Jane.

'What about you?'

'I got a few hours on the sofa.' Jane looked out of the passenger window as Dixon accelerated up the northbound slip road on to the M5. 'Any news?' she asked.

'If you assume the number plate had been doctored with insulating tape, then the van belongs to Ted Buckler, the TV weatherman.'

'And rapist.'

'You've heard of him?'

'Safeguarding isn't just about vulnerable people; we also identify those who pose a risk. It's about collating intelligence and risk management.'

'Is he a risk?'

'The psychiatrists say not, which is why he got parole. He was only released from prison two years ago, though, so he's still monitored quite closely. There's an internet banning order in place too. He says it's damaging his business and he's trying to get it lifted.'

'Have you met him?'

'No.'

'I'm meeting Potter at his place at nine. Then we'll interview him later this morning.'

'Where is he?'

'He'll be at Express Park by now.'

'Any sign of the girls?'

'Not yet.' Dixon slid his phone out of his pocket and handed it to Jane. 'Not as far as I know.'

'No messages,' said Jane, looking down at the screen. 'They're probably miles away by now, if they're still alive.'

'Oh, they're still alive,' muttered Dixon.

He glanced across at Jane leaning on the door pillar, her eyes closed. Two minutes' silence was all it had taken and she was fast asleep. It must be the new engine. She'd never have managed that in his old Land Rover.

Twenty minutes later he was paying for diesel at the Shell station on the Berrow Road when he noticed Jane yawning in the passenger seat. He smiled. The smell of the fuel woke her up, probably.

'What are we doing here?' she asked, as he opened the driver's door and climbed in. 'I thought we were going home?'

'We are. We'll have a quick look for Sailes on the way.'

'Where?'

Dixon was turning out of the petrol station. 'What route did he take from Tanya's to his mother's?'

'The main road. They both said he always used the main road.'

'And that was checked?'

'Yes. On foot and by the helicopter with its thermal imaging camera. Potter even put divers in the River Axe.'

Dixon sighed. 'He was drunk when he arrived at Darryl's place. He had a few more beers there, strong ones, then he turned up at Tanya's where he had half a bottle of vodka and some of her methadone. How far would you get with that lot inside you?'

'I'd be unconscious, probably,' replied Jane, shaking her head.

'Me too, but Kevin is used to it, so he can still function, still drive, and maybe, just maybe, he thinks he'd better go the back way, just in case he gets breathalysed. What say you?'

'We sent a patrol car that way. You're talking about Red Road?'

'I am.'

'They found nothing.'

'Were they on foot?'

'No, I don't think so. We checked the main road on foot, but not the back way.'

Dixon went straight on into the single track country lane when the main road turned sharp left towards Berrow church. He glanced down at the deep ditches on either side.

'You'd see him straightaway if he was in one of them,' muttered Jane.

They followed Red Road in silence, Dixon watching the ditch on the driver's side and Jane the passenger side.

'There's Brean Golf Club,' she said. 'They'd have seen anything along here.'

'It'll be at the end of the long straight along the railway line, if I'm right. Accommodation Road, it's called. I looked it up on Google Maps.'

'You think he missed the bend?'

'We'll soon see,' replied Dixon, turning right at the first T-junction, then left at the next.

Once over the railway line the road turned sharp right. It had been widened and a car missing this bend would have been clearly visible in the field beyond.

'There are no ditches along here,' said Jane.

Dixon put his foot down on the long straight alongside the railway line.

'You'd never outrun a train in this old heap.'

'Thank you, Sergeant.'

He slowed for the chicane on the bridge over the River Axe, then accelerated again towards the railway bridge at the far end of the straight.

'He left Tanya's after midnight in a Renault Clio V6.' Dixon shook his head. 'He could've got up to a ton along here.'

'Don't you try it.'

'Yes, Mother.'

He slowed on the approach to the apex of the bend, a sharp right hand turn that took the road back over the railway line, and pulled into a lay-by on the nearside.

'Let's have a look then,' Dixon said, switching off the engine.

'Are you sure?'

'No.' Monty jumped over on to the passenger seat when Jane got out. 'Not you, old son.'

'There aren't any skid marks,' said Jane, walking over to the nearside kerb on the bend.

'That just means he didn't brake.' Dixon squatted down and peered at the kerbstones. 'What's this?' he asked, pointing at gouge marks in the concrete.

'Could be anything.'

He scrambled down the steep bank beyond the kerb, stepped over a low barbed wire fence at the bottom and peered into the dense undergrowth. A small weed covered pond was just visible through the vegetation, surrounded by bushes on all sides that all but obscured it from the air.

Four wheels were sticking out of the weeds, one at each corner of the underside of a car, the twin exhaust pipes covered in green slime. Enough of the chassis was visible to confirm the car was black.

Dixon straightened up.

'What is it?' asked Jane.

'D'you want to have a look?'

He held the barbed wire down with his foot while he helped her over the fence. Then he pointed through a small gap in the branches. 'Look through there.'

'Oh, shit, you were right.'

'A lucky guess.' He shrugged his shoulders. 'It's the back way to Weston. I'd take it if I'd had a few. He missed the bend, hit the kerb sideways on and the car flipped, landing upside down in there. It would've cleared these bushes easily if he had his foot down.'

'Are you sure he's in there?'

'Where else is he going to be? If he wasn't killed in the crash, he'd have drowned within minutes of it.'

'Can you get out to it?'

'Not through that lot. They'll need cutting equipment,' replied Dixon.

'Let me get round there and see if I can see the rear number plate,' said Jane. 'The bumper's sticking out of the water, so . . .'

'I'll go. I'm dressed for it.' He managed to find a gap in the bushes adjacent to the back of the car. 'OY01 XJN.'

Jane was looking in her notebook. 'That's it. That's Darryl's. All that bloody fuss and he's been here all the time.'

Dixon scrambled back up the bank to the road, then he reached down and pulled Jane up. 'Better call it in,' he said.

'You'd have thought the bloody idiots in the patrol car would've seen him. Potter'll do her nut,' muttered Jane, fishing her phone out of her handbag. 'Where are you going?' she asked, as Dixon walked back to the Land Rover.

'I've got to be over at Watchfield by nine.'

'But—'

'You'll be fine. I'll catch up with you at Express Park.'

Chapter Fourteen

Tanner's Farm, Westhill Lane, Watchfield was hidden behind high, corrugated iron fencing. The gates were open, but blocked by Scientific Services vans, so Dixon left his Land Rover in the lane, behind Potter's BMW. The tops of the polytunnels were visible behind a red brick bungalow and there were several sheds off to the left, a forklift truck parked outside.

'Been busy, I gather,' said Potter, striding over to meet him as he walked into the yard. 'You've shaved and changed too. I rather liked the mountain man look.'

'Was he in the car?' asked Dixon.

'Yes.'

He nodded.

'How did you know?'

'He was never going to get far with all that booze and methadone inside him. And he'd probably have gone the back way to avoid us. It's not rocket science.'

'Don't tell Sally Guthrie that.'

'I won't.'

'It does mean her team can concentrate on Buckler now, which is good.' Potter smiled. 'You may also be interested to know that Dave Harding has fessed up, so we have you to thank for this too.'

Dixon shrugged his shoulders.

'Where's Jane?' he asked.

'Still over at Lympsham. They're waiting for a crane to get the car out. I've told her to meet us at Express Park.'

'What about Sailes?'

'They haven't got him out yet.' Potter grimaced. 'A diver's been in. It looks like his neck's broken so he was probably killed instantly.'

'And here?'

'We've not found anything yet, but the sniffer dogs have only just arrived. Scenes of Crime are in the house at the moment.'

'Is it connected to mains drainage?'

'No. We've checked the septic tank.'

'Ma'am!'

The shout came from the far corner of the yard, just inside the corrugated iron fence. Louise was standing behind a dog handler waving her arms.

'What is it?' asked Potter, as she ran across with Dixon close behind her.

'A beaded bracelet,' replied the dog handler.

'It's an anklet,' said Louise. 'It's a bit longer than a bracelet.'

Potter waited until the dog handler pulled his spaniel clear and then squatted down. 'It looks broken.'

'It's just like Alesha's, isn't it, Ma'am?'

'It is, Louise, yes.'

Dixon looked around. 'We'd better get these pallets moved,' he said, 'and those two old cars. These oil drums will need opening too.'

Potter turned to Louise. 'What's the senior SOCO's name?'

'Donald Watson, Ma'am.'

'Get him out here, will you?'

'Yes, Ma'am.'

'And be careful where you're treading.'

'Where's the van?' asked Dixon, his eyes darting around the yard.

'In that barn,' replied Potter, pointing over her shoulder. 'SOCO haven't got to it yet.'

'I thought you were in the Lakes,' said Watson, appearing around the stacks of pallets. He was wearing a one-piece white protective suit with blue latex gloves and overshoes.

'I was.'

'Bet you wish you'd stayed there.'

'Not this time.'

'Yeah.' He turned to Potter. 'What can I do for you?'

She pointed to the anklet lying on the gravel. 'Bag it up and get it tested.'

'Yes, Ma'am.'

'Then tear this fucking place apart.'

Dixon started walking towards the barn.

'Wear gloves if you're going in there,' shouted Watson. 'And don't touch anything.'

Once inside the barn Dixon walked around the van, taking photographs of it from various angles on his iPhone. He was careful to step over the tyre tracks in the soft earth floor and, while he opened the doors and photographed the passenger compartment, he touched nothing even though he had stopped to put on a pair of latex gloves. He squatted down and took close-ups of the number plates too, front and rear.

'There's a lorry on the way to pick it up,' said Potter, standing in the doorway. 'We won't know anything until SOCO have been over it, though.'

Dixon opened the rear doors and took a photograph of the back of the van.

'Is it empty?' asked Potter.

'Looks it.'

Dixon walked past Potter and out into the sunlight.

'Where are you going now?'

'The house. I want to see what sort of man he is.'

'And you can tell that from his house?'

'Haven't you ever watched *Through the Keyhole*?'

'No.'

'Me neither,' said Dixon, smiling.

He started in the kitchen, Potter following him every step of the way. The cupboards: ordered, jars and tins facing front. The fridge: nothing out of place. Jane would have appreciated the cutlery drawer. Maybe Buckler had a touch of obsessive compulsive disorder too?

A faint smell of bleach, perhaps?

'It's been cleaned,' said Watson, watching them from the serving hatch.

'There's nothing you'd feed a child, is there?' asked Dixon.

'Beans on toast, perhaps?' replied Watson. 'There are some beans in the cupboard.'

'If you were going to kidnap a ten year old child, you'd stock up with stuff to keep her happy, surely? Crisps, sweets, fizzy drinks, crap like that.'

'Maybe she's dead.'

'Which one?' snapped Potter.

'Both of them.'

Dixon shook his head. 'You really can be a git sometimes, Donald.'

'Just doing my job.'

He pushed past Watson and into the dining room.

'He hasn't used this room for months,' said Watson, following him. 'It's covered in dust. Even the bottles on the sideboard. The tonic's flat too; best before September 2016.'

'How old is he?' asked Dixon.

'Sixty-one,' replied Potter.

The curtains were closed in the living room, the scene lit up by arc lamps.

'We got a few fibres off the sofa that have gone off to the lab,' said Watson. 'There must be a cat somewhere too.'

'An old fashioned TV,' said Dixon. 'Not internet enabled.'

'He's subject to a banning order,' said Potter.

Dixon picked up four DVDs lying on the coffee table, all rented from Burnham library and all of them Westerns. 'These aren't bad if you like that sort of thing,' he said, holding up *The Outlaw Josey Wales* and *Unforgiven*.

He picked up two photographs on the mantelpiece, one in each hand, both of Ted Buckler in happier days, reading the weather forecast beside a map of the south west. On the left, a younger man, presumably at the start of his career; and on the right, an older man being presented with various gifts, on his retirement, no doubt.

'I'll wait outside,' muttered Potter, when Dixon switched on the TV.

BBC News. He switched it off again. 'Have you finished upstairs?'

Watson nodded.

By the time Dixon had finished going round the house, SOCO were dismantling the piles of rubbish in the yard, bit by bit. The cars had been moved, as had the forklift.

'No, before you ask, there were no trapdoors underneath,' said Watson, raising his eyebrows.

'What did you learn in the house then?' asked Potter.

'Nothing,' replied Dixon, peeling off his gloves.

'Can I call you Ted?'

'I use Edward now.'

'You've declined a solicitor, Edward,' continued Potter. 'Is that right?'

'I've done nothing and I have nothing to hide.'

Dixon watched Buckler in the reflection on the tape machine. Closely cropped white hair, clippers probably, and a white goatee; he bore little resemblance to the TV weatherman he had seen in Google Images. There were no flowery shirts now.

'You've been arrested on suspicion of the abduction of Alesha Daniels and Harriet Renner.'

'I had nothing to do with it.'

'You're a convicted rapist, Edward. What have you got to say about that?'

'Read the file.'

'Put it into context for us,' said Potter.

'I was found guilty by a jury. It's happened to innocent people before and it will again. That's all I have to say about it.'

'So, you're saying you didn't do it?'

Silence.

'But the jury didn't believe you, did they?'

Buckler took his reading glasses out of his breast pocket and began cleaning the lenses on his shirt tail.

'How d'you explain that, Edward?'

'Read the file. It's all set out in the grounds of appeal.'

'The appeal failed,' said Potter.

'I was refused leave to appeal. There's a difference.'

'The jury got it wrong then?'

'Look, I'm saying nothing more about it. It's finished with. So, I suggest you move on.'

'All right, Edward, let's move on,' said Potter. 'Where were you on Saturday?'

'What time?'

'Talk me through the whole day.'

'I had a delivery of tulips from Amsterdam.'

'Is that a wind up?'

'Why would it be?' snapped Buckler. 'I'm a flower wholesaler. I import all sorts.'

Dixon sighed, as silently as he could manage.

'What time was that?' asked Potter.

'The lorry got to me about ten, I suppose. We unloaded the tulips into the cool shed and he was gone again within the hour.'

'Where to?'

'Back to Harwich for the ferry.'

'Then what?'

'It took me a while to sort them out, I suppose. I put the freshest ones to the back. Then I had a couple of deliveries to make. Ellen collected some flowers before that too, when the lorry was there. You can check with her if you need to.'

'Ellen?'

'Ellen's Flowers in Burnham. She had a wedding that afternoon.'

'And the deliveries?'

'Weston and Wells. I deliver a couple of times a week.'

'On a Saturday?'

'It depends what they've got going on. Wells was flowers for the cathedral. Weston they had a marquee to decorate. I don't know what for; it wasn't a wedding anyway.'

'And you do the deliveries yourself?'

'I do.'

'You used to have a delivery driver, didn't you?'

'Kevin, yes. I had to let him go.'

'Why?'

'I don't want to get him in any trouble.'

'He's dead, Edward,' said Potter, matter of fact.

'Doesn't surprise me, to be honest.' Buckler put his reading glasses on and then slid them on to the top of his head. 'Overdose, was it?'

'Road traffic accident.'

'Did he take anyone else with him?'

Potter ignored the question. 'When did you last see him?'

'The day I sacked him.'

'When was that?'

'A year ago maybe? It'll be in my records.'

'You had a lot in common,' said Potter, tipping her head to one side.

Buckler was sucking his teeth, watching Dixon watching him in the reflection on the tape recorder.

'He told me what had happened to him, yes.'

'And you believed him?'

'I had no reason not to.'

'When did you last speak to him?'

'I told you, the day I sacked him. Check my phone if you don't believe me.'

'We are.'

'Look, what's Kevin go to do with this?'

'He was in a relationship with Alesha's mother.'

No reaction, but Dixon would check the CCTV footage again later to be on the safe side. The new interview room layout was a pain in the arse for a whole host of reasons, not least because he couldn't look Buckler in the eye.

'I still don't see what that's got to do with me.'

'OK, let me spell it out for you then, Edward,' said Potter, turning on her seat to face him. 'You're a convicted paedophile, and a known associate of another convicted paedophile, who just happens to be in a relationship with the mother of a missing ten year old girl.'

Buckler took a deep breath. Dixon glanced across at him over Potter's shoulder, noticing beads of sweat on his forehead that hadn't been visible in the reflection.

'I've not seen Kevin for a year. More, probably.'

'Let's go back to Saturday then,' said Potter. 'What about the rest of the day?'

'I was open to the public in the afternoon. I sell a bit direct to a few regular customers. Not enough to piss off my shop customers.'

'Cash in hand?'

'No.' Indignant.

'D'you have a card machine?'

'Yes.'

'What time was the last transaction on Saturday?'

'Must have been nearly five. The receipt will be in the till.'

'Then what?'

'I closed the gates and spent the rest of the day in front of the telly. Fed the cats.' He shook his head. 'How much detail d'you want?'

'What did you watch?'

'Two Clint Eastwood films.'

'All right,' said Potter. 'Talk me through the route you took for the deliveries.'

Buckler frowned. 'I went to Weston first, up the A370. Then across to Wells and back via Wedmore.'

'Did you go on the M5?'

'No. Over it twice, but not on it.'

Potter handed a black and white photograph to Buckler, who slid his glasses down on to the end of his nose. 'This was taken on Saturday at two twenty-four p.m. It's a still from the traffic camera on the southbound off slip at junction twenty-two.' Potter waited for a reaction.

None came.

'Would you agree this is your van?'

'It can't be. I didn't go on the M5.'

'It's your number plate.'

'No, it isn't.' Buckler handed the photograph back to Potter, shaking his head as he did so. 'Mine ends in ALG and this one's AEG.'

'So, let me be quite clear. You're saying it's not your van, despite the *almost* identical registration – which, I might add, is clearly visible.'

'Yes.'

'How long d'you think it would take to change an "L" to an "E" with a bit of black insulating tape and a pair of scissors?'

'You're not seriously suggesting . . .' Buckler's voice tailed off.

'That's exactly what I'm suggesting, Ted. Do you own any black insulating tape?'

'It's Edward.' Buckler hesitated. 'Yes.'

'That's the right answer, because we found it.' Potter nodded. 'And you can take it that we'll be checking your number plate for traces of glue residue.'

Silence.

'A van fitting this description was seen by a witness in Marine Drive shortly before Alesha disappeared,' continued Potter. 'What have you got to say about that?'

Buckler folded up his glasses and dropped them into his breast pocket. 'It must have been the van in the photo then, because it wasn't mine.'

Potter glanced at Dixon and sighed.

'You seriously expect us to believe that, Edward?' she asked.

'Yes.'

'This is your chance to tell us what happened and where the girls are.'

Silence.

'Where are they?'

Buckler looked up at the camera in the corner of the interview room, just under the ceiling, and then back to Potter.

'I've told you.'

'Are they still alive.'

'I really don't know.'

'You'll need your glasses again,' said Potter, sliding another photograph out of the file on her knee. 'This is a white beaded anklet identical to the one Alesha was wearing when she disappeared.'

Buckler took the photograph from Potter's outstretched hand and peered at it. Then he took out his glasses, put them on and looked at the picture again.

'Have you seen it before, Edward?'

'No.'

'It was found this morning in your yard.'

Buckler sat up sharply, arching his back. 'Where?'

'In the corner by the empty pallets.'

Buckler tried to hand the photograph back to Potter, but he was trembling now. She ignored his outstretched hand, instead watching the photograph fluttering as if in a strong breeze.

'It's being tested for her DNA, Edward,' she said. 'Is there anything you want to tell me now?'

Buckler hesitated, then slumped back in his chair and sighed. 'I'd like to see my solicitor.'

Chapter Fifteen

'What d'you think?' asked Potter, stepping into the lift.

'I think we're no nearer finding the girls,' replied Dixon, shaking his head. 'Dead or alive.'

'He'll crack. Especially if we get a DNA match off the anklet. We've got enough to charge him then, probably.'

Dixon was watching Poland steaming along the landing towards the lift, with Jane running to catch up. It was one disadvantage of glass walls.

'Sailes is dead?' asked Roger, as the lift doors opened.

'Who told you that?' snapped Potter.

Poland looked at her and then turned back to Dixon. 'And you've arrested Ted Buckler. Has he said anything?'

'Dr Poland—'

'Leave this to me, Ma'am,' interrupted Dixon. 'I'll catch up with you later.'

Potter sighed. 'I'll call you when we get the DNA results.'

'Thank you.'

Dixon glared at Jane, his eyes wide.

'Don't look at me. I didn't tell him.'

'We'll talk in the car.'

'Where are we going?' asked Poland.

'Catcott.'

'I can't.'

'Yes, you can,' replied Dixon, stepping back into the lift.

'Look at that lot,' sneered Poland, as the lift doors closed. 'Patting themselves on the back.'

Dixon watched a small group of officers on the far side of the Incident Room. They were smiling and shaking hands. At least there were no high fives this time.

'It's a breakthrough, Roger,' said Jane. 'They're just letting off steam.'

'I know, I know.'

'Everyone's trying to find Hatty.'

Poland turned to Dixon as he stepped out of the lift on the first floor. 'Tell me about Ted Buckler, then.'

'In the car.' He wrenched open the back door to the staff car park.

'I know how this works, Nick.'

'I know you do.' Dixon was peering into the back of his Land Rover.

'Is Monty asleep?' asked Jane.

'I left him at home. I've got the back seats down.'

'I'll drive,' said Roger, rummaging in his pocket for his keys. 'Mine's over there.'

'Buckler's denying everything,' said Dixon when the last of the car doors slammed shut. 'He says the van in the photo isn't his and he hasn't seen Sailes for twelve months.'

'What about the anklet?'

'You *are* well informed, Roger.'

Poland shrugged his shoulders.

'He clammed up when Potter put that to him. Asked to see his solicitor.'

'So, we're no nearer finding Hatty?'

'We'll find her, Roger.' Jane leaned forward and put her hand on Poland's shoulder.

'You keep saying that.'

'What are we going to find at Catcott?' asked Dixon, changing the subject.

'I spoke to Adele this morning. She's not good. Jeremy's in a bit of a state too.'

'Is Geraldine there?'

'She'd gone home to feed her cats, but she'll be back by now, I expect.'

'You know what to do,' said Dixon.

'What?'

'Take a deep breath and count to ten. You tell me to do it often enough.'

Poland parked behind a Mercedes two-seater in the lay-by opposite Old School House. 'That's Geraldine's,' he muttered. 'I'm still paying for it.'

'This is about Hatty, Roger.'

'I know.'

'I'll get someone to shift that lot too,' said Dixon, frowning at a small group of journalists and photographers hovering at the far end of the lay-by.

Poland rang the doorbell, at the same time looking through the stained glass window in the door, Dixon and Jane standing behind him, peering over his shoulder. 'Who's this, I wonder?'

'Family Liaison,' said Jane. 'Down from Bristol.'

The officer was dressed casually; windproof trousers and a fleece. Potter would approve, thought Dixon. He stepped in front of Poland, warrant card in hand.

'Detective Inspector Dixon,' he said, when the door opened. 'This is DS Winter and Dr Poland, Adele's father.'

'Oh, come in, Sir. I'm Richard Page, FLO, just filling in, really.'

'We know.'

'Is there any news?' whispered Page.

Dixon shook his head. 'Lead on.'

They followed Page into the living area. Adele jumped up, ran over and threw her arms around Poland, sobbing into his shoulder. 'I thought you were coming yesterday,' she gasped.

'I rang and was told not to.' He glanced around the room and up at the galleried landing. 'Where's your mother?' he asked.

'In the garden with Ros.' Jeremy had been sitting with his back to them and stood up, his eyes bloodshot, his face ashen behind a thin layer of stubble.

'This is Nick Dixon, the police officer I told you about, Adele,' said Roger.

'Have you found her?'

'We've made an arrest,' replied Dixon, 'but there's no connection with Hatty at the moment. Possibly Alesha, but there's still a long way to go.'

'Who is it?' asked Jeremy.

'I really can't divulge—'

'Dad?'

'He doesn't know, Adele.' It was a white lie Dixon could live with, if it saved Roger from lying to his daughter. Or worse still, telling her more than he should.

'Mum wants to bring in a clairvoyant.'

'She would,' muttered Roger.

'She knows someone, apparently. It can't do any harm, can it?'

'No,' replied Dixon. False hope was still hope, if they were lucky to get even that.

Poland glared at him, but was distracted by Geraldine appearing in the doorway, brushing leaves off her long skirt.

'Oh, *you're* here,' she said, glaring at Roger.

'We all are, Mrs Poland,' said Dixon, noticing the holes in the elbows of her cardigan and the small tattoo on her right wrist, not quite hidden by the bangles. The beads were quite something too.

'And you'll be the police officer?'

'Detective Inspector Dixon.'

'Well, it's *Ms* Crosby, if you don't mind. I use my maiden name now. And this is Ros Hicks,' she replied, looking over her shoulder. 'A neighbour.'

'I just popped in to see if there was anything I could do,' said Ros, hesitating in the doorway. 'I'll leave you to it, Adele, if the police are here.'

'Thank you.'

Then Ros stepped back out of the French windows into the garden and disappeared around the side of the house.

'Has Hatty ever gone missing before?' asked Dixon, walking round to the fireplace and looking at the pictures on the mantelpiece.

'No. Never,' replied Jeremy.

Innocuous family photos: Hatty on a pony, grinning from ear to ear; on a beach building a sandcastle; on her father's shoulders with several donkeys in the background; a wedding photograph. Dixon raised his eyebrows – Roger and Geraldine were holding hands in that one.

'Are you here to ask the same questions we've been asked countless times already?'

Dixon's association with Roger would be enough to account for the immediate hostility. 'Ms Crosby, I'm here to find Hatty. Either you want to help or you don't.'

'You can't speak to me like that.'

'Yes, he can,' snapped Poland. 'Just shut up for once in your life.'

'Cup of tea, anyone?' asked Page.

'Thank you.' Jeremy sighed. He knelt in front of Adele, who had collapsed on to the sofa, sobbing. 'It's going to be fine,' he said, his eyes wide. 'We'll get her back. I know we will.'

'Have you been able to think of any connection between Hatty and the other girl, Alesha Daniels?' asked Jane.

'No,' replied Jeremy. 'Nothing. Does there have to be one?'

'Not at all.' Dixon turned around with a photograph in each hand, taken off the built in shelves by the fire. 'It's just that if the girls are connected then it's reasonable to assume there's some connection between them and whoever might have got them.'

'Reasonable to assume?' sneered Geraldine.

'It's a starting point.' He looked back down at the picture in his left hand. 'Who's the skier?' he asked.

'That'll be me,' replied Jeremy. 'That's the Hahnenkamm. Took me twenty minutes to get down. They do it in less than two when they're racing.'

'What about this one?' Dixon asked, looking at the photograph in his right hand: four lads and a girl in a bar, several empty champagne bottles on the table in front of them. 'Celebrating something?' he asked, holding it in front of Adele.

'That was the old champagne bar on Paddington station. It's gone now. That was years ago; we'd just sold our internet company.'

'He doesn't want to hear about that now, Adele,' said Jeremy.

'Yes, I do.'

'We sold it for just under eleven million pounds. I had ten per cent. But we were locked in as founding directors. We couldn't sell our shares for two years and the internet bubble burst in the meantime.' Adele shrugged her shoulders. 'We came away with enough for a round of drinks in the end, but it was a lot of fun.'

'And this was before you met?'

'Yes, thank God,' mumbled Jeremy.

'What about birthday parties?' asked Dixon, replacing the photograph on the shelf amongst the family snaps. 'Is it possible the girls were at the same party at some point?'

'I bloody well hope not.'

'Shut up, Mother,' snapped Adele. 'For God's sake.'

Geraldine stormed into the kitchen. Poland looked at Dixon and rolled his eyes.

'You've been asked about a white van?' continued Dixon.

'We've not seen one,' said Adele, shaking her head.

'Excuse me.' Dixon reached into his jacket pocket and took out his phone. 'I need to go, I'm afraid.'

'Has she—?'

'I'm sorry, no. It's lab results, that's all.'

Adele jumped up off the sofa and took hold of his wrist. 'Don't stop looking for her. Please.'

'He won't,' said Poland.

'Only, she's alive. I know she is.' Tears were streaming down Adele's face now. 'Or, at least, I'd know if she was dead. I'd know that.'

'I'll give you a lift.'

'Can't you stay, Dad?'

'Well, I . . . er . . . yes, of course.' Poland threw his car keys to Dixon. 'Here, take it.'

'I'll bring it back in one piece.'

'Just bring Hatty back in one piece.'

Chapter Sixteen

'It's a bloody automatic,' muttered Dixon, looking down at the pedals.

'D'you want me to drive?'

'No, I'll be fine.'

'What are the lab results?' asked Jane, putting on her seatbelt.

'It's Alesha's anklet, so Potter wants to interview Buckler again.'

'Roger's ex is a bit of a dragon, isn't she?'

'He did warn us.'

'And a clairvoyant?' Jane shrugged her shoulders. 'Can't do any harm, I suppose.'

'That depends on what she says. It could be a waste of bloody time.'

'What d'you mean?' Jane was looking over her shoulder. 'You can turn left and then left again takes you back out to the main road.'

Dixon was staring in the rear view mirror, doing a three point turn outside the house.

'Clear at the back,' said Jane.

'What if she says Hatty is, I don't know, in Scotland, say. She hears "Mull of Kintyre" and sees a vision. Are we supposed to drop everything we're doing and go look for her on Mull?'

'Kintyre.'

'Whatever.' Dixon turned out on to the main road. 'Because the family will soon jump on us if we don't.'

'Why didn't you say that?'

'The mother'd probably do it anyway. And it might give them some comfort.'

'Potter won't like it.'

'She'll get over it.'

'What did you make of the husband?' Jane frowned. 'There's a speed camera along here.'

'I don't know.' Dixon stamped on the brakes just before he reached the yellow speed gun. 'What did you think of him?'

'Just as you'd expect really. Trying to hold it together for Adele's sake, I suppose.'

Dixon left Roger's Volvo in the visitors' car park outside Express Park and they ran in the front door.

'Superintendent Potter is waiting for you in the custody suite, Sir,' said the receptionist.

'Thank you.'

Jane swiped her ID card and opened the security door. 'I'll see if I'm needed upstairs, then nip home and sort Monty out.'

'Bring him back, will you?'

'Yeah, fine.'

◆ ◆ ◆

'A prepared statement.' Potter slammed the door behind her. 'A bloody prepared statement.'

'What was the solicitor's name again?'

'Holt. From some bucket shop in Taunton.'

'Sharp, though,' muttered Dixon, making a mental note of the name in case he ever needed a solicitor himself.

'He's lying, Ma'am,' said Chard, emerging from a door behind them. 'We were watching on the CCTV.' Superintendent Guthrie followed him out into the corridor.

'What d'you think, Sally?' asked Potter.

'Lying,' she replied. 'He has to be.'

'And you?' Potter turned to Dixon.

'Everything he says is plausible.'

'You believe him?' snapped Chard.

'He says it's not his van and we can't prove it is,' continued Dixon. 'We say he disguised the number plate; he says someone else did it to make it look like he was disguising it, casting suspicion on him. And if he's right, it's worked.'

'Someone went to the trouble of getting an identical plate and then changed it?' asked Guthrie.

'That's what he's saying, yes. They'd know we'd be looking for it and it makes him look bad, doesn't it? Is there any glue residue on his number plate?'

Guthrie frowned. 'No.'

'Had it been cleaned?'

'No.'

'Whose fucking side are you on?' snapped Chard.

Dixon glared at him. 'Alesha and Hatty's.'

'How d'you explain the anklet then?' asked Potter.

'I don't. Not yet. But he says someone must've thrown it over his fence, which ties in with where we found it.'

'For fuck's sake.' Chard turned away.

'He's a high profile convicted sex offender. If you wanted to snatch a child and set someone up to get us barking up the wrong tree then he's your man, isn't he?'

'Bollocks.'

'What about the insulating tape?' asked Potter.

'I've got some at home somewhere,' replied Dixon. 'I used it to mark my rock climbing gear. Mine was black and Jake's red.' He shook his head. 'You can get it at B&Q.'

Potter folded her arms and let out a long sigh. 'We've got some too. God knows what my husband uses it for, but it's in the drawer with the spare batteries.'

'My husband's an electrician so don't look at me,' said Guthrie, shrugging her shoulders.

'Well, I'm not letting him go. At least, not until SOCO have finished the search and if that means a custody extension then so be it.'

'Thank God for that.'

'When I need your opinion, Simon, I'll ask for it.' Potter scowled.

Chard blushed. 'Yes, Ma'am.'

'Sally, your team can stay on him. Look for any recent contact with Sailes.'

'Yes, Ma'am.'

'What do we tell the press, Ma'am?' asked Chard. 'They know we've made an arrest and Vicky Thomas is coming under pressure to give them an update.'

'You didn't say whether you believed him, Nick,' said Potter, turning to Dixon.

Dixon felt Chard's eyes burning into the back of his head. As if glaring at him was going to make a difference. Still, there was a time and place for everything, and this was not it. Not yet.

'I don't know, Ma'am,' he said.

Potter leaned back against the wall. 'We tell the press nothing for the time being. And if Buckler's name gets out I'll want to know who leaked it.'

'This just came in,' said Potter, perching on the corner of Dixon's workstation. She handed him a colour photograph. 'It's from the speed camera at Woolavington. Yesterday morning just before nine. I'm getting it blown up and enhanced to see if we can see the tape on the number plate.'

He leaned back in his chair and looked at the image, holding it up in front of him.

'Buckler's van's come back clear too,' continued Potter. 'There's no trace of Alesha or Hatty.'

'It must be the same van from the M5 traffic camera,' said Dixon. 'Makes you wonder whether Hatty's in the back.'

'Buckler said he didn't go out at all yesterday, but we've got a trace on his mobile phone, so we'll soon see.'

Dixon sighed. 'All that will tell us is that his phone stayed at home. Doesn't mean he did.'

'We're checking for CCTV along the route,' said Potter. 'You never know, we may get a look at the driver.'

Dixon slid his iPhone out of his pocket and opened 'Photos', then began scrolling through the pictures he had taken of Buckler's van in the barn at Watchfield. He stopped at an image of the back of the van and used his fingers to zoom in on the number plate.

He nodded, then handed the colour photograph from the speed gun back to Potter. 'It's definitely not Buckler's van,' he said.

'How d'you know?'

'I took this photo of his number plate yesterday. It must be the original – you can see the two screws holding it on where the little yellow plastic caps have come off.' He passed his phone to Potter. 'Now look at the image from the speed camera.'

Potter had Dixon's iPhone in her right hand and the photograph in her left. 'No screws,' she said.

'That's right, which means that number plate's been stuck on. There'll be another one behind it.'

'So, Buckler is telling the truth?'

'Possibly.'

'What d'you mean "possibly"?'

'He's telling the truth about the van. That's all we can say with any degree of certainty. Someone has doctored that number plate . . .' Dixon was pointing at the image from the speed camera. 'To make it resemble his. If it was him, then why would he do that? If it was someone else, then who and where are they? Because if we can find them I'm guessing we'll find Alesha and Hatty as well.'

'Maybe it's some sort of elaborate alibi?' asked Potter.

No reply.

'Nick?'

'You have to ask yourself why the driver got himself caught on this speed camera too. It's a bloody great big yellow box on top of a pole. There are even signs warning you it's there. If you're making your getaway with a child in the back you're not going to draw attention to yourself like this, are you?'

'Unless it's deliberate?'

'Exactly. We were meant to see this.' Dixon frowned. 'It's more evidence against Buckler on the face of it.'

'If you accept it's his van.'

'Which we're supposed to but don't.'

'Which *you* don't.'

'And you doubt.'

Potter nodded.

'Let him go and put a tail on him. That's what I'd do,' continued Dixon.

'You're kidding?'

'It's about finding the girls now, and we're not going to do that with him sitting in a cell. That's assuming he's got anything to do with it at all.'

'And if he hasn't then we've lost nothing anyway.'

'What's going on?' asked Jane, running along the landing.

'What d'you mean?' Dixon was standing in the doorway of the canteen.

'Chard's having a fag up in the car park, cussing and swearing at the top of his voice.'

'Potter's letting Buckler go.'

'What the hell is she doing that for?'

'I told her to.'

'You what?'

'He's a diversion. Nothing more.'

'You believe him?'

'Between you and me, I do.'

'And as far as everyone else is concerned?'

'I'm hedging my bets. He'll have a tail on him and you never know where he might lead us.'

Jane shook her head as she pushed past Dixon into the canteen.

'It's closed,' he said.

'Marvellous.'

'Did you bring Monty?'

'He's in the back of my car.'

'C'mon, I thought we could call in on Tanya. We can have a bag of chips on the seafront and Monty can have a quick run on the beach at the same time.'

'Does Potter know you're going?'

'We'll be back before she notices I've gone.'

'So, Buckler's being framed,' said Jane, accelerating along the dual carriageway towards the motorway roundabout.

'It's not his van and the anklet was probably just lobbed over his fence.'

'What would anyone hope to gain by that?'

'Time.'

'For what?'

'Let's not go there.'

Jane nodded. 'Who then?'

'I don't know. A paedophile gang would just grab the girls and they'd be miles away by now. They're hardly likely to worry about setting up Buckler to take the blame, are they? And if it was a sexual predator we'd probably have found their bodies by now, much as I hate to say it.'

'Random girls, snatched by the same people . . .' Jane was peering in her wing mirror, as she drove down the slip road on to the M5. 'What about Sailes?' she asked, as she flicked the indicator and pulled out.

'It's no coincidence that Sailes used to work for Buckler. It can't be.'

'What does that mean?'

No reply.

Jane glanced over at Dixon. He was staring out of the window at the remains of the furniture factory looming up on the nearside, on the banks of the River Brue.

'Is it still smouldering?' she asked.

'The rain put it out days ago.'

'Don't dwell on it. It was one of your nine lives and that's an end of it.'

'You're the one who mentioned it. I didn't.'

Jane rolled her eyes.

Ten minutes later she turned into Princess Street and parked on the double yellow lines opposite Burnham library.

'Salt and vinegar?' asked Dixon, opening the passenger door.

Dixon snapped the letterbox shut and stood up.

'Vomit,' he said, grimacing.

He stepped back and brought his left foot up, ready to kick in the door.

'Don't!' The voice was shrill and came from behind them at the bottom of the steps.

Sonia was carrying two bulging Tesco carrier bags in each hand and struggling up the steps. 'Who the hell are you?'

'Detective Inspector Dixon, and this is—'

'I know who she is.'

'Where's the Family Liaison officer?' asked Dixon.

'I told her to piss off. She's about as much use as a chocolate teapot.'

'I get the picture.'

'Smells like she's been sick,' said Jane.

'She's always sick on methadone.' Sonia dropped the carrier bags at the top of the stairs and fumbled in her pocket for the door key.

'There was supposed to be an officer on duty too.'

Sonia looked over her shoulder. 'There were two of them in a car when I left. Probably nipped down the pub.' She opened the door and began gathering up the handles of the carriers to lift them inside.

'Here, let me,' said Dixon.

'I can do it,' snapped Sonia.

Tanya was lying on the sofa with a blanket over her legs, a bowl on the floor next to her. Dixon winced. Some sort of chicken curry – marinated in vodka after it had been eaten, by the looks of things. And rice, there was definitely rice in there.

'Let me get that,' said Sonia, pushing past him.

'How did she take the news about Kevin?' asked Dixon.

'I haven't told her.'

'Why not?'

'I think she's got enough to deal with at the moment, don't you?'

Dixon nodded.

'At least your lot have been keeping the press away.' She picked up the bowl and carried it out of the living room, bringing it back seconds later, the sound of a toilet flushing in the background.

'Were you here when Kevin arrived?'

'I'm always here.'

'Always?'

'I go to the shops, yes. And I pop home every day to feed my dog.'

'Where's home?'

'I live on a canal boat in Bridgwater docks.'

'And your dog?'

'An elderly greyhound. She sleeps all day.' Sonia sighed. 'It's fine, before you go ringing the RSPCA.'

'What did they talk about?' asked Dixon. He was looking down at Tanya, looking for signs of life. 'Is she still breathing?'

'She's fine,' snapped Sonia.

'Should we call an ambulance?' asked Jane.

'No. This is perfectly normal for her.' Sonia gave Tanya a prod and she rolled over on to her side. 'See.'

'If you're sure.'

'I am. The doctor only came this afternoon. And to answer your other question, I left them to it and had a lie down on Alesha's bed. I can't stand to be around them when they're drinking and taking . . .' Her voice tailed off.

Dixon pulled back the blanket and looked out of the window. 'Which is your car?' he asked.

'It's an old Nissan Micra, down the road a bit.'

'And you live on a canal boat?'

'It's cheap.'

'Can I see Alesha's room, please?'

'She's seen it,' replied Sonia, pointing at Jane with her thumb.

'And I'd like to see it too.'

Jane was standing behind Dixon, peering over his shoulder. 'The goldfish has come back to life,' she said.

'I got her another one. For when she comes home, y'know.'

'It smells damp,' said Dixon.

'I put the poster back up.' Sonia took hold of the corner of the Girls Aloud poster and pulled it, revealing the mould on the wall behind it.

Jane frowned. 'You want to get that seen to.'

'I've been on to the council about it.'

'Let him have the name of the person dealing with it,' said Jane, nodding towards Dixon. 'He's good at shouting at people.'

'I will, thank you,' replied Sonia.

Dixon looked out of the window at the back garden, the swing just visible in the failing light. 'How often d'you see Alesha?'

'Every day. Usually. I try to anyway. Someone's got to keep an eye on the poor little bugger.'

'And your relationship with her?'

'Good. Why wouldn't it be?'

'No reason.'

Jane opened the wardrobe. The pile of dirty clothes in the bottom had gone, replaced by washed and ironed clothes, neatly folded on the shelves.

'I did her washing.' Sonia shrugged her shoulders.

Dixon's phone buzzed in his pocket. 'A text from Roger,' he said, handing it to Jane.

Clairvoyant coming later. Want to be here?

'I'll find out what time.' Jane tapped out the message and hit 'Send'.

Roger's reply arrived before she handed the phone back to Dixon.

He. Xander Dolphin. 9

'We'd better go,' said Jane. 'We'll only just get there as it is.'

'Thank you, Sonia,' said Dixon, as she closed the front door behind them, a faint cry of 'Mum' coming from the lounge.

They were out on the M5 before Dixon spoke.

'Anything strike you as odd about that?' he asked, looking up at the first of the stars to appear in the darkening sky. 'That one must be a satellite. It's far too bright and low for anything else.'

'Odd about what?'

'Sonia's behaviour.'

'Not really. She likes to make out she's Alesha's guardian angel, though, and yet she's not mentioned in any of the Social Services reports. Tanya seems to be hitting the methadone hard too, but you can hardly blame her, I suppose.'

Dixon said nothing more until Jane was parking the car in the lay-by outside Old School House in Catcott.

'What time is it?'

'Five to,' replied Jane.

They looked up at the house when the front door opened, a shaft of light reaching across the road and lighting up the passenger compartment of Jane's car.

'It's Roger,' said Dixon. 'Just make a mental note of the first thing he says. All right?'

Jane frowned.

'Then compare it to what Sonia said.' Dixon nodded. 'Or didn't say.'

Poland strode across the road and wrenched open the driver's door before Jane had taken the key out of the ignition.

'Any news about Hatty?'

Chapter Seventeen

'Xander, this is Detective Inspector Dixon and . . .' Geraldine frowned. 'I'm sorry, I've forgotten your name.'

Poland sighed. 'Detective Sergeant Winter.'

'Yes, sorry. Ros Hicks you know, and this is our local vicar, Reverend Julia Morgan.'

Dixon hadn't expected an audience, all three of them sitting around the dining table. It reminded him of a seance.

'I think I'll leave you to it,' said the vicar, standing up. 'I'm not altogether sure I should be here for this.'

'The Lord wouldn't approve, you mean?' Xander had been sitting on the sofa with his arm around Adele. He stood up. Blue jeans, a sleeveless T-shirt under a black leather waistcoat, both arms covered in tattoos from the shoulder to the wrist. He'd have to stand still if Dixon was going to count those earrings. A nose stud in each nostril; he probably had his tongue pierced too. Dixon winced.

'What were you expecting, Inspector?' Xander grinned.

'I wasn't expecting anything, Sir.'

'No, I meant . . .' The vicar hesitated, then walked towards the front door, avoiding eye contact with Geraldine.

'I'll go too,' said Ros, following the vicar towards the front door. 'It should be family only. Ring me if you need anything.'

'We will.' Adele spoke without looking up.

'Shall we get on with it then?' said Dixon, spinning round. 'What do we do?'

'I detect a note of cynicism.' Xander frowned.

'Not at all. If you think you can help, I'm listening.'

'Well, I do think I can help.'

'So, what happens now?' asked Poland.

'Can I see Hatty's room?'

'I'll show you, Xander,' said Geraldine, gesturing to the stairs that led up to the galleried landing. 'This way.'

The Family Liaison officer, Karen Marsden, appeared behind Dixon and whispered in his ear. 'I have warned the family that it may be a waste of time.'

'Thank you,' said Dixon, turning around.

'Is there any news?'

'No.'

'I'm in regular contact with Express Park and have been keeping them informed.'

Dixon nodded.

'What do we do now?' asked Jeremy. He stood up and began pacing up and down in front of the fire. 'It's all a bit . . .' His voice tailed off.

Poland sat down next to Adele.

'She's had to be sedated again, Sir,' said Karen, raising her eyebrows.

'This is fucking ridiculous,' snapped Jeremy. 'I can't believe we're doing this. He'll be doing bloody card tricks on *Britain's Got Talent* next.'

'We've got nothing to lose,' said Adele, her voice low and slow.

'Well?' asked Jeremy, when Xander and Geraldine appeared at the top of the stairs.

'I need to be alone.' Xander was carrying a teddy bear.

'That's Letty,' mumbled Adele. 'Hatty's favourite.'

'I'll bring her back. I'm just going for a smoke.'

'Wacky baccy probably,' muttered Jeremy. 'How much is this costing us?'

'Nothing,' snapped Geraldine.

'A bloody good thing too.'

'Jeremy, please.'

'I'm sorry, darling,' he said. He leaned over and kissed Adele on the cheek. 'What d'you think, Inspector?'

'I'm with your wife, Sir. It can't do any harm.' Dixon looked out of the window into the darkness, the outline of Xander sitting on a low wall on the far side of the patio just visible in the light from the windows; so too the unmistakable glow of a long, slow drag on a joint.

'Is he taking the piss?' whispered Jane.

'What d'you want to do, nick him for possession?'

'I suppose not.'

'Not now anyway.'

'She's alive,' said Xander, stepping in through the sliding door.

'Thank God,' muttered Geraldine.

'She's definitely alive.'

'What makes you think that?' asked Jeremy.

'I don't think it,' replied Xander. 'It's a fact.'

'Where is she?' asked Roger.

'I see a castle . . . and flowers . . .' He shook his head. 'That's all.'

'What sort of castle?' asked Dixon.

'I don't know.'

'Is it a ruin?'

'I can't see.'

'Is there a roof on it?'

'I don't know.'

'Where is it?'

Xander shook his head.

'What sort of flowers?'

'All sorts. They're not clear.'

'Well, that's a fat lot of fucking good, isn't it,' snapped Jeremy.

'I'm doing my best,' said Xander. 'I can only see what I can see.'

'So, what happens now?' asked Jeremy.

'We'll get the local castles checked.' Dixon frowned. 'But unless Xander can come up with anything else, it doesn't really take us much further forward.'

'But, you'll check the castles?' asked Geraldine.

'We will.'

'Thank you.'

Dixon brushed aside Poland's apologies as they walked across the lane to Jane's car. 'Really, Roger, it's fine,' he said.

'And thank you for not nicking him.'

'It was tempting.' Dixon smiled.

'You'll let me know as soon as you hear anything?'

'Of course we will.'

Dixon was searching the internet on his phone while Jane turned left at the end of the lane.

'There are twenty-four castles in Somerset, according to Wikipedia,' he said. 'I bloody well told you, didn't I?'

'At least he didn't say a Scottish castle.'

'That's something, I suppose.'

'Will you get them checked?'

'Yes.' Dixon rolled his eyes. 'What was the first thing Roger said then?'

'"Any news about Hatty?"'

'That's right. Something Sonia never asked about Alesha. Not once.'

'You're right, she didn't.' Jane turned out on to the main road. 'Where to now?'

'Express Park.'

'Why would that be, d'you think?'

'There are only two reasons I can think of,' replied Dixon. 'One is she doesn't give a shit.'

'Which can't be right.'

'Can't it?'

'And the other?'

'She already knows exactly where she is.'

Chapter Eighteen

'Where the hell have you been?' demanded Potter, as Dixon and Jane appeared at the top of the stairs.

'Catcott, Ma'am,' he replied.

'What for?'

'The family got a clairvoyant in and I thought I ought to be there.'

'You thought wrong.' Potter threw her reading glasses on to the desk in front of her. 'What'd she say?'

'Hatty's alive.'

'Anything else?'

'He saw a castle and flowers.'

'He?' Potter sighed. 'I suppose we've got to waste time checking the local castles now, have we?'

'Would you like to tell the family we're not going to bother, or shall I?'

Potter clenched her jaw, breathing slowly through her nose. 'Organise a search with uniform,' she said.

'I already have, Ma'am.'

'Just make sure it doesn't interfere with the reconstruction tomorrow morning.'

'Reconstruction?'

'If you'd been here, you'd know.' Potter sighed. 'Catcott, tomorrow morning at eight thirty. We've got a girl following Hatty's route to school. The press will be there and so will you.'

'Have you told the parents?'

'Family Liaison are going to keep them indoors.'

'Is there another press conference afterwards?'

'The mother's not up to it, apparently.'

'Sounds about right.'

'Aren't they missing you in Safeguarding?' asked Potter, turning to Jane.

'I was supposed to be on holiday this week anyway, Ma'am.'

'Any news about Ted Buckler?' asked Dixon.

Potter shook her head. 'The search turned up nothing we didn't already have. He went straight home when we released him and hasn't budged since.'

'Anything else?'

'The phones have been pretty steady. The public are doing their best, but nothing of note, sadly.'

'What about Sailes?'

'You'll need to speak to Sally Guthrie about him.'

'Yes, Ma'am.'

Potter picked up her reading glasses and turned back to her computer screen.

'You didn't tell her what you said about Sonia?' said Jane, following Dixon as he weaved in and out of the workstations looking for Guthrie.

'She'd think I was mad as a hatter.'

'She's not the only one.'

'Thank you, Sergeant.'

'I'm going down to my office for five minutes,' said Jane. 'Then I'm going home, I think. If I don't get some sleep . . .'

'I'll catch you up.'

◆ ◆ ◆

It was just before midnight when Dixon crawled into bed.

'Where've you been?' asked Jane, rolling over, the duvet wrapped around her shoulders.

'On the beach.'

'In the dark?'

'It's a full moon and the tide's out.'

'What did Guthrie say about Sailes?'

'She'd buggered off, but Dave was there,' replied Dixon. 'The car's gone for forensics at Portishead.' He moved his legs so Monty could jump on the end of the bed. 'The post mortem gave the cause of death as a broken neck, which is what we expected. Did you know he dialled 999?'

'When?'

'Eleven o'clock that night.'

'What'd he say?'

'Nothing. He rang off.'

Jane sat up. 'Anything else?'

'A witness near the Shell station on the Berrow Road saw the car being driven erratically and said the driver appeared to be in distress. It was only a glimpse, mind you. "Crying his eyes out" was the phrase Dave used.'

'What's the plan for tomorrow then?'

'Portishead first,' replied Dixon, setting the alarm on his phone. 'Then I'd like to catch Tanya conscious for a change.'

'Don't hold your breath,' muttered Jane, sliding down under the duvet. 'Wait a minute.' She rolled over on to her back. 'What about the reconstruction at Catcott?'

But Dixon was already asleep.

◆ ◆ ◆

'We can watch it on the telly,' Dixon had replied, as he sped down the northbound on slip at junction twenty-two on to the M5 the following morning. Jane had asked him about the reconstruction twice, while there'd still been time to get there, and the answer had been the same both times.

Now they were standing side by side, wearing white overalls, gloves and masks, staring at a black Renault Clio with a flattened roof and shattered windows. Both doors had been removed with cutting equipment, presumably to get Sailes's body out.

'What exactly did you want to know?' asked the technician.

'Have you finished with it?'

'Pretty much.'

'What caused the accident?'

'That's for the motor engineer, really, but the wheels are both buckled on the nearside, so he spun, hit the kerb and took off.'

Dixon squatted down and peered in. 'What was in it?'

'It's over here.'

They followed the technician over to a locked cabinet. He opened it and took out a box, setting it down on the bonnet of the car. Each item taken from the car had been documented and sealed in an evidence bag.

'There was a small amount of cannabis resin,' he said, rummaging in amongst the plastic bags. He pulled one out with a flourish and dropped it on the bonnet in front of Dixon.

'Anything else?' he asked.

'This was under the seat.' The technician was holding up a second bag.

Dixon leaned forwards. 'It's an iPhone.'

'An iPhone 7 to be precise. Still sealed in its box, so it should be fine.'

'What does it say on the label?'

'Just the standard stuff, but it was in this bag, if that helps?' The technician was holding up yet another evidence bag, this one containing a single Vodafone carrier bag. 'There was nothing else in it.'

'No paperwork, receipt, anything like that?'

'No.'

'Can I take it?' asked Dixon.

'You'll have to sign for it.'

Less than an hour later Dixon screeched to a halt on the pavement outside Lloyds Bank in the middle of Bridgwater.

'The Vodafone shop's just down there,' he said, reaching over and picking up the iPhone and carrier bag off the back seat, both still in their evidence bags. 'I'll be back in a minute.'

'And if a traffic warden comes along?'

'Enjoy the moment.' Dixon grinned.

'I could just move the Land Rover.'

'Where's your sense of adventure?'

'I left it on Striding Edge,' said Jane, smirking.

Dixon ran along Fore Street and through the front door of the Vodafone shop.

'I need to speak to whoever sold this iPhone,' he said, holding up the evidence bag in one hand and his warrant card in the other.

The shop assistant tucked her iPad under her arm and took the evidence bag from Dixon. 'You know it was sold from here?' she asked, rolling over the box inside the bag.

'No.'

'I should be able to trace it from the IMEI number.'

'Whatever that is.'

'International Mobile Equipment Identity.'

'You live and learn.'

'You do.'

Dixon followed her to a computer terminal at a standing desk in the back corner of the store.

'Are you on Vodafone?'

'I'm in a bit of a hurry,' replied Dixon, stifling a sigh.

'Sorry. Force of habit.' She typed in the IMEI number. 'Here it is. It was only the day before yesterday.' She sat back on her bar stool. 'Actually, should I be giving you this information without a search warrant?'

'Have you been watching the news lately?'

'Yes.'

Dixon raised his eyebrows.

'The girls?' she asked.

He nodded.

'Sonia Lamm. *Golden Fleece*, Kingfisher Marina. That's a boat then, presumably?'

'Is it on a contract?'

'Yes. D'you need the details?'

'How much is it?'

'Fifty pounds a month for two years.'

'Does it give the name of who it's for?'

'Er . . .' Dixon watched her eyes scanning the screen. 'Here it is. Alesha Daniels. That's one of them, isn't it?' She looked up, but he was already halfway to the door.

'Well?'

'Sonia bought it for Alesha,' replied Dixon, jumping in the driver's seat. 'The day before yesterday.' He threw the evidence bag on the back seat and started the engine.

'So?' Jane shook her head. 'She's bought Alesha a new phone for when she gets back. What does that tell us?' she asked.

'Oh, come on, Jane. When Alesha gets back, then you go and buy the phone, and sign up for the contract. Do you really do that before you know she's coming back at all? It's fifty quid a month.'

'Maybe she was planning to keep it for herself if—?'

'Bollocks.'

'Just be careful, that's all I'm saying. You've got no evidence and you're gonna look a right dickhead if you go wading in there accusing the bloody grandmother of being in on it.'

Dixon accelerated on the long straight out of Bridgwater.

'Where are you going now?'

'Burnham.'

'You'll have to drop me at Express Park. I've got things to do.'

'Make sure they send a Family Liaison officer over to Worston Lane, will you,' said Dixon, pulling in on the edge of the roundabout at the entrance to Express Park.

Jane looked at police centre, a couple of hundred yards away along the service road. 'Is that it?'

'The exercise will do you good.'

'Cheeky sod.'

'Tell no one where I'm going with this. All right?'

'No bloody fear. You can tell 'em yourself.'

Richard Page was standing on the garden path outside Tanya's flat with his mobile phone clamped to his ear when Dixon arrived in Worston Lane.

'What's going on?' he asked, winding down the window.

'She won't let me in.'

'Who won't?'

'The mother.'

Dixon smiled. 'Come with me,' he said, climbing out of his Land Rover.

'You again?' Sonia was leaning on the front door. She had her hand on the frame, blocking the way.

'Me again.'

'She's out of it again, so there's no point coming in.'

Dixon fixed Sonia with his best stare and waited.

'Oh, for fuck's sake.' She stepped back. 'If you must.'

'This is Richard, Sonia, he's a Family Liaison officer and it's important he stays here all day in case Tanya wakes up. All right?'

'It's a waste of time.'

'Well, it's his not yours so let's not worry about that.'

Sonia frowned.

Dixon was standing in the lounge looking down at Tanya asleep on the sofa. 'Does methadone usually have this effect on her?' he asked.

'Yes.'

'When were you going to tell us that Kevin stole the iPhone you bought for Alesha?'

'How d'you . . .' Sonia hesitated. 'I didn't want to get him in trouble.'

'He's dead, Sonia,' said Dixon.

'Yes, but—'

'It's a nice gift for a ten year old, isn't it?'

'She's always wanted one to go with her iPad. I was going to give it her when she got back.' Sonia lit a cigarette. 'You are going to find her, aren't you?'

'Yes, Sonia. I am.' Dixon loosened his tie and puffed out his cheeks. 'Sorry, have you got anything sweet, a biscuit or something. I'm diabetic, you see, and my blood sugar's dropping . . .'

'There'll be something in the kitchen,' said Sonia.

Dixon followed her into the hall and watched in the reflection of a glazed kitchen cabinet as she reached into a Tesco carrier sitting on the worktop. She slid her hand down the side of a stack of Heinz baked beans and took out a packet of sweets.

'Will these do?' she said, handing them to Dixon. He was leaning on the door frame. 'They're coated in sugar.'

'Thank you.' He ripped open the packet and stuffed a handful in his mouth, breathing deeply through his nose as he chewed.

'Better?'

'It'll take a minute or two.'

'D'you want to sit down?'

'No, thank you.' His breathing slowed as he walked into the kitchen, straightening his tie in the reflection from the same glazed kitchen cupboard. He glanced around the kitchen, noticing the washing up bowl back in the sink. He winced, wondering if Sonia had bleached it first.

'Can I see Alesha's room again, please?'

'Really?'

'Just for a second.'

Sonia sighed, then opened the door, watching Dixon carefully as he looked around the room. He opened the drawers and the wardrobe, even looking under the bed.

'Where's her iPad?' he asked.

Sonia frowned. 'It must be at her father's.'

Dixon nodded. 'Thank you, Sonia,' he said. 'I'll leave you to it.'

He was halfway down the steps when Page caught up with him.

'Are you all right, Sir?'

'Fine, thanks.'

'But, you were having a hypo—?'

'Was I?' Dixon grinned. 'Whatever gave you that idea?'

'Where the hell have you been?'

Dixon winced. He had thought he'd avoided Potter, but Chard must have pointed him out to her as he crept in at the back of the Incident Room.

'You were supposed to be at the reconstruction.' She threw her reading glasses on to the workstation in front of her. Again.

I hope they're a cheap pair.

'I got sidetracked, Ma'am. Did anything come of it?'

'A couple of sightings of the white van again. Both of them out on the A39 though.'

'Anything else?'

'We've narrowed the search down to thirty-seven vans and we're tracing them now. That's just the south west, though. If we come up with nothing then we'll have to take it national and that's three hundred and twelve to track down. Nothing has changed hands recently according to DVLA and one's not been reported stolen either. Apart from that, no.'

'What about Buckler?'

'Still nothing.' Potter frowned. 'You were going to tell me where you were?'

'Was I, Ma'am?'

'I saw Jane earlier and she dodged the question too.'

'She's well trained, Ma'am.'

Potter sighed. 'You're up to something.'

'Just give me a few hours.'

'What d'you need?'

'Dave Harding.'

'Be my guest,' muttered Potter, gesturing towards Harding's workstation, his head popping up from behind his computer at the mention of his name.

'Yes, Sir.'

Dixon leaned over and dropped a piece of paper on to his keyboard. 'I need mobile phone tracking on this number and traffic cameras on this registration. It's a silver Nissan Micra.'

'All cameras?'

'Just the number plate recognition for the time being. That'll be quicker won't it?'

Harding nodded. 'Whose is it?'

'D'you need to know?'

'Not really.' Harding shrugged his shoulders.

'When can you let me have it by?'

'Give me a few hours.'

Dixon nodded. 'Thanks.'

'Where will you be?'

'Downstairs.'

'There you are,' said Jane, as Dixon walked past the canteen a few minutes later. 'Have you eaten?'

'I won't need to eat for the rest of the day after all that bloody sugar.'

'What sugar?'

'Don't ask.'

'Coffee then?'

'Is there an FLO with Alesha's father?'

'I think so.'

'Find out what Alesha's favourite meal is, will you?'

'That's easy.' Jane smiled. 'Beans on toast.'

Chapter Nineteen

Dixon spent the rest of the afternoon catching up with the call logs and witness statements on the system, not an easy task when there were already more than 400 logged. He made up his mind whether to read the whole statement or just scroll straight down to the end from the first few paragraphs. He even applied the same technique to the statements that had been flagged as high priority, most of them sightings of the white van here, there and everywhere. Some members of the public had even emailed in photographs and video footage.

He was leaning back in his chair, rubbing his eyes when he heard someone sit down on the chair at the vacant workstation in front of him.

'Thought I'd find you down here, Sir,' said Harding, smiling.

'How'd you get on?'

'I've got her on the—'

'Her?'

'I looked it up. Sorry. Shouldn't I have done?'

'Just don't tell anyone. Yet.'

'Anyway, I've got her leaving Burnham on the ANPR cameras. That's no problem. And here she is arriving in Bridgwater. She comes right past here, presumably going home.' Harding handed Dixon a photograph. 'Same routine every day.'

'She feeds her dog.'

'Then something odd happens.'

'What?'

'She heads south out of Bridgwater, here she is on the camera at the motorway roundabout at junction twenty-four, but she doesn't show up on another traffic camera for an hour and a half. And that's at junction twenty-three. It takes her an hour and a half to go one junction north.'

'What does the mobile positioning say?'

'I checked that. She's picked up on the Vodafone mast at junction twenty-four, and the O2 mast at Huntworth, but she can't be on the motorway, can she? She stays in the vicinity for the whole time, but where does she go?'

'When does this start?'

'I checked that too.' Harding smiled. 'First time is Sunday morning. Then it's twice a day since. First thing in the morning and then late afternoon.'

'And she stays an hour and a half each time?'

'There or thereabouts. Then it's back to Burnham.'

'Well done, Dave.'

'What happens now?'

'Just keep it under your hat for the time being, will you?' Dixon stood up and was rummaging in his pockets for his car keys. 'What time's she getting to junction twenty-four each day?'

'Between five and five thirty.'

Dixon looked at his watch. 'Bags of time.'

'You haven't said where we're going.'

'Don't know yet,' replied Dixon, pulling into the lay-by at the entrance to the industrial park. He parked behind the bushes, screening his Land Rover from the road. 'Keep an eye out for a silver Micra.'

'Not Sonia?' Jane rolled her eyes.

'Did you bring a hat?'

'What for?'

'You're going to need something to eat.'

'Oh, come on!'

'Did you notice what was missing when we were in Alesha's bedroom yesterday?'

'No.'

'Her iPad. Sonia tried to spin me some crap about it being at Ryan's, but we know that's not true.'

'So, where is it?'

'Alesha's got it. It's the first thing a ten year old kid's going to want.'

'Where?'

'That's what we're going to find out, isn't it? Every day between five and five thirty, after she's fed her dog, Sonia heads out of town this way and disappears.'

'And you think she's going to see Alesha?'

'This time she'll have a carrier bag full of sweets and baked beans. I faked a hypo to get a look in the kitchen at Tanya's.'

'But she went shopping yesterday, didn't she?'

'She did. And she put the rest of it away except that one bag.' Dixon raised his eyebrows. 'Nice sweets they were too. Sort of tangy.'

'Yes, but—'

'Think about it. She's never once asked for news of Alesha, then there's the iPhone, the iPad, the food. And why is she keeping Tanya sedated?'

'Is she keeping Tanya sedated?'

'She must be. The poor bugger's never awake. That'll be because she knows what Sonia's up to and Sonia doesn't want her blurting it out. It'll be why she doesn't want Family Liaison in the flat too. And what about Kevin? I bet that's what the row was about before he—'

'There she is,' said Jane, pointing at a Nissan Micra heading south towards the motorway roundabout.

'You look worried,' said Dixon, starting the engine.

'I've never eaten hat before,' muttered Jane.

'She's staying in this area according to the phone signal, so my guess is she'll be going left at the roundabout,' said Dixon, spinning his wheels on the grit in the lay-by as he accelerated towards the exit. 'Right'll take her out to the A38 and we know she's not getting on the motorway. Yet, anyway.'

'You've got it all worked out.'

Dixon raced up to the roundabout and screeched to a halt. 'She's not there, is she?' he asked, glancing off towards the A38.

'Nope.'

'Huntworth it is then.'

Dixon raced across the roundabout, then slowed on the approach to a fork in the lane on the far side of the motorway.

'There she is,' said Jane, pointing to the back of a small silver car disappearing around a bend at the bottom.

'It had to be left,' said Dixon, accelerating again. 'The right fork's a dead end.'

'So's the left.'

'No, it isn't. You can follow the canal back through the industrial estate.'

Jane frowned. 'You'd better get a bit closer then.'

Engine screaming, Dixon raced down through Huntworth in second gear with his foot down hard on the accelerator.

'She's put her lights on.' Jane was pointing beyond the houses where the trees were overhanging, plunging the lane into darkness.

'What's round the back of the industrial estate?' Dixon shook his head. 'It's either that or over the canal bridge to the Boat and Anchor.'

'I know where she's going.' Jane nodded. 'Stay back a bit,' she said when Dixon raced around the corner, the canal bridge visible ahead. 'You remember when we were down here for the pillbox? When was it, February?'

'It was bloody cold, that's for sure.'

'Think about what's under the M5 flyover.'

Dixon smiled. 'Caravans.'

'Must be fifty at least behind that bungalow,' said Jane. 'There she is, look.'

Dixon crept up to the small wooden canal bridge just in time to see Sonia opening a steel five bar gate. She unlocked the padlock, allowing the heavy chain to drop to the ground. Then she ran back to her car.

'We can watch from over there.' Dixon allowed the Land Rover to roll back off the bridge, then turned left and parked under the motorway on the opposite side of the canal, screened from the bungalow by dense undergrowth on the canal bank. 'Is it a caravan store or a graveyard?' he muttered.

'Store, I think,' replied Jane. 'Some of them are motor homes down the far end.'

Dixon climbed out of the Land Rover and walked over to the bushes, crouching low as he crossed the road. 'There she is,' he said, when Sonia appeared from behind the bungalow, this time on foot.

'She's got the carrier bag,' said Jane, peering over his shoulder.

'Well, she sure as hell won't hear us,' said Dixon, glancing up at the underside of the M5, the drone of the traffic above their heads all but drowned out by the staccato roar of a motorcycle accelerating hard.

Beyond the towpath on the far side of the canal two lines of caravans and motor homes were parked in between huge concrete pillars on either side, sheltered from the elements by the motorway above. Some of the caravans were covered in tarpaulins, the rest taking their chances.

At the far end of the lines of caravans the railway embankment rose up behind a high steel fence, a train rumbling past under the motorway.

'It goes on for miles, this bridge,' said Jane. 'It takes the M5 over the River Parrett further down as well.'

'If she's in one of the caravans she should be all right, but this end is more like a bloody scrapyard.' Dixon watched Sonia weaving in and out of piles of rusting, tangled metal – old garage doors, gates, corrugated iron, cement mixers and ride on mowers – pallets, tyres, even rusting tractors and abandoned horse trailers, towards an old shipping container.

'She can't be in that,' said Jane, 'there're no doors on it.'

'Behind it,' replied Dixon. 'There's a canal boat up on bricks.'

'A canal boat?'

'You can see it from here,' he said, pulling her towards him by the elbow.

Jane peered through the bushes. 'There are steps up to the back.'

Dixon nodded. 'It's only a small one, thirty foot maybe, but that's enough, isn't it?'

'I suppose it is.' Jane frowned.

'That must be it,' said Dixon, as Sonia reached the bottom of the steps. 'Look, see that yellow cable on the ground? I bet it goes to the bungalow.'

'That means whoever owns it knows about Alesha.'

'It does.'

'What happens now?' asked Jane.

The back doors opened from the inside and Sonia disappeared. 'We wait.'

Dixon had ignored three texts from Potter by the time Sonia emerged from the back of the canal boat, the doors locked behind her from the inside.

'You'd better move the Land Rover,' he said, handing Jane his car keys. 'She may come this way and recognise it.'

'Where shall I go?'

'The lay-by, wait ten minutes, then come back.'

'What are you going to do?'

'Check we've found what we're looking for.'

'There might be someone in the bungalow.'

'I'll go through the scrapyard, don't worry.'

Dixon watched Jane drive off and then ducked back into the bushes, careful to avoid falling in the canal. He peered through the undergrowth when he heard the rumble of wheels coming across the wooden bridge and watched Sonia's car turn back towards Huntworth.

Then he ran across the bridge and along the towpath. Careful to avoid the barbed wire wrapped around the top of the gate, he climbed over into the scrapyard and weaved his way through the junk, crouching as low as he could until he was behind the shipping container, the canal boat on the far side.

An oil drum would do.

Seconds later he was on top of the container, looking down at the canal boat. All of the curtains were closed, but the skylight window gave him a clear view into the cabin below – and a clear view of Alesha wandering about with her headphones in, her left hand thrust deep into a bag of crisps.

Jane was back from the lay-by by the time he sprinted across the bridge.

'Well?' she asked, winding down the window.

'The curtains are closed, but I got a look through the skylight. She's in there.'

'You saw her?'

'Plain as day,' said Dixon, grinning. 'Hop out. I need to get back to Express Park.'

'Out?'

'You need to keep an eye on her while I get everything set up.'

'You're leaving me here? On my own?'

'Good point.' Dixon opened the back of the Land Rover and Monty jumped out. 'He'll look after you.'

One junction north on the M5, Dixon was back at Express Park in ten minutes. He left his Land Rover in the visitors' car park and ran in to reception.

'You're supposed to use the staff car—'

No time for that, thought Dixon, the receptionist cut off mid-sentence by the security door slamming shut behind him.

He was running along the landing on the first floor when he noticed meeting room 2 was full, the faces turning towards him as he ran past the glass partitioning. Potter was sitting nearest the door. She jumped up and wrenched it open.

'Where've you been?'

'Finding Alesha.'

'In here. Now.'

Dixon closed the door behind him and glanced around the room. Assistant Chief Constable David Charlesworth was sitting at the far end of the table, next to Chief Inspector Bateman, both of them in uniform. Detective Superintendent Sally Guthrie was sitting to Bateman's right and Bob somebody to Charlesworth's left, all of them glaring at him. The press officer, Vicky Thomas, was glaring at him too, but the smirk on DCI Chard's face was something to behold. He must have been working on it.

'Inspector Dixon has some good news for us,' said Potter, sitting down.

'Progress, hopefully,' said Charlesworth. 'That's what we're here to talk about, after all.'

'Detective Sergeant Winter and I have found Alesha.'

Dixon glanced at Chard. Smirk gone.

'She's in a canal boat under the M5,' continued Dixon. 'DS Winter is watching her now.'

'Thank God for that,' said Charlesworth.

The glares had been replaced by smiles all round, apart from Chard, who was now glaring at Dixon. He'd been working on that too.

'You've seen her?' asked Potter.

'Yes. The boat's out of the water on bricks. There's a bungalow nearby.'

'Who's got her?' asked Bateman. 'D'you know?'

'Her grandmother, Sonia.'

'The fucking grandmother?' Guthrie shook her head.

'She's gone back to her daughter's flat in Burnham,' said Dixon. 'So we'll need a unit to pick her up there. If I'm right, she's been keeping Tanya sedated, so they'll need an ambulance in attendance. At the same time another unit can search her canal boat in Bridgwater docks. Then there's the bungalow and canal boat under the M5. It's a caravan store so every one of them will need to be searched too.'

'We can organise that easily enough, can't we?' asked Chard.

'Yes, we can,' replied Bateman.

'When?' asked Potter.

'The sooner the better,' said Dixon. 'We'll need the social worker too, but Jane's met Alesha before so we don't have to wait for her if—'

'Hang on a minute; let's think this through,' interrupted Charlesworth. 'If we know where she is and she's safe, shouldn't we leave her there and keep the narrowboat under surveillance? Does rescuing her jeopardise Hatty?'

'We can't risk it, Sir,' said Potter. 'If something happened—'

'The press would crucify us,' interrupted Vicky Thomas.

'At the very least there needs to be an absolute press blackout then,' said Charlesworth. 'Whoever has Hatty can't find out we've got Alesha.'

'We can do that, Sir,' said Vicky.

'D'you know who's got Hatty, Dixon?'

'Not yet, Sir, but I'm hoping that Sonia may be able to help us with that. Or the owner of the bungalow.'

'What the bloody hell's the grandmother playing at, I wonder?' Charlesworth shook his head. 'Kidnapping your own granddaughter . . .'

'My guess is it's a diversion, Sir,' said Dixon. 'We've had one already.'

'Buckler, you mean?'

Chard sneered.

'Yes, Sir,' continued Dixon. 'Hatty is the target and Alesha was taken to make it look like a random child abduction.'

'Why, though?'

'I don't know yet, Sir.'

'And how the hell am I going to tell Roger Poland we've found Alesha but not Hatty?'

Dixon grimaced. 'Leave that to me, Sir.'

Chapter Twenty

'Two minutes to go.' Dixon leaned back against the container and took a deep breath. He glanced across to the bungalow and watched several uniformed officers taking up position by the back door, the lead officer armed with a battering ram. The same would be happening around the front.

Dog handlers were getting into position amongst the caravans further along under the motorway bridge, moving silently from concrete pillar to concrete pillar. The trains had been stopped too. Charlesworth had authorised it.

'Control to all units, sixty seconds.'

That was the roads sealed off – Bridgwater docks, Worston Lane and Huntworth.

Dixon glanced across at Jane. 'How do I tell Roger we've got Alesha and not Hatty?'

'It's progress.'

Dixon nodded. 'Remember, knock three times. It's what Sonia did.'

'Control to all units. Go!'

Jane ran around to the back of the canal boat and up the short step ladder to the rear cabin door, Dixon following close behind. She knocked three times and listened, crouching down with her ear to the door, the drone from the traffic overhead worse now, if anything.

'She's coming.'

Two bolts, one left, one right, then the door opened, just a crack. Dixon lurched forward, grabbed the leading edge and wrenched it open.

Alesha turned and ran towards the front of the boat, dialling a number on a mobile phone. Jane jumped down into the cabin and ran after her, reaching her just as she put the phone to her ear.

'I don't think so.' Jane snatched the phone and disconnected the call. 'And besides, your grandmother will be in custody by now,' she said, looking at the number.

Alesha threw herself on the sofa, buried her face in the duvet and started to cry. 'She made me do it,' she gasped.

'What is that?' asked Dixon, pointing to an iPad on the arm of the sofa.

'Candy Crush.'

He raised his eyebrows. 'You've been here too long already,' he said.

Alesha smiled, wiping the tears away with the palms of her hands.

'Am I in trouble?'

'No, you're not.'

But your grandmother bloody well is.

'There's someone here to see you,' continued Dixon, gesturing to the door at the back.

'Dad!' screamed Alesha, jumping up and running into Ryan's arms.

Dixon stepped back out on to the stern deck, watching the sniffer dogs going from caravan to caravan, their handlers close behind them. Two Scientific Services vans had pulled up outside the bungalow and officers in white overalls were already carrying equipment inside. Another van was negotiating its way through the piles of junk to reach the canal boat.

Ryan was carrying Alesha, her arms and legs wrapped around him, to a waiting ambulance; hospital first for a medical examination, then to the Bridgwater Contact Centre for interview by two specially trained officers down from Bristol. They'd know what to ask by the time Dixon had finished with them.

'Sonia's on her way to Express Park and the ambulance took Tanya to Weston,' said Jane, sliding her phone back into her pocket as she climbed out of the rear cabin on to the stern deck.

'Anything from the docks?'

'Sonia's washing machine is full of Alesha's clothes.' Jane raised her eyebrows. 'A *Walking Dead* T-shirt, amongst other things.'

Dixon shook his head.

'I wonder what the hell Sonia hoped to gain from it?'

'It has to be money,' replied Dixon. 'The only question going round in my head is who was paying her?'

'Answer that and we find Hatty,' said Jane.

'We do.'

'We'd better get back to Express Park.' Jane climbed down the step ladder on to the bare earth and gravel under the motorway bridge. She picked up the yellow cable and pulled it, lifting it out from under the stones, flicking dirt and dust up as it revealed itself, heading directly towards the bungalow.

Dixon followed her, then held the step ladder for a Scientific Services officer carrying a metal briefcase. He watched him drop down into the cabin and then close the doors.

He hesitated, then frowned.

'What is it?' asked Jane.

'What did that clairvoyant say?'

'A castle and flowers.'

Dixon climbed back up on to the stern deck of the canal boat and opened the doors. 'Tell me what you see?' he said, gesturing to the faded artwork on the inside of the door panels.

'A castle and some flowers . . .' Jane's voice tailed off.

Dixon took out his iPhone and photographed the inside of both doors, each an elaborate painting of red, yellow and pink flowers – roses probably – set in a garland around a gothic castle with several towers, each flying a pennant from a red tiled roof.

'Don't tell anyone about this.'

'But—'

'Just don't.'

Chapter Twenty-One

'Where's Jane?'

'Gone home,' replied Dixon. He ripped the corner off a small packet of sugar and emptied the contents into a mug of coffee on the desk in front of him.

'I thought you were diabetic?' asked Potter.

'I haven't eaten yet.'

'D'you want to get something from the canteen?'

'It's closed.'

'Have you briefed the team interviewing Alesha?'

Dixon nodded. 'Jane gave them Alesha's background too. They're just waiting for the social worker to get there now.'

'Are you going to watch it?'

'I'll watch the tape later.' He took a swig of coffee. 'I can tell you what she's going to say, though: my gran told me to do it; offered me a new iPhone if I just stayed there for a few days watching DVDs and stuff; she brought me food and—'

'I get the picture,' interrupted Potter.

'It'll be useful to know if she saw anyone else while she was there, or if she can give a description of the man who took her.'

'That wasn't Sonia?'

'Probably not. It had to look like the real thing, didn't it?'

'Are you ready to brief the team?'

'I thought you were doing it.'

'You need to be there,' said Potter. 'You *are* part of it, whether you like it or not.'

The Incident Room on the second floor was packed – standing room only at the back – a ripple of applause starting at the front when Dixon reached the top of the stairs.

'That's for you,' whispered Potter over his shoulder.

Dixon was blushing when he perched on the corner of Louise's workstation.

'Well done, Sir,' she said.

He smiled.

'Right then.' Potter clapped her hands. 'Today has been a good day, thanks to DI Dixon and DS Winter. But, we're only halfway to where we need to be. We still have to find Hatty Renner.'

'Are you sure about the press blackout, Ma'am?' asked Guthrie.

'Yes. And if anybody, and I mean *anybody*, is found to be leaking anything to the press, that'll be treated as gross misconduct. Is that clear?'

Some nodded; some said, 'Yes, Ma'am' – almost in unison, but not quite.

'We have Sonia Lamm in custody. She's Alesha's grandmother. There's no evidence yet that she abducted Alesha, but she knew where she was being held and certainly conspired with person or persons unknown in her abduction. She's been looking after Alesha since Sunday morning, according to what we have so far. I think most of you know the details. So, interviews . . .' Potter's phone buzzed on the table next to her. She picked it up and looked at the screen. 'Tanya's woken up at Weston hospital. Sally?'

'Yes, Ma'am.' Guthrie turned to the officer sitting next to her and nodded.

'It would be useful to know what she's saying before we interview Sonia.'

'Yes, Ma'am.'

'Nick Dixon and I will be interviewing Sonia in an hour or so and a child team are down from Bristol to interview Alesha. That'll be taking place elsewhere, of course, but the footage will be available on the system pretty much straightaway. Where did you get to with the bungalow, Bob?'

'It belongs to a Jeffrey Alexander Savage, Ma'am,' replied Bob, standing up. 'There's a photo of him on the system, but it's a couple of years old now. He's known to us – three convictions for crap, really: two theft and a possession of cannabis. He's unemployed, drives an old VW Passat estate, according to DVLA, although the insurance and MOT have run out so it may be off the road.'

'Is it a caravan store or a graveyard?'

'A store, Ma'am. It's registered with the Caravan Club, although the registration is in the name of Edith Savage. She died five years ago, so it's probably Jeffrey's mother and he inherited it.'

'Anything on social media?'

'Nothing yet, but we're working on it. Traffic cameras, mobile phone, the usual stuff. We're targeting known associates too, and he has a sister in Clevedon. It's all on the system and there's a shout out for him too.'

'He must be known to Sonia somehow,' replied Potter. 'See if you can find out how.'

'Yes, Ma'am.'

'We're extending the search to all narrowboats on the Bridgwater and Taunton Canal from dawn tomorrow, and the Tivvy probably. I've put a call in to Devon and Cornwall.'

'What about the motive, Ma'am?' asked Guthrie. 'Do we know why Alesha was taken?'

'Not yet. The best theory we have so far is that it was a diversion, the real target being Hatty, but we'll see what Sonia's got to say for herself.'

'A diversion?'

'Nick, maybe you can chime in at this point?' asked Potter, turning to Dixon and raising her eyebrows.

He stood up and turned to face the officers sitting behind him. 'We thought we were dealing with random child abductions: unconnected children, the motive sexual, the work of a predator. Great care was taken to send us in Buckler's direction, don't forget, and that was a dead end.'

'We don't know that,' said Guthrie.

'Buckler was set up, a diversion; and so is Alesha – she was just sitting there watching DVDs and playing Candy Crush while her grandmother made a few quid out of it, a smokescreen to hide the fact that Hatty was deliberately targeted. Think about it: kidnap another girl and then point us in the direction of a known child sex offender.'

'Why, though?'

'We can rule out a sexual motive. If that was it then Alesha would've been attacked too, particularly given that she was snatched first.'

'He's talking out of his arse.' A man's voice, whispering, somewhere near the back.

'Have we had the results of the medical examination?' asked Guthrie.

'Yes, and she's fine,' replied Potter.

'Maybe they just hadn't got to her yet.' The same man, whispering.

Dixon grimaced. 'I can't believe even Sonia would've cooperated if the motive was sexual.'

'Good point,' said Potter.

'So, why would you kidnap a ten year old child?' continued Dixon, frowning. 'Ransom perhaps, but there's been no sign of a demand so far and the family don't appear to be unusually well off. Hatty's father works for a bank, though, so it's possible. That leaves an attempt to get at the parents somehow – revenge possibly – or the grandfather even. Remember, he's the Home Office pathologist for this area so maybe someone has a grudge against him.'

'A grudge against a pathologist?' asked Guthrie.

'You're assuming she's still alive, though, Sir?' said Louise.

'I am. Because if they were just going to kill her, why bother kidnapping Alesha at all? Why the smokescreen?'

'Has anyone told the family?' asked Potter.

'I've told Roger there have been some developments and I'll get over there as soon as I can.'

'So, you think she's being held by someone to get at the family?' asked Guthrie.

'Let's hope so,' replied Dixon. 'Because that means she's still alive.'

'You've declined a solicitor, is that right?'

Potter was sitting in between Dixon and Sonia, all of them facing the tape machine.

'I don't need one.'

'Are you sure?'

'I'm going to go "no comment" to all your questions anyway, so . . .' Sonia's voice tailed off. She was busy peeling the red polish off her nails and flicking it on the floor.

'And why is that?'

'No comment.'

Potter turned to Dixon and sighed.

'Tanya has regained consciousness and given a statement confirming your involvement in the abduction of her daughter. What have you got to say about that, Sonia?'

'No comment.'

'Perverting the course of justice, conspiracy to do God-knows-what. I'd suggest you start talking.' Potter puffed out her cheeks. 'Still, it won't be the first time you've gone to prison, will it, Sonia?'

Silence.

'Theft. You were a carer stealing from an elderly patient with dementia that time, weren't you?'

'No comment.'

'How d'you know Jeffrey Savage then?'

'No comment.'

'How much did the paedophile ring pay you, Sonia,' snapped Dixon, 'to set up your own granddaughter?'

'Paedophile ring?' She sat bolt upright.

'That's what this is about, isn't it? Selling your own granddaughter for sex with the promise of an iPhone.' Dixon dropped an evidence bag on the floor in front of Sonia. 'This was at the post office for collection. We found the card at Tanya's flat.'

'What is it?'

'It's a cover for an iPhone 7.'

'I . . . I got it on eBay. It's got *The Walking Dead* on it.'

'The same iPhone 7 that we found in the car that Kevin was driving.'

'He found out about it and flew off the handle. He said he was going to be blamed for it.'

'And when did Tanya find out about *it*?'

'That night.'

'Which is why you've kept her sedated ever since?'

Sonia nodded. 'Just a few sleeping pills, that's all.'

'How much were they paying you?'

'It wasn't for sex. I'd never do that. I love Alesha.'

'What was it for then?'

Sonia took a deep breath. 'Nothing. I just had to keep her there for a week at most, they said.'

'Who said?'

'Jeff.'

'Did he say why?'

'No.' Sonia shook her head. 'Just that Poland had a lot to answer for and was going to suffer.'

'Poland?'

'I thought he meant the country. I didn't fucking know what he meant, did I?'

'D'you know what he meant now?'

'No.'

'How d'you know Jeff?'

'He used to have his boat on the canal, till his mum died and he took it out of the water. We used to have a thing going.'

'Bit young for you isn't he?' Potter raised her eyebrows.

Sonia grinned, revealing at least three missing front teeth, although it was difficult to tell in the reflection on the tape recorder.

'Look, he's a nice lad. All right?' Sonia glanced at Potter and then looked away. 'He's just easily led, y'know.'

'Who by?'

'No comment.'

'You still haven't said how much he was paying you.'

'Five grand.'

Sonia had moved on to the skin at the base of her nails now, tearing it off and dropping the strips on the floor, thin streaks of blood licked off as soon as they appeared.

'Are you still in contact with Jeff?'

'I've not seen him since last week.' Sonia shook her head. 'Look, he told me he'd leave Alesha in the boat and I just had to keep her there for a week, maybe more.'

'And he'd tell you when she could go?'

'No. I'd just know, he said.'

'And Alesha knew about this?'

'I told her it was my plan to try and shock Tanya into stopping the drugs. She loves her mum and would do anything for her. I even told her to scream when Jeff picked her up to make it sound realistic. I left some food and a duvet on the boat for her and she was fine with it.'

'Wasn't she worried about what Tanya might think? That she might panic?'

'Alesha said she probably wouldn't notice, but if she did it might give her a reason to stop the drugs.'

'So, Alesha doesn't know about Hatty?'

'Who's Hatty?'

Chapter Twenty-Two

Potter waited until the door closed behind the custody officer collecting Sonia from the interview room. 'You crossed a line,' she said, turning to Dixon.

'It was a perfectly reasonable theory to put to her based on the information we have available to us.'

'A paedophile ring?' Potter frowned. 'But you don't believe it yourself.'

'That's not the point.'

'What is?'

'A girl is missing.'

'All right, all right. You heard what she said about Poland?'

'I'll speak to him. I'm going over there now.'

'But it's nearly midnight.'

'He'll be up,' muttered Dixon.

'I'll see how far we've got with Savage.'

Jane left Monty eating his supper in the kitchen and slumped down on to the sofa with the living room lights off. She closed her eyes, listening to the sound of a metal dog bowl scraping across the kitchen floor. Then a strange knocking. Either Monty was pushing it up against the kitchen units, or someone was at the back door. Then the scraping stopped and the barking started.

'Priorities – finish your food first, then start barking.' She shook her head as she walked into the kitchen, a figure visible behind the frosted glass of the back door.

'Who is it?' she asked, leaning over the sink and peering out of the window.

'Rob from the Red Cow.'

'I thought you'd be closed,' said Jane, opening the door. 'Otherwise I'd have popped over for a gin and tonic.'

'We are closed,' replied Rob, 'But we've got someone you might be interested in. She came in earlier looking for you and has been asleep in the corner ever since.'

'Looking for me or Nick?'

'You. She says she's your sister.'

'Lucy?'

'I could only give her Diet Coke because she's fifteen. Fed her, though. She was starving.'

Jane sighed. 'How much do I owe you?'

'Nothing, really. She's a nice kid. Been on the road all day.'

'On the road?

'Hitched down from Manchester, she said.'

'I'd better come and get her.'

'Thanks,' replied Rob, smiling. 'We can't close up and leave her there.'

Jane leaned over the bench seat in the pub and looked down at Lucy. She hadn't dyed her hair since their mother's funeral, that much was clear from the blonde streak under the jet black. No more piercings, by the looks of things. A shower and some clean clothes might be an idea too.

She was about to wake Lucy up when Monty leaned over the seat and licked her nose.

'What the—?' Lucy sat up with a start, rubbing her mouth with the back of her hand. 'Oh, hi.'

'What are you doing here?' asked Jane.

'I thought I'd come and see you.'

'Do your foster parents know you're here?'

'Yes.'

'Really? They let you hitch-hike down here just like that, did they?'

'You don't want me here?'

'I didn't say that.' Jane took her phone out of her pocket and handed it to Lucy. 'Ring them now and tell them where you are.'

'And if I don't?'

'Then I'll have to ring them myself.'

'You haven't got their number.' Lucy smirked.

Jane raised her eyebrows. 'Have you forgotten what I do for a living?'

Lucy snatched Jane's phone and dialled the number, making the call as they walked back across the road to the cottage.

Jane listened to Lucy's end of the conversation.

'It's me.' . . . 'Somerset. With my sister.' . . . 'I hitch-hiked.' . . . 'I was fine. Stop worrying.' . . . 'Well, you can't stop me.'

'She wants to speak to you.' Lucy was holding the phone out to Jane as she opened the front door of the cottage.

'Hello, Judy.'

'Jane, look, I'm sorry about this. She just took off. We didn't know she was—'

'It's fine, really. I just got home from work and found her in the pub over the road.'

'The pub?'

'They know me in there and looked after her. They even fed her.'

'Good, because she's got no money.'

'It's just a bit of a bad time, that's all,' said Jane. 'We're right in the middle of a big case.'

'We saw it on the news.'

'I've just got in from work and I've got to be back at seven in the morning. Nick's putting in even longer hours. Any other time and it'd be fine.'

'I did try to explain that to her.' Judy sighed. 'Dave can't get down till the weekend to pick her up, though, that's the problem. Can you put her on a train?'

Lucy was sitting on the sofa next to Monty, scratching him behind the ears. 'I'm not going back,' she said. 'They can just piss off.'

Jane held the phone to her shoulder. 'We're going to be out at work all day, every day, Lucy. What are you going to do? Sit here and watch DVDs all day?'

'Yes.' Lucy slid off the sofa and crawled across to the DVD rack next to the TV. 'Maybe not,' she muttered, looking it up and down.

'The weekend is fine, Judy,' said Jane. 'If we put her on a train she'll just get off at the next stop. I would.'

Lucy grinned.

'It'll be Sunday then if that's OK,' replied Judy. 'Dave'll leave about nine and get to you for lunchtime, I expect.'

'We'll see him then.'

'And tell her not to get in any bloody trouble.'

'She's going to be staying with two police officers, Judy.'

'I know, I know.'

Jane rang off. 'Sunday it is then.'

'Judy said two girls have been snatched now.' Lucy was sitting cross legged on the floor with her back to the TV.

Jane nodded as she dropped on to the sofa.

'And you know one of them?'

'She's the granddaughter of a friend of ours,' replied Jane.

'Is she still alive?'

'Nick thinks so.'

'Are you two getting married then, or what?'

'God knows.'

'I've never been to a wedding,' said Lucy, smiling.

'You were going to tell me about our mother,' said Jane. 'I only met her twice.'

'Lucky you.' Lucy's smile evaporated in a sneer. 'There's nothing to tell. You know what she was.'

'What about you?'

'Judy and Dave are my fourth foster family. I get by.'

'It's not about getting by, though, is it. There's more to life than "getting by".'

'Is there?'

'When are your exams?'

'In a couple of months, but I'm not doing 'em.'

'Good thinking,' muttered Jane. Her eyes were closed and she was leaning back on the sofa. 'Drop out, leave school, then you can be a fuck up just like our mother.'

'Fuck you. What d'you know about our bloody useless mother?' Lucy jumped up.

'Nothing,' replied Jane. 'I was hoping you might tell me.'

'You're just like the rest of them. What d'you want me to do, pass my exams so I can be a pig like you?'

'You don't have to be a police officer.' Jane opened her eyes and smiled. 'I just want you to be happy, that's all.'

Lucy sat on the arm of the sofa.

'You're my sister,' Jane said, shaking her head. 'Takes some getting used to, doesn't it?'

'My sister, the copper.' Lucy grinned. 'Yes, it bloody well does.'

Dixon looked up at Old School House as he switched the engine off. Only one light was on downstairs, the curtains closed; the upstairs dark. Poland was waiting up for him, but hopefully the rest of his family were asleep. This was not a conversation they needed to hear. Not yet.

The front door opened as Dixon walked up the steps to reveal Poland, unshaven and with bloodshot eyes, leaning on the frame, a bottle of Scotch in one hand and a half-empty glass in the other.

'Where is everybody?' asked Dixon.

'Gone to bed.'

'How much of that stuff have you had?'

'This is my first,' replied Poland, closing the door behind Dixon. 'You said there'd been some developments?'

'Adele doesn't need to hear this yet, Roger, all right?'

'What is it?'

'May I?' Dixon gestured to the bottle of Scotch in Poland's hand.

'Er, yes, of course.'

'We've found Alesha.'

'But not Hatty?'

'Not yet.'

Poland was standing in front of the sideboard, pouring a glass of Scotch. 'Where?' he asked, turning around and handing a glass to Dixon.

'In a canal boat under the M5.'

'Is she all right?'

Dixon nodded. 'Fine.'

'Who found her?'

'I did.'

Poland forced a smile. 'And who'd taken her?'

'We don't know yet, but her grandmother was looking after her.'

'Her grandmother?'

'She'd been paid, Roger. We think it was done to make it look like Hatty's kidnapping was random.'

'But, it isn't?'

'No.' Dixon shook his head. '*Poland's going to suffer* was the phrase used.'

'Me?'

'It looks like it.'

'This is my fault?' Poland leaned forwards over the sideboard, the empty decanters rattling as he steadied himself. 'Oh God, Hatty.'

'Has anyone been in touch with you?' asked Dixon.

'A ransom demand, you mean?'

'Or a threat.'

'I'd have told you if they had.'

'Can you think of anyone who might have a grudge against you?'

Poland sighed. 'There have been a couple over the years, I suppose. I'd need access to my records to give you the details.'

'Tell me about them.'

'There was a husband who'd murdered his wife. Thought he'd got away with it, too, until I examined her. This is going back twenty years to when I was in Birmingham, longer probably. Malcolm Muir, his name was. You don't think he's been released from prison, do you?'

'We'll check.' Dixon took a swig of Scotch. 'Anyone else?'

'Barnard. It was a hit and run. A boy was killed and the driver was charged with causing death by dangerous driving. This must be eight years ago now.' Poland grimaced. 'I was asked to do a second post mortem by the defence – it was before I was Home Office pathologist. Anyway, a congenital heart defect caused the death, so the CPS accepted a plea of driving without due care and attention and the driver walked out of court with a few points and fine. The father was furious. Threatened all sorts. I needed a police escort to get out of the court building.'

'Where did they live?'

'Burnham. The accident was out on the Berrow Road by the old putting green. Names and addresses will be on the file at the hospital, but you've still got my car, remember?'

'It's still in the visitors' car park at Express Park.' Dixon thrust his hand into his coat pocket and took out a key. 'Sorry, Roger.'

'I haven't needed it. You'll need to give me a lift over there, though.'

'Now?'

'My granddaughter's been kidnapped and it looks like it's my fault.' Poland shrugged his shoulders. 'Of course now.'

'Tell me about the accident,' said Dixon, unlocking his Land Rover.

'The boy was on his bike on the zebra crossing there. The car was speeding and didn't stop. Simple, really.'

Dixon frowned. 'How old was the boy?'

'Ten.'

Chapter Twenty-Three

'We've got a visitor,' said Jane, as Dixon opened the back door of the cottage. He let Monty out into the yard and watched him in the lights from the kitchen window.

'Who?' he asked.

'Lucy. She's asleep in the spare room. Hitch-hiked down here, would you believe it.'

'Do her foster parents know?'

'We rang them. Dave's coming down on Sunday to pick her up.'

Dixon sighed. 'I need some sleep.'

'How did you get on with Sonia?'

'She was paid. Whoever it is has a grudge against Roger, it looks like. She was told "Poland's going to suffer".'

'How did he take it?'

'Not good. He's down at Musgrove Park now, going back through his records to see what he can find.' Dixon opened the fridge and took out a can of lager. 'There are a couple of possibles we're looking into already: a bloke whose son was killed in a hit and run and a man convicted of murder thanks to Roger's evidence. Looks like he's been released on parole within the last six months.'

'What did Alesha have to say?'

'I haven't watched the tape yet,' replied Dixon, closing the back door behind Monty. 'It'll have to wait until the morning.'

'D'you mind Lucy being here?'

'Of course not.' Dixon frowned. 'Why would I? It's your home and she's your sister.'

'Thank you.'

'You don't have to thank me.' Dixon leaned back against the sink and took a swig from the can.

'Anyway, it's given us a chance to have a proper talk. She's a good kid, really. I think I've even persuaded her to go back and sit her exams.'

'How?'

'Bribery,' replied Jane. 'Have you eaten?'

'Not for a while.'

'How's your blood sugar?'

'It feels all right. I'll check it in a minute.'

'I don't know what she's going to do all day,' said Jane, shaking her head. 'We're both busy and—'

'She's welcome to watch any of my DVDs.'

'I'll be sure to let her know,' muttered Jane.

◆ ◆ ◆

A spare door key, twenty quid and a note telling her to stay out of trouble. It had been the best they could do.

'She'll be fine,' said Dixon, as they waited for the steel gates at the entrance to the staff car park to open. 'She probably won't wake up until midday. You know what teenagers are like.'

'I'll ring her a bit later and find out what she's up to.'

'She'll go into town and push it all in the fruit machines, I expect.'

'What's first?' asked Jane.

'I want to see where we've got to with Roger and watch Alesha's interview.'

'Roger's here.' Jane was looking over her shoulder at the visitors' car park in front of the police centre.

'What time is it?'

'Seven.'

'He probably came straight here from the hospital.'

Dixon parked on the top floor of the car park. 'We'll try the canteen first,' he said, as they walked along the landing.

Poland was sitting in the corner, leaning against the wall with his eyes closed, a cold cup of coffee on the table in front of him.

'I'll get him another,' said Dixon. 'D'you want one?'

'Better had,' said Jane, pulling a chair out from the under the table.

Poland woke up with a start.

'What time did you get here, Roger?'

'Six,' he replied, through a yawn.

'Here,' said Dixon, handing him a mug of coffee. 'That one's stone cold.'

'Thanks.'

'Did you come up with anyone else?'

'Just one. I gave the details to Deborah Potter. Ken Mitchell. He tried to claim a shotgun went off by accident when his wife was cleaning it, but it was a suicide, pure and simple. She put the gun in her mouth. Anyway, her life insurance policy was less than twelve months old so the insurers refused to pay. There'd also been non-disclosure of mental health issues. Of course, it was all my fault as far as he was concerned.'

'Where is he now?'

'The address I had on file is nine years old, but Potter's tracing him now.'

'And there's no one else?'

Poland shook his head.

'I'll be back in a minute.'

Dixon ran along the landing and up the stairs.

'Ah, there you are,' said Potter.

'How are we doing?'

'Muir is in custody in Birmingham and the local lot are checking his alibi now.'

'And Barnard?'

'We picked him up . . .' Potter checked her watch. 'Twenty minutes ago. And we've tracked Mitchell down to an address in Yeovil. Someone will be knocking on his door right about now.'

Dixon nodded.

'What about Savage?' he asked.

'Nothing yet.'

Jane appeared at the top of the stairs.

'Where's Roger?' asked Dixon.

'He's gone home to shower and change. Then he's going back to Catcott. He said he's not going to tell them what's going on yet.'

'Good idea.'

'I think he's hoping you'd do it.' Jane raised her eyebrows.

'I don't blame him,' muttered Potter. 'Where are you going now?' she asked when Dixon headed for the stairs.

'To watch Alesha's interview.'

'I can tell you what she said.'

'I'd like to see it for myself, Ma'am,' said Dixon. 'If you don't mind.'

'Hello, Alesha, I'm Trish and this is Jenny.'

Alesha smiled.

'What's your favourite TV programme?' asked Trish.

'*The Walking Dead.*'

Dixon winced. Maybe he'd read the transcript instead. He leaned forward, pressed 'pause' and shook his head.

The Walking Dead. *At your age?*

The child interview suite was at the contact centre in Bridgwater. Purpose built, with posters on the walls and boxes of toys on the floor. A large red sofa with Alesha and Ryan sitting together was the focus of two of the cameras. Trish and Jenny were sitting opposite on another sofa, dressed casually – they looked more like children's TV presenters than police officers, but then that was the idea.

Dixon pressed 'Play' then started flicking through the transcript on the desk in front of him with the interview playing on the computer monitor.

'Aren't you a bit young for that?' continued Trish.

'It's just a bit of fun,' replied Alesha. 'It's not real.'

Dixon reached for the mouse and scrolled forward to twenty-one minutes eight seconds.

'Whose idea was it?' The camera was on Alesha, but Jenny asked the question this time, according to the transcript.

'My nan's. She'd worked it all out with Jeff.'

'And what did she say?'

'She said all I had to do was sit in the canal boat for a few days. I could watch what I wanted on the TV and she'd bring me food and sweets and stuff.'

'You weren't scared?'

'No.'

'It's a spooky place at night, down there under the M5, isn't it?'

Alesha grinned. 'Nah, I just locked myself in and listened to music on my headphones.'

'Did she promise you anything for helping her?'

'An iPhone 7.'

'Why were you doing it? What was it all about?'

'Nan said it would shock my mother into stopping the drugs, or getting help anyway. If she thought I was missing. She's going to die if we don't do something.'

'Who said that?'

'Nan.'

Tears were rolling down Alesha's cheeks now.

'D'you want to take a break?' asked Trish.

'No, I'm fine.'

'Did you see anyone else when you were on the boat?' Jenny again.

'No.'

'So, you were doing it to help your mum?'

Alesha nodded.

'And how long was it to go on for? How long did you have to be there?'

'Until my nan came for me. She said it would be a few days. Just till my mum came to her senses, she said.'

'Didn't you think it might scare your mummy?'

'That was the idea.'

'And what about the police? Did your nan tell you we were out looking for you?'

'No.'

'And hundreds of local people?'

Alesha shook her head.

'Your mummy and daddy have even been on the telly. Did you see it?'

'I could only watch DVDs. There's no aerial.'

'What did your nan tell you to say if the police found you?'

'Just that Poland has a lot to answer for and is going to suffer.'

'Do you know what that means?'

'No.'

'Why did she tell you to say that?'

'I don't know.'

Dixon pressed 'Stop' and closed the transcript on the keyboard in front of him.

'Seen enough?' asked Jane standing behind him.

'Yes.'

'Mitchell has arrived from Yeovil, but it's looking like Muir's alibi is good. They're double checking it, but the Birmingham lot may have to release him.'

'That just leaves Barnard and Mitchell then.' Dixon switched off the computer and stood up. 'C'mon, we've got time to get over to Catcott and back before the interviews.'

◆ ◆ ◆

'You'd better come in.' Geraldine stepped back, allowing Dixon and Jane into Old School House.

'Is Roger here?' asked Dixon.

'He's told us it's all his fault. I told him what would happen when he took on the Home Office work.' Geraldine slammed the front door behind them. 'Karen had to nip back to Bridgwater. She said she'd be back in half an hour.' She sneered. 'That was over an hour ago.'

Poland was sitting on the sofa with his back to them when Dixon and Jane walked into the living room. 'If something's happened to Hatty, I'll never forgive myself,' he said.

'Don't be ridiculous, Dad,' snapped Adele. 'I don't care what Mum says; it's not your fault.' She was pacing up and down in front of the open French windows, dragging on a cigarette. She inhaled the smoke and held it in, before blowing it out through her nose.

'There have been some developments,' said Dixon.

'About bloody time,' Jeremy sneered and looked away.

'You'll have to forgive them, Inspector,' said Ros. She was sitting at the dining table, under the galleried landing. 'Things are getting a bit fraught.'

'I understand.'

Jeremy turned to Dixon. 'What developments then?'

'We've identified three individuals who may have a grudge against your father-in-law, Sir,' replied Dixon. 'All three of them are being spoken to and their whereabouts checked.'

'Spoken to?' Adele threw her cigarette out of the open window into the flower bed.

'Two are at Express Park and I'll be interviewing them when I've finished here.'

'And the third?'

'He's in Birmingham.'

'Are they under arrest?' asked Geraldine.

'They're cooperating with us at the moment, so there's been no need to arrest them yet.'

'No need?' Jeremy jumped up from the armchair, walked over and put his arm around Adele. She wriggled free and sat down on the sofa next to Poland.

'It's all right, Dad,' she said. 'It'll be all right.'

'Bloody typical,' mumbled Geraldine. She walked into the kitchen behind Dixon and switched on the kettle.

'Who are these people?' asked Adele, looking at Dixon over her shoulder.

'I'm afraid I know no more than Roger's probably already told you, but we have teams of officers looking at all three of them now. We'll be tracking their mobile phones, cars, bank accounts, following up their friends and associates, checking at their places of work. No stone will be left unturned.'

'We get it.' Jeremy stepped out into the garden.

'There's a huge team on this and we will find—'

'No, you won't,' interrupted Adele. 'You won't find her.' She stood up and lit another cigarette.

'D'you really have to smoke those filthy things?' Geraldine's shrill voice screeched from the kitchen behind Dixon. 'They'll kill you one day.'

'D'you think I care about that now?' Adele stepped out into the garden and stood beside Jeremy, staring at the daffodils and cigarette butts.

Jeremy looked at her, shook his head and then turned back to the daffodils.

This time she dropped her cigarette on the floor, stubbed it out with her toe and then kicked it into the flower bed. She glanced at Jeremy and whispered something through gritted teeth. Dixon frowned. Whatever it was, it was well beyond his lip reading skills. Then she walked off down the garden.

'D'you want tea, Jeremy?' Geraldine was shouting from the kitchen.

'That's your answer for everything, isn't it?'

Jane sat down on the sofa next to Poland and put her arm around him. 'We're doing our best, Roger.'

'I know.'

'You didn't have to tell them.'

'Yes, I did.'

'Has anyone been in touch with them?' asked Dixon turning to Geraldine, who was handing a mug of tea to Ros behind him. 'A ransom demand, anything like that.'

'Why would they?' replied Ros, 'If it's him they're after.' She pointed at Poland with her teaspoon.

'No,' said Geraldine. 'No one's contacted them.'

Dixon nodded.

'What happens if these three all have alibis?' asked Jeremy, stepping back into the living room. Adele was visible over his shoulder, at the bottom of the garden, pulling at her hair.

'Then we widen the search, Sir,' replied Dixon.

'Oh, God, she's pulling her hair out again,' said Ros.

Jeremy turned towards the door.

'Let me.' Geraldine pushed past him and ran down the garden.

'Why don't you just go, Roger. It's not helping, you being here.' Jeremy flicked on the television and turned to BBC News.

'There'll be nothing on the news, Sir,' said Dixon. 'We don't want whoever has Hatty to know we've found Alesha.'

'And you think someone's still got Hatty?'

'I do.'

'And what makes you say that?'

Dixon looked at Poland and Jane, who were both staring at him over their shoulders, and then back to Jeremy. 'Because we haven't found a body yet, Sir.'

'Is that it?' asked Ros.

'For the time being.'

Poland stood up. 'I'd better go.'

'No, don't go, Dad.' Adele was standing in the doorway, tears streaming down her face. 'I'm sorry.'

'What for?'

'Everything.'

'It's his fault.' Geraldine was in the garden, hidden behind Adele, but her voice was unmistakable.

'No, it isn't, Mum. And I want him to stay.'

'We'll go then,' said Dixon, looking at Jane and gesturing to the door, his eyebrows raised.

Poland followed them out to Dixon's Land Rover. 'You were supposed to be finding Hatty,' he mumbled.

'You just stay there, Roger, and let me know the minute anyone gets in touch with you or them.'

'Them?'

'Adele or Jeremy.'

'But—'

Dixon started the engine and accelerated away, waiting until the end of the lane before he turned to Jane. 'Check their phones, will you? They gave us permission to monitor them.'

'Whose?'

'All of them.'

'Including Roger's?'

'Especially Roger's.'

Chapter Twenty-Four

'Get this for me, will you,' said Dixon, handing Jane his phone as he sped down Puriton Hill towards the M5 roundabout.

'It's Deborah Potter.' Jane answered the call and held the phone to her ear. 'Yes, Ma'am.' . . . 'He's driving.' . . . 'Chew Valley? Yes, I know it. We're on our way.' . . . 'Just getting on the M5 now.' Jane pointed to the northbound slip road. 'Catcott, Ma'am.' . . . 'Not good.'

'She rang off.' Jane shook her head. 'She said you're supposed to be finding Roger's granddaughter, not holding his bloody hand.'

'What's at Chew Valley?' asked Dixon.

'Savage. Floating face down with the back of his skull bashed in.'

'Well, he can't tell us much now, can he?'

'What's that supposed to mean?'

'We're going to waste precious time on a dead body.' Dixon sighed. 'Why can't we just read the post mortem report later?'

The lay-by at the top of the reservoir had been sealed off by the time they arrived, two Scientific Services vans parked either side of a silver VW Passat estate, a flatbed lorry pulled in on the opposite side of the road waiting to pick it up. Dixon spotted the senior Scenes of Crime officer, Donald Watson, and parked behind the lorry.

'Well?' he asked, striding across the road.

'He was killed down at the water's edge and pushed in,' replied Watson, straightening up. He had been looking in the glove compartment of the car. 'The water level's risen a bit overnight but there's still some blood visible.'

Dixon peered over the dam wall and looked down at the water. 'Where is he then?'

'See those boats in the distance?' Watson was pointing to the far end of the reservoir. 'That's Denny Island. He's there. Must've drifted in the night.'

Jane frowned. 'Really?'

'It's quite possible,' replied Watson. 'It was windy last night and there are some strong currents in such a huge expanse of water.'

'Wouldn't he sink?'

'Not if he went in face first. There'd be no way for the air in the lungs to get out.'

'It's the water supply for Bristol, presumably?' asked Dixon.

'I know.' Watson shrugged his shoulders. 'Don't drink the tea.'

'Anything in the car?'

'Nothing of note. No blood or anything like that anyway. Looks like he drove here and got out to meet whoever killed him.'

'What about in the back?'

'We'll look in there at Portishead.'

'How do we get out there then?' asked Dixon, gesturing towards the island.

'The boats are down at the lodge. Keep going and the entrance is on your right. Deborah Potter's down there with the pathologist from Bristol.'

'Thanks.' Dixon waved as he crossed the road back to his Land Rover.

'At last,' muttered Potter, doing up her lifejacket as Dixon screeched to a halt in the gravel car park. 'This is Leo Petersen, the Bristol pathologist. We're going out in a boat.' Potter smiled. 'You're just in time.'

Dixon frowned. He was watching Petersen trying to wriggle into his life jacket, which seemed at least two sizes too small for him.

'You'll need one of these,' continued Potter, throwing Dixon a life jacket.

'What about me, Ma'am?' asked Jane.

'You can wait here. The lodge is open for breakfast.'

Jane looked at Dixon and smiled, then helped him into his lifejacket.

'One of the dive team is going to take us out there,' continued Potter.

'While you have a nice breakfast,' muttered Dixon, glaring at Jane.

'This is Dixon, Leo,' said Potter. 'The one I told you about.'

'All good.' Petersen smiled and shook Dixon's hand.

'Donald Watson said if the body went into the water face down it would stay afloat?'

'That's right. It's the air in the lungs.'

'Is he face down?'

'Yes,' replied Potter. 'According to the fishermen who found him.'

Dixon followed Potter and Petersen down to the pontoon where several Bristol Water motor boats were tied up. 'You look like you know where you're going, Dr Petersen,' he said.

'I do a bit of fly fishing when I can.'

'Who found the body?'

'Those two up there,' replied Potter, gesturing to two men sitting at a picnic table on the veranda overlooking the lake. 'We've got statements from them.'

'What are they waiting for then?'

'The all clear to go back out.'

'But the body's still in the water.'

'Gives the trout added flavour,' said Petersen, grinning.

Dixon was last on to the motor boat and sat down in the bow, facing forwards. Potter and Petersen were behind him, with a dive team officer sitting at the back next to the outboard engine.

'Everybody ready?' he shouted.

'Let's go,' said Potter.

A second dive team officer on the pontoon untied the rope and threw it into the boat, then it reversed out into the lake and turned towards the island. Two boats were visible in the distance, close to the island, the occasional camera flash going off.

'SOCO are already out there,' shouted Potter over the noise of the engine.

Dixon nodded. He looked back at the lodge, already several hundred yards behind them, and thought about his last boat trip. The water had been shallower that time, and mixed with mud and slurry. They'd been following flooded roads too.

'How long would it take a body to get that distance?' asked Potter. 'It must be two miles or so.'

'Four hours maybe, depending on the wind,' replied Petersen. 'We drift in the boat when we're fishing and it takes a couple of hours to get across Stratford Bay. Denny Island must be the same distance again. He probably went in late last night, but I can give you a more detailed time of death when I get him back to the lab.'

'That's after we found Alesha,' said Dixon. 'So they probably know we've done that.'

'Who's *they*?' asked Potter.

'Whoever's got Hatty.'

Rolling countryside all around, the occasional aircraft flying overhead – on the way into Bristol airport probably – the sun glinting on the surface of the water, Dixon even spotted a fish jumping. He could understand the attraction, not that he was that keen on trout. Proper fish comes in batter with a sprinkling of salt and vinegar. Still, he could always put it back if he caught one.

The boat slowed on the approach to Denny Island. Two Scenes of Crime officers were visible in the trees, standing in knee deep water, one holding a lamp, the other taking photographs.

'The level's up a bit,' said Petersen. 'Usually it's an island, but when the water's up, the trees look like they're growing out of the lake.'

'Are they dead?' asked Potter.

'No. You can just see the buds, if you look carefully.'

'He's in amongst the trees.'

'Good thing I brought my waders.' Petersen smiled.

'I'll get you in as close as I can,' said the dive team officer, slowing down still further.

Dixon watched the boat edging ever closer to the trees until he was forced to duck under the branches. He leaned over the bow, took hold of the nearest tree trunk and pulled them into the island until he heard the sound of rock scraping on the bottom of the fibreglass hull.

'That'll do,' said the dive team officer.

Savage was floating face down in the water, his torso wedged between two tree trunks. The blood had been washed clear of the back of his skull, revealing the bone fragments that had been driven into the brain tissue beneath. *Pulverised* was the word that sprung to Dixon's mind.

'Looks a frenzied attack,' said Petersen, stepping over the side of the boat.

Potter was standing up to get a better view, holding a tree trunk to steady herself and the boat.

Petersen turned to a Scenes of Crime officer while he filled a small vial with water. 'Have you taken the water temperature?'

'Yes, Sir.'

He leaned over the body as he tightened the lid. 'Repeated blows with a blunt instrument of some sort.' Then he took a torch out his pocket and leaned over still further. 'Can't see any wood or anything like that, so probably metal.'

Trainers, blue jeans and a black leather jacket; the body was moving gently backwards and forwards on the current as the small waves driven on the light wind rolled through the trees.

'Let's get him on a stretcher and roll him over,' said Petersen.

The Scenes of Crime officers slid a stretcher under the body and then lifted it out of the water, careful not to trip on submerged tree roots.

Petersen leaned over and shone his torch at the side of the face. Then he straightened up and puffed out his cheeks. 'We won't roll him over here. His face doesn't look much better than the back of his head. His own mother wouldn't recognise him.'

'We don't know it's Savage then, do we?' said Dixon. 'We assume it's him, because his car is parked at the top of the lake, but we won't know it's him for some time yet.'

'True.'

'Anything in his pockets?'

'His wallet and two sets of keys,' replied a Scenes of Crime officer, holding up a clear plastic bag. 'There are bank cards and a driving licence. It's Savage's wallet; we can say that much.'

'What about a phone?'

'No, Sir.'

'He's got a kid in Bath so we can do a DNA test if we have to,' said Potter. 'Although he's probably on our database, come to think of it.'

'Well, you won't get any dental records.' Petersen shook his head. 'His teeth have been well and truly smashed in. Whoever did this has got some serious issues.'

'Either that or it's another attempt to delay us. And it will, even if it's just for a day or two.'

'It's a theory,' said Potter.

Fifteen minutes later they were back at the lodge, having left their lifejackets in the drying room. Dixon watched the Scenes of Crime officers carrying a body bag to a waiting van, the windows blacked out.

'I'll do the PM this afternoon and let you have my report via email,' said Petersen. 'Cause of death will be fairly straightforward. He couldn't have survived that so was almost certainly dead before he went into the water. The only question is whether I can give you any idea of the sort of weapon used.'

'And how many people,' said Dixon.

'Quite.'

'The dive team will be searching the top end of the reservoir near where he went in,' said Potter. 'So we'll see what they come up with.'

'Have we found any connection between Savage and Barnard?' asked Dixon.

'No.'

'What about Mitchell?'

Potter grimaced. 'No,' she muttered.

◆ ◆ ◆

'Nice breakfast?'

'Yes, thanks.' Jane shrugged her shoulders. 'Where to now?'

'Back to Express Park,' replied Dixon. 'I've got an hour to see what I can find on Barnard and Mitchell before we interview them.'

'You haven't eaten.'

'I'll stop for a sandwich on the way.'

'What did he look like then?'

'I didn't get too close, but he'd been pulverised. I've never seen anything like it.' Dixon sighed. 'It was a bloody good job I hadn't eaten.'

'Whoever did it would have been covered in blood,' said Jane.

'Good point. Unless they went for a swim afterwards.'

'In there?' Jane glanced across at the reservoir as Dixon raced south past the lay-by, the flatbed lorry and Savage's VW long gone, leaving Scientific Services officers in white overalls combing the water's edge.

'Why not?'

'It'd be bloody freezing.'

'Better that than getting pulled over by a traffic officer covered in blood.'

They stopped off at the cottage to give Monty a run in the field. Lucy and the £20 note had gone, but then that was to be expected perhaps.

'I tried ringing her when you were out on the lake but she wasn't answering.'

'How much trouble can you get into with twenty quid?'

'Enough.'

'You sound like her older sister.'

'I *am* her older sister!'

They arrived at Express Park before Deborah Potter, giving Dixon time to find out all he could about Barnard before the interview. Guthrie would be interviewing Mitchell, apparently. The whiteboard was a good place to start; it held a photograph of Barnard and various arrows leading to family members, each giving their age and occupation. Several statements had already been uploaded to the system too.

'Potter's called a briefing at two and the interviews have been put back to two thirty,' said Jane, appearing next to Dixon in front of the whiteboard.

He was still standing in front of the whiteboard when Potter clapped her hands behind him.

'Right then, everybody!'

Dixon shook his head. 'Every step we take we get further away from Hatty.'

'What makes you say that?' Jane whispered.

'We've got a preliminary time of death for Savage between ten and two last night,' continued Potter. 'So, let's get the traffic cameras checked and I want a list of mobile phones registering on the nearest phone masts during that time.'

Dixon followed Jane along the back wall of the Incident Room to a vacant workstation.

'He had his brains bashed in with a blunt instrument. And I mean bashed in. Avoid the photographs.' Potter winced. 'We've got divers in the water and boots on the ground looking for the murder weapon, but so far, nothing.'

'Any witnesses, Ma'am?' Dixon didn't see who asked the question.

'House to house won't take long. It's a fairly remote area. But, we're stopping traffic on the main road and checking with anglers who hired boats yesterday, so maybe that'll turn up something. There might be the odd dog walker too, but don't hold your breath.' Potter leaned on the desk behind her. 'We'll be interviewing Barnard and Mitchell in the next half an hour or so and that should give us their alibis to check. Anything else?'

'We've found the van, Ma'am,' said Bob. 'A man took it into White Horse Car Breakers over at Midsomer Norton yesterday afternoon and offered them cash to crush it.'

'And did they?'

'No.'

'What time was this?'

'The owner of the yard had just got back from lunch, Ma'am. So, just after two.'

'Have we got a description?'

'It's looking like it was Savage.'

'And he left on foot?'

'He did.'

'Where's the van now?'

'On the way to Portishead, Ma'am. We've traced it to a bloke in Stoke. The buyer – Savage – paid cash. He said he'd fill in and send off the V5, only he never did.'

'Well done, Bob. That gives us a start for the timeline. Where did Savage go after that? He walked out of the yard, so who picked him up? Someone must've seen him.'

'We're checking the CCTV and traffic cameras now.'

Potter nodded. 'What else do we know about Savage?'

Bob somebody stood up behind a workstation in the middle of the Incident Room. 'He's forty-two years of age and lives alone. He's got very few friends, no social media presence at all, although there's one child living in Bath. Doesn't have much contact with her, apparently, and is well behind with his maintenance payments. After that relationship broke down he lived on a boat on the Kennet and Avon Canal until his mother died and he inherited her bungalow. That's when he moved his boat to Bridgwater. Then a year or so later he took it out of the water and put it up on bricks under the M5.'

'He kept it on a marina on the K and A?'

'Yes, Ma'am.'

'Find out if it's the same one that Sonia kept her boat on, will you? British Waterways or the Canals and Rivers Trust or whatever it is these days will have the records.'

'It was the same one, Ma'am. Kingfisher Marina, it's at Dundas Wharf at the junction with the old Somerset Coal Canal. I've got the dates too.'

Potter nodded. 'Was he unemployed?'

'Sort of, Ma'am. He runs the caravan store, but he used to work as a delivery driver for a vintners in Trowbridge.'

'Have you spoken to anyone at the vintners?'

'On the phone, Ma'am. He left there over a year ago, though, and lives off the caravan store rentals.'

'Lived.' The voice came from behind him, dripping with sarcasm.

'Lived, thank you,' said Bob, raising his eyebrows. 'We've got his bank statements and it's about eight hundred quid a month.'

'Anything else?'

'Not really, Ma'am.'

'Sally, are you ready to interview Mitchell?'

'Yes, Ma'am.'

'Right then, let's get on with it. Dixon, you're with me. And remember, people: Hatty is still alive unless and until we know otherwise. All right?'

Chapter Twenty-Five

'Well that was a complete waste of bloody time.' Potter switched off the monitor and dropped the remote control on the table. 'No connection with Savage. Whatsoever. And, on the face of it, alibis for every damn thing.'

Dixon shrugged his shoulders.

'And he said Poland was just doing his job! It wasn't *personal*, whatever that means.'

'Did you believe him?' asked Dixon.

'Did you?'

'Yes.'

'Me too.' Potter sighed. 'We'll have to let Mitchell go, which just leaves Barnard.'

'He's not under arrest so he could just walk anyway, Ma'am,' said Jane.

'Let him.' Potter was distracted by voices in the corridor. 'Sounds like they're out. Our turn.'

Dixon followed Potter to the interview room next door, watching Jane switching the monitor back on as the door of the anteroom closed behind them. Seconds later Barnard was escorted in and sat down next to Potter, facing the tape machine.

'You lot like to keep people waiting, don't you?'

'I'm sorry about that, Mr Barnard, something came up; but thank you for your patience.'

'I'm not under arrest, am I?'

'You're not, and you're free to go at any time.'

Barnard nodded. 'Is that thing on?' he asked, gesturing to the tape machine.

'No. You're just helping with our enquiries at this stage, but the interview is being filmed.' Potter pointed to a camera mounted on a bracket just under the ceiling.

'Do I need a solicitor?'

'I don't know, do you?'

Dixon winced. It was a cheap shot and Potter should have resisted the temptation.

'No, I don't. Look, I know I kicked up a stink at the time but the pathologist—'

'Dr Poland.'

'Yes, him, was just doing his job. Any other pathologist would've said the same thing. I know that now.'

'You've been advised that we are investigating the disappearance of Dr Poland's ten year old granddaughter?'

'Yes.'

'How old was your son when he died?'

'Ten.' Barnard folded his arms tightly across his chest. 'For fuck's sake, is that why I'm here?'

'You're here because of the remarks you made at the time, Mr Barnard. They're recorded in the transcript of the court hearing.'

'I was angry.'

'Poland's going to pay for this.' Potter was reading from her notebook. 'This is Poland's fucking fault.'

Dixon glanced across at Barnard, who was rubbing his stubble, flakes of dry skin falling like snow on to his black trousers.

'I told you I was angry. My son was dead.'

'He had a congenital heart defect. Is that right, Mr Barnard?'

Barnard sighed. 'Yes. We had a second post mortem done when we were considering a civil claim and it found the same thing.'

'And the CPS dropped the causing death by dangerous driving?'

'Careless bloody driving. My son was dead and he walked out of court with six points and a three hundred quid fine.' Barnard wiped his eyes on his sleeve.

'I'm sorry if this is bringing it all back, but I'm sure you can understand why we'd be interested to speak to you in the current situation.'

'I haven't kidnapped his granddaughter. All right?'

'If you say so, Mr Barnard.' Potter looked at Dixon and raised her eyebrows.

'Can you account for your whereabouts last Saturday afternoon, Mr Barnard?' asked Dixon. 'Between two and six.'

'I watched my son . . .' He sighed. 'My other son, Niall, playing football for Burnham. That was at the BASC ground. Kick off was at three then we went in the bar for a few beers. Lots of people will have seen me.'

'What about Tuesday morning? Early, say between eight and nine.'

'That's not early. I'd finished milking by then and we were out over Edithmead fixing a fence. My lads'll vouch for that.'

'And last night between ten and two?'

'At home with my wife.'

'Does the name Jeffrey Savage mean anything to you?'

'No.'

'Maybe Jeff Savage?'

Barnard puffed out his cheeks. 'I told you, no.'

'Are you familiar with canal boats, Mr Barnard?'

'I went on a holiday once and was bored shitless. It was my wife's idea.'

'Where did you go?'

'We hired a boat at Bath and went along the Kennet and Avon. All those bloody locks. One after the other.' He shook his head. 'Never a-bloody-gain.'

'When was this?'

'Five years ago, maybe. Something like that.'

'What about Edward Buckler. Does that name mean anything?'

'You mean Ted the weatherman?'

'Yes.'

'Lives over Watchfield way. Everybody knows Ted, or knows *of* him, I should say. Why?'

'Have you ever met him?'

'No.' Barnard looked at his watch. 'Have you finished? It'll be milking time again soon.'

'The search of your premises is still going on, Mr Barnard,' replied Potter, standing up. 'But you're free to go.'

'How much longer is that going to take?'

'They'll be finished today and all being well we can eliminate you from our enquiries.'

'Good,' muttered Barnard. 'I wouldn't want you wasting any more of your time. And mine.'

Potter dropped her notebook on the workstation and picked up her handbag, rummaging inside for a packet of cigarettes. She took one out and held it between her teeth while she found her lighter.

'I'll be in the car park,' she said.

'Petersen rang, Ma'am,' said Guthrie. 'Savage's eardrums had both been pierced. Perforated was the word he used.'

'Perforated eardrums?'

'Yes, Ma'am.'

'Why the fuck would anyone do that?'

'He thought you ought to know.'

'Does Mitchell's alibi check out?'

'Yes, Ma'am.'

'Let's get Barnard's checked as soon as we can.' Potter was halfway down the stairs now. 'There's a possible connection with Savage. They were both on the canal at the same time.'

'With thousands of other people,' muttered Dixon.

'And he knows of Ted Buckler.'

Doesn't everyone?

He waited until the door slammed behind Potter and then went down to the Safeguarding Unit, where Jane was catching up with her emails.

'It's not Barnard, is it?' she said, looking up when he appeared by her workstation.

'Or Mitchell.'

'Oh, for God's sake!' Jane was looking past him through the glass partition to the landing on the other side of the atrium.

Dixon spun round to see PC Cole leading Lucy by the arm. He leaned over and banged on the window.

'What the hell's she been up to?' Jane wrenched open the door. 'In here,' she said.

At least the Safeguarding Unit's soundproofed, thought Dixon.

Jane slammed the door behind them.

'What the blood—?' Jane stopped abruptly when she noticed that Cole was smiling at her. 'What?'

'It was her idea,' he said, letting go of Lucy's elbow. 'Thought it might wind you up.'

'No shit.' Jane glared at Lucy. 'Where've you been all day?'

'Over at Catcott, helping with the search.'

'Been a great help,' said Cole. 'Lots of the public turned out and we've covered a huge area. No sign of Hatty though, sadly.'

'How did you get there?'

'Taxi,' replied Lucy. 'You left me the money.'

'That was supposed to be for food.' Jane frowned. 'Have you eaten?'

'No. You told me to stay out of trouble, so I did. And besides, lots of people went out looking for me when I went missing so I thought I ought to do the same for her.'

'You went missing?'

'I ran away . . .' Lucy hesitated. 'Once or twice.' She grinned. 'I was thinking I might be a police officer one day too.'

'Are you taking the piss?'

'She asked me to print off the application forms for her,' said Cole.

'You need to pass your exams for that.'

'I know, but you said—'

Jane's glare stopped Lucy mid-sentence. 'Not now.'

Lucy nodded.

'I can drop you both off at home, if you like,' said Dixon, smiling.

'Where are you going?'

'You wouldn't believe me if I told you.'

Chapter Twenty-Six

The sickly sweet smell was unmistakable, even to someone who had never worked the drug squad. Dixon sighed. An old fashioned bobby-on-the-beat would have soon smelt it and been knocking on the door.

He stood on the pavement outside the small terraced house in Glastonbury and listened to the muffled voices in the front room; laughter, shouting, a flame flickering, more laughter. And God knows what that pentangle thing hanging up at the window was supposed to be. Kicking the door in and nicking the lot of them was tempting. But this is Glastonbury, thought Dixon. Best go along with it. And besides, he needed Xander Dolphin's help.

He knocked and waited, his finger over the spy hole just above the door knocker. The pentangle moved – someone was trying to peer out of the front window – then footsteps and a dark figure looming up behind the small frosted pane of glass in the front door.

'Who is it?'

'Detective Inspector Dixon.' Loud and clear. He shook his head, listening to the low muffled whisper of 'plod' then the sound of people – two, possibly three – running and the back door slamming shut.

'I'll be out in a minute,' shouted Dolphin, followed by a flame flickering and an aerosol.

'You're wasting your time,' said Dixon. 'I can smell it from out here.'

Dolphin shrugged his shoulders as he opened the door.

'And besides,' continued Dixon, 'if that was why I was here, I'd have kicked the door in.'

'Good point.'

'Can I come in?'

'Why?'

'We found Alesha,' replied Dixon. 'In a canal boat under the M5. This was painted on the inside of the back doors,' he said, handing Dolphin his phone.

'Shit.' Dolphin was staring at the photograph of the castle and flowers. 'I was right.'

'You were.' Dixon winced. 'Much as it pains me to say it.'

Dolphin smiled. 'And you want my help again?'

'Hatty is still out there somewhere.'

Dolphin stepped back. 'You'd better come in.'

'What the blood—' The words caught in the back of Dixon's throat as he coughed and spluttered on a mixture of joss sticks, marijuana and pine air freshener in the living room.

'Sorry,' mumbled Dolphin. 'I got a bit carried away with the Febreze.'

Dixon picked up the joss sticks and dropped them in an open can of lager. Then he picked it up and shook it. 'Can you open a window? Much more of this and I won't be fit to drive.'

'Yeah, sure.'

'And the back door. Get a bit of air in this damn place.'

'We haven't talked about my fee,' shouted Dolphin from the kitchen as he opened the back door.

'Fee?' Dixon picked up a carved wooden box on the coffee table.

'The other night was a freebie for Gerry, but I usually charge . . .' Dolphin's voice tailed off when he walked back into the living room and saw Dixon holding the box.

'You usually charge for what? This?' He pulled a clear plastic bag out of the box and held it up to the light. 'Because that would make it possession with intent to supply.'

'No, for a reading,' mumbled Dolphin, tugging at one of the earrings in his left ear.

'Looks like good stuff.' Dixon nodded. 'There's probably enough here for possession with intent anyway.'

'I use a lot. It's medicinal, you understand?'

'Of course it is.'

Dixon pushed the plastic bag back into the box, closed the lid and put it on the coffee table. 'Your fee, Xander, is not getting nicked for this lot.'

Dolphin nodded.

'And that's on the strict understanding you tell no one I was here. Ever.'

'Worried that people will take the piss?'

'Something like that.'

'It'll be our little secret.' Dolphin sat down on the sofa and picked up a half burnt joint from the ashtray.

Dixon frowned. 'Don't push your luck.'

'Let me have another look at that photograph.' Dolphin dropped the joint back into the ashtray and snatched Dixon's phone, which he was holding in his outstretched hand. 'Roses and castles,' he muttered, peering at the screen. Then he used two fingers to zoom in on the flowers. 'They're definitely roses.'

'If you say so.'

'And she was on a canal boat?'

Dixon nodded. 'It was out of the water on bricks.'

'That explains it.'

'What?'

'It was after last time at Catcott, the next night maybe,' Dolphin shook his head, 'I saw a boy, drowning. There was a stone wall and a big wooden gate, so maybe it was a canal lock. It makes sense if it was a lock, but there was no water in it.'

'D'you see anything else?'

'A horse.' Dolphin leaned back on the sofa and closed his eyes.

'What colour?'

'Black, but that's from coal dust.' He took a deep breath through his nose. 'She's covered in dust and I can smell the burning coal.'

Dixon sniffed the air. 'All I'm getting is pine air freshener.'

'You asked me and I told you,' snapped Xander. 'You don't have the gift. How can you expect to see what I see?'

'Is that it?'

'I don't control it. I have to be able to smoke too, and I can't do that with you here.'

'So, you're high when you get these visions?'

'It opens the doors of the mind.'

'Well, if it opens any more, you let me know. All right?'

'Where've you been?' asked Jane. She was sitting on the sofa with Lucy, both of them watching the TV, the film on pause.

'Glastonbury,' replied Dixon.

'Not to see the hippy?'

'He's more wizard than hippy.'

'What'd he say?'

'A boy drowning in an empty lock and a horse covered in coal dust.'

'What does that mean?'

'No idea.' Dixon was squatting down in front of the fridge. 'You eaten?'

'We went to the pub.'

'Have you fed Monty?'

'Yes.' Jane sighed. 'Of course we have.'

'*Dr Zhivago*, eh?' said Dixon, walking into the living room eating from a tub of olives, the microwave going in the kitchen behind him.

'I've not seen it before,' said Lucy. She frowned. 'It's a bit slow.'

'What's your fav—?'

'Don't ask her that,' interrupted Jane. 'For God's sake.'

Lucy grinned. '*The Walking Dead*.'

Dixon rolled his eyes.

'I told you not to ask,' said Jane.

Dixon was distracted by the ping from the kitchen; he took his curry out of the microwave, stirred it and then shoved it back in.

'You look dead to the world,' said Jane. 'You need some sleep.'

'Can't sleep while Hatty's still out there,' muttered Dixon. 'I think I'll take Monty for a walk when I've had this. I've got a horrible feeling I'm barking up the wrong tree, so we can do it together.'

Jane got up and stood in the kitchen doorway. 'What d'you mean the wrong tree?'

'Everyone with a grudge against Roger has a cast iron alibi.'

'Everyone we know about. There may be others.'

Dixon nodded. 'Either that or we've been sent in the wrong direction.' The microwave pinged on the worktop next to him. 'Again.' He dragged the curry out on to a plate and picked up a fork.

'Have you done your jab?'

'Yes.'

'So, it's got nothing to do with Roger?'

'Think about what Sonia and Alesha said. Both of them used exactly the same words. Exactly.'

'It was rehearsed?'

Dixon nodded. 'Must've been.'

'Have you mentioned this to Potter?'

'Not yet.'

'So, what's going on?'

'God knows.'

Twenty minutes later Dixon parked on the beach at Berrow. The tide was coming in, the waves rolling up the mud flats several hundred yards out. That gave him a couple of hours until the sea reached his Land Rover, if it came in that far. He hadn't checked but it was plenty of time anyway. He opened the back, letting Monty jump out, his white coat seeming to glow in the moonlight, and followed the dog towards Burnham.

He couldn't sleep knowing that Hatty was still out there, somewhere, but taking his dog for a walk seemed almost as crass. Or at least it would to someone who didn't know him. Poland would understand. He knew.

'Poland's got a lot to answer for and is going to suffer.'

Roger was certainly suffering. Dixon didn't doubt that for a minute. But, as for a reason . . .

He kicked Monty's ball along the sand and tried to follow it in the moonlight as it rolled towards a pile of seaweed.

It was definitely rehearsed. Both Sonia and Alesha had used the identical phrase. 'Going to suffer' was unusual wording to use too. Most people would say 'going to pay', surely? And what does 'has a lot to answer for' mean? Poland had been through his files and identified everyone who might have borne a grudge against him, anyone who'd suffered as a result of his findings and might wish him to suffer too.

Potter had asked him to go through his files again. Clutching at straws, thought Dixon, as he fumbled in his pockets for a dog bag.

'I thought Jane had let you out?' he muttered, flicking on the torch on his phone.

At least she had been able to spend some time with her sister, and they seemed to be getting on. Dixon frowned. What was it with girls and *The Walking Dead*?

Detective Sergeant Jane Dixon. It had a certain ring to it. He smiled. The ring was still in the top pocket of his rucksack and it would have to stay there for the time being. Poland had even agreed to be his best man before all this had kicked off, despite protesting that he was old enough to be Dixon's father.

'I've got one of them, thanks.'

And he had reminded him that he perhaps ought to consider asking Jane first. It had been a good idea, but the moment had been lost.

Random thoughts were popping into and out of his head as he walked along the beach. At night was best too. Then he didn't have to worry about avoiding other dogs in case they went for Monty.

Find Hatty first, then ask Jane, and make sure it was before another case came along.

He noticed a light down at the tide line, some distance off to his right. A fisherman, probably, after flatfish on the incoming tide. Then the lighthouse silhouetted against the seafront beyond and the lights of Hinkley Point power station on the other side of the estuary.

He wondered whether Jane would stick with her maiden name when they got married. Some people did.

Oh, fuck it.

Chapter Twenty-Seven

It was just before midnight when Dixon burst into the cottage, startling Jane and Lucy sitting on the sofa.

'You still watching *Dr Zhivago*?'

'I was asleep,' mumbled Lucy.

'It's a long film,' replied Jane. 'And we keep getting interrupted. How far did you get?'

'Far enough.'

Jane knew the signs. 'Well?' she asked.

'Poland's going to suffer . . .'

Jane nodded. 'And?'

'What's Adele's maiden name?'

Jane frowned. 'Oh, shit,' she muttered, her eyes widening. 'What made you think of that?'

'You did.'

'Really?'

'Don't ask.'

'Yeah, but if someone had kidnapped Hatty to get at Adele, wouldn't she say something?'

'Would you?' Dixon was pacing up and down in front of the television. 'Someone takes your child and tells you they'll kill her if you talk to the police. What're you going to do?'

'Say nothin',' said Lucy.

'Exactly. You'd leave us following the dead ends.'

'And you could be forgiven for that,' said Jane. She switched off the television. 'So, what happens now?'

'I need to speak to Sonia and Alesha again before I say anything,' replied Dixon. 'Then we need to have a close look at Adele and Jeremy Renner.'

'Without telling Roger.'

Dixon had managed five hours' sleep, at Jane's insistence. 'You're no good to Hatty if you're like a bloody zombie,' had been her exact words, and she had a point. The first seventy-two hours after Hatty's disappearance had come and gone, but he never had believed that crap anyway. Every case was different. Either way, the next twenty-four hours would be critical and he needed to be able to stay awake. For Hatty's sake, and for Roger's.

Now he was sitting at a workstation in the Incident Room on the second floor of the police centre at Express Park. Everyone was drinking coffee: those officers who had been on duty all night, and those who had just arrived, including Potter and Chard.

'We need to interview Sonia again, Ma'am,' said Dixon, standing by her workstation.

'You're too late,' Chard sneered. 'She's being charged now and it's not a terrorism offence so you won't get leave from a judge.'

'The Chief Crown Prosecutor approved it overnight, Nick,' said Potter, frowning. 'Why? She's refused to give us anything else. Says she can't.'

'I need to ask her about something she's already said.'

Potter shrugged her shoulders.

Dixon ran down to the Safeguarding Unit on the first floor and wrenched open the door. 'You got a minute?' he said, looking at Jane with his eyes wide.

'Er, yes.'

She followed him down to the custody suite.

'Sonia's being charged now, so it's my last chance to speak to her,' he said, running down the stairs.

'You're too late already, by the sounds of things.'

'Bollocks.'

Once through the door, Dixon and Jane blinked furiously in the glare from the bright strip lights and spot lamps on the ceiling. Everything was white or light grey, which didn't help – the floor, the ceiling and the desks, arranged in a circle in the middle of the room and each separated from the next by a curved soundproofed partition. The only colour in the entire room came from an illuminated red strip on the wall at waist height that looked much like a dado rail.

'She's in the next bay,' said Jane, peering around the soundproof partition at the custody desk to their right. 'I can't tell whether she's already been charged or not.'

'I need you to go over to that far wall and lean against the red strip. All right?'

'What does that do?'

'D'you remember when I gave our local MP a guided tour of this place?'

Jane nodded.

'I found out that it's a panic strip. If you hit that all the cameras in the whole suite turn to that spot.' Dixon grinned. 'And I get a chance to speak to Sonia.'

'What about the custody sergeant?'

'I'll take my chances with her.'

'We could get in deep shit for this.'

'Deeper than Hatty?'

Jane sighed. 'Over there, you mean?'

'That'll do.'

Dixon watched Jane walk over to the far wall and lean back against it. Then she hit the red strip with the palm of her hand, triggering the alarm. He sprinted around to the custody desk in the next bay, pushed past the custody officer and appeared next to Sonia.

The custody sergeant's eyes narrowed.

'Remember me, Sonia?' asked Dixon.

'Yes.'

'Hatty's still out there.'

Sonia turned at the sound of footsteps as two more custody officers ran past behind them.

'And she doesn't have her grandmother to look after her,' continued Dixon.

'Sixty seconds,' said the custody sergeant, glancing up at the camera above her head.

'"Poland's got a lot to answer for." You were told to say that, weren't you?'

Sonia nodded.

'Who by?'

'Jeff.'

'Those exact words?'

'He made me learn them and I had to teach them to Alesha too. She was to say them if we got caught.'

'And it was "*is* going to suffer"?'

'That's it.'

'Not *he* or *she*?'

'No, just "*is* going to suffer".'

'Who is Poland?'

'I told you, I don't know.'

'Thank you, Sonia.'

Dixon stepped back from behind the soundproof partition to find Jane being helped to the door by two custody officers.

'I felt faint,' she said, 'and must've leaned against the alarm by mistake.'

'I'll take her,' said Dixon. 'Too much gin last night, I reckon.'

Jane waited until the door closed behind her. 'Too much bloody gin,' she said, hitting Dixon on the arm. 'Did you get what you needed?'

'Yes.'

'What about the custody sergeant?'

'She'll be fine.'

Jane puffed out her cheeks as she followed Dixon up the stairs, two at a time. 'What happens now?'

'I need to persuade Potter to let us investigate Adele and Jeremy. Hopefully, she'll give us some help too.'

'And if she says no?'

'We do it anyway.'

'You did what?' Potter threw her pen on to the table in meeting room 2.

'I spoke to Sonia and she confirmed it,' said Dixon.

'You spoke to Sonia?'

'I bumped into her down in the custody suite.'

'So, let me make sure I understand this correctly, you're saying Roger Poland has nothing to do with this?'

'Sonia and Alesha were both schooled to say it if they were caught. "Poland's going to suffer." Think about it. As soon as we find Alesha we know Hatty's kidnap is anything but random and we start looking at the family. This sends us in the wrong direction. Again. It was another smokescreen. It's not about Roger at all.'

'Yes, but it would hardly throw us off the scent for long.'

'Maybe it doesn't have to. Look, it's about Adele and Jeremy.'

'Someone has a grudge against them now?'

'Or wants them to do something. Don't forget, he works for a bank.'

'They would've said something, surely?'

'Would they?' asked Dixon. 'Would you, if someone had your daughter and was—'

'I get it.' Potter folded her arms.

'Jane put in a request for their mobile phone records.'

'I cancelled it.' Potter sighed. 'Which maybe I shouldn't have done. What else d'you need?'

'Some help. Louise, Dave and Mark will do.'

'What about Roger Poland?'

'I'll deal with Roger.'

'All right. I'll arrange it.' Potter sighed. 'What if you're wrong?'

'Then you haven't lost much. You're not committing any real resources to it, are you? And if I'm right . . .'

Potter nodded. 'Fuck it up and you're on your own,' she said, raising her eyebrows.

'I never doubted it for a minute.'

Chapter Twenty-Eight

'This is more like it,' said Louise.

'Putting the band back together.' Pearce grinned.

'Shut up, Mark.'

'Yes, Sir.'

It *was* more like it, though. Dixon smiled as he looked around meeting room 2 at people he knew and trusted: Jane, Louise, Dave Harding and Mark Pearce. 'Right then,' he said, 'we're going to be working on the assumption that the reference to Poland in what Sonia said is Adele's maiden name. It's not Roger at all.'

'Adele's maiden name?'

'Yes, Dave.'

'For fuck's sake . . .' His voice tailed off.

'I want full mobile phone records and I want to know where their cars have been since Tuesday morning. Include Roger's ex-wife's in that.'

'I'll do it,' said Harding.

'Er, thanks, Dave.'

'That's a first,' said Pearce. 'I've never known you volunteer for anything.'

Harding frowned. 'It's Roger's grandkid.'

'Mark, can you concentrate on their internet profiles, social media, anything like that. Usual drill.'

'Yes, Sir.'

'Louise, you take their finances. I want bank statements, past and present directorships, anything like that. Check the Land Registry too.'

'Will do.'

'Jane, you're with me.'

'Where are we going?'

'Catcott. Walking on thin ice, treading on eggshells, and any other clichés I can think of.'

◆ ◆ ◆

'No Roger?' asked Dixon as he stepped in through the front door of Old School House.

Geraldine sneered. 'He's down at the hospital going through his records again.'

Dixon and Jane followed her into the living room, where Adele was sitting alone in front of the wood burner, watching the flames flickering behind the glass. The television was on in the background, BBC News, with the sound switched to 'Mute'.

'Hello Adele,' said Dixon, employing his best disarming smile.

She stood up, snatched a packet of cigarettes off the sideboard and walked out into the garden through the open French windows.

Dixon looked at Jane and raised his eyebrows.

'They had a row, as far as I can gather,' said Geraldine. 'We left them alone last night, which was probably not a good idea. Jeremy wasn't here when I arrived this morning and Adele's not said a word.'

'What about the Family Liaison officer?' asked Jane.

'She sent them home. Adele wouldn't let Ros in either. I bumped into her in the lane when I arrived.'

Dixon hoped no one else could hear the alarm bells going off in his head. 'Where's Jeremy gone, do we know?'

Geraldine shrugged her shoulders. 'His car's gone; that's all I can tell you.'

'D'you know what time he left?'

'No.'

Dixon walked towards the French windows, noticing out of the corner of his eye Geraldine following him. 'Did you say tea?' he asked, spinning round.

'No.'

'Oh, that's a shame.'

'Would you like tea?'

'Coffee for me, please,' said Jane, walking towards the kitchen. Geraldine followed, her sigh as loud as humanly possible.

Once out in the garden Dixon sat down on the low wall next to Adele. She reached behind her and flicked her ash into the pond. Two small fish surfaced to investigate, but soon turned away.

'Poland's got a lot to answer for,' said Dixon, nodding.

Adele looked at him, her eyes narrowing.

'Is there anything you want to tell me?' he asked.

She took a long, slow drag on her cigarette, then dropped it into the pond behind her as she blew the smoke out through her nose. 'Why, should there be?'

'You tell me.'

'There's nothing,' she said, lighting another cigarette.

'How did they make contact with you?'

Adele frowned. 'Who?' The end of her cigarette bounced in the flame of the lighter as she spoke, the orange glow reflecting in her already bloodshot eyes.

'Whoever's got Hatty,' said Dixon, matter of fact.

Silence.

He waited while Adele puffed on her cigarette.

'What do they want?' he asked.

'No one's contacted us.' She flicked her ash on the patio this time.

'Yes, they have. And they've told you not to tell me or they'll harm Hatty.'

'That's not true.' She shook her head. 'You've got that wrong.'

She was staring at the broken paving stones in front of her, watching a small spider walking towards her bare feet. That's if she was focusing on anything at all, thought Dixon. Her eyes looked glazed over, although it was difficult to tell with all the lost sleep and pills.

'Where's Jeremy?'

'We had a row.'

'What about?'

'Nothing.'

'And where's he gone?'

'He said he had to go to work.'

'What time did he leave?'

'Who fucking cares?' Adele sighed. 'He's gone. I have no idea what time he left. And no idea what bloody time it is now.'

'What time will he be back?'

'God knows.'

'Hatty's an only child?' asked Dixon, changing the subject.

'It just turned out that way,' replied Adele. 'We tried and I miscarried a couple of times. It just never happened.'

'Did you try IVF?'

'No. I wanted to, but Jeremy wouldn't. He said *it wasn't meant to be.*' Another cigarette butt behind her in the pond. 'So, how come you get on so well with Dad?'

'Not sure, really. We just do,' replied Dixon.

'He said you're the best he's ever known in thirty years on the job.'

Dixon smiled. 'He's prone to exaggeration, is Roger.'

'You and Jane are getting married too?'

'I haven't asked her yet.'

'He's really cut up about Hatty. Blames himself, but I keep telling him it's not his fault.' A tear appeared in the corner of Adele's eye. 'He was only doing his job, wasn't he?'

'It's nobody's fault, Adele. And certainly not Roger's.' Dixon spotted the sideways glance. 'Tell me this,' he said. 'When you've done whatever it is they want, or paid them whatever it is they want, how d'you know they're going to give you Hatty back?'

Adele took a deep breath, watching the flame on her lighter as she flicked it on and off again. 'We . . . look, we don't . . .'

'Did they prove to you she's still alive somehow?'

'I . . . I don't . . .'

'Your tea's here,' shouted Geraldine, her head appearing around the patio door.

Dixon grimaced.

'I don't know what you're talking about,' snapped Adele, standing up.

'I'm sorry, we don't have time for tea, after all,' said Dixon, following her back indoors. 'Please ask Mr Renner to contact me when he gets back from the office.'

'He's gone to work?' asked Geraldine, spinning round to glare at Adele.

'May I?' Dixon took a biscuit off the side plate on the dining table. 'In the meantime, I'll arrange for a Family Liaison officer to come back.'

'We don't need . . .' Adele's voice tailed off.

'They'll be here round the clock from now on.' Dixon turned towards the door. 'We'll show ourselves out.'

'What was all that about?' Jane had waited until Dixon switched the engine on. 'They're getting on fine without Family Liaison.'

'I want them there for our benefit, not theirs.' He did a three point turn in the lane outside Old School House and raced back towards the main road. 'Jeremy's gone to work.'

'Work? With his daughter kidnapped?'

'Adele knows – she bloody well knows who's got Hatty. I'm sure of it. They've been in touch somehow and that must be why Jeremy's gone to work.'

'Nothing's shown up on the phone tap or the email, so how are they communicating?'

'We'll find out. In the meantime, we get a warrant and then turn up at the bank when he's gone home. I want to see what he's been up to.'

Chapter Twenty-Nine

'Parkway North Business Park is a bit of a mouthful, isn't it?' said Jane, looking at the map on her phone. 'It's probably quicker to go along the M4 and M32.'

'I hate office parks,' muttered Dixon.

'We know.' Jane rolled her eyes.

'What did Lucy say when you rang her?'

'She's gone over to Catcott again, would you believe it?' Jane shook her head. 'I rang Cole and he's going to keep an eye on her. It's a sod of a long way for Jeremy to come every day, isn't it?'

'It's maybe fifty minutes if he goes round the motorway, and he won't be doing it every day. He's business development director, so he'll be out and about seeing customers.'

'Clients.'

'Bollocks. Banks have customers.'

'If you say so.'

Dixon reached into his inside jacket pocket and took out his phone. 'Get that for me, will you.' He said, passing it to Jane sitting in the passenger seat. 'It's an 01278 number so it's probably Jeremy telling me he's at home.'

Jane put the phone to her ear. 'Detective Sergeant Winter.' . . . 'He's driving, Mr Renner.' . . . 'Yes, I know he wants to speak to you so I'll get him to call you back.' . . . 'Thank you for calling.'

'He sounded nervous,' said Jane, ringing off.

'He'll know that I know. Adele will have told him by now.'

'You think you do.'

Dixon shook his head. 'I know, and she knows that I know. And if that bloody tea had taken another few minutes, she'd have told me.'

'What?'

'Who's got Hatty. She knows. Not the "where", maybe, but the "who" and "why" she knows all right.'

'And she can't tell us?'

'Not without risking her child's life.'

'But won't they think she's told us if we go wading in—'

'We won't. We're just making routine enquiries, no arrests.'

'Yet,' muttered Jane.

'They all look the bloody same,' said Dixon, turning into Parkway North Business Park twenty minutes later. 'What number is it?'

'It's called Park House.'

'Are you taking the Mickey?'

'Just look for a Svenskabanken sign.' Jane sighed.

'Park House, Parkway North Business Park. You're not going to forget that in a hurry, are you?'

'Down there,' said Jane, pointing to a side turning. 'It's at the end.'

'What do you do for lunch in these bloody places?' muttered Dixon.

'The same as we do,' replied Jane.

'Go to the pub.'

'Tesco's is over there.'

'That's all right then.' Dixon stopped across the entrance and wrenched on the handbrake; a rather grand glass revolving door set in an atrium of sandstone and yet more glass, the rest of the building red brick. 'Svenskabanken AB' in bright red lettering above the door.

'Are you going to leave it here?'

'Why not? There are no yellow lines and the place is deserted.'

The revolving door was locked so Dixon banged on the window next to it. A man perched on the edge of the reception desk folded up his newspaper and walked across to the door, a bunch of keys jangling in his hand.

'Are you the manager, Sir?' said Dixon, his warrant card in his hand as he emerged from the revolving glass.

'Alan Price, yes.'

'Detective Inspector Dixon, Sir. It's good of you to turn out on a Saturday.'

'I wasn't aware that I had a choice.'

'You didn't, Sir. I was being polite.' Dixon smiled. 'And this is Detective Sergeant Winter.'

Price locked the door behind Jane.

'What's this all about then?' asked Price.

'We're investigating the disappearance of Hatty Renner, Sir. She's Jeremy Renner's daughter.'

'I've seen it on the TV.'

'And the murder of Jeffrey Savage. He was found in Chew Valley Reservoir.'

'They're connected?'

'They are. And this is a search warrant.' Dixon handed the document to Price. 'Mr Renner came in to the office this morning, Sir. I'm assuming you can check that?'

'I can. He'll have used his code for the staff entrance at the back of the building.'

'Good. We need to know what he did when he was here. I need copies of any and all emails he sent and received, details of any phone calls he made, files he looked at, any memos or letters he dictated. Everything.'

'That's all—'

'Confidential?' Dixon raised his eyebrows.

Price nodded.

'Of course it is, Sir. That's why I got the search warrant. And I would remind you that a ten year old girl is missing and a man dead.'

'This has got nothing to do with Jeremy, surely?'

'You mean apart from the girl being his daughter?'

Price was looking at the search warrant, but his eyes were focused elsewhere. Buying time rather than reading it: Dixon knew the signs.

'I'll need my IT guy to access the stuff on the computers and the phone system.'

'Presumably he's just a phone call away, Sir?'

Price nodded.

'You ring him, Sir – impress upon him the urgency – and then we'll do what we can until he gets here.'

Price used the phone on the reception desk but spoke quietly; his voice was muffled and only raised once throughout the call: 'bloody search warrant'. Anyway, it seemed to do the trick.

'He's on his way,' said Price.

'How long?'

'Ten minutes.'

'Good. Can we see Mr Renner's office while we wait?'

'Er, yes, follow me.'

Price opened the double doors at the top of the stairs to reveal glass cubicles around a central open plan area, much the same as Express Park. The idea of promotion to an office job sent shivers down Dixon's spine.

'This one's Jeremy's.'

First door on the left; it was open. Jane sat down behind the desk while Dixon looked at the photographs on the wall; various certificates, a picture of Adele with Hatty, both of them smiling at the camera. Several pictures of a small yacht, on a trailer and then again on Durleigh Reservoir.

'What does business development director involve?' asked Dixon.

'Developing business,' replied Price. 'I'm sorry, that's not meant to sound flippant, but that's his job: finding new clients, new business. Jeremy's mainly on the corporate side. He's got company clients in Somerset, Dorset, Devon and Cornwall. That's his patch. He's only here once or twice a week. The rest of the time he's out and about or working from home. Sometimes he's down at the Plymouth office too.'

'Is the network secure?' asked Jane.

'He connects via the internet to a secure server, yes,' replied Price. 'Adam can explain it when he gets here.'

'What about everybody else?' asked Dixon, gesturing to the offices further along the first floor.

'Business development this end and that's the enforcement team down the far end. Things don't always go to plan, sadly.'

Jane was holding the pad of paper that had been on Renner's desk up to the light, turning it this way and that. Then she took an evidence bag out of her handbag, dropped the pad in and sealed it.

'Excuse me,' said Price, answering his phone. 'Upstairs in Jeremy's office.' Then he rang off. 'Adam's here.'

Dixon nodded.

Adam still had his cycling helmet on when he burst through the double doors at the top of the stairs. 'I came as quick as I could.'

'We need access to Jeremy's computer,' said Price.

'I thought you would so I brought the master password list from my office. May I?' he asked, gesturing to the chair Jane was sitting on.

'Yes, of course.'

'What do you need?' he asked, logging on.

'Emails, sent and received. Anything he typed, documents he worked on, copies of any voice files he dictated. Web history,' replied Dixon. 'Basically, anything he did when he was here this morning.'

'And phone calls made and received,' said Jane.

'I can get that, but I'll need to log on again as administrator.' Adam dropped his cycle helmet on his rucksack beside the desk. 'How do you want the emails?'

'Printed,' said Dixon.

Adam slid across to the sideboard on the swivel chair and switched on the printer.

'He logged on at four minutes past nine and off again at ten fifty-seven, which corresponds with the door entry records.'

'Can you print—?'

Adam pointed to the printer behind Dixon, which began churning out paper. 'The emails are on their way too.'

'What about recent documents?' asked Dixon.

'Four. I'm just sending them to print now.'

Dixon glanced at Jane, who was standing behind Adam watching the screen. She nodded.

'No voice files. Web history's just BBC News and the Western Daily Press – articles about his daughter, by the looks of things. Let me just check the calls.'

Dixon picked up the emails and flicked through them. Then the four documents: two memos, a loan agreement and a confidentiality agreement. The door entry records showed only Renner, Price and Adam had clocked in that day, which was not surprising for a bank on a Saturday perhaps.

Adam shook his head. 'No calls, made or received from this extension. None at all.'

'What about the others?' asked Dixon. 'I'd use somebody else's phone, wouldn't you?'

'You have a suspicious mind, Inspector,' said Price.

'Thank you.'

'No, none.' Adam leaned back in the swivel chair. 'The only call was made from reception to my mobile about half an hour ago.'

Jane glanced at Dixon and nodded.

'Is that it then, Inspector?' asked Price. 'He wasn't here long, as you can see.'

'If we give him two minutes each for the emails sent and received, that's forty-four minutes. Say, twenty for the documents and another twenty on the internet, and he was here for two hours, what was he doing for the other thirty-six minutes, I wonder?'

'On his own,' said Jane. 'We know that because no one else signed in.'

'He could have let them in?' Dixon looked at Price.

'Yes, he could. He doesn't have keys to the front door, but there's the back.'

'Any CCTV?'

Adam stood up. 'It's in my office.'

A room with no windows. Dixon grimaced. It made a glass cubicle on the open plan floor look positively desirable, even if it was just inside the back door.

'It's motion activated, so it only kicks in—'

'We know,' said Dixon.

Adam scrolled through the footage, which showed only Renner arriving and then leaving two hours later, followed by Price and himself arriving.

Dixon was sucking his teeth. 'Well, thank you for your help. It goes without saying that the execution of this warrant is highly confidential. This is an ongoing investigation and no one is to hear about this. Is that clear?'

'Certainly, Inspector,' replied Price. 'Isn't it, Adam?'

'Yes, yes, of course.'

They stood on the pavement listening to Price locking the revolving door behind them and then walked across to Dixon's Land Rover.

'It must be in here then,' said Dixon, handing Jane an envelope containing the pile of emails and documents.

'Or here,' she said, holding up the evidence bag. 'There's a handwritten note. You can see the imprint on the pad.'

'We'll stop off at Portishead on the way back and drop it off with Scientific.'

◆ ◆ ◆

'What've we got then?'

Jane was sitting in the passenger seat of Dixon's Land Rover as he sped south on the M5. 'Nothing in the emails. It's all just crap.'

'What sort of crap?'

'Office stuff,' replied Jane. 'And he's emailed some loan application forms to a couple of people. The rest is notes to his secretary telling her what to say to people who've rung in.' Jane sighed. 'Mainly that he'll call them back as soon as he can.'

'Mainly?'

'She's to tell Barry Davenport of Metcalfe Electrical that he's not to worry. He'll sort it out when he's back in the office. Whatever that means.'

'We need to find out.'

'Simon Gregson from Markhams South West Limited has rung six times, apparently.'

'What's the message for him?'

'There isn't one.' Jane frowned. 'He says to ignore him.'

'And there's another here that might be interesting. "Malcolm Clarke has to give a personal guarantee for the mortgage."' Jane was reading from the email. '"Tell him that, with regret, it simply can't be done without."'

'What's the email address?'

'Malcolm dot Clarke at Hawkridge Cycles.'

'We can google it later,' said Dixon. 'What about the documents?'

'Two memos.' Jane glanced down the pages, speed reading. 'More crap. The loan's for Hawkridge Cycles Limited and there's a confidentiality agreement. That last one's blank.'

'How long did SOCO say it would take to get a copy of the handwritten note off the pad?'

'Later on today.'

'Let's start with Hawkridge Cycles then. If it's a bike shop it'll be open on a Saturday.

Jane took out her phone and opened a web browser. 'They're in Weston,' she said. 'On that new retail park on the way in.'

Dixon managed to avoid the three small children cycling up and down the car park on shiny new bicycles, closely watched by their parents and a shop assistant, and parked outside the front entrance of Hawkridge Cycles.

'We should get some bikes,' Jane said. 'It'd be nice.'

Dixon sighed.

'What?'

'The only place I'd want to cycle is the pub,' muttered Dixon.

'But that's only fifty yards from the cottage.'

'Exactly.' He opened the driver's door and climbed out of the Land Rover. 'Let's go and see what Mr Clarke has got to say for himself.'

The staff were easily identifiable in their matching green polo shirts. 'I'm looking for Mr Clarke,' said Dixon, picking on the tall one staring blankly at a computer screen behind the counter.

'Give me a minute.'

'If I had one, I would.' He leaned over and held his warrant card in front of the screen.

The shop assistant looked up. 'What's it about?'

'Are you Mr Clarke?'

He shook his head. 'I'll, er . . . just go and get him.'

'Thank you.'

He watched the shop assistant hovering behind another man in a green polo shirt showing off an expensive looking racing bike to a man with thighs the size of tree trunks. The shop assistant soon summoned up the courage to tap the second man on the shoulder. A frown, a glare, then Clarke, presumably, came weaving his way towards them through the bikes on display.

'Yes?'

'Is there somewhere private we could talk, Mr Clarke?'

'Is it about that stolen bike?'

'No, it isn't.'

Clarke frowned. 'Follow me.'

They ducked under more bikes hanging from the ceiling and into a small office at the back of the shop. Clarke closed the door behind them, kicking a box out of the way to do so.

'We're investigating the disappearance of Jeremy Renner's daughter, Hatty, Mr Clarke. We're just making routine enquiries with his customers at the bank.'

'I heard about that,' said Clarke, sitting down.

'I gather you are dealing with Mr Renner at the moment?' asked Dixon.

'I'm trying to negotiate a commercial mortgage through my company.'

'What for?'

'So I can buy the freehold of this place and take a lease on a new unit in Bath.'

'Is there some problem with the mortgage?'

'Not really. The bank are insisting on a personal guarantee from me. I don't mind that, but my signature needs to be witnessed by a solicitor and I can't seem to find one who'll do it without charging me a huge fee.' Clarke sighed. 'Apparently, it's not just a case of witnessing my signature. They have to advise me on the bloody thing and confirm that advice in writing before we even sign it. Three hundred quid plus VAT, they want.'

'So, you rang the bank?'

'I wasn't expecting to speak to Mr Renner. I was just hoping someone might tell me I needn't bother with the personal guarantee. After all, the freehold of this place will more than cover the borrowing, let alone the stock.'

'And that's the only issue outstanding with the bank?'

'Yes. Apart from that, they've been great.' Clarke smiled. 'Will you be seeing Mr Renner?'

Dixon nodded.

'Tell him, I hope it works out and she comes home safe.'

'I will, Sir.'

Dixon slammed the door of the Land Rover and switched on the engine.

'You're hardly going to kidnap Hatty over a three hundred quid bill,' said Jane, climbing into the passenger seat.

'What about Metcalfe Electrical?'

'Give me a minute.' They were arriving at the motorway roundabout before Jane spoke again. 'Torquay.' She looked up. 'I suppose he does cover the whole of the south west.'

'What about the other one?' asked Dixon. 'Markhams South West.'

'They're Torquay too, according to Companies House, but that's just the registered office.'

'That's probably their accountant.'

'They've got a listing on Yell. It says they're a commercial wine merchant supplying the trade in Avon and Somerset. You're hardly going to do that from Torquay.'

'A wine merchant?'

'Isn't that the same as a vintner?'

Dixon nodded. 'They'll be closed on a Saturday, I expect. See if you can find a home address for Simon Gregson.'

'I'll ring Lou.'

Much of Jane's call to Louise passed him by. He pulled into a lay-by on the A370 and sat listening to the diesel engine idling. It was more of a hum than a rattle and you could hear yourself think. Much better than the old one. He shook his head. A commercial wine merchant? The world was suddenly getting smaller.

Jane rang off. 'He's at Marston Farm Barn, Marston Farm Lane, Combe Hay. Where the hell's that?'

'Over Radstock way.' He reached into the footwell behind the front passenger seat, picked up a road atlas and dropped it into Jane's lap. 'I'll head for Bath while you find it on the map.'

'Aren't you going to ring him to let him know we're on the way?'

Chapter Thirty

The road atlas took them to Combe Hay, and Google Maps on Jane's iPhone the rest of the way. Marston Farm Lane was not marked on the map, but Marston Farm was, so they took the left turn just beyond the pub and had gone no more than a couple of hundred yards before the road forked again, a sign for Marston Farm Barn pointing down a track to the left.

The grass growing in the middle of the track didn't quite reach the underside of the Land Rover as Dixon bounced over the ruts, but it would have had the exhaust off Jane's car.

'I hope he's got a four wheel drive,' she said.

The track ended at a gravel turning circle, a large Volvo XC90 blocking the entrance to a courtyard beyond.

'There's your answer,' said Dixon. 'I'm guessing the XC stands for cross country.'

'No shit.'

'At least we know he's in.'

'Are you going to ask him about Savage?'

'In a roundabout, routine enquiries sort of way,' said Dixon. 'We're speaking to all Mr Renner's customers etcetera etcetera. All right?'

'He'll know we're here, anyway,' said Jane, without looking up. 'There's a camera on the wall above your head.'

They squeezed past the Volvo into a small courtyard where they were surrounded by a single storey barn conversion, probably old stables or a cowshed even. There were two front doors to choose from, each with its own letterbox, but lights behind only one of them. Dixon and Jane were walking towards it when it opened.

'Can I help you?'

'I hope so, Sir,' said Dixon, his arm outstretched, warrant card in hand. 'We're looking for Mr Simon Gregson.'

'That's me.' He looked like he'd just taken his dog for a walk: red corduroys with mud splattered up them, a navy pullover; he was even holding a dog's lead. Late thirties, possibly early forties, there was no grey to be seen in amongst the thick curly dark hair. The car may be on tick, but Dixon doubted the Rolex was.

'May we come in, Sir?'

'Er, yes.' Gregson stepped back. 'Look, what's this all about?'

'Just routine, Sir,' replied Dixon. 'We're investigating the disappearance of Jeremy Renner's daughter and we're speaking to all of his customers at the bank.'

'I heard about that. I hope she's all right.'

'We all do, Sir. We all do.'

'I was just having a cup of tea. Would you like one?'

'Thank you, Sir. That would be very nice.'

Dixon and Jane followed Gregson into the kitchen. He slammed the microwave door shut and set it going then flicked the kettle back on. 'I'm just doing Henry a bit of food too,' he said. Then he reached into a cupboard for two more mugs, placing them on the worktop next to the one with the teabag already sticking out of it. The elderly West

Highland terrier on the dog bed in the corner opened his eyes, looked at Dixon and then went back to sleep, his brown stained muzzle twitching.

'Hope you don't mind decaff,' said Gregson. 'It's all we've got.'

'That's fine,' said Jane.

'D'you live alone?' asked Dixon.

'No, my wife's gone into Bath for the day with a friend.' He rolled his eyes. 'Spending money we haven't got.' He dropped a teabag into each mug and then leaned back against the worktop, folding his arms.

'How long have you been a customer of Svenskabanken?' asked Dixon.

'Oh, six years or so. We switched when my father died and I took over.'

'Family business then, is it?'

'I'm the managing director and my wife and I own sixty per cent. My brothers have ten per cent each, then there's an aunt with ten and her two children each have five per cent. We only see them once a year at the AGM. We do get the odd phone call too, usually around dividend time.'

'And you're a vintners?'

'Commercial, trade only. Pubs and restaurants, hotels, anywhere with a drinks licence, really. We cover the whole of Avon and Somerset. A bit of Wiltshire too.'

'And is the business doing well?'

'Fine, yes. We're making a profit.'

'Only you rang Mr Renner six times last week so I was wondering whether some issue might have arisen?'

Gregson turned back to the kettle when it finished boiling and poured the tea.

'We're refinancing,' he said, placing the mugs on the table where Jane was sitting making notes. 'Sugar's there and I'll just get you some milk.'

'And what does refinancing involve?' asked Dixon.

'We've an overdraft we're moving to another bank. The interest rate is better. There's no hard feelings.' Gregson shrugged his shoulders. 'You have to shop around when you're running a business. Even the smallest difference in the interest rate can mean a lot of money.'

'And is Mr Renner helping you with that?'

'I wouldn't say helping – after all, we're leaving Svenska. I think he was hoping we'd stay with them, to be honest, but they can't match the terms we're being offered. It includes invoice finance too, and we're raising some capital to fund an expansion.'

'What's the current extent of your borrowing with Svenska?'

'Borrowing?'

'You said you had an overdraft, Sir.'

'Yes, there's a loan too. It's . . . er . . . four hundred and seventy thousand pounds in total. Just over, actually. It sounds a lot.'

'It does, Sir.'

'But it's manageable and we still turn a healthy profit, as I said.'

'It is secured?'

'They've got a floating charge over the company assets and personal guarantees from me and my wife.'

'And a mortgage?'

'On this place, you mean?'

Dixon nodded.

'Yes.'

'What about your premises?' Dixon was stirring his tea. 'In Trowbridge aren't they?'

'We lease a unit on the industrial estate.'

'How many staff d'you have?'

'Two in the office, two sales, and two in the warehouse. The rest are delivery drivers. Maybe six of them, so what's that?' Gregson nodded. 'Twelve or so, but it fluctuates.'

'Does the name Jeffrey Savage mean anything to you?'

Gregson turned away and emptied his mug into the sink. 'I don't keep a track of the drivers; some of them are agency staff at busy times too.'

'Only we pulled his body from Chew Valley Reservoir. You may have seen it on the news?'

Gregson rinsed his mug under the tap. 'No, I've not seen that.'

'He was a delivery driver for a vintners in Trowbridge until about a year ago.'

'Must be us,' said Gregson. 'There aren't any others. I can check, if you like?'

'That would be most helpful, Sir, if you don't mind.'

'It won't be until Monday now, I'm afraid.'

'That's fine, Sir.' Dixon drained his mug, walked over and put it on the sideboard, then he looked out of the kitchen window. 'Nice view,' he said. 'I hadn't appreciated you were on a hill. It's the high hedges in the lane.'

'It's why we bought it, really. We own the land between here and the road,' said Gregson. 'It's about ten acres in all.'

'And where's the road?'

'Down there, the other side of the cut.'

'The cut?'

'The old canal. Long since abandoned and derelict now, but you can still see the old locks in the trees. We've got three of them on our land.' Gregson was rinsing the mugs under the tap. 'It's the old Somerset Coal Canal.'

◆ ◆ ◆

'He wasn't too keen on us walking down here, was he?'

Dixon held open the five bar gate at the bottom of the paddock for Jane. 'He knew damn well that Savage was a driver too; although that might be understandable, I suppose, if the other staff haven't changed recently.'

Jane jumped over the mud on the other side of the gate on to a tuft of grass beyond. 'We should've changed into our wellies.'

'Is he still watching us?'

She glanced up at the house. 'He's in the kitchen window now.'

'This must be the path he was talking about,' said Dixon, ducking under the bare branches and stepping over a low barbed wire fence at the same time.

The path shelved away steeply through the trees down an embankment of bare earth covered in dead leaves, a line of puddles and a chicken wire fence at the bottom marking the old canal.

'I never knew there were coal mines in Somerset,' said Jane, as she slid down holding on to Dixon's arm.

'A bit before our time.'

Dixon was hanging on to a branch to steady himself as they teetered their way down the muddy track until it opened out into a small meadow at the bottom, tufts of thick grass growing almost up to the level of the 'Private: Keep Out' sign on the fence on the far side. They blinked in the bright sunlight as they emerged from the undergrowth and looked down at the line of the canal.

The ground shelved away to their left, thick stone walls either side of dark chasms in the ground marking the abandoned locks, the sun striking the top line of stone blocks poking out of the grass, recently cut by the looks of things.

'Someone's been out with a strimmer,' said Jane.

'The road must be beyond those trees.' Dixon was pointing to the embankment on the far side of the small meadow.

'You can hear the cars.' Jane was craning her neck. 'Just.'

Dixon headed for a gap in the fence and stood on the edge of the nearest lock, looking down into the void at his feet.

'Difficult to imagine this full of water with a canal boat going through it,' he muttered.

At the far end the thick wooden skeleton of an old lock gate was leaning over, still hanging from one hinge at the top, the panels long since rotted away.

'I'm surprised that's not gone for firewood before now.'

'The brambles must be holding it up,' said Jane, peering down at the dense vegetation in the bottom of the lock, a thin trickle of water just visible in the middle.

Dixon looked down the flight of locks, which followed the contours of the land like stone steps, taking the boats down the hill a few feet at a time – the sights, sounds and smell of the working canal replaced by a silence only broken by birdsong and the low hum of traffic in the distance.

He sighed. 'A stone wall, a big wooden gate, and a boy drowning.'

'The wizard?'

'A lock with no water in it and a horse covered in coal dust.'

'What does it mean?'

'A boy drowned in a lock, I suppose.'

'When?'

'Not recently, that's for sure.'

'And what's it got to do with Hatty?'

Dixon closed his eyes and breathed in through his nose. 'Can you smell burning coal?'

Chapter Thirty-One

'Someone's been cutting the grass,' said Dixon.

'That'll be the Somersetshire Coal Canal Restoration Society,' replied Gregson, holding the gate open for them at the top of the paddock. 'They want to restore it, as the name suggests.'

'And will they?'

'They've done bits of it near the junction with the Kennet and Avon, but down here there are too many different landowners to deal with and most of us don't want it opened up.' Gregson shrugged his shoulders. 'Would you?'

'Why not?'

'Hundreds of holidaymakers going past the end of your garden? No thanks.'

'Not in my backyard,' said Dixon, smiling.

'Exactly. And I'm not ashamed to admit it. It's my land and that's an end of it as far as I'm concerned.'

'When does the refinancing go through?'

'Next few days, I hope,' replied Gregson.

'And which bank are you moving to?'

'Er . . .' Gregson hesitated. 'It's not a done deal yet. I'm just waiting to hear from them.'

'Who?'

'I'd rather not say. Will you be contacting them?'

'No, Sir. It was just out of interest really,' replied Dixon, handing his car keys to Jane. 'It's not important.'

Gregson nodded. 'Well, if there's anything else I can help you with.'

'We'll let you know.'

'Which way now?' asked Jane, having safely negotiated the farm track.

'Express Park.' Dixon was holding his phone just under the roof of the Land Rover, moving it from side to side. 'Somewhere we get a signal would be good too.'

'What did you make of that?'

'The only thing I'm left wondering is why he wouldn't tell us the name of the bank he's moving to.'

'Maybe he was worried we'd contact them and it might put them off.'

'Possibly. Ah, at last.' Dixon flipped his phone sideways and opened a web browser. Then he typed in 'Somerset Coal Canal' and hit 'Search'. The first result came from the Somersetshire Coal Canal Society so he clicked on it to open coalcanal.org.

'"A ten mile long amenity corridor",' he said, reading aloud. 'That's their plan for it, and it's hardly at the end of his garden is it? Here we are: it was built to carry coal from the Paulton and Radstock coal fields.' He scrolled down. '"The drop of one hundred and thirty-five feet from Paulton to Dundas was concentrated in a lock flight at Combe Hay."'

'When was it opened?'

'It doesn't say. It closed in 1900, I can tell you that much,' replied Dixon, scrolling back up. '"Researching the history of the canal as an educational resource." Let's try that,' he said, clicking on the link. 'There's a PDF file,' he said.

'Open it.'

'There are lots of technical drawings.' Dixon frowned.

'Scroll down,' said Jane.

'By 1854, one hundred and sixty thousand tons a year.' Dixon shook his head, still flicking the screen with his index finger, scrolling down through the PDF file. 'I don't understand most of this. There's caisson locks and inclined planes, whatever the hell they – oh shit.'

'What is it?'

'There's a section here, "Death on the Canal." It's from the *Bath Chronicle*, October fourteenth, 1830. Listen to this. "Saturday afternoon, as a lad, engaged in a barge from Devizes, was winding the windlass to let the water through the locks, near Combhay, he lost his balance and fell in; he was not missed for a space of 4 or 5 minutes when, in apprehending some accident caused by his absence, the bargemen dragged the water and found the body with life extinct."'

'A drowning boy,' said Jane, raising her eyebrows.

'The bloody wizard must've seen this before.'

'You reckon?'

'Don't tell me you believe he had a vision?'

'He saw the castle and flowers.'

'He did.' Dixon sighed. 'All right, there's some significance to it. We just have to find out what it is.'

Dixon spent the rest of the journey back to Express Park reading the educational resource and felt like an authority on the Somersetshire Coal Canal by the time they arrived back at Express Park.

'If it ever comes up at a pub quiz, we'll be quids in,' he muttered.

It had been interesting, but the best he could come up with to answer the substantive question was that it was the third time that the Kennet and Avon Canal had come up in the investigation into Hatty's disappearance.

'Everything connects to the Kennet and Avon,' he said, as Jane drove up the ramp into the staff car park. 'Sonia kept her boat there and so did Savage. And now we find Gregson living on the Coal Canal.'

'You'll have to do better than that.'

'I know.'

Jane parked on the top floor and they were walking across to the back door when it flew open, Potter standing there waving a piece of paper at them.

'We've had a complaint,' she said.

'That was quick.' Dixon smiled. 'Who from?'

'Jeremy Renner.' Potter stood her ground, leaving Dixon and Jane standing in the drizzle that had started to fall. 'Says you've been pestering the bank's clients.'

'Only some of them.'

'What the hell are you playing at?'

'Trying to find his daughter.'

'And why does that involve his clients?'

'His daughter's been kidnapped and he goes into work.' Dixon scowled. 'Don't you think that a bit odd?'

'So, what do I tell him?'

Dixon was looking at the piece of paper in Potter's hand. 'What's that?' he asked.

'It's come over from Scientific. A handwritten note they got off the pad you took from the bank.'

'The pad was on Jeremy's desk, Ma'am,' said Jane.

'What does it say?' asked Dixon.

'Here, you take it,' said Potter, handing the piece of paper to Dixon. 'It's your "Get Out of Jail Free" card.' She smirked. 'And what's Markhams?'

He smiled at Jane. 'A vintners in Trowbridge.'

'Not the same one Savage worked for?' asked Potter.

'Yes, now can we come in out of the rain?'

Meeting room 2 was more crowded than usual, Potter sitting at the head of the table, with DCI Chard standing behind her.

'What've you got, Louise?' asked Dixon.

'They're—'

'Who's "they"?' snapped Chard.

'Mr and Mrs Renner, Sir,' replied Louise. 'They paid five hundred and fifty thousand for Old School House two years ago, according to the Land Registry, and they've got a mortgage with Svenskabanken. That's probably at preferential staff rates, but I can't tell how much is outstanding on it. I can't find any other loans and there's cash in the bank. Their credit score is good too.'

'What about directorships?' asked Dixon.

'None current for either of them, Sir, but she's got Polgen Communications Limited and Vectra Network Technologies Plc; both companies have since been wound up, though.'

'Do full company searches against both.'

'Yes, Sir.'

'What about their cars, Dave?'

'Nothing, Sir. The cars haven't moved except for Jeremy's trip to work, which we know about anyway.'

'And phone calls?' Dixon frowned. 'Someone must've rung him and told him we were looking at his customers.'

Harding shrugged his shoulders. 'Someone at the bank, I reckon. It was a Bristol landline number.'

Dixon sighed. 'What did you find out, Mark?'

'Not a lot, Sir. There are a few old press releases archived on some of the news sites mentioning Adele Poland and a release announcing that Jeremy is joining Svenskabanken. Even that's ten years ago now.' Pearce looked down at his notes. 'He's on LinkedIn, which you'd expect for a banker. I've printed off a list of who he's connected to.'

'Is there a Simon Gregson on the list?'

'Who's he?' asked Potter.

'The owner of Markhams, Ma'am,' replied Jane.

Pearce scanned down the list. 'Yes, he's here, Sir.'

Dixon nodded.

'And he's got an Instagram account,' continued Pearce, 'but it's mainly sailing photos. She's on Twitter with seven followers. Never tweeted, though.'

'Facebook?'

'Nothing, Sir.'

'Tell us about the handwritten note,' said Potter.

'It came from a pad of paper in Jeremy's office at the bank. In it,' said Dixon, 'Jeremy is ordering a junior colleague to withdraw a winding up petition scheduled for hearing in the Bristol District Registry of the High Court on Monday.'

'That's the day after tomorrow,' said Louise.

'The company in question is a vintners in Trowbridge, the same one Savage used to work for.'

'And the "or else" is killing Hatty, I suppose?' asked Chard.

'He went into the office for one reason – and one reason alone – to send this.' Dixon picked up the email with the transcribed handwritten note taken from the pad. '"Miriam. Please fax the court withdrawing the Markhams petition first thing Monday morning and text me to confirm you have done so. I will take full responsibility for this decision. Jeremy."'

'So, we know who's got her,' said Chard. 'What are we waiting for?'

'We don't know who's got her, or where she is,' snapped Dixon. 'All we have is the motive. If we wade in now and pick up Gregson, God alone knows what might happen to Hatty – and I sure as hell am not explaining to Roger that his granddaughter's dead because we fucked up.'

'Nick's right,' said Potter. 'We wait.'

'Gregson can't know we're on to him. When we've got Hatty then we pick him up, but not before.'

'How can we help?' asked Potter.

'A tail on Gregson would be useful, but it's a remote rural area so it's not going to be easy. Two cars pointing in different directions and a spotter hidden in the trees, ideally.'

'We're not the bloody SAS,' muttered Chard.

Potter ignored him. 'Just organise it.'

'Yes, Ma'am.'

'Phones too,' said Dixon. 'Dave?'

'Leave it with me.'

'We also need surveillance on the other shareholders in the vintners. Gregson's wife, two brothers, aunt and her two children. You never know, one of them may lead us straight to Hatty.'

'I can do a company search,' said Louise.

Potter nodded. 'I can authorise all of that.'

'I'm sorry if this sounds a bit dim, but what happens if the bank won't agree to withdraw the petition and the hearing goes ahead on Monday?' asked Jane.

Potter raised her eyebrows. 'The company gets wound up.'

'We need to find Hatty first,' said Dixon.

'At least we know she's alive,' said Louise.

'What happens now?' asked Potter.

'I'm just waiting for a copy of the winding up petition to arrive,' replied Dixon. 'Then I'm going back over to Catcott.'

'Be careful.' Potter frowned. 'He's already complained about you once.'

Chapter Thirty-Two

The front door opened as Dixon reached up for the bell.

'I was just leaving, Inspector,' said Ros Hicks, her voice raised. 'Would you like me to let them know you're here?'

'I think you just did.'

She stepped back to allow Dixon and Jane into the hall, then left, closing the door behind her.

'Any news?' Roger was striding across the living room towards them, his stubble almost a beard now; the same clothes too. Probably hasn't been home for days, thought Dixon.

Poor sod.

'Where's Geraldine?'

'Gone home.' Poland frowned. 'What's going on?'

Karen Marsden put her book down and got up from the dining room table. 'Anything I can do, Sir?' she asked.

'The journalists have reappeared outside in the lane. Get someone to move them on, will you?'

'Yes, Sir.'

'And show Dr Poland out,' said Dixon. 'It may be better if you went home too, Roger.'

'Why?' Poland was rubbing the back of his neck.

'You'll just have to trust me, Roger.'

Jeremy and Adele were sitting on the sofa with their backs to the door, both of them looking over their shoulders.

'I do,' muttered Poland.

Dixon's eyes widened. 'This might get a bit—'

'I don't care. I'm staying. I want to hear it. Whatever it is.'

Jeremy stood up, nudged by Adele. 'What are you doing here?' he asked. 'I spoke to DCS Potter and she said—'

'What d'you mean, you "spoke to DCS Potter"?' snapped Poland.

'There have been some developments, Sir,' said Dixon.

Jane sat down at the dining table and took out her notebook.

'What developments?' Jeremy glanced at Adele, then back to Dixon.

'Sit down, Sir.' Dixon walked around the front of the sofa and stood with his back to the wood burner. 'Now.'

Jeremy sat down next to Adele and took her hand, both of them staring at the rug on the floor in front of them.

'When did they make contact with you?' asked Dixon.

Silence.

Dixon waited. He glanced at Karen, who shook her head.

'Who?' asked Poland, hands on his hips. 'Will someone please tell me what is going on?'

'I'm hoping someone will tell me, Roger.' Dixon was looking down at Jeremy and Adele. 'All right then, I'll tell you.' He slid a piece of paper out of his jacket pocket and unfolded it. 'This is a transcript of a handwritten note lifted from a pad of paper. I get it. I do. If someone had my daughter and told me they'd kill her if I contacted the police, I'd do what they said. Really.'

'So would anyone,' said Jane.

Adele leaned forwards over her knees, her shoulders heaving. Jeremy started rubbing her back.

'"Miriam."' Dixon was reading from the note. '"Please fax the court withdrawing the Markhams petition first thing Monday morning and text me to confirm you have done so. I will take full respons—"'

'All right, all right.' Jeremy stood up.

Adele was sobbing uncontrollably now.

'You know who's got Hatty?' asked Poland.

Dixon nodded.

'And so do you?' Poland glared at Jeremy.

'We do, Dad,' gasped Adele. 'We both do.'

Poland shook his head. 'Who the hell are Markhams?'

'They're a vintners in Trowbridge, Roger,' said Dixon. 'The same one that Savage worked for. I've got the winding up petition here.' He unfolded another piece of paper. '"The petition of Svenskabanken AB. Company subject to the petition; Markhams South West Limited. The grounds on which a winding up order is sought is that the Debtor is indebted to the Petitioner in the sum of four hundred and seventy-one thousand, five hundred and twelve pounds and seventeen pence. A statutory demand was served on the company on—"'

'Enough,' snapped Jeremy.

Adele lit a cigarette.

'"For the reasons stated in the statement of truth of Jeremy Renner filed in support . . . "' Dixon turned over the page. '"This petition . . . will be heard at Bristol District Registry of the High Court on Monday—"'

'Enough, I said.'

'Where is Hatty then?' asked Poland.

'We don't know,' replied Dixon. 'We know who's behind it but not who's got her or where she is. Yet.'

'How did you find out?' asked Jeremy.

'You went to work, which seemed a bit . . . odd, so – as you know – we followed you there.' Dixon frowned. 'Then we made a few routine enquiries. We spoke to Malcolm Clarke, who sends his best wishes. And Simon Gregson.'

'Oh God, not Simon.'

'That was before we saw the winding up petition. He rang six times to speak to you last week. Unusual that, in the circumstances, wouldn't you say?' Dixon raised his eyebrows. 'Or maybe he was just behaving normally, or trying to make it look like he was behaving normally.'

'Did he suspect anything?'

'We told him it was just routine enquiries. He has no idea we're on to him or that we're watching his house.'

'He'd better not.'

'He seems to think he's refinancing?' Dixon frowned. 'Any day now, apparently.'

Jeremy shook his head. 'It's not happening. No other bank will touch him.'

'But he says he's making a tidy profit. If that's true, why are you winding up the company?'

'Profit? Three or four years ago maybe, but not since then. His losses are growing each month and his overdraft's just getting bigger and bigger. His gross profit's hardly covering the interest now.'

'Why?'

Jeremy sighed. 'Pubs are closing, people's drinking habits are changing and his income's falling every month. He was breaking even a couple of years ago, but not since then; and the longer we leave it, the bigger the debt. His assets will just about cover it now, but not for much longer.'

'And the bank has a floating charge over the company assets so you can step in and take everything?'

'There isn't much. The vans are leased and the unit is rented. There's just the stock.' Jeremy shrugged his shoulders. 'We have the personal guarantees, too – although there's a mortgage of over three hundred thousand on his house to take into account.'

'Which means you get his house too?' asked Dixon.

'It'll be sold.'

'And the land?'

Jeremy nodded.

Poland pulled a chair out from under the dining table opposite Jane and slumped down on to it. 'More than enough motive, I'd have thought,' he muttered.

Adele looked up, her eyes full of tears. 'But he's got no idea you're on to him?'

'None at all. It was just routine: we're speaking to all Mr Renner's customers; that sort of thing,' replied Dixon. He turned to Jeremy. 'So all that stuff about refinancing any day now was bollocks?'

'Yes.'

'And will he go bankrupt?'

'I can't see how he can avoid it.'

'I can,' said Poland. 'Kidnap your daughter and get you to withdraw the court case.'

'How many people will lose their jobs?' asked Dixon.

'There are twelve employees, plus Simon and his wife too, I suppose.'

'Is it your decision?'

'Simon thinks it is, but it isn't. Decisions like that are taken by the board.'

'And you saw no sign of Hatty when you went to his house?' asked Poland.

'None at all,' replied Jane.

'How did you meet him?' Dixon turned back to Jeremy.

Adele stood up, turned her back on him and walked over to the patio window, blowing her smoke out into the garden.

'He was introduced to me at a business networking event. Said he knew . . .' Jeremy's voice tailed off.

'Hang on a minute.' Poland jumped up. 'Simon Gregson? Wasn't he an ex-boyfriend?'

Adele stepped out into the rain.

Dixon spun round and snatched a photograph off the bookshelves behind him. He nodded. 'The champagne bar at Paddington station,' he muttered. Five smiling faces, two of whom he now recognised: Adele and Simon Gregson.

'Is it him?' asked Poland.

Dixon nodded, as he walked over and handed the photograph to Jane.

'Yes, it's him,' she said.

'So, your ex-boyfriend has kidnapped your daughter.' Poland clenched his teeth. 'My granddaughter.'

'And killed the man who organised the kidnap of Alesha,' said Dixon.

'Do we know Simon killed him?' asked Jeremy.

'No, we don't,' replied Dixon, 'but the two events are connected.'

'Get in here now,' shouted Poland.

Adele appeared in the doorway. She dropped her cigarette on the patio and stubbed it out with the toe of her shoe, before stepping inside. Poland slammed the door behind her, then locked it.

'We don't want the whole bloody village knowing our business,' he muttered.

'When did he contact you?' asked Dixon, watching Adele sitting down on the sofa, the tears gone.

'The night before last. There was a note on the doormat.'

'Pushed through the bloody letterbox?'

Dixon glared at Poland.

'All right,' he said, returning to his seat at the dining table.

'Where is this note?'

Adele looked at Jeremy and nodded. He walked over to the shelves, opened a large hardback book and took out an envelope. He handed it to Dixon, who had put on a pair of latex gloves.

'There's a photograph of her in there,' he said.

'A photograph?' Poland jumped up. 'Let me see it.'

'She's holding Thursday's *Western Daily Press*,' mumbled Adele.

Dixon opened the envelope and looked first at the note. It was short and to the point: 'Wind up the company and she dies. Tell the police and she dies. Withdraw the petition and you get her back in one piece. Try anything and you get her back piece by piece. Issue another petition and we will be back for her. And you.'

He looked at the photograph, taken on a phone and printed on an inkjet printer. Hatty was looking at the camera, her eyes red and wide – pleading – the mark of a gag recently removed across her mouth. She was holding a newspaper in her left hand, her right tied to the arm of the chair she was sitting on.

'How many people have touched this?'

'Just me and Adele.'

'And Mum.'

'She knows?' Poland sighed. 'Why the bloody hell didn't you tell me?'

'Because you'd have told *him*,' said Jeremy, pointing at Dixon. 'And we couldn't risk that. It was my decision, Roger.'

Jane held open an evidence bag that she had taken from her handbag and Dixon dropped the note and envelope into it. He held the photograph in front of Poland, before dropping it into the bag, watching a tear appear in the corner of Poland's eye.

'Start at the beginning,' he said, sitting down on the arm of the sofa. 'And tell me everything.'

Adele sighed. 'We met at university.'

'I knew it,' muttered Poland.

'I was doing business studies and he was doing computer sciences. We were friends and . . .'

'A couple,' said Jeremy, his voice dripping with sarcasm. 'Why don't you just admit you were a couple and be done with it?'

'We were a couple.' Adele smirked. 'Happy now?'

'How long for?'

'We split up two years after we left, I suppose. But we kept in touch and he asked for my help when he was starting Anytimenow. He wanted me to form a company and organise some funding, which I did.'

'That's Polgen Communications Limited?' asked Dixon, glancing across at Jane scribbling in her notebook.

'Yes. The product was called Anytimenow. It was an internet based email, calendar and document storage website. It sounds old hat now but you have to remember this was nearly twenty years ago. We were the first company in the world to get email working on a mobile phone via the old Wireless Application Protocol.' Adele shrugged her shoulders. 'I can't pretend to understand the tech side of it, really; that was Simon's bag. I just dealt with the business end.'

'Who are the others in this photo?' asked Dixon, handing her the framed photograph from the champagne bar.

'That's me and Simon. That's Liang on the end. He'd come over from Hong Kong for the meeting.' She pointed to another smiling face. 'That one's Bill Luhrmann. He was over from Canada. And the last one's Paul Goggins. He was our solicitor.'

'Were there any others?'

'A couple of techies. It was all done remotely. That was the first time I'd met Liang and Bill, and I've never seen them since either.'

'And what were you celebrating?'

'We'd just sold the company.' Adele shook her head. 'I was a millionaire on paper for a while.'

'What exactly did you do for the company?' asked Dixon.

'I formed it and then got seed funding from a group of angel investors based in Wells, of all places. The internet bubble was inflating fast at that time and investors were throwing money at you, even if your company wasn't making a bean. There were some ridiculous valuations doing the rounds. We got seventy grand to get us going and that cost us ten per cent.'

'Then what happened?'

'Simon and the techies set about building the product and I tried to get some clients. The idea was to let other companies put their own brand on it and offer it to their customers. Nokia were looking at embedding it on their phones too and we had several meetings in Finland. Then we did a second round of funding in 1999 and that's when it got really exciting.'

'How much?'

'We got another two hundred and fifty thousand for twenty per cent, but it brought with it the Engine Room, a corporate finance specialist – called themselves an "accelerator" – retained by the venture capitalist. Their job was to put together an exit, either a trade sale or float us on the stock exchange.'

'Is this making any sense to you?' asked Jeremy, frowning at Dixon.

'He's a solicitor,' said Poland.

'Oh, sorry.'

'Who was the venture capitalist?'

'Sajeed Sohail. He was based in New York. Never met him.'

'And did the Engine Room put together an exit?'

Adele nodded. 'They did. They merged several small tech businesses like ours into a shell company listed on the Alternative Investment Market. Then the idea was to raise some more money on the stock exchange – only it didn't work out quite like that.' She hesitated.

'Just tell him,' said Jeremy.

'They got an empty shell listed on AIM – Vectra Network Technologies Plc, it was called – and we sold out to it for just under eleven million in shares. No money changed hands. We just got shares to the value of eleven million quid. Then, just as we were raising money on the stock exchange, the bubble burst and investors started moving away from internet companies, so we didn't get the cash.'

'And that left you owning shares in a company worth nothing?' asked Dixon.

'Exactly.' Adele sighed. 'Not only that, but we couldn't sell them for two years because we were founding directors. When we finally sold them we got enough for—'

'A round of drinks,' sneered Jeremy.

Adele glared at him. 'It was like sticking a pin in a balloon. I resigned as a director and that was that. I went back to what I'd been doing before.'

'Which was?'

'Training to be an accountant.'

'And then we met,' said Jeremy.

'And when was the last time you saw Simon Gregson?'

Adele hesitated. 'Just after it all collapsed.'

'Just tell him,' said Jeremy.

Poland sat up.

'About six years ago, longer maybe,' said Adele, her eyes closed. 'It wasn't long after Hatty started nursery, possibly.'

'After?' Poland shook his head.

'Yes, Dad, after. And nothing happened. It wasn't like that.'

Poland raised his eyebrows.

'Anyway, I'd just gone back to work part time,' continued Adele. 'His father had died and he'd taken over the wine business. He said he wanted some advice, so I met him for lunch. I think it was just an excuse, really.'

'What did happen, then?' asked Dixon.

'Nothing. When he found out I was with Jeremy I never heard from him again.'

'But he used the connection to move to Svenskabanken?'

Jeremy nodded. 'And we gave him a good deal to move too. At that time, the business was flying.'

'And now he's got your daughter.' Dixon was sucking his teeth.

'He won't do anything to her,' said Adele. 'I'm sure he won't.'

'Poland's got a lot to answer for,' muttered Dixon.

'That's what the other girl and her bloody grandmother said.' Poland stood up and peered through a gap in the curtains.

'What does it mean, Adele?' asked Dixon. 'What have you got to answer for?'

Adele lit another cigarette, leaned over, picked up an ashtray off the floor and placed it on the arm of the sofa.

'It sounds to me like you have nothing to answer for,' continued Dixon. 'Unless it was your decision to sell to Vectra Network Technologies?'

'No.' She took a long drag, blowing the smoke out through her nose. 'That was unanimous. We all agreed. Even the small shareholders.'

'What have you got to answer for then?'

Jeremy tipped his head to one side and frowned at Adele.

'I can guarantee you,' said Poland, 'whatever it is, it's going to come out – so you might just as well spit it out now.'

She sighed. 'I'm not even sure it's relevant.'

'You let *him* be the judge of that,' said Jeremy, jabbing his finger at Dixon.

'D'you know what it is, Sir?'

'If I did, I'd tell you.'

'All right, all right.' Adele shook her head. 'The corporate financier at the Engine Room, Sid Farooq, came down to Combe Hay for a meeting at Simon's place after we sold to Vectra and before the fundraising on the stock exchange. He said there were material non-disclosures in the sale of Polgen to Vectra and demanded that we give up a chunk of shares or he'd sue. That would mean the fundraising couldn't go ahead either.'

'What happened?'

'I told him to get stuffed. We'd rather burn the whole bloody thing down than do that. And if there really were any material non-disclosures, he should put them in writing and I'd get our lawyers to look at it.'

'So, you called his bluff?'

'I did. His little scam had worked with the other companies going into the scheme. They'd had family members and everybody relinquishing shares, but I told him no way. Anyway, I got up and walked out of the meeting. And that was the last time I, or anyone else for that matter, saw Sid Farooq.'

'What happened to him?' asked Jeremy.

Adele shook her head. 'I've no idea. There was a police investigation, but nothing came of it. I had to give a statement.'

'Who else was at the meeting?' Dixon stood up and walked over to the wood burner.

'Just me and Simon. He said that Farooq had left in a taxi not long after me.'

'And why should you have to answer for that?'

'Simon blamed the failure of the fundraising on the publicity. It was a murder investigation and he was a suspect. He said we should've just handed over the shares and got on with it.' Adele shrugged her shoulders. 'It was all my fault, apparently.'

'We'd better have the file out, Jane,' said Dixon.

She got up and walked into the kitchen with her phone clamped to her ear.

'What happens now?' asked Poland.

'We've got Gregson and the other shareholders in Markhams under surveillance, so one of them may lead us to Hatty. Then there's Polgen. We'll see if Scientific can get anything off the note too. But you must let us know if any further contact is made. Immediately.'

'We will,' replied Jeremy.

'What about the hearing on Monday?' asked Adele.

'We can look at that on Monday morning,' said Dixon. 'If needs be we can get the directors to withdraw it. After all, they can always issue another winding up petition later.'

'He won't hurt Hatty.' Adele shook her head.

Jeremy grimaced. 'A man is dead, for fuck's sake.'

'Two,' muttered Dixon.

'What d'you mean?' asked Poland.

'Sid Farooq.'

Chapter Thirty-Three

'Hatty first, Roger.'

Poland nodded. He was leaning on the door of Dixon's Land Rover, watching him putting on his seatbelt. He slammed the door and Dixon wound down the window.

'And if we can't find her by Monday we get the petition withdrawn and see if they release her.'

'I'm not holding my breath.'

'Me neither.'

'D'you think Gregson's got her?'

'No.' Dixon switched on the engine. 'But he's behind it.'

'I met him a couple of times, years ago. He seemed a nice lad.' Poland sighed. 'What can I do?'

'Keep your phone on and your fingers crossed.'

'All right.'

Dixon accelerated along Old School Lane.

'Poor bugger's going round the bend,' said Jane, watching Poland in the wing mirror as he trudged back across the lane to the house. 'What now?'

'Back to Express Park.'

The Incident Room was deserted apart from Dave Harding, Mark Pearce and Louise, sitting at workstations at the front, near the whiteboards.

'Where is everybody?' asked Jane.

'Some have gone home, the rest are on surveillance duties,' replied Louise. 'We're watching Gregson and the other shareholders in Markhams.'

'Phone records?'

'On their way,' replied Pearce.

'Here's what I've been able to find,' said Louise, handing Dixon a bundle of papers. 'You've got a full company search, plus accounts and whatever else I could get from Companies House. Svenskabanken have provided copies of the stuff they've got too.'

'That'll be the third time Price has gone in today.'

'Funnily enough, he did say something along those lines.' Louise shrugged her shoulders. 'A couple of times.'

'What did you find on Polgen and Vectra?'

'You can still find Polgen on the Companies House website under "dissolved companies". It was a voluntary dissolution in 2003. Vectra Network Tech is still current and listed on the Alternative Investment Market, although it's changed its name to Erbeum Plc and doesn't seem to have any assets.'

'What about past directors?'

'Adele is there. She resigned on twenty-fourth of July 2001. Simon Gregson is listed too.'

Dixon smiled.

'I printed off everything I could find on both,' continued Louise, handing Dixon a folder over an inch thick. 'Cost a few quid on the Companies House website too.'

'Any sign of Lucy?' asked Jane.

'Cole was going to drop her at the Red Cow. That was an hour or so ago maybe.'

'The night before last, Dave,' said Dixon, 'a note was pushed through the letterbox at the Renners' place in Catcott. Check the nearest traffic cameras and see if any cars on your watch list show up around that time.'

'What time?'

'Early evening.'

'Yes, Sir.'

'Give me a few minutes to flick through this stuff then, Jane, and I'll drop you home.'

She sat down on the corner of Louise's workstation and folded her arms. 'What are you looking at?' she asked, as Dixon thumbed through the pile of papers.

'Just the shareholders for now,' he replied. 'Here, Lou, look. One of the shareholders in Polgen is listed as Bluewater Nominees Limited at an address in Wells. That'll be the first round of funding they got.'

'Leave it with me,' she said.

'And I need a complete list of all Markhams employees in the last five years.'

'Where am I going to get that at this time on a Saturday?'

'HM Revenue and Customs have an emergency number. I'll be back in an hour.' Dixon tucked the papers under his arm. 'Where's Potter?'

'She had to go back to Portishead for a meeting with the Chief Constable. She said she was going to ring you.'

'Well, she hasn't.'

'Aren't you going to ring her?' asked Jane, following Dixon as he hurried towards the stairs.

'No bloody fear.'

'You'd better have something to eat while you're here,' said Jane, holding open the door of the pub. 'You can't keep going on fruit pastilles.'

'Fish and chips then.'

'She's by the fire,' said Rob, pushing a glass under the gin optic at the first sight of Jane.

'Has she eaten?'

'Not yet.'

Jane leaned around the pillar and shouted across to Lucy. 'Fish and chips all right with you?'

'Whatever.'

'Three lots, by the sounds of things,' muttered Dixon, reaching for his wallet.

'How's it going?' asked Rob.

'We're getting there.'

'Someone said you'd found the first girl?'

'Who?'

'Just someone at the bar. Last night I think it was. News travels fast.'

Dixon frowned. 'Well, it bloody shouldn't. There's a news blackout, or supposed to be.'

'Sorry.'

'It's not your fault.'

'Who found her?' asked Rob.

'He did,' said Jane, nodding at Dixon.

'Just keep it under your hat, will you? The fewer people who know about it the better, for the sake of the second girl.'

Rob nodded. 'I'll bring your food through.'

'How was your day?' asked Jane, sitting down next to Lucy.

'Cold.'

'Find anything?'

'Nobody did.' Lucy glanced across at Dixon, sitting in the corner, thumbing through a thick wad of paper. 'What about you?'

'We're getting closer,' replied Jane. 'I think.' She shrugged her shoulders. 'You won't get a word out of him when he's like this. He goes to another place.'

'Where?'

'Buggered if I know.' Jane smiled. 'Don't think he does either, but when he comes back he's got the answer more often than not.'

'Weird.' Lucy grimaced, her voice a whisper. 'And you want to marry him?'

'I heard that,' muttered Dixon.

Jane's eyes widened, glaring at Lucy. 'What time's Dave picking you up tomorrow?'

'He said he'd be here about lunchtime.'

Jane nodded.

'When this is over,' said Dixon, looking up, 'we'll be going back to the Lakes to finish our holiday. You should come.'

'Really?' said Lucy.

'Why not?'

'Are there any nightclubs?'

'Mountains,' muttered Jane. 'Lots of them. And lakes.'

'Does that mean you're getting married?' asked Lucy, turning to Jane. 'Don't forget, you said I could be your bridesmaid if I passed my exams.'

'Did she now?' Dixon smiled. 'Did she really?'

Jane blushed.

'Two fish and chips,' said Rob, appearing behind them. 'I'll just go and get the other. Any sauces?'

Dixon left Jane and Lucy in the pub and raced back to Express Park with Monty in the back of the Land Rover, more in hope than expectation of a chance to give him a run somewhere.

'Potter's been on again,' said Louise, as Dixon appeared at the top of the stairs. 'She said your mobile must be switched off or something.'

'I was driving.'

'Yeah, right.' Louise grinned. 'Anyway, she wants you at a meeting with the Chief Constable.'

'When?'

Louise looked at her watch. 'Twenty minutes.'

'What did you find on Bluewater Nominees?'

'Here's everything I could get off the Companies House website.' She handed Dixon another bundle of documents. 'I've stapled each document separately.'

'Anything leap out at you?'

'There are four shareholders. Are we going to speak to them?'

'We can't just go wading in rattling cages. We need to find Hatty first.' Dixon shook his head. 'Anything else?'

'Savage's post mortem report is in your email.'

'Well?'

'Dead before he went into the water,' continued Louise. 'But, it's the comments about the murder weapon that are interesting.'

'Have they found it?'

'No.'

'Can you print me off a copy?'

'Give me a minute.' Louise pointed to a printer on the far side of the room. 'It'll be on that end one in a sec. Did you find anything in the other stuff I downloaded?'

'Not really. Simon Gregson is the only one who was a shareholder in both Polgen and Markhams. I need to go through it again.' Dixon was standing by the printer, watching the paper churn out.

'D'you want the photos?'

'No, thanks. What about the employees?'

'No luck so far,' replied Louise. 'It's the weekend and we may have to wait until Monday. A couple of them are listed on their website. The sales team are named and so is the office administrator and credit controller. None of them known to police. That just leaves the warehouse staff and the drivers.'

Dixon sighed. 'Check and see if any of their vans have been involved in an accident in the last five years. The police accident report will name the driver, won't it?'

'It will.' Louise nodded. 'It's a long shot, but . . .'

'Try their motor insurers too. The drivers may be named on the policy.'

'Will do.'

'Did SOCO get anything off the note?'

'We won't know until the morning.'

'I'll be in the canteen if Potter rings again.'

Louise frowned. 'It's closed.'

'Where are you?'

Dixon winced. His phone had been buzzing on the table for several minutes before he finally succumbed to temptation.

'Driving.'

'I wanted you up here for a meeting with the Chief Constable. It's going on now and he was expecting you.' Potter sighed down the phone. 'What do I tell him?'

'Tell him we know who's behind the kidnap of Hatty and why. You've seen the note?'

'A copy of it.'

'Ask him to speak personally to the directors of Svenskabanken and get them to agree the withdrawal of the winding up petition on Monday, if we don't find her first.'

'And will you?'

'We're going to have to. Word's got out that we've found Alesha and if that gets back to whoever's got Hatty, God knows what they'll do.'

'How the hell did that happen?'

'I don't know, but it's only a matter of time before it's all over the internet.'

'He wants to know how long we keep up this level of surveillance. It's the overtime bill, if nothing else.'

Dixon had missed a few meetings in his time, usually when being there would have been far worse than the consequences of absenting himself. This was one of them.

Git.

'Tell him as long as it bloody well takes and if he pulls the plug, he can explain it to Roger.'

'That's what I was going to say, in a roundabout sort of way.' Potter hesitated. 'How close are we then? I mean really.'

'We're on the right track; that's the best I can say for now. It's not helping that it's a weekend.'

'Whatever you need . . .'

'Thanks.'

Dixon rang off and turned back to the documents in front of him. The canteen was deserted and he had pushed several tables together, the documents spread over them all in a multitude of different piles.

Something in amongst them was significant. He knew that. But what it was and when he had seen it wouldn't come, no matter how many times he shuffled them around. Nothing for it but to start at the beginning. Again.

He was halfway through the Polgen documents when Louise appeared in the doorway holding up a plastic document wallet.

'You were right,' she said. 'Three years ago, a rear end shunt in Somerton. Here's the accident report. A guy named Anthony Steiner was driving a Markhams van. He hit the back of a . . .' Louise was watching Dixon.

He closed his eyes and took a deep breath through his nose, puffing out his cheeks when he exhaled. Then he stood up, walked around to the far corner of the tables and picked up a pile of documents.

'Are Mark and Dave still here?' he asked, flicking through the bundle.

Louise nodded. 'They wouldn't go home.'

'Better get them.' Dixon slid a document out of the bundle and dropped the rest back on the table. 'Anthony Kurt Steiner. An employee of Markhams, previously a shareholder in Polgen. What d'you make of that, Lou?'

'I'll go and get Dave and Mark.'

Dixon looked up, his jaw clenched. 'It's going to be a long night.'

Chapter Thirty-Four

Dixon switched off the engine and listened to the chime of the church bells: ten, eleven, twelve. He looked up at Old School House, lights still on, but then he had expected that.

The front door opened as he walked across the road, the growl of his diesel engine and the slam of the Land Rover door alerting Poland, who was standing in the doorway, his large frame silhouetted in the shaft of light from the hall, the light glinting on the glass in his hand.

'What is it?' he asked.

'Where's Adele?'

'She took a sleeping pill and went to bed.'

'Get her up.'

'She's not going to be in a fit state.'

'She'll have to be.'

'What is it?'

Dixon looked up at the sound of footsteps on the galleried landing above his head. Jeremy was leaning over the balustrade, naked apart from his underpants.

'What's going on?'

'I need to speak to Adele.'

'She's taken a—'

'Get her up.'

'I'll put some coffee on,' said Roger, disappearing into the kitchen.

'Has he found Hatty?' Adele's voice was low and slurred.

'I don't know,' replied Jeremy, their voices carrying down the stairs over the sound of the kettle. 'Have you found Hatty?' asked Jeremy, peering over the balustrade.

Dixon shook his head.

'No, he hasn't, Adele.' A bout of coughing. 'Here, drink this.' Then they appeared at the top of the stairs, Adele wearing a blue bathrobe that was far too big for her. Jeremy's probably.

She was holding the banister with both hands as she teetered down the stairs. 'What is it?'

Dixon waited until she slumped down on to the sofa.

'Look, is this important?' asked Jeremy, pulling a T-shirt over his head.

'He's hardly going to be turning up at this time of night if it isn't, is he?' snapped Poland, handing Adele a mug of black coffee.

Dixon sat down on the arm of the sofa, watching Adele take a sip from the mug. Then she handed it to Jeremy.

'Tell me about Anthony Steiner,' said Dixon.

Adele blinked and then turned her head slowly. 'Tony?' she asked.

Dixon nodded.

'I never met him. He was a friend of Simon's. He had a text messaging system that we integrated into Anytimenow at the start. Simon gave him some shares in return. Five per cent, or something like that, but then we dropped it when the mobile phone companies started offering free texts anyway. After that he was just one of the minority shareholders. Why?'

'Where did he live?'

'Near Midford, I think.'

'And how far's that from Combe Hay?'

'A couple of miles, I don't know.'

'What happened to his text messaging system?'

'He had to shut it down.' Adele shook her head. 'Last I heard he had a gardening website. He was a techie, really, so it was one computer project after another, I suppose.'

Dixon leaned forwards. 'When did you find out they'd killed Sid Farooq?'

'I didn't!' Adele sat bolt upright.

Dixon stared at her, until she looked away and reached up for the mug of coffee with both hands.

'Where did they bury the body?'

'I don't know.'

'But you knew they killed him?'

'No!' She was shaking now, tears streaming down her cheeks.

'That's enough!' shouted Poland.

'When I left that meeting he was alive and sitting in Simon's living room.'

'And Simon never told you what happened?'

Silence.

'Never confided in you?'

'No.'

Dixon nodded. He got up and stood with his back to the wood burner. 'When was the last time you saw Steiner?'

'I told you, I never met him.'

Adele leaned back and closed her eyes.

'She's telling the truth,' muttered Dixon.

'Of course she is,' snapped Poland. 'You're supposed to be putting my family back together, not tearing it apart.'

'I'm supposed to be finding Hatty, Roger.'

Poland turned away.

'Who is Steiner?' asked Jeremy.

'His business was shut down, Adele was right about that. Trading whilst insolvent. Then he finally went bankrupt when he went to prison for five years.'

'What for?'

'Fraud. Every type of online scam imaginable. He's industrious, I'll give him that. Millions, he took, but it was all confiscated. He was banned from using the internet as a condition of his parole, so he pops up working as a driver for Markhams. Gregson gave him a job when he got out.'

'Why?'

'You tell me,' said Dixon. 'Maybe he owes him?'

'What for?'

'Killing Farooq, or helping him dispose of the body perhaps. There's a lot of guesswork in here, but if Farooq ever left Combe Hay I'd be very surprised. It'd take Steiner, what, twenty minutes to get there from Midford along the line of the old canal?'

'But why would Steiner kill Farooq?'

'His text message business is failing and Farooq is demanding he hand over some of his shares in Polgen. Five per cent of eleven million quid is a sod of a lot of money.'

Poland nodded. 'A powerful motive.'

'So, you think Steiner's got Hatty?' asked Jeremy.

'I do.'

'Why?'

'If Markhams goes bust he'll lose his job and with his past he's unlikely to get another. Gregson may have paid him too – but they're partners in crime already, if I'm right about Farooq.'

'Find him,' said Poland.

'We will, Roger. We will.'

'He's a named driver on the Markhams motor insurance policy, Sir,' said Louise, when Dixon appeared at the top of the stairs in the Incident Room at Express Park, Monty running along in front of him. 'It's current so it means he must still be working there.'

Dixon nodded. 'Anything else?'

'He's got a Honda CRV, according to DVLA,' said Harding. 'You know, the small four wheel drive thing.'

'Cameras?'

'I'm checking that now.'

'What about a mobile phone?'

'Just waiting on that now, Sir,' replied Pearce.

'We'd better get his medical records too.'

'It's gone one on a Sunday morning, Sir,' said Louise.

'I know that.' Dixon was pacing up and down in front of the whiteboard. 'What about the banks?'

'The requests have gone in but we won't get anything until Monday now,' said Pearce.

'What did Adele have to say?' asked Louise.

'Not a lot,' replied Dixon. 'She never met him, but she was quite clear she never knew what became of Farooq.'

'I reckon it'd take twenty minutes tops from Midford to Gregson's place, that's running along the line of the old canal,' said Harding. 'It can't be more than two miles.'

'What about the place in Midford?'

'Changed hands several times since he lived there, according to the Land Registry website,' replied Louise.

'And now for the big question.' Dixon took a deep breath. 'Do we have a current address for him?'

Louise smiled, held up a piece of paper and waved it. 'Number twelve Paulton Terrace, Radstock. He's on the electoral roll, would you believe it?'

'That matches the address I got off DVLA,' said Harding.

'It's registered for multiple occupation so he's unlikely to have Hatty there, I'd have thought.' Louise shrugged her shoulders.

'Let's go and kick the door in anyway,' said Dixon. 'Better rustle up some armed response for backup, just in case.'

Chapter Thirty-Five

The streetlights were off when they turned into Paulton Terrace just after 2 a.m., a flashing blue light at the far end and a set of headlights penetrating the darkness. The patrol car was parked on the nearside, the only light coming from a house opposite. Light sleepers, thought Dixon.

'Talk about announcing your bloody arrival,' said Harding, sitting in the back of Dixon's Land Rover. 'I suppose we should be grateful they haven't got their siren on.'

'They don't look like Armed Response either,' said Louise.

Dixon pulled up alongside the patrol car and Louise wound down the window. 'Where's Armed Response?' she asked.

'I sent them home,' said the officer sitting in the passenger seat of the patrol car.

'Why?'

'You'll see.'

Dixon parked behind it, climbed out of his Land Rover and looked around. Then the smell hit him. The familiar smell.

'That's burning,' said Pearce. 'Can you smell it?'

'Me too,' said Louise.

'Over here,' said the uniformed officer, shining a lamp along the pavement. They followed him, Dixon glancing up at the houses on either side set back from the road behind iron railings, cars parked on both sides. Three or four storeys – he couldn't see in the darkness – steps down to a basement and another set up to a front door.

Then they arrived at a gap in the parked cars marked off by police cones and blue tape, the smell stronger now.

'There's number twelve,' said the officer, shining his lamp up at the house. 'We've had to evacuate the ones either side too. The engineers can't get here until tomorrow – later today, I mean.'

The glass in the bay windows had blown out and was strewn across the road, small shards glinting in the torch light.

'We swept up, but there's still a lot of glass around.'

'Did everyone get out?' asked Dixon, clenching his fists.

'Are you all right, Sir?' asked Louise, watching the beads of sweat on his forehead in the flickering torchlight.

He nodded.

'Thanks to the fire brigade. One's in hospital with smoke inhalation,' said the officer.

'How many people lived here?'

'Seven, but only three were in at the time. We've traced them all except one.'

'Anthony Steiner?'

'How could you know that?'

'What about the cause?' asked Harding.

'There were traces of accelerant in the kitchen and a first floor back bedroom so the preliminary finding is arson; that's to be confirmed when they can have a proper look. Engineers have to declare it safe first.'

Dixon ducked under the blue tape across a gap in the railings.

'You can't go in there.'

'You don't have to, Sir,' said Louise. 'I'll go, with Mark.'

Dixon shook his head. 'I'll be fine.'

'It's a crime scene,' said the uniformed officer.

'It is,' said Dixon, sliding his phone out of his pocket and switching on the light. 'And I am a police officer investigating a crime.'

Halfway up the steps to the front door he stopped and took a deep breath.

'What's the matter with him?' asked the officer.

'He was caught in a factory fire a month or so ago,' whispered Louise. 'Only just got out.'

The officer nodded.

'Go with him, Mark, for fuck's sake,' said Louise.

'All right, all right.'

'Which bedroom?' asked Dixon, turning around on the steps.

'Next floor up, the first door on the landing. They said it was number five, but I'm not sure if the door's still on.'

Dixon nodded and turned back to the house, listening to Pearce's footsteps behind him.

'Got any evidence bags, Mark?'

'A couple.'

'Better put on some gloves too.'

The front door had been smashed off its hinges and was lying on its side up against the wall at the bottom of the stairs. Dixon glanced up at the front of the house, the sandstone bay windows stained black from the smoke, the curtains gone – torn down probably or burnt.

'Pretty much gutted, by the looks of things.'

'I don't like the look of those stairs,' said Pearce, peering over his shoulder.

'Get that bloody lamp, will you?'

Pearce ran down the steps and snatched the lamp from the uniformed officer's hand.

'Thanks,' said Pearce, raising his eyebrows.

The banister had been burnt away, so Dixon checked the handrail on the wall to his left. It felt secure, so he tiptoed up the left side of the stairs, holding the handrail with both hands.

'It's fine, Mark,' he said, when he reached the top. 'Just keep left and hold the rail with both hands.'

'Have you done a risk assessment?' asked Pearce, his smile nervous.

'Yes.'

'Written?'

'Just get on with it.'

Dixon looked down at his hands, the blue latex gloves black from the wet smoke dust that had been coating the handrail, the stair carpet beneath his feet saturated. On the landing puddles were lying on the lino, which had melted in the doorway of room five. Several of the floorboards had collapsed, leaving only the joists. Dixon shone the lamp down into the kitchen below, watching the water dripping down electric cables that were hanging in the void.

'D'you think the electrics are off?' asked Pearce, grimacing.

'Yes, of course they are. It's the first thing they do.' Dixon smiled. 'After the gas.'

'Where do we go now?' asked Pearce.

'Hold the door frame, walk along the joists,' said Dixon, shining the torch at Pearce's feet.

'Oh, for—'

'Either that or wait here.'

'I'll wait here.'

Holding on to what was left of the door frame, Dixon took two steps along the joists to a fireplace on the side wall, where he stopped, holding on to the mantelpiece. He shone the lamp round the room. All that was left of the mattress was metal springs and melted foam lying on the floorboards. The bedside table was intact, saved by water from a fire hose in the back garden, probably. The curtains had been torn down and were lying in a sodden heap in the corner in front of the wardrobe.

He sniffed the air. Petrol – just – over the reek of saturated curtains. It had been the smoke last time, but this was worse, if anything, the water adding a sickly chemical tinge to the burning. He closed his eyes and the vision of flames all around him snapped into his mind.

'Are you all right, Sir?' Pearce was leaning around the door frame.

'Fine.'

The floorboards were intact nearer the window, so Dixon stepped on to them and walked around what was left of the bed to the bedside table. On the other side was a sink with a mirror above it, and a small table, the remains of a Camping Gaz stove on it, the gas canister having exploded.

The charred handle came off when he tried to open the drawer so he squatted down and reached underneath, pulling it open from the back. An open bar of chocolate had melted in the heat and run on to a small box of paracetamol, next to a packet of plastic razors. A tube of toothpaste completed the contents of the drawer.

'Bollocks,' muttered Dixon, shining the lamp behind it and on the floor at the side.

Then he retraced his steps back to the wardrobe, kicked aside the curtains on the floor and opened it. He frowned. Nothing. Not a single item of clothing. He shone the torch around the room – not a single picture on the walls either.

'Louise is saying something, Sir.'

'Go and see what she wants.'

Dixon turned to leave when he noticed a ball on the floor by the fireplace, under the corner of the wardrobe – rolled off the mantelpiece, perhaps. He picked it up and looked at it. Charred, it left a black streak on his blue gloves where it rolled around in the palm of his hand. Too big for a squash ball, too light for a golf ball, and too small for cricket or tennis. He frowned.

'She says—'

'What the hell is this?' asked Dixon, shining the lamp at the ball in his hand.

Pearce shook his head. 'No idea, Sir.'

'Let me have an evidence bag, will you?'

'She says the duty inspector at Bath wants us out of here now. He's on his way, apparently.'

Dixon dropped the ball into the evidence bag and looked up. 'Let's make sure we're gone before he gets here, then.'

The first hint of dawn was appearing when Dixon parked in the road outside his cottage and looked at his watch. He sighed. A couple of hours sleep and back to Express Park by eight. It would have to do.

He was feeding Monty by the open back door when Jane appeared in the living room doorway, rubbing her eyes.

'What time is it?'

'You don't want to know.'

'How'd you get on?'

'We're looking for a man named Tony Steiner.' Dixon flicked on the kettle. 'He's a friend of Gregson's, an original shareholder in Polgen and an employee of Markhams.'

'Where is he?'

'Gone. His bedsit in Radstock was burnt out last night.'

'What did Adele have to say?'

'She's never met him, which I can believe. I gave her a hard time about it and Roger got a bit . . .' Dixon's voice tailed off.

'What?'

'We had words.' He rolled his eyes.

'What's going on?' Lucy was standing at the top of the stairs.

'Nick's back,' said Jane. 'Tea?'

'Yes, please.' Lucy sat down on the top of the stairs and yawned.

'Was there anything left at the bedsit?' asked Jane, turning back to Dixon. He was standing in the back door watching Monty sniffing around Jane's car, his white coat just visible in the lights from the kitchen window.

'Nothing except a ball of some sort.'

'A ball?'

'A tube of toothpaste, some painkillers, a bar of chocolate and a ball, which had been burnt in the fire anyway.'

'What was it made of?'

'Cork,' replied Dixon. 'I broke it open back at the station.'

'No clothes?'

'Nope.'

'What the hell's that all about?'

'Crikey,' said Lucy, standing behind them yawning, 'you can tell there aren't many canals down south.'

'Eh?'

'A cork ball?' She shrugged her shoulders. 'It makes your keys float. Everybody knows that. Don't they?'

Chapter Thirty-Six

'Right then, everybody.'

Dixon was listening to the briefing from the bottom of the stairs, leaning on the banister. Two hours' sleep had been it, then back to Express Park. Still, it had been the same for the others.

'Tony Steiner,' continued Potter. 'Find him and we find Hatty.'

I bloody well hope so.

'We've spoken to the other residents at twelve Paulton Terrace and they've given us a description. IC1 male, aged late forties, early fifties, five eleven, shaven head, no facial hair, no visible tattoos. Everybody got that?'

'Yes, Ma'am.'

'And we're going to have to do this without speaking to any of the other employees at Markhams, for obvious reasons. Right, what about traffic cameras?'

'Nothing yet, Ma'am.' Dixon recognised Dave Harding's voice.

'His car and the Markhams vans, all right, Dave?'

'Yes, Ma'am.'

'Mobile phones?'

'He's got a contract with Vodafone, Ma'am, but the phone's dead. It's not showing up anywhere. He must've taken the battery out.'

Or chucked it in the canal.

'Where's Inspector Dixon?'

'Probably on the beach with his bloody dog, Ma'am.'

Dixon smiled. Chard was up early on a Sunday.

Twat.

'His team has been on this most of the night, so the rest of us are playing catch up. Everybody else, focus on known associates, social media, anything you can find. It's reasonable to assume he knows we're on to him because he torched his flat last night so let's find the bastard before he does anything else really bloody stupid.'

'Yes, Ma'am.'

'Anything from the surveillance overnight?'

'No, Ma'am,' said Guthrie. 'All quiet. Gregson's not moved.'

'I want surveillance on the other Polgen shareholders and get local police to check out those living abroad. There's one in Hong Kong and another in Canada. Let's see if they're still there, shall we? And tell Dixon I'd like to see him as soon as he gets in.'

'Ma'am,' said Louise, pointing to the top of the stairs.

'Ah, there you are,' said Potter. 'Where have you been?'

'On the beach with my bloody dog, Ma'am.' Dixon smiled at Chard, who ducked down behind his computer.

'We've got it all under control, I think. Everything that can be done is being done.'

Dixon nodded.

'And well done.'

'Thank you, Ma'am.'

Louise appeared next to Dixon and handed him a file. 'It's the missing persons file on Sid Farooq, Sir,' she said, grinning. 'You're going to love it.'

'Love what?' snapped Potter.

'Nothing in particular, Ma'am,' replied Louise, walking back to her workstation.

Dixon followed her. 'That cork ball is to make your keys float, apparently. Check with the Canal and River Trust and see if Steiner is the registered keeper of a narrowboat. Or any boat, for that matter.'

'Yes, Sir.'

'I'll be in the canteen.'

'Want another coffee?' Jane dropped her handbag on the table.

'I thought you'd be staying with Lucy,' said Dixon, looking up. 'Dave's driving down today.'

'She understands. I said we'd pick her up on the way to the Lakes, whenever that is. I left her with my door keys and she's going to leave them in the pub.'

'She's a good kid.'

'In spite of everything.'

'And she's going to be your bridesmaid, is she?' Dixon smirked.

Jane picked up a menu and pretended to look at it. 'She wasn't supposed to say anything,' she mumbled, blushing.

'And there was me thinking I did your head in.'

'You do.' She smiled, 'Now, do you want that bloody coffee or not?'

Dixon turned back to the file in front of him and listened to the whirr of the coffee machine. 'Read this,' he said, sliding the file across the table when Jane sat down. 'And tell me what you notice about it.' He stirred his coffee while he watched Jane flicking through the witness statements.

'Adele's is crap,' she said. 'No mention of what Farooq was wearing, no timeline, nothing.' She looked at Dixon. 'Is Gregson's the same?'

He nodded.

'And he was the last person to see Farooq alive.' Jane shook her head. 'Unless he really did get in a taxi.'

'They found a taxi driver who remembered dropping him off at Combe Hay, but not one who collected him.'

'Even so.' Jane was glancing down Gregson's statement. 'There's not even any background.'

'Well, we know it now,' muttered Dixon. 'Notice anything else?'

Jane shook her head. 'What?'

'The investigating officer?'

'Bath police station,' said Jane, turning to the front cover of the file. 'Detective Constable . . .' She smiled. 'Simon Chard.'

Dixon nodded.

'He's going to look a right dickhead when this comes out,' continued Jane.

'I could do without the hassle, to be honest,' said Dixon. 'And whatever happens . . .' He took a swig of coffee. 'We must try not to enjoy it too much.'

'Or not look as though we are.' Jane grinned.

'Quite.'

'I said you'd love that.' Louise was standing in the doorway of the canteen, smiling. 'Nothing from the Canal and River Trust, I'm afraid.' She shook her head. 'No boat registered in Steiner's name.'

'Thanks,' said Dixon.

'You had breakfast, Lou?' asked Jane.

'Not yet. I'll get something a bit later.'

'I wish I was on the beach with my bloody dog,' muttered Dixon.

'Eh?'

'It was just something Chard said.'

'You've got Monty in the Land Rover?'

Dixon nodded.

'Take him for a walk then,' said Jane. 'Fuck Chard.'

'The wizard said he saw a boy drowning in a lock with no water in it – and a boy did drown, didn't he?'

'It was in the *Bath Chronicle*.'

'He was winding a windlass when he slipped and fell in.' Dixon slid his phone out of his pocket and opened a web browser. Then he typed 'windlass' into Google and hit 'Search'.

'What are you looking at?' asked Jane.

'Windlass. It's a winch, especially one on a ship or in a harbour, according to this.' Dixon frowned.

'Try "canal windlass".'

He started typing. 'It's giving me "canal lock windlass" as a search term.'

'Try that then.'

Dixon clicked on it, then switched to an image search. He passed his phone to Jane as he stood up. 'I'll be back in a sec,' he said.

'What's that?' asked Jane, when Dixon sat down five minutes later.

'Savage's post mortem report and this . . .' Dixon held up a yellow Post-it note. 'Is the pathologist's mobile number.' He started flicking through the report. 'Here it is.'

'Read it out then.' Jane shook her head.

'Er . . . "blunt instrument, metal, possibly steel or aluminium, with square edges. Therefore a spanner of some sort, possibly a box spanner with two heads side by side."'

'A windlass,' muttered Jane.

Dixon picked up his phone and dialled the mobile phone number he had stuck to the table.

'Dr Petersen.'

'This is Detective Inspector Dixon, Sir. I wanted to speak to you about—'

'It *is* Sunday morning, you know.'

'There *is* a ten year old girl missing, you know.'

'All right, all right, get on with it.'

'Can you get to a computer, Sir?'

Dixon pressed the phone to his ear, straining to hear muffled voices in the background.

'Pass me that.'

'Must I?'

'Yes, you must.'

Then Petersen came back on the line. 'I've got my wife's iPad. What do you want me to look at?'

'Go to Google and type in "canal lock windlass", then select "Images".'

'Give me a sec.'

'Anybody would think I'd just got him up,' whispered Dixon, his hand over his phone.

'You probably have,' said Jane.

'Yes, that's it. The first one with the spanner heads side by side. Well done.'

'Thank you, Sir,' replied Dixon.

'What put you on to it?'

'Don't ask.'

'Tell DCS Potter I'll let her have an amended report on Monday.'

'Yes, Sir.'

'It's a new murder weapon on me.'

'Probably the first thing that came to hand,' replied Dixon.

'Well, it left a distinct imprint on the skull. And there's a first time for everything, I suppose.'

'Thank you, Sir.'

'My pleasure.'

He rang off and turned to Jane. 'Savage had his brains bashed in with a windlass,' he said, nodding.

'So the wizard was right?'

'The wizard was right about the wrong thing for the wrong reasons.'

'Wrong then?'

'Pretty much.' Dixon stood up. 'C'mon then, don't just sit there.'

'Where are we going?'

Chapter Thirty-Seven

'We're in the outside lane of the M5, Lou.' Jane had Dixon's phone clamped to her right ear, her other hand over her left. 'Doing about ninety, I think. I can hardly hear you.' She glanced at Dixon. 'Yes, I'll tell him.'

Jane rang off.

'She said you were right. There's a canal boat registered in Simon Gregson's name, called *Anytimenow*.' Jane shook her head. 'How could you possibly . . . ?'

'A fridge magnet.'

'The units were built in.'

'It was on the side of the microwave.'

'Sometimes, I think you operate on a different plane to the rest of us.'

'Thank you, Sergeant.' Dixon smiled. 'What else did she say?'

'He keeps it on the Kennet and Avon at Kingfisher Marina.'

'It stands to reason when you think about it. Savage kept his boat there and so did Alesha's granny. Nice and cosy, all three of them, I bet.'

'And you think Hatty's on the boat?'

'Got to be worth a look, wouldn't you say?'

'He may have left the marina, of course.'

'How far's he going to get at three miles an hour?'

'Depends when he left.'

Jane felt sick by the time Dixon turned into the entrance to Kingfisher Marina. It had felt like a lifetime being thrown around the country roads in his new Land Rover but it had only taken just under an hour from junction twenty-two on the M5. They were probably on every speed camera along the A38 too.

'I preferred your old Land Rover,' muttered Jane. 'It was slower.'

Dixon peered over his shoulder into the back. 'He slept through it all right,' he said, looking at Monty curled up on his bed.

'Lucky sod.'

Further progress was blocked by large steel gates so Dixon left his Land Rover in the visitors' car park and tried the shop door. Locked.

'The gates are too,' said Jane, rattling them.

Dixon looked up.

'You can't climb over them.' Jane's eyes widened. 'There's a camera.'

Lines of canal boats moored to pontoons were visible beyond private car parking, a single boat moored on the far side next to a diesel pump.

'It would be a bloody Sunday,' muttered Dixon. He tried the door of the shop again, before knocking on it as loudly as the pain in his knuckles would allow.

'Yes?' A man leaned out of a window above his head.

Dixon held up his warrant card.

'Oh.' The window slammed shut and seconds later a light came on at the back of the shop.

'Are you the owner?' asked Dixon, when the man opened the door. Corduroys and a very fetching cardigan. Nice.

'Caretaker. My name's Jim Hendry.'

'We're looking for a boat called *Anytimenow*,' said Dixon.

'Pulled out a few days ago.'

'When exactly?'

'Monday night, I think. He was gone when I got up on Tuesday morning, any road.'

'Who was?'

'Tony.'

'Describe him for me,' said Dixon. Jane was making notes.

'Bald. Shaves it, y'know. Scruffy too. Not a nice fella. Bloody rude he is, most of the time.'

'Facial hair, tattoos?'

Jim shook his head.

'So, the last time you saw him was Monday?'

'No. Yesterday evening. He cycled in on his bike and checked his post box. All the residentials have boxes and use the marina address for their post. He used the phone too.'

'Phone?'

'There's a payphone on the wall in the laundry area.'

'Has it been used since?'

'No way of knowing. Sorry. It's quite popular, though. Not much of a signal around here for the mobiles.'

'Is his car here?'

'Aye,' replied Jim. 'D'you want me to show you?'

The back door of the shop opened out on the inside of the steel gates and a short walk across the gravel car park revealed a grey Honda CRV. On a 2005 number plate and covered in dents and scratches, it reminded Dixon of his old Land Rover.

'Shall I—?'

'We'll leave it where it is for now, Jane.' Dixon turned to Jim. 'What does his boat look like?'

'She's a fifty-five footer. That big,' he replied, pointing to the canal boat filling up with diesel. 'She's blue with a red roof. Oh, and a skylight too. Only a low one, mind, so he can get through the tunnels.'

'Anything else?'

'He's got a couple of solar panels, and then there's his bike, which he puts on the roof. Locks it to the side rails.'

'Where will he be now, d'you reckon?'

Jim grimaced. 'He likes to moor up out in the country, so he's maybe out towards Trowbridge. That's only a couple of miles on his bike. He used to do that at weekends anyways.'

'And if he left last night, how far will he have got by now?'

'Not past Caen Hill, that's for sure.'

'What's at Caen Hill?'

'Locks. Twenty-nine of them in two miles on the way up to Devizes. They'll take him most of the day, if he's on his own.'

'That's east. Would he have gone west instead?'

'Nah. The canal ends at Keynsham and beyond Hanham Lock it's the River Avon. Tidal, that is. East takes you to the Thames at Reading and you can go pretty much anywhere in the country from there.'

Dixon looked at Jane and smiled. 'You got any large scale maps in that shop of yours, Jim?' he asked.

◆ ◆ ◆

'Fancy taking Monty for a walk?'

'Eh?'

'I'll drop you at bridge one-four-two on the A361 and you walk along the canal looking for him,' said Dixon. 'Then I'll pick you up at bridge one-four-eight. That's the A365.' Dixon had the map spread out across the steering wheel and dashboard of his Land Rover.

'How far is it?' asked Jane.

'A couple of miles.'

'What do I do if I see him?'

'Act like a dog walker, find a bench, sit down and ring me. Then pretend to be walking back the way you came and keep an eye on him. If you can get a look in the boat then so much the better.'

'And what if he's not there?'

'We try lower down. And if he's not there either then we try the other side of Caen Hill.'

Jane sighed. 'Why me?'

'You'll look less suspicious than me.'

'I'll take that as a compliment.'

Dixon folded the map, leaving it open at Caen Hill, and slid it down the side of the passenger seat. 'Ready?'

'Just go.'

'You got poo bags?'

'You think of everything, don't you?'

He screeched to a halt across the entrance to the footpath. 'The towpath's just there.'

Jane jumped out of the Land Rover and waited for Monty to hop over on to the passenger seat. Then she clipped on his lead and was gone, slamming the door behind them.

A boat was in the lock under the road bridge, the sound of a diesel engine echoing under the arch, so Jane walked up and looked down into the chamber.

Green with a red roof. And pointing the wrong way too.

Then she walked back along the towpath to the top of the hill.

'Bloody hell,' she muttered.

The flight of locks shelved away beneath her in a series of steps, each marked out by the huge black painted beams and a white painted footbridge. Several boats were in the top locks in the flight, all pointing down the hill, though, and Steiner would be coming up. If he'd got this far.

She tried counting the locks, but soon lost the thread. Then she tried imagining the horse, pulling a boat laden with coal up this lot. Poor sod.

'Right then, you. Let's make like dog walkers,' she muttered, Monty sniffing along the undergrowth on the end of his long lead.

Sixteen locks, one after the other; she counted them on her way down the hill. And three boats near the bottom, all going up. People milling about, windlasses in hand, the cranking of the paddles making a loud metallic clack that even Monty had got used to by the time they reached the bottom.

Plenty of other dog walkers too, enjoying the spectacle. Dixon had been right: she didn't look out of place.

Jane looked back up the flight and tried to imagine the derelict locks on the Somersetshire Coal Canal in the same state. Maybe restoring them wouldn't be such a bad thing?

A hundred yards or so separated the bottom of the flight and the next lock going down the hill. She spotted figures standing either side of the top gate, windlasses in hand. That couldn't be Steiner, unless he had help. Either that or two boats were going through the lock at the same time. The locks were wide enough to take two side by side.

The water had brought the boats almost level with the top of the lock chamber and the men on the other side of the gates were leaning against them, trying to push them open. Both were hire boats, green with a red roof.

Jane walked on.

The locks were evenly spaced out now, perhaps a hundred yards between each, and all of them empty. She walked up on to a footbridge and looked along the canal. Nothing.

Then she checked her phone.

Bollocks.

No signal either.

The towpath crossed the canal at the next lock, bridge one-four-six, according to the sign. Not far to go now until Dixon picked them up at one-four-eight.

She stopped in the middle of the bridge and looked down at a boat in the lock below, deep in the bottom, the chamber only just beginning to fill, the now familiar clack of the paddles being ratcheted open and the water swirling.

Jane glanced at the man cranking the windlass. A red baseball cap. Odd that there was no hair sticking out at the sides.

Solar panels, a bike chained to the top rail. And a skylight. Jane froze.

A girl lying curled up on a bench seat, her knees tucked under the dining table; she was just visible in the gloom, the curtains on both sides of the cabin drawn.

Jane looked up and watched the man tiptoeing across the top of the lock gates to the other side. Then he attached the windlass to the paddle and began cranking it.

She walked on, breathing hard now. Fifty yards to a bend in the canal. She looked back. No one coming, so she checked her phone again.

Still no fucking signal.

Then she began to run.

Dixon parked on the grass verge with his hazard lights flashing and walked back to the bridge. He sighed. Dense undergrowth on a bend in the canal obscured his view, so he dropped down on to the towpath and walked around the corner, keeping pace with a narrowboat that had emerged from under the bridge. Black with a purple trim, and no bike on the roof.

Several canal boats were moored on the nearside, some of the boaters enjoying the Sunday morning sunshine with breakfast on deck. Dogs running around loose too.

And Jane sprinting towards him, with Monty running off the lead alongside her.

Dixon checked his phone. No signal.

That explains that.

She stopped in front of him, breathing hard, her hands on her knees, so Dixon took the lead hanging around her neck and clipped it on to Monty's collar.

'Well?'

'The fucker went right underneath me at Lower Foxhangers. Just around the bend back there.' More gasping for breath. 'There's a bridge over the lock. One-four-six.'

'Did you see her?'

'She was lying on the bench seat behind the dining table. The curtains are closed but I could see her through the skylight. Asleep, I think.'

'Drugged, probably. And you're sure it's her?'

'I was looking straight at her. And him.' Jane straightened up, sweat dripping off the end of her nose. 'And it's the right boat.'

'I got a signal up on the bridge,' said Dixon, checking his phone again.

'What're you going to do?'

'Call for backup.' He grimaced. 'I'm not taking any chances with Roger's granddaughter.'

Jane nodded. 'We're in Wiltshire here, don't forget.'

'I'll ring Potter and she can sort it out.'

Once sitting in the passenger seat of the Land Rover, Jane leaned back and closed her eyes, so Dixon reached behind her into the passenger footwell and picked up a bottle of water.

'Here,' he said, handing it to Jane. 'Just make sure you leave him some.'

'Is it Monty's?' she asked, frowning at the bottle.

Dixon shrugged his shoulders. 'He won't mind, seeing as it's you.' Then he unfolded the map across the steering wheel and dialled Potter's number.

'This had better be good.'

'We've found her,' said Dixon.

'Oh, thank fuck for that.' The sound of Potter clicking her fingers at someone in the background. 'Where are you?'

'Caen Hill Locks, just west of Devizes on the Kennet and Avon Canal. She's on a narrowboat with Steiner heading east between bridges one-four-six and one-four-five at a place called Lower Foxhangers.'

'How the hell did you find her?'

'Can we worry about that later?'

'Yes, of course. What d'you need?'

'We can't let him get up into the main flight of locks, and we've got about an hour until he reaches the pound in between lock twenty-eight and the bottom lock of the main flight. That'll be just east of bridge one-four-four.'

'Hang on a minute – Devizes is bloody Wiltshire, isn't it?'

'It is.'

Potter sighed. 'All right, leave it to me.'

'I want to take him in the bottom lock. Going up the hill it'll be empty when he goes in and the water will be at its shallowest. Plus we can close the gate behind him and we'll have him surrounded.'

'Armed Response?'

'Yes. I want dogs too and we'll need to seal off the A361 and the B3101.'

'I'll ring my opposite number at Wiltshire and call you back.'

'Tell them no bloody sirens.'

'Will do.'

Dixon rang off.

'What happens now?' asked Jane.

'I'm gonna drive round and park at bridge one-four-four. You get to go for a walk.'

'Another one?'

'Get ahead of him and keep him in sight. Dawdle a bit if you have to; watch boats in the locks, that sort of thing. When he's in lock twenty-seven, come and find me. All right?'

Chapter Thirty-Eight

Dixon looked down into the empty lock chamber beneath him, the water perhaps ten feet below, the huge gates to his right closed and holding back the canal above. The sound of running water masked the pounding of his heart, a trickle leaking around the sides of the gates and from a tiny gap in the middle where the two met, the pressure of the water above not quite sealing them shut.

The lower gates were open, turned back into recesses in the stone walls, weeds clinging on in the sludge that had collected on the beams between the panels.

He looked down at a set of metal rungs set into the stone walls. A ladder of sorts with a handrail at the top – just like at a swimming pool, only painted white. One on each side of the lock. Dixon grimaced. He hoped it would all be over before he needed to climb down.

The walls flared at the entrance to the lock, the curved red brick bearing the scars of the boats needing help to get lined up, lichen growing where water was seeping through from above and more weeds sprouting in the cracks.

The dark green water in the pound below the lock reflected the trees on the far side and the few clouds in the sky, the only ripples on the surface coming from tiny fish rising in the sun.

The grass around the lock made a stark contrast with the old Somersetshire Coal Canal: carefully mown – manicured even – rather than strimmed; the wooden footbridge and gate arms freshly painted too.

Away to his right, the next lock up the hill and the ones above were empty, the lock keepers holding back the boats coming down the hill. They were blocking the towpath too, dog walkers diverted across the footbridge over lock forty and into the woods.

Giant black beams with white painted handles on the end marked each set of gates on the sixteen locks in the flight stretching away up the hill, thirty-two pairs in all, looking like giant oars sticking out of the side of a Viking longship. Or giant piano keys maybe. Dixon frowned. Perhaps not.

Below him the towpath was blocked at bridge one-four-five, now well behind Steiner, with dog walkers and other pedestrians being intercepted and sent back to Foxhangers. No traffic on the now closed B3101, blocked at its junction with the A361; might be a bit of a give-away, Dixon thought, but then it was a Sunday and they'd just have to take that chance.

He looked back across the lower pound to lock twenty-eight. No sign of Jane or Steiner. Yet.

Two narrowboats moored on the nearside in between the locks had been checked, and the anglers who had been fishing in the pound when he arrived told to clear off. The campsite on the far side of the pound had been evacuated too. Otherwise, it looked like a perfectly normal Sunday morning at Caen Hill.

But it wasn't.

Dixon felt his hands shaking and thrust them into his trouser pockets. Then he perched on the edge of the gate arm and tried to look casual.

Was Steiner armed? Jane hadn't seen a gun but that didn't mean . . .

He took a deep breath and puffed out his cheeks. They'd find out soon enough.

He looked across at the dense undergrowth on the other side of the lock and the four Armed Response officers kneeling in the stinging nettles. Four more were lying in the bushes behind him below the tow-path. The dog handler was in there too. And the duty inspector from Devizes. All well hidden.

No helicopter was a bit of a shame, and not even on standby. Grounded for maintenance, apparently. Still, they shouldn't need it.

That's Monty!

Movement under the bridge, in the shadows. Then Jane appeared, running behind him, glancing over her shoulder.

'He's in the pound just below the lock,' she said, when she reached Dixon.

'Both still on board?'

Jane nodded.

'I'm parked in the farm on the other side,' he said, handing Jane his car keys. 'Over the footbridge and follow the path. There's a gate. You can't miss it. There should be some water left too.'

'Good. I'm parched.'

'Not for you, for Monty.' Dixon rolled his eyes. 'I got this for you,' he said, handing her a can of Diet Coke from his coat pocket. 'And tell the lads in the bushes on the other side that Steiner's on his way.'

'All right.'

'Then you'd better keep out of sight. He'll expect to see you with a dog.'

Jane sighed and trudged across the footbridge.

The metal clanking of the windlass alerted Dixon to Steiner's arrival in lock twenty-eight, his boat in the bottom of the chamber. A red base-ball cap leaning over the paddle capstan cranking the handle; he could see that from over a hundred yards away.

Dixon wondered where Poland was now. Catcott, probably, staring into the bottom of an empty coffee mug, or a whisky glass.

It'll soon be over now, old son.

The roof of the canal boat began to appear over the top of the gate, a bicycle lying on its side, solar panels too. Blue with a red roof. Dixon couldn't see the name on the side but it must be *Anytimenow*.

This is it.

Then the metallic clang of the rear doors being opened on another boat. Nearer.

What the fuck?

The hatch cover slid back and a figure stepped out on to the rear deck of the first canal boat moored in the pound. Seconds later the front doors opened and a woman stepped out on to the front deck and began untying the rope.

Dixon stepped back and spoke in a furious whisper over his shoulder.

'I thought you lot cleared those boats?'

'We did,' came the reply from the bushes. 'They must've been asleep or deaf. Nobody answered when I knocked.'

Dixon gritted his teeth.

For fuck's sake.

Engine on now, the boat crept away from its mooring, heading towards the lock directly below Dixon, the woman sauntering along the towpath, windlass in hand, ready to operate the paddles.

He stepped forward, holding his warrant card to his chest, with his back to Steiner, who was now at the tiller of *Anytimenow* as it emerged from lock twenty-eight. 'Give me the windlass, keep walking and don't look back.'

'What?'

'This is a police operation,' said Dixon, his eyes wide. 'Now keep walking as if everything's perfectly normal.'

'How far?'

'Someone will intercept you. Now go.'

The woman handed Dixon the windlass and walked on up the towpath, the temptation to look back too strong, obviously.

The rumble of a diesel engine echoed from the bottom of the chamber below him and he looked down to see the narrowboat edging into the lock, an elderly man holding the tiller and looking all around the top, trying to find his wife, presumably.

Dixon ran across the footbridge, climbed down the metal rungs set into the lock wall and jumped across on to the roof of the boat, which was lying at an angle across the lock. Then he stepped over the solar panels and skylight before dropping down on to the rear deck.

'Who are you?'

'I'm a police officer,' replied Dixon, his warrant card in the palm of his hand. 'Get down in the cabin and lie on the floor.'

'But—'

'Now, Sir.'

'Where's my wife?'

'She's safe.'

Dixon took hold of the tiller and turned to watch Steiner's approach on *Anytimenow*, the boat lining up to come into the lock alongside him.

A stab vest might have been a good idea. Dixon sighed.

Too bloody late now.

Then *Anytimenow* stopped in the middle of the pound between the two locks, drifting sideways on the breeze.

Chapter Thirty-Nine

Jane knelt down behind the stinging nettles and looked along the top of the lock.

'Where's Inspector Dixon?'

'He went down the ladder,' replied the Armed Response officer kneeling in the nettles in front of her. 'Another boat pulled in.'

'He's on another boat? Where the hell did that come from?'

'Just over there.'

Jane frowned. She watched through a gap in the undergrowth as Steiner edged his boat towards the lock, lining it up with the entrance and the space next to Dixon. 'And what's he looking at?' she whispered.

'He won't hear you. He's standing on top of a diesel engine, don't forget.'

'He's seen something over there,' said another, pointing to the bushes on the far side of the towpath.

Jane looked across, just in time to see a uniformed officer duck down. The drone of the diesel engine slowed, the wake at the back of *Anytimenow* all but disappearing, leaving it drifting sideways on what little breeze there was.

'He's stopped,' muttered Jane. 'What the fuck's he doing?'

She watched him lift the floor of the rear deck and lean down into the engine compartment, cranking a handle of some sort. Then he crawled forwards and reached up for the throttle, the water churning forwards under the boat this time.

Jane looked up at a lock keeper sprinting down the towpath. He stopped at the edge of the lock and shouted down to Dixon in the bottom.

'He's going to sink the boat!'

That was all she heard and all she needed to hear.

She glanced across as she sprinted across the footbridge, watching *Anytimenow* sinking at the back as the water gushed into the engine compartment. It was up to the back doors by the time she cleared the bridge, the stern resting on the bottom and the nose settling inch by inch.

She raced down the grass bank on the far side and ran along the towpath, past the Armed Response officers still pointing their weapons at Steiner, who was up to his neck in water at the back of the boat.

'No shot!' shouted one.

'Hold your fire,' shouted another. 'He's not armed.'

The dog handler was ahead of her, running along the towpath towards the road bridge. Then, when she was level with the sinking boat, Jane dived into the water. A flat racing dive, just like she'd been taught at school; she surfaced five yards from the bank, grateful that she hadn't hit anything under the water.

She struck out for the sunken boat now resting on the bottom of the canal, only its roof still visible, the skylight poking out of the water, the bicycle still chained to the railings at the front.

A diesel engine revving hard off to her right – she glanced across to see Dixon on the rear deck of the other canal boat, roaring backwards out of the lock.

Hang on, Hatty. We're coming!

Someone was in the water on the far side of the *Anytimenow*, swimming towards the far bank. Must be Steiner.

Bastard.

Then she felt the handrail on the back of *Anytimenow* and pulled herself into a standing position on the deck at the back of the boat, holding on to the roof. She tried the steel doors, but they were bolted from the inside, the sliding hatch above them open. Two pillows and a duvet had floated to the surface, so she threw them clear, took a deep breath and slid down into the gloom, feeling her way with her feet and hands.

Steps. She missed the top one and pitched forward, her arms flailing in the murky green water.

Then the edge of a bed. She felt the wooden slats, but where was the mattress?

Shafts of light were streaming in from the windows on either side, everything tinged green by the water.

The bathroom on her left now, a tin of shaving foam above her head, banging against the underside of the roof. She followed the passageway, pulling herself along using the window frames on one side and the open bathroom door on the other, until she reached a locked door; fumbling for the lock, the clock ticking, lungs bursting. And Hatty had been in the water even longer.

Then her fingers closed around a bolt and she slid it open.

The kitchen. It must be. The curtains were closed now, but she could make out a loaf of bread floating above her head, just under the roof, a box of cornflakes, empty cartons of milk and apples bobbing; bottles and tins rolling about on the floor at her feet too, as she pulled herself along the worktop.

Light was streaming in from above now. The skylight. It must be the skylight!

Odd that the light was flickering. Then she saw the legs of a child – *Hatty's legs* – kicking out in the water in front of her, the girl's face pressed to the glass of the skylight above her.

An air pocket, it must be an air pocket!

Jane felt the edge of the dining table against her thigh and stepped up on the bench seat, wrapping her arm around Hatty's waist to hold her up. Then she fumbled for the lock on the skylight with her free hand.

It opened. Just a couple of inches, but that was enough. She was standing on the dining table now, pushing Hatty up towards the gap, and heard her coughing and spluttering as she filled her lungs with air. Hatty turned and wrapped her arms around Jane's neck, sobbing and gasping for air at the same time.

Then Jane lurched upwards towards the light, her face pressed against the glass as she too gasped for air, one arm still around Hatty's waist, the other holding on to the edge of the roof.

'Can you hold on to the roof, Hatty? I won't let go of you.'

The child slid her hands from around Jane's neck and took hold of the edge of the roof, pulling herself up and turning her face towards the opening.

'I've got you,' said Jane. 'See if you can find the dining table with your feet.'

'I . . . I can't.'

'It's all right.' Jane felt Hatty's legs flailing in the water. 'I can hold you. We're going to be fine. The boat's stopped sinking and help's on the way. All right?'

Hatty nodded. If she was still crying then her tears were being washed away by the water that was washing over the roof of the boat and in through the skylight, the wake of Dixon's boat, probably.

Jane took a deep breath. She tried to turn her head to look towards the front of the boat.

Nick, where are you?

Then she heard the dull thud of footsteps running along the roof above them.

Chapter Forty

Dixon watched Steiner looking all around him, no more than thirty yards away now, his eyes darting from side to side. Then he disappeared down behind the back cabin and lifted the engine cover.

'Armed police. Stay where you are!'

Dixon peered around the wall at four Armed Response officers edging along the towpath, their weapons raised and pointing at *Anytimenow*. More on the top of the wall above him.

'He's going to sink the boat!'

He looked up to see a lock keeper running along the top of the lock. He stopped adjacent to Dixon and shouted down to him: 'If he removes the cover on the rudder housing and puts it in reverse, it'll sink like a stone.'

The sound of the armed police officers shouting was drowned out by the revving of a diesel engine, then the water started churning at the back of *Anytimenow*, bubbling forwards under the boat.

'That's it,' shouted the lock keeper. 'That's reverse.'

'How do I reverse this one?' shouted Dixon.

'Press the red button, lever back, point the tiller in the direction you want to go.'

The nose of *Anytimenow* was rearing up in the water as the narrowboat sank at the stern. Arms were flailing in the water on the far side: Steiner was swimming for it.

Dixon looked up at the sound of footsteps on the bridge directly above him just in time to see Jane sprint across, run down the grass bank and dive into the canal. She surfaced five yards out and started swimming towards the stricken canal boat now sitting on the bottom of the canal, only the roof and bike visible.

He slammed his boat in reverse, roaring backwards out of the lock towards *Anytimenow*, and had cleared the lower wall by the time Jane arrived at the sunken narrowboat. He watched her take a deep breath and drop down inside the cabin through the top hatch.

'Can I help?' shouted the elderly man over the noise of the engine. He had crept to the top of the back steps and was peering out on to the rear deck.

'Get me over there, as quick as you can,' replied Dixon. 'There are people on board.'

'Oh, good God.'

The man stepped out on to the deck and took hold of the tiller, adjusting it so they were heading directly for the front of the sunken *Anytimenow*.

Dixon climbed over the back rail, ready to jump across, and waited, watching the bicycle on the roof getting ever closer.

He spotted movement on the far bank and watched Steiner climb out of the canal and run across the campsite towards the road. Dixon grimaced. Sirens were all around him now – even over the sound of the engine – Armed Response officers and dog handlers sprinting along the towpath towards the road bridge and through the farm on the other side too. They should be able to cut him off.

'That's close enough,' he shouted. Then he jumped, landing on the roof of the sunken boat.

'Nick!'

Jane's voice, coming from the open skylight, her fingertips just visible, holding on to the edge of the frame.

Dixon picked up the barge pole and ran along the roof, jumping over the bicycle chained to the side rail. He stopped when he reached the open skylight and looked down at the two faces pressed to the Perspex beneath him, eyes wide open. Jane clinging on with one hand, her other arm wrapped around Hatty, both of them gasping for air.

'You'll need to take a deep breath and duck down, just for a second. All right?'

'Yes,' replied Jane.

'Can you do that, Hatty?' asked Dixon.

She nodded.

'With me, Hatty. OK?' said Jane. 'Ready?' She took a deep breath, turning her head to watch Hatty do the same. Then she nodded and they both ducked down under the water.

Dixon slid the pole under the skylight, braced it against the single hinge and levered it open, snapping the metal bracket off the frame. The skylight flew open. Then he reached down into the water and took hold of Hatty by the wrists, lifting her clear of the water up on to the roof.

She rubbed her eyes.

'Are you all right?' asked Dixon.

'Yes.' Sobbing now.

Then Jane appeared, both hands on the edge of the frame, kicking with her feet and trying to climb out of the skylight. Dixon reached down, put his hands under her arms and lifted her out of the water.

Hatty lunged forwards, clamping her arms around Jane's waist.

'It's going to be all right,' said Jane, wrapping her arms around Hatty. 'You're safe now.'

'I'm Nick and this is Jane.' Dixon smiled. 'Your Grandad Roger sent us.'

Chapter Forty-One

'He what?'

'He got away, Sir.' The uniformed officer took a step back.

'How?'

'I'll deal with this, Quinn, thank you.' The duty inspector appeared behind Dixon. 'He hijacked a car at knifepoint, rammed the patrol car blocking the road and sped off.'

'They should've bloody well shot him.'

'Oh, c'mon, Dixon, you know the rules of engagement. There was no immediate threat.'

'You're in pursuit? At least tell me you're in pursuit.'

'We were.' The duty inspector was rubbing his hands together. Nervously. 'We called it off on the outskirts of Chippenham,' he said. 'It was becoming a danger to the public.'

'And what the fuck d'you think Steiner is?' Dixon kicked the gravel on the towpath, sending small stones spraying across the canal. 'And who's "we"?'

'I called it off. I'm the duty inspector and it was my decision. We've got the Avon and Somerset helicopter en route and we'll try to pick him up once he clears the town.'

'*If* he clears the town.'

Dixon walked over to the ambulance parked on the towpath. Jane was holding hands with Hatty in the back, both of them wrapped in space blankets.

He smiled. 'How are they?' he asked, turning to the paramedic standing at the back of the ambulance.

'They're both fine.'

'Has Hatty been assaulted?'

'She says not, but she'll need to be examined properly.'

Dixon nodded.

'She's a bit groggy, but it seems to be wearing off,' continued the paramedic. 'She swallowed some water, so we'll need to watch she doesn't vomit and choke on it, but her lungs are clear. We'll be taking them both to Bath A&E.'

Dixon nodded.

'Can you follow us there?'

'Yes.' Dixon smiled. 'Her mother's already on the way there.'

'Your DCS Potter is on the way, Dixon,' said the duty inspector, sliding his phone into his breast pocket. 'She'll be here in ten minutes.'

'Thank you for the warning.' He turned back to the paramedic. 'C'mon, then, let's get them to the hospital. I'll follow in my Land Rover.'

◆ ◆ ◆

Blue lights.

The curtains at the front of Old School House had been closed day and night since Tuesday, but Poland could still see the blue lights outside, reflecting off the ceiling even in broad daylight. He walked over to the window and peered around the side of the curtain, expecting to see the now familiar gaggle of photographers and journalists in the lay-by opposite the house.

Instead his view was obscured by an Avon and Somerset Police four wheel drive pursuit vehicle parked directly outside the house, its engine still running, the driver's seat empty.

The knock at the door was loud and slow.

'Who is it, Dad?' asked Adele, looking up.

'It's the police.'

He walked over to the front door, with Adele and Jeremy close behind him, and opened it. Geraldine was sitting at the dining table, doing a jigsaw puzzle. She stood up, craning her neck to listen.

'What is it, Cole?' he asked.

'May I, Sir?'

Poland stepped back, allowing Cole into the hall, before closing the door behind him. He swallowed hard. 'Is it Hatty?' he whispered, his eyes wide.

'We've found her. She's fine, Sir.' Cole grinned. 'She'll be on her way to Bath A&E in the next few minutes. We're to meet them there.'

Adele dropped to her knees behind Poland and began to sob. He turned around and helped her to her feet, holding her up with an arm around her waist. 'Them?' he asked.

'She's with Jane Winter, Sir. Inspector Dixon will be following in his Land Rover.'

Poland nodded. 'Who d'you want then?'

'All three of you, I think, Sir. There's room in the car.'

'What about Mum?' gasped Adele.

'You go,' said Geraldine. 'Just go!'

Poland climbed in the back of the BMW with Adele, Jeremy sitting in the front passenger seat. They ducked low behind the car to avoid the photographers, but several cameras were still held out in front of them as Cole accelerated away.

Adele leaned over, her head on Poland's shoulder, the tears soaking into his shirt.

More blue lights up ahead. Cole slowed at the junction – the traffic stopped by police motorcycles – before sweeping out on to the A39 and accelerating hard towards the motorway. Seconds later the motorcycles flashed by, taking up position in front of them, ready to stop the traffic again at the bottom of Puriton Hill.

'Why Bath?' asked Jeremy.

'It was the nearest A&E, Sir,' replied Cole.

Jeremy looked over his shoulder at Adele. 'Where was she?' he asked, turning back to Cole.

'In a narrowboat on the Kennet and Avon Canal, Sir.'

'And she's not been . . . ?'

'She says not, Sir, but she'll need to be examined.'

'Of course she will,' said Poland. 'Let's worry about that later, shall we?'

The motorcycle escort stayed with them as they raced north on the M5, Poland watching the familiar landmarks flashing by on the nearside, tears rolling slowly down his cheeks.

A burnt out factory; that had been quite a night. And Brent Knoll. He smiled. He had some good friends who lived there. Some damned good friends.

◆ ◆ ◆

Hatty was still, at last, lying on a stretcher in the back of the ambulance, holding Jane's hand. Cried herself to sleep, probably, thought Dixon as the paramedic closed the back doors of the ambulance, the last vestiges of whatever drug it was in her system taking effect.

He was following the ambulance along the A4 when he spotted the blue lights, coming up fast behind them in the outside lane of the dual carriageway. He looked in his rear view mirror and watched the cars approach, sirens wailing. One pulled in behind his Land Rover, the other coming alongside in the outside lane. The driver looked up at Dixon and nodded, then accelerated, taking up position in front of the ambulance, matching their speed.

He thought about Steiner and wondered where he was. Hiding under a bush, perhaps, or even in custody by now. He slid his phone out of his pocket and glanced at the screen. No messages, so he dropped it on the passenger seat, waking up Monty, who was asleep in the front passenger footwell.

Two walks today. Good lad. We might get another later, old son. If we're lucky.

Dixon followed the ambulance into the small car park outside the A&E department, which was deserted apart from a police BMW X5 and two motorcycles parked on the double yellow lines opposite the entrance. The car doors opened; Adele and Jeremy took each other's hands, Poland standing behind them on the grass verge.

The ambulance stopped in front of the double doors and Dixon coasted to a stop behind it. He switched off his engine, got out and waited for the paramedic to open the back doors. Hatty slid off the stretcher and Jane helped her to the back of the ambulance when the doors opened, so Dixon picked her up and carried her across to Jeremy and Adele, who ran forward, their arms outstretched.

'She's fine,' said Dixon, gently placing Hatty in Jeremy's arms.

'Thank you,' he said, tears streaming down his cheeks.

'She needs to be checked over.'

Adele nodded. She tried to say something, but shook her head, the words lost in the sobs.

Poland stepped off the kerb and put his arms round Adele, who had her arms around Hatty. Then he walked over to Dixon and stood in front of him with his hand outstretched.

'I don't have the words,' he mumbled.

'Save them for your best man's speech.' Dixon smiled.

'Thank you.'

'Don't thank me, thank Jane.'

'What happened?' asked Poland.

'The boat sank. She went in and got Hatty out. I may have found her, but Jane saved her life.'

Poland walked over and put his arms around Jane, who had climbed out of the ambulance under her own steam.

'You're soaking wet,' he said, smiling.

'Er, yes . . . sorry.' Jane shrugged her shoulders.

'You need to get Hatty inside,' said Dixon. 'Cole will go with you. A paediatrician and the police surgeon are waiting to examine her.'

They watched Poland follow Adele and Jeremy into the hospital, Jeremy still carrying Hatty who was waving at them over his shoulder.

'Now what?' asked Jane, waving back.

'Aren't you going in?' asked Dixon. 'You might as well let them check you over, seeing as you're here.'

'I'm fine.'

'Well, you need a change of clothes.' Dixon was watching Hatty still waving as the double doors closed behind them. 'We've got to drop Monty off anyway.'

'I need a shower too, if we've got time.'

'I wasn't going to say anything.' Dixon grinned.

Jane put her arms around his waist and kissed him.

'And you, going down into that boat. You could've drowned,' he said, smiling. 'You're doing my head in, you really are. You go out sometimes and I never know whether you're coming back. I'm not sure I can—'

She pressed her index finger over his lips, silencing him mid-sentence. 'Shut up,' she said, before kissing him again. 'And don't you ever mention a canal boat holiday to me. All right?'

'I thought maybe for our honeymoon?'

'Piss off.'

Chapter Forty-Two

They were back at the cottage an hour later, Dixon feeding Monty while Jane was in the shower.

'Isn't it a bit early?' she asked, standing in the doorway, wrapped in a towel. 'What time is it?'

'Five.' Dixon was watching Monty pushing his bowl around the tiled floor. 'I'll give him a bit more later.'

'Anything from Potter?'

'She wants us over at Combe Hay as quick as we can. They're going to pick Gregson up.'

'I'd better throw some clothes on then.'

Dixon listened to the thump of Jane's footsteps running up the stairs as he slid his phone out of his pocket and tapped out a text message to Dave Harding.

Any sign of Gregson or Steiner's cars on the traffic cameras Tuesday morning near Catcott?

The reply came just as Jane appeared in the kitchen doorway, fully clothed this time.

None at all. Not in any direction. No Markhams vehicles either. Just the van on the speed camera at Woolavington

What about Hatty's DNA in the van?

Clear. Just Alesha's

Dixon sighed.

'What's that?' asked Jane.

'Nothing really,' replied Dixon. 'Just something that doesn't seem to add up.'

They were driving east on the A368, Jane looking out at Blagdon and Chew Valley reservoirs, before either of them spoke again. He had been deep in thought long enough. 'What doesn't add up?' she asked.

'Eh?'

'Back at the cottage, you said something didn't add up.'

He nodded. 'The van wasn't seen in Catcott at all. How many statements were taken from the village?'

'Over twenty.'

'And not one of them saw the van the morning Hatty was taken.'

'That doesn't mean—'

'And yet it was caught on the speed gun at Woolavington.'

'You said you thought that was deliberate.'

'I did.' Dixon nodded. 'And it could well have been, just to make us think it was in the area. And yet when we found it there was no trace whatsoever of Hatty's DNA. Nothing. It hadn't been cleaned either because Alesha's DNA was in it. Which means Hatty was never in it.'

'What about Gregson or Steiner?'

'There's no sign of them on any of the traffic cameras, in the vehicles we know about anyway, which makes me think about the mechanics of how she was snatched.'

'And who by.'

'Exactly.'

'Can you hear what I can hear?' asked Jane, frowning as Dixon dropped down off the main road into the back of Combe Hay.

'Sirens.'

An ambulance flashed by on the main road just as Dixon pulled up at the junction at the bottom of the hill. 'I'm guessing it didn't go according to plan.'

The farm track was blocked by a patrol car and a uniformed officer he didn't recognise.

'DCS Potter is on scene, Sir. She's expecting you.'

'What happened?' asked Dixon, throwing his warrant card on to the dashboard.

'They were dead when we went in.'

'They?'

'Mr Gregson and his wife, Sir.' The officer winced. 'It's not a pretty sight.'

'Shift the car, will you?'

'Yes, Sir.'

The Land Rover bounced along the farm track.

'Who killed them?' asked Jane.

'Steiner. He'll have come in on foot along the old Coal Canal.' Dixon shook his head. 'And all the time, we were watching the road.'

'How can you be so sure?'

'You never asked me if I was sure.'

Jane rolled her eyes.

Dixon squeezed past the patrol cars parked on the verge and parked behind Gregson's Volvo. 'You'd better move those two,' he said to a uniformed officer leaning on the bonnet of one of the patrol cars. 'Scientific'll never get their vans through there.'

'Yes, Sir.'

'Potter's here,' said Jane. 'That's her car.'

Dixon walked around the outside of the single storey barn conversion and peered in the French windows overlooking the garden and beyond that the walk down through the field to the canal. Potter was standing in the doorway on the far side of the living room surveying the scene, Superintendent Guthrie craning her neck to look at something on the floor that was upside down. Both were wearing latex overalls, overshoes and gloves.

Potter gestured to Dixon and Jane to stay where they were on the patio. 'It's like a bloody abattoir in there,' she said, appearing around the corner. She let the picket gate slam behind her. 'I've never seen anything like it. They even killed the dog, would you believe it?'

Dixon grimaced. 'They?'

'Whoever did it.'

He gestured to the path down to the old canal. 'Better get SOCO to look for footprints down there,' he said, the long grass beyond the stile at the bottom of the garden recently flattened, by the looks of things.

'Steiner?'

'My guess is he came along the old canal. We'd have seen him if he'd come by road.'

Potter nodded. 'How's Hatty?'

'She'll be all right, Ma'am,' said Jane. 'She's at Bath hospital being checked over.'

'Well done, the pair of you, anyway.' Potter smiled. 'I'm recommending you for an award, Jane.'

'Thank you, Ma'am.'

'You too,' she said, turning to Dixon, 'And I may not give you any choice about that transfer.'

'Let's finish this first,' muttered Dixon.

'It is finished, surely?' Potter frowned. 'We've just got to catch Steiner and I've got every available—'

'I'll be inside,' said Dixon, ripping open a packet of latex overalls as he walked around the corner of the house.

Potter looked at Jane and raised her eyebrows.

'Don't look at me, Ma'am. He never tells me anything.'

The front door was standing open, the lock intact. Gregson, or his wife perhaps, had let Steiner in. Dixon glanced around the hall, at the blood spattered up the walls, mainly on the left. Steiner was right handed, according to Petersen's post mortem of Savage, and it looked like he'd struck the first blow from the doorstep, blood spattered across the coats hanging just inside the door.

He stepped over the blood trail in the hall and followed it along the corridor to the living room. Gregson must have crawled, trying to hide under the dining table, possibly; more blood on the floor and was that skull fragments? The dining table lying on its side against the drinks cabinet.

Blood was spattered up the back of the sofa too. Perhaps a few more blows had rained down on Gregson's skull there, before he made one last effort to crawl away, his life ending on the rug in front of the sofa.

He was lying on his back, rolled over by Steiner probably, the wooden handle of a steak knife sticking out of his chest. Dead before he was stabbed, thought Dixon, judging by the lack of blood on the paper. That would be Petersen's problem though.

'Beaten, then stabbed to death,' said Guthrie, watching Dixon peering at the body.

'Beaten to death.' Dixon straightened up. 'The knife was inserted later to hold that document in place.'

Guthrie nodded.

Dixon craned his neck to look at the document pinned to Gregson's chest by the steak knife, just as he'd seen Guthrie doing. A loan agreement, dated almost exactly two years ago. Dixon recognised the names.

'Where's his wife?'

'Back bedroom.'

By the time he emerged from the living room the corridor had been covered in plastic to preserve any bloodstained footprints, and a Scientific Services officer was laying down stepping plates to the back bedroom. The kitchen door was open, so Dixon peered in. The elderly terrier was hanging out of his bed in the far corner, a large carving knife sticking out of his side and a small trickle of blood from his nose puddled up on the quarry tiled floor in front of him.

Dixon squatted down next to the dog's bed and stroked him on the back of his head. Stone cold.

Poor old lad.

Henry, according to the tag on the collar. He flipped it over and looked at the name and phone number on the back.

Helen Gregson was lying face down on the double bed in the back bedroom, a small incision in her blouse evidence of the single stab wound that had killed her. Or had it? Dixon noticed a trickle of blood coming from each ear, running down her cheeks and dripping off the end of her nose on to the carpet.

Then he retraced his steps back to the living room, squatted down next to Gregson and looked at his ears. The same – possibly – although it was difficult to tell, what with the savagery of the beating.

'Petersen's here,' said Jane. She had tiptoed along the stepping plates and was standing in the living room doorway.

'All right, everybody out.'

Dixon recognised the senior Scientific Services officer's voice. 'Bit out of your area, aren't you, Don?' he asked, smiling.

'It's a Sunday,' muttered Watson.

'Tell me about it,' said Dixon. 'We're still on holiday.'

'You found the kid, I gather?'

'Yes.'

'About bloody time.'

Dixon smiled. 'Get Petersen to check their ears, will you?' he asked, heading for the front door.

'Where are you off to?' shouted Potter, wriggling into a set of white overalls in the car park.

'Express Park, Ma'am,' replied Dixon, throwing his car keys to Jane.

'Where are you off to, Dave?' asked Dixon, stopping in front of Harding on the stairs up to the Incident Room.

'Home, Sir.' Harding shrugged his shoulders. 'You've found Hatty and the hunt's on for Steiner. What else is there to do?'

'Track this car last Tuesday,' replied Dixon, handing him a piece of paper. 'Mark in?'

'Yes, Sir.' Harding frowned. 'Whose car is it?'

Dixon ran up the last couple of steps to find the Incident Room deserted, except for Louise and Mark.

'Where is everybody?' he asked.

'They all went to the pub when the news came through, Sir,' replied Louise.

'Gits,' muttered Pearce.

'We'll go to the pub when we've got Steiner,' said Dixon. 'In the meantime, Mark, track these mobile phone numbers last Tuesday, will you?'

'Whose are they?'

'I'll be in the canteen.'

'It's closed, Sir.'

◆ ◆ ◆

Dixon and Jane were sitting in the canteen, Dixon leaning back in his chair, eyes shut, Jane reading several documents that he had ripped out of the lever arch files in the Incident Room, when DCI Lewis walked in holding a mug of coffee in each hand.

'Here,' he said. 'I got you these from the machine.'

'Thank you, Sir,' said Jane, smiling.

'All over bar the shouting, is it?' Lewis pulled a chair out from under the table and sat down.

Jane shook her head. 'We're waiting for a phone trace and Dave's tracking a car on the cameras.'

'Whose?'

'Dunno.'

'So, how did Steiner get away?'

Dixon's eyes opened and he sat bolt upright. 'I'll tell you how Steiner got away. Those fuckwits from Wiltshire didn't check the moored boats properly and then . . .' He gritted his teeth. 'Then they let him see them skulking about in the bushes.'

'That's when he sank the boat,' said Jane.

'Deliberately?'

Dixon nodded. 'Take the cratch cover off the rudder housing and stick it in reverse. The backwash floods it in seconds. We were supposed to trap him in the bottom lock, but he never got that far.'

'He hijacked a car.' Jane rolled her eyes. 'Then they called off the chase on the edge of Chippenham. It was becoming a danger to the public.'

'I've called off a chase in that situation before,' said Lewis. 'It happens.'

'When you're in pursuit of a child snatching multiple murderer?' asked Dixon.

'Maybe not, then, no.'

'He even killed the bloody dog.'

'He'll turn up in a B&B somewhere, or sleeping in a tent in the woods. His face is all over the TV news. It'll be in every newspaper in the morning too. And at least you got Hatty out unscathed.'

'Jane did that.'

'So I heard.' Lewis smiled at Jane.

'Looks like you were right, Sir.' Dave Harding was standing in the doorway with Mark Pearce. 'The car's picked up on the A39 heading north east. It's on the number plate recognition cameras in Glastonbury and Wells, then again on the A36 just south of Bradford-on-Avon, so it must've gone across country to get there.'

'What time?'

'Glastonbury's first, just after nine.'

'What about the phones, Mark?'

'There's not been time to triangulate, so it's not going to be an accurate location. Vodafone have got back to me first, and it's showing up on the base stations at Glastonbury and Wells, then again at Radstock; that's a weaker signal, so I reckon they went along the B3139. Then again on the mast at Farleigh Hungerford. That's on the A36, that one. Then it's Bradford-on-Avon.'

'Whose is it?' asked Dixon. 'His or hers?'

'Hers.'

Chapter Forty-Three

'Have you rung DCS Potter?' asked Lewis. He was sitting in the back seat of Dixon's Land Rover.

'Yes, Sir,' he replied. 'She's on her way back from Combe Hay and should be at Express Park by the time we get back.'

'Good.'

'D'you think they know what's happened to the Gregsons?' Harding had rung Louise, who had raced back to Express Park and jumped in Dixon's Land Rover just as he was leaving.

'No.'

'What are we waiting for?' asked Jane. She looked along Old School Lane and then back to Dixon.

'Backup to get in position.'

The streetlights flickered, the wind blowing the branches of the trees all around them. They'll be a fat lot of good in the summer when the trees are in leaf, thought Dixon, as he watched four figures creeping along the far end of Old School Lane. Then a flatbed lorry drove past the top end of the lane.

He checked his watch. 'Right, let's go.'

Dixon and Jane paused at the front door and watched Lewis and Louise creep along the side of the house, ready to take up position at the French windows. Then he knocked on the door.

'Ah, the heroes of the hour,' said Geraldine, stepping back to allow Dixon and Jane into the hall.

'Have you got him?' asked Poland, getting up from the armchair by the wood burner.

'Not yet, Roger,' replied Dixon. 'How's Hatty?'

'The children team are interviewing her tomorrow, but they won't get much. She can't remember anything before she woke up on the boat.'

Dixon saw Ros Hicks sitting at the dining table in front of a glass of wine and a jigsaw puzzle, a second glass of wine in front of the empty chair next to her.

'She's going to be fine,' said Jeremy, walking over to the drinks cabinet. 'She got a clean bill of health from the consultant.'

'Where is she?'

'She's asleep upstairs. Adele's with her.' Jeremy shrugged his shoulders. 'She can't bring herself to leave her on her own.'

'Who can blame her,' said Jane.

'Nobody.' Jeremy was waving a bottle of Scotch in his hand. 'Drink?'

'No, thank you, Sir. Better not,' replied Dixon.

'I can't begin to tell you how grateful we are, Inspector,' said Jeremy. 'Roger was right. You are—'

Dixon held up his hand, silencing Jeremy mid-sentence.

'I should clarify that this isn't a social call, Sir,' said Dixon. He looked up at the sound of footsteps above to see Adele leaning over the balustrade.

'What's going on?' she asked.

Geraldine sat down at the dining table next to Ros.

'I regret to inform you, Mrs Renner,' said Dixon, turning back to look up at Adele, 'that Simon Gregson and his wife were both found dead this afternoon at their home in Combe Hay.'

'Dead?'

'Murdered, we believe by Steiner, sometime last night.'

Ros Hicks slumped forwards across the dining table, scattering jigsaw puzzle pieces on to the floor.

'I'm sorry, Mrs Hicks.' Dixon picked up several pieces of the puzzle and looked at them in the palm of his hand. 'That's no way to find out your son is dead, is it?'

'Your son?' Adele came running down the spiral stairs.

'A canal boat?' Dixon leaned over the puzzle, before dropping the pieces on to the table. 'How apt,' he said, matter of fact.

'You took Hatty?' screamed Adele. Poland ran forward, wrapping his arms around her.

Dixon stepped forward. 'Rosalind Hicks, I am arresting you on suspicion of the abduction of Harriet Renner.'

Ros lunged across the dining table, reaching for the knife on a cheese board, but Jane beat her to it, knocking it on to the floor. Instead she snatched her wine glass, smashed it on the edge of the table and then held the jagged edge to Geraldine's neck, her left arm clamped around her throat.

'For God's sake, Ros,' gasped Geraldine, as she was wrenched back in her chair.

'And how far d'you think you're going to get, Ros?' asked Dixon.

'Far enough.'

'The place is surrounded,' continued Dixon. 'Your husband'll be in custody by now and your car's on a flatbed lorry.'

Ros's eyes darted around the room. 'Don't try anything,' she mumbled, as she stood up and backed away towards the French windows, dragging Geraldine off her chair.

'Did Simon kill Sid Farooq?'

'Steiner did. And they buried him in the bottom of lock sixteen.'

'And you knew?'

'I fucking helped them, didn't I?' Her face flushed now, her teeth gritted as she held Geraldine by the throat.

'I don't know, you tell me.' He took two paces forwards, more to cover DCI Lewis's approach in the French windows.

'Stay back,' screamed Ros, watching Dixon's every move.

'For God's sake, Ros, put her down,' snapped Jeremy.

'You were going to tell me about Farooq,' said Dixon.

'He was dead when I got there. The lying bastard. Material non-disclosures? It was a rip off and he got what he deserved.' She sneered. 'It was my husband's money. *His* shares. Why should he have to give them up?'

'What about Markhams, then?' asked Dixon. 'There was a loan agreement pinned to Simon's body.'

'I lent him the money and he lent it to the company.'

'Whose money was it?'

'My husband's. It was all Bob's. My first husband left me penniless when he died. Useless bugger.'

'What part did Bob play in all this?'

'None. He knows nothing about it.'

Dixon frowned. 'You didn't tell him you lent two hundred thousand pounds of *his* money to your son?'

'Of course I bloody well didn't!'

'So you snatched Hatty?'

Ros sneered at Jeremy. 'It was that or let these bastards wind up the company and lose everything. Bob's money and then my marriage when he found out what I'd done.'

Dixon hesitated. The sound of a child crying. Softly. But from where? He looked up to see Hatty standing at the top of the stairs in her pyjamas, rubbing her eyes with her right hand and holding a teddy bear in her left.

'I'm sorry, Hatty,' said Ros. 'No one was going to hurt you, you do know that, don't you?'

Ros relaxed her grip on Geraldine's neck, not much, but enough, lowering the jagged stem of the wine glass. DCI Lewis lunged through the open French windows and took hold of her right wrist, snatching it away from Geraldine's neck.

Ros let go of Geraldine and she slumped to the floor while Lewis wrestled Ros to the ground and handcuffed her.

'You do not have to say anything,' continued Dixon, 'but it may harm your defence if you do not mention when questioned something that you later rely on in court.' He paused while Lewis dragged her to her feet and sat her down on a dining chair. 'Anything you do say may be given in evidence.'

'I'm all right, Dad.' Adele stopped wriggling in her father's arms; Roger let her go so she could intercept Hatty, who was running down the stairs, her arms outstretched. Then he walked around the dining table and helped Geraldine up.

'How did you know she was Simon's mother?' asked Adele, cradling Hatty in her arms.

'Henry told me.'

Ros looked quizzically at Dixon.

'Simon Gregson's dog,' he said.

'My dog,' spluttered Ros. 'Bob doesn't like dogs. He wouldn't let me have him in the house.'

'The tag on his collar still has your old surname on it. Ros Gregson. And your mobile number's the same too.' Dixon looked down at Ros, her head bowed now as she sobbed quietly. 'I'm sorry to tell you that Henry was killed as well.'

No reply.

Louise, along with two uniformed officers, stepped in through the French windows and led her away.

'You really never knew she was Simon's mother?' asked Jeremy, shaking his head at Adele.

'I didn't have that sort of relationship with Simon. And he didn't have that sort of relationship with her. He never told his parents about me, or any of his girlfriends for that matter.'

'Didn't you think that a bit odd?'

'Yes, but he said she was a bit odd.'

'No shit,' muttered Jane.

'All the time she was sitting here drinking coffee and telling us it'd be all right in the end,' said Geraldine, picking up the cheese board and the rest of the jigsaw puzzle pieces. 'And she bloody well knew.'

'How did you find out?' asked Poland.

'In amongst the documents we got from Svenskabanken, there was a Director's Loan Note dated two years ago under which Simon loaned his company two hundred thousand pounds.' Dixon spun round to face Jeremy, still standing by the drinks cabinet. 'Did you ever find out where that money came from?'

'The company burned through it and that was that.' Jeremy shrugged his shoulders. 'We never asked where it came from.'

'Well, it came from his mother.' Dixon grimaced. 'Pinned to his chest with a steak knife was a loan agreement dated the same day as the loan note.'

'So, with the bank foreclosing, she stood to lose her two hundred grand.' Adele nodded.

'Her husband's two hundred grand. And much more besides. We'll get their car checked, but I'm guessing we'll find Hatty's DNA in the boot. She lives a few doors up. It was easy. Grab her as she walked past the house, straight in the boot and away. It explains why no one saw the van in the village on Tuesday morning.'

'It was never here?' asked Jeremy.

'Exactly. She delivered the note too. You bumped into her in the lane, Ms Crosby. Remember?'

'I do.' replied Geraldine, nodding. 'Did Bob really not know?'

'He may not, but I'm hoping he'll know something about the murder of Sid Farooq.'

'So, Steiner killed Farooq . . .' muttered Adele.

'We'll be able to confirm that if and when we find the body.' Dixon shook his head. 'The Bluewater Nominees shareholders, your angel investors. Did you ever know who they were?'

'No.' Adele frowned. 'We dealt with an accountant in Wells.'

Dixon reached into his pocket and unfolded a piece of paper. 'There were four shareholders.'

'Bob Hicks?' asked Jeremy.

'Robert Archibald Hicks,' replied Dixon, handing the piece of paper to Adele.

'And you never knew that either?' Jeremy glared at Adele.

'No, I bloody didn't!'

'Simon's bloody stepfather and he never said a thing?' Jeremy sneered. 'I find that hard to believe.'

'He didn't. I don't know, maybe he didn't want me to know he fixed it.'

'The family connection explains the reluctance to relinquish shares,' said Dixon. 'And we may never know exactly what happened after you left that meeting in Combe Hay, but what it does do is explain their determination to stop the bank winding up the company and bankrupting Gregson.'

'Does it?' asked Jeremy, frowning. 'It's just money.'

'It's not just the money, though, is it?' replied Dixon. 'What would the bank do with the house and land?'

'Sell it.'

'And a new owner might allow the canal to be dug out and the Restoration Society to restore the old locks.'

'Perhaps.'

Dixon smiled. 'And you wouldn't want that if you'd buried a body in the bottom of lock sixteen, would you?'

Chapter Forty-Four

'Still no sign of Steiner?'

Dixon shook his head.

'It's been a week now,' said Poland.

'How's Hatty doing?' asked Jane.

'She's getting there and it'll be easier now the interviews are out of the way. They've taken a holiday cottage in Cornwall and Adele's going to home-school her for the rest of this term.'

'Have the local police been notified?' asked Dixon.

'Yes, they're being very good, apparently. A Family Liaison officer has gone with them and Armed Response are on high alert. They've had alarms fitted too.'

'Good idea,' said Jane, nodding.

'The bank has told Jeremy to take as much time as he needs.' Poland shrugged his shoulders. 'They'll stay there until you've got Steiner, I expect. Safely out of the way. They're not even allowed visitors, in case we're followed.'

'It won't be long, Roger.'

Poland smiled. 'What shall we drink to then?'

They were sitting at their usual table in the Zalshah,
rite Tandoori restaurant in Burnham-on-Sea, although it had been Jane's choice when Poland had said he wanted to take them out to dinner.

Dixon held up a pint of Kingfisher. 'How about Detective Sergeant Jane Winter, Queen's Police Medal.'

'Fine with me,' said Poland, clinking glasses with Jane in the middle of the table.

Jane drained her gin and tonic. 'Shall we order?' she asked.

'We're still waiting for one more,' said Dixon, snatching the menu out of her hand.

'Who?'

'You were going to tell me what Ros had to say for herself,' said Poland, changing the subject.

Dixon grimaced. 'She admits pretty much everything.'

'What about Farooq?'

'He was dead when she got to Combe Hay and we can't prove otherwise. Gregson's dead and that just leaves Steiner. We found Farooq's body, though, buried in the bottom of lock sixteen on the old coal canal.'

'Was it the lock where the boy drowned?' asked Jane.

'I don't know,' replied Dixon. 'I haven't been able to find anything more about him, anywhere. Not even a name.' He sighed. 'Poor lad.'

'You knew Farooq would be there, though.' Poland frowned. 'How did you know?'

'I suspected,' muttered Dixon.

'Ask him about the wizard.' Jane smirked.

'No, don't ask him about the wizard,' snapped Dixon. 'You wouldn't believe me if I told you anyway.'

Poland shook his head. 'What about her husband, Bob?'

'The husband knew nothing about any of it,' said Jane. 'Or so he says.'

'She backs him up on that,' said Dixon. 'It was his money and she persuaded him to invest in Polgen. He lost the lot, of course. Then she lent his money to her son so he could prop up Markhams. He'd told her it was to fund an expansion, only it didn't work out quite like he said, and she fell out with him over it – which explains why Adele never saw him visiting his mother,' continued Dixon. 'It's another reason why Ros was so keen the vintners shouldn't go bust.'

'And Farooq's post mortem?'

'Stabbed to death. There are cut marks on the ribs and the side of the skull. Had his eardrums pierced too, right through the skull, just like Savage and both Gregsons.'

'A myringotomy of sorts then.' Poland nodded. 'That's an incision in the eardrum, to you. I wonder what that's all about?'

'When I catch up with Steiner, I'll ask him.'

'I bet you will.'

'She gave us a bit more on Hatty's kidnap too,' continued Dixon. 'She says she stepped out from behind the tree in her front garden. Swears blind she did it on her own, but went "no comment" when I pressed her on it. I'm still not sure why Hatty didn't scream.'

'She doesn't remember a blow to the head, but there was a small needle mark on the right side of her neck,' said Poland. 'So, she must've been drugged.'

'Are Adele and Jeremy going to be all right?' asked Jane.

'They'll work it out. We're getting on better too.' Poland took a swig of beer. 'Whose idea was it to kidnap Alesha then, and all that rubbish about Ted Buckler?'

'Steiner's. Alesha's grandmother knew that Sailes used to work for Buckler, so the plan to kidnap Alesha and set them up was hatched over a beer, at a cosy canal side pub of all places. We were supposed to waste days investigating Buckler and Sailes. Only we didn't.'

'Thanks to you.' Poland raised his glass.

Dixon smiled. 'Once the petition had been withdrawn they would have handed Hatty back and that would've been that, provided Jeremy kept Markhams afloat using the bank's money. If he didn't Steiner would pay them another visit and this time it'd be—'

'I get it,' interrupted Poland.

'He's quite the criminal mastermind, apparently. As well as being a psychopath. But we'll get him.' Dixon slid his phone out of his pocket and looked at the screen. 'It's the biggest manhunt I've ever . . .' His voice tailed off. 'I'll be back in a sec.'

Jane watched him walk out of the restaurant. 'Where's he going?' she asked.

'Don't look at me.' Poland smiled.

Then Dixon reappeared carrying a small rucksack, with Lucy walking along behind him. 'Your bridesmaid's here,' he said, grinning at Jane.

She jumped up and threw her arms around Lucy. 'I didn't know you were coming.'

'I didn't want to miss the party.' Lucy grinned. 'My sister, the hero.'

'Your bridesmaid?' Poland winked at Dixon. 'Does that mean you've asked her?'

'Has he hell,' muttered Jane.

'Oh, so I'm not going to be your best man, then?'

'Hang on a minute.' Jane glared at Dixon. 'You've already asked him to be your best man?'

'Well, I—'

'The bloody grief you gave me.'

'So, when *are* you going to ask her?' demanded Lucy.

Dixon slid his hand into his jacket pocket and his fingers closed around a small velvet covered jewellery box.

'Oh, y'know,' he said, smiling. 'Anytime now.'

Author's Note

I wanted to say a few words, while I have the chance, about the character 'Nat' who features in the Prologue and then later in the narrative.

He is – or was – a real person, just one of many thousands of boys working on the canals 200 years ago; and, despite extensive research, I have been unable to find out anything more about him. The only information available comes from the *Bath Chronicle* and is quoted verbatim in *Dead Lock*. I haven't even been able to find out his name and so, for these purposes, I have christened him 'Nat'.

I would like to have found his last resting place – even his age would have been something – but alas I have found nothing. So, if by any chance you do happen to know anything more about him, please get in touch via my website. Otherwise, he must remain a mystery, just one of many lost in the passage of time.

The remains of the Somersetshire Coal Canal are well worth a visit if you are ever in the area. Abandoned locks loom out of the trees as you walk up through the woods behind Combe Hay, testament to a way of life long since consigned to history. It is a truly atmospheric spot!

I would also like to take this opportunity to thank my old (and long suffering) biology teacher, Dr Roger Poland, for lending his name to my Home Office pathologist. I did warn him what happened this time!

As always, I would like to thank the team at Thomas & Mercer for their patience and support. It would be wrong to single out any individuals from such a great bunch of people, but I'm going to do it anyway. So, a huge 'thank you' to Emilie Marneur, Laura Deacon, Hatty Stiles and, of course, Katie Green.

And lastly, I would like to thank *you* for reading *Dead Lock*. I do hope you enjoyed it.

Damien Boyd
Devon, UK
January 2018

About the Author

Damien Boyd is a solicitor by training and draws on his extensive experience of criminal law, along with a spell in the Crown Prosecution Service, to write fast-paced crime thrillers featuring Detective Inspector Nick Dixon.